Cigar Box

By

**Wilbur Witt
&
Pamela Woodward**

This book is a work of fiction. Places, events, and situations in this story are purely fictional. Any resemblance to actual persons, living or dead, is coincidental.

© 2003 by Wilbur Witt and Pamela Woodward.
All rights reserved.

No part of this book may be reproduced, stored in a retrieval system, or transmitted by any means, electronic, mechanical, photocopying, recording, or otherwise, without written permission from the author.

ISBN: 1-4140-1491-0 (e-book)
ISBN: 1-4140-1490-2 (Paperback)

This book is printed on acid free paper.

1stBooks – rev. 10/25/03

To the girl from Commerce Street.

Christmas Morning

The old, West Texas barn was cold on Christmas morning as the two men huddled around the little hibachi grill glowing red with coals. It was a white man and a Mexican who found comfort in each other's company this day. The Mexican put a ragged cigar box on the table before them and spoke, "This is the smoke I told you about. It has special power. I wanted to smoke it only with you, for I trust you."

The white man opened the cigar box and saw within it was a bag of herb, bulging at the seams. Tucked neatly within its confines were various rolling papers. Gingerly he took a pack of papers out and withdrew the bag. Then he took two papers from the packet and sealed them together, even though they were "double-wide" according to the packets.

"Looks like good stuff," the white man said.

"It comes from deep within Mexico. Very few Anglos get to see this, or smoke it. It releases the spirit, and the spirit goes where it wants."

The white man began to roll the herb, and then put it into his mouth and sealed it so none of the particles could fall from the cigarette. Then, reaching into the glowing fire in the pot on the floor he withdrew a twig, still glowing and placed it onto the end of the cigarette, drawing the smoke that was produced deep within him, and passed the cigarette over to the Mexican. The Mexican man was old, but carried it well. His hair was already showing streaks of white, lacing the once black strands. His face was as timeless as the Virgin of Guadalupe itself, yet older in many ways. He took the cigarette from the Anglo and drew the smoke within his lungs, holding it there for what seemed to be an eternity, and then slowly released it back into the air.

"How long you been around here?" the white man asked.

"Forever! I have been here since way back. The spirit has been good to me. I buried two wives, and have a fine daughter now.

"How old? C'mon, how old are you?"

The old Mexican peered at his friend, "I can't tell you 'cause I don't know. There ain't no paper on me. All I know is I been around a while, and I know I remember Poncho Villa."

The barn began to fill with the smell of marijuana as the two men passed the joint back and forth between them. The white man began to feel the drug and settled back, but the Mexican man sat upright and began to stiffen, and grow glassy-eyed. He then grew silent and didn't move for the longest time; all the while the Anglo slowly finished the joint by himself and watched his friend go into a meditation. He had seen this in his friend before and it didn't alarm him. He just waited until the Mexican came back to his senses.

Cigar Box

*   *   *

The night was clear and cool a thousand miles from the barn as an old Chevy moved steadily down the gravel road just outside of Memphis. The radio was blaring out the sounds of a local station, complete with scratchy bass, and fading in and out. The driver, intent on being home for Christmas, ignored the exhaustion creeping into his mind. All he could focus on was being home with his little girl that next morning. It had been a big week; big month actually and tonight's party wound down the events leading up to his older brother's departure for sea duty. They drank a lot of beer, ate a lot of bar-b-que and now all that was left to do was be home when the little girl opened her presents on Christmas morning. He would be cutting it close, and would arrive most likely as the child rose to greet the biggest day of the year. Sherman Road was like all rural roads in Tennessee in that it wound, and wound like a snake through the trees; a snake with a bite for the unwary traveler who didn't pay attention to its winding ways. Its rough gravel complained beneath the tires as the car lumbered on through the darkness. The head lights frequently glaring off into nothingness, causing the driver to slow down and check out the turn. Then the road seemed to go straight for a little while, so he picked up speed. Any time he could gain would be valuable. He simply could not let the little girl get out of bed and he was not there. Then, suddenly the form of an old man, with long gray hair with black streaks ambled across the road with a stick in his hand appeared before his lights. Stopping in the middle of the road, the old man stood there, and stared at him as if he didn't care if the car struck him or not. The driver swerved to miss the old man, and the car lost its grip on the loose gravel, plunged through an intersection and through a fence surrounding a local equipment rental business, coming to rest against a telephone pole. His head smashed against the windshield, and he lost consciousness amid the blare of the radio, and the hissing of the escaping steam from the radiator. The old man who had been walking across the road came over to inspect the car. Looking inside at the unconscious driver, he reached into a bag slung across his shoulder and retrieved some sand. Taking one of the driver's hands, and then the other he placed the sand into them. Bending over he whispered into his ear, "You are now *Dreamwalker.* You stay *here*! Someone is coming. You will be my eyes, my ears, and my will. You will see that my will is carried out. And you will not leave this place until I tell you to go. Your soul is bound by my magic, and by my will. The driver's hands clenched the sand. The old man stepped back, inspected his handiwork, turned and walked down Sherman Road, disappearing into the darkness.

It was hours before they found the driver, and by then the injury to the brain was too massive to be reversed. Paramedics noticed that his hands were clenched tightly, but didn't bother about it because of all the other injuries he had suffered that night.

His mother was summoned to the hospital and was told of the condition of her son. She was a simple woman of good Baptist roots who didn't want to hear that her son was gone, but the body was still here. It

Cigar Box

was like some macabre scene from an old horror movie. A true night of the living dead. The doctors explained in detail how the brain stem had been damaged, but she took that to mean that he was still "there" but just couldn't communicate with anyone. Then, one of the doctors took the breather off the man in the bed.

"See?" he reasoned, "He doesn't breath without the respirator. The brain stem no longer has the capacity to demand oxygen. There's nothing left. Let me explain it this way, the brain, as you know it, can actually be dead, and yet this area beneath that we know as the stem will still make the reflex actions work. Breathing is one of these actions. You son's brain stem no longer works. Your son is dead. I'm sorry."

"Could I be alone with him a moment?"

The doctors all nodded and left the room. She pulled a chair over to the bed and looked at her son. All the promise, and all the hope was still there for her, but the doctors said that it was gone. She wasn't a great theologian. She was a simple woman from Tennessee who believed that a person was alive until their heart stopped beating. The doctors thought differently though, and after all, she was just one old woman from Tennessee. Her family, such as it was, sat outside in the hallway without the intelligence or conviction to even come into the room. It had been this way all of her life. Ever since she was a little girl she'd had choices put on her that no one wanted, and this was just one more.

"Mike," she began, "I know you can hear me, son. I can't do nothing about this. They say you ain't here.

Inside I know you are, but I don't know if even you would want to stay here like this. They told me that you are paralyzed now and that you'll never be the same. They even told me that you would be an idiot if you ever come out of this. Son, I'm gonna have to let you go. I'm gonna do it, 'cause I'm the only one with the strength to do it. It's better to be with our Lord than to be here like this. I know you'll understand. Please forgive me, son. I gotta do what I gotta do."

She looked up at the ceiling but her eyes peered beyond it, and into the heavens beyond human sight, or understanding. "Lord, let this sin be upon me, and not my other children or my husband. I do this on my own. Lord, please take my Mike to your bosom and take care of him 'till we all get there. He's a good boy, Lord, and I know he'd done a bit of drinking, but that don't make him bad. You use my boy Lord, and I think you'll see that he has a use. He'll come in right handy if you let him. He's got a quick mind, Lord, and I'm sure that you'll find something for him to do that he can make you proud of."

She got up and went to open the door. "I think ya'll need to come in and say good bye to your brother now."

One by one, the brothers and sisters filed in and talked to the unconscious man. Each one had some heart felt statement to tell him, and none of them could tell if he could hear them. All except Claudette, a thin girl with a persistent pained look on her face. She stood there with her husband, Ed; a fat man with a red face who breathed in short labored gasps. As each person leaned over she watched her brother lying on

Cigar Box

the bed, but she would not draw near to him, when just then she thought she noticed something.

"His hand moved!"

"What?"

They all looked intently at the man's hands, but could not discern any movement. The hands were still clenched just as they had been since the ambulance brought him in that morning.

"It did move. I saw it," she insisted.

Claudette was a tall, Tennessee woman who only owned two dresses and about five pairs of jeans. Her black, stringy hair hung unkempt to her shoulders, and her teeth needed work. To be honest she was the mirror image of her mother at her age, but she had other issues her mother did not have. Dyslexia clouded her reason and in this back woods community that was equal to retardation. Her mother had been glad to see her married, even to Ed, because an "idiot girl" was hard to marry off. Back in school she'd been given to fits, and fainting, and the family had grown used to her outbursts.

"Nervous reaction, that's all," one of the attending doctors said. "His hands are still as they have been all along. The reaction has given his hands that grip you see."

Claudette looked back at her brother lying in the bed. She could sense a struggle going on within him. He was trying to open his hands; she saw it! He was trying to show everyone in the room something that was in his hands as if that had something to do with his condition. It was then she realized that he *could* hear her! He *could!* "Mike, I ain't no part of this. You know that! I saw it!" She looked at the people in the room, "You do this and I'm leaving. I'm leaving forever, and I ain't ever coming back here to this trash!"

Her red-faced husband told her, "Just pipe down Claudette! No body wants to hear your retarded nonsense today."

She turned on him, "I put up with you all these years. Had two boys by you, and all you can do is make fun of me. Well, if you're a part of this I'm gonna put you in the pot with the rest of them. I'll just leave you here with them!"

The fat man shrugged his shoulders and looked at the others, "Hey, ya'll know how she is. Heck, she can't even read! Just a retard, that's all."

Claudette leaned over, kissed her brother, and left the room. One by one they all left and the old woman was finally alone with one doctor in the room.

"She said he moved. You sure there ain't nothing can be done?"

The doctor looked at his feet. "The man is brain dead. What your daughter saw was a nervous reaction. His hands have been clenched like that since they brought him in. It doesn't mean anything. Only that the brain is damaged. He can go on like this for years. You don't need to put yourself, or your family through this."

"All that drinking. That's what done it. Partying all them nights, but he never hurt nobody. He always made people laugh. You would have loved him. He learned to walk on stilts, and ride one of them one-wheeled bicycles just to make us all laugh. Will he suffer?"

Cigar Box

"No ma'am. He's already gone. He doesn't know anything right now."

The old woman sadly shook her head, "Yeah he does, Doc. Yeah he does." She looked one last time at her son and said, "Just do it."

The doctor leaned over and disconnected the life support, and as he did the man's hands unclenched, letting a small bit of sand fall to the hospital floor.

Christmas Morning Twenty Years Later

Christmas day dawned clear and cold in the little neighborhood just north of Memphis. Children all over were waking, and running to the room that held the tree. Joy had descended on Memphis, Tennessee. In a small, two-bedroom apartment, June Montgomery rose and sat on the couch that she'd slept on last night, staring at the morning. The morning stared right back at her. How many mornings had she been through? How many Christmases had come and gone? The last Christmas was but a dim memory. It was a Christmas with a small tree in her old apartment, the one with *one* bedroom. There were very few gifts, and not even a card from her mother or little sister. For June, Christmas had lost its magic a long time ago. It was a day just like all the others. It was no different from any other day. But how could anyone call it just another day? Her Pentecostal upbringing told her that it was a very special day, but the last three years told her that tomorrow would just be the day after, and that life, with all of its heartache, and misery, would crash in. No one and nothing could stop that. June had lost

Cigar Box

it all! But she was coming back. She felt as if she had "bottomed out," and that there was no way to go but up from this point.

How had she come to this place in her life? The years began to reel into a blur in her mind. She had never been the prom queen, but she'd stolen the prom queen's thunder. She'd been married into the best family with the biggest reception in town. She had scaled that wall that separated the elite from the common people, and she had walked with the giants that sculpted history. June Montgomery was beautiful! She looked like a movie star, or like one of those expensive porcelain dolls you could find in an antique shop. A fine little doll with all of her features etched into the memory of everyone who'd seen her that day so long ago back in west Texas. She remembered the long tables set up with all the food on them. She could still see the line of beer kegs that had graced the porch after her wedding. She could recall the blue of the west Texas sky, turning red in the early evening, and then the bright stars coming out with the moon shining down upon her reception. Shining down on the greens of the golf course that wound through the neighborhood. She had walked those greens many times. One time too many! Her entire life had been changed one night on one of those greens. The passion had taken her and led her into something that was irreversible. Her eyes began to tear a bit. Her eyes were blue, like that sky had been. Yes not a shade of blue that you could see, but a blue that was almost transparent as if you were looking through two actual windows to her soul. And that soul was marked, and as unfathomable as only the soul of an innocent child could be when it had been too far and seen too much! As a child in church she'd learned that sins may be forgiven, but she was now discovering that the mark of those sins remains forever on the soul, maiming it, and staining it in a way that only God knows, and holds one accountable for on that last day. How many times had she looked up at heaven and pleaded for forgiveness? How many times had she wished that she simply had made *different* choices? She had found that forgiveness was a precious commodity and while *God* may forgive, but men don't! She was finding that men did not forget, either. Back in west Texas she was known as "The Catter." And she was the Catter. She'd learned the game too well, and played it too often. She'd discovered that the thrill had long since worn out and that she was playing the game simply because she *could*! Men had *buttons* on them, and she knew how to push those buttons with a learned hand. And all men would react the same way, *every* time!

Her hair had been naturally blonde, and hung down to the middle of her back. Now she had it cut to shoulder length. Cut, as it was it began to curl a bit and draw up. But if her eyes were bluer than the Texas sky the color blonde isn't the word that would really describe her hair. The description didn't do justice. Golden because gold has value, and this gold stemmed from the head of a goddess. She was a perfect five foot, two inches tall, with just enough "baby fat" to round her out. Her pregnancy had done her figure justice, and rounded out the areas that were still "girlish." Her breasts were well formed, but not too large. Her butt was a perfect heart shape and on her face was a look of constant surprise. Her lips formed a

Cigar Box

natural "pout," that was even there when she was asleep. A pout waiting to be kissed by her lover. It was almost as if she were puzzling over something over, and over again. This face had gotten her over the imaginary wall and into the "Bend," that exclusive section where she'd been married. This face had split her family and inspired love and hate. This face was not scorched, and lined like so many other girls from west Texas. They looked far older than their years, tired and worn out way before their time. The image of the lovely cowgirl on a horse was but a myth, for they all looked harsh, driven by the west Texas sand with their faces of leather.

But while June's face was far prettier than these, she had come to consider it a liability. For all of her beauty, her clothes were wrinkled, and they had that "slept in" smell to them. After her return from Texas, her boyfriend, a man she called the "Doc," because he was a pre-med student at a local college, refused to even sleep with her, and he put her on the couch. It was a new experience for June. She'd never seen a man that could walk away from the promise of her love. What's more, the boyfriend had made other moves even before her arrival. When she'd arrived home the night before she discovered that he had already evicted her clothes and would shortly evict her. He had thrown her clothes out on the porch. Then he called her husband's biological father, known to her as "Real Daddy" to come and get her "possibles" if he wanted them. She called some friends last night, and sent them to "Real Daddy's" house to fetch her clothes. "Real Daddy!" God! She wished she'd never started *that* one! It seemed an eternity since she and her husband had been, sitting by a cow pond back at her stepfather's ranch talking about "Real Daddies." Her husband, Mike, lived with his "Real Daddy" in a shack across town. June loathed "Real Daddy." Her mother in law, Claudette Montgomery, had left this ogre years ago and remarried. Claudette's husband, Bill was Junes father in law, and not this toad known as "Real Daddy!" She'd lied to her boyfriend about her true intentions in going back to Texas for the holidays, but really she'd not known that her soon to be ex husband would be there when she arrived. Because of this she'd avoided contact with the Doc during her trip, and thought that it would be no matter because she really expected him to take off to Little Rock to see his family anyway. But, having heard no word for several days after she'd left for Texas the Doc had called "Real Daddy" to see if she had in fact arrived, only to discover that Mike had flown to Texas for the holidays also, contrary to what she'd told the Doc before her departure. June was to be condemned for one mistake that she really didn't make. That's when the Doc threw her clothes out of the apartment. For all of her planning and scheming June came home with only the clothes on her back. She had in fact; left the clothes she'd taken to Texas with her hanging in her old closet back in her bedroom in the mansion at the Bend. Her plans had been laid out well. Her meeting with Claudette had actually solidified her choices, and soon her long sentence in this purgatory of a town would come to an end and she'd be back on the porch of the big house, drinking strawberry wine, and gazing out over the greens of the golf course. The greens! How far they seemed right now, looking into

Cigar Box

the mirror as she passed the bathroom, and seeing the tangled mess her hair had become. Back in Texas, she'd never have let her hair go like this. She never let anyone see her like this. Still, her options were open! West Texas was still waiting for her, and her deal with Claudette was a good one. Screw the Doc! Him and his family of Arkansas hill-billies! She'd grown tired of his ever-present reminder of how great his family was, and how small she was. Poor dumb bastard! Then, looking into the mirror again the reality of the situation overcame her. For June was still a young girl. If she didn't play this hand correctly she'd have to live in this god-forsaken town forever! She had to get back to west Texas, and the Bend. She *had* to!

She paused for a moment. *"What has happened to me?"* The thought ran through her mind. She looked at her eyes. How could these eyes be only twenty years old? These eyes had seen the burning oil wells of Kuwait, and the bodies of the dead Iraqi soldiers lying beside the road as she traveled with Claudette around the Middle East rebuilding what the war had torn apart. It seemed so long ago. When she had been sixteen those eyes had been so much younger. How much could happen in just three years to dull the blue eyes. Sky blue. Pale blue. Her son had the same eyes. Funny how eyes can tell so much even when there are no wrinkles. The age of the soul is timeless. How many lifetimes? How many years had it been? Only two? Only three? She looked away. Then, she looked back. She was still June Montgomery. She was only twenty, and she would still come back and be home again.

Wilbur Witt and Pamela Woodward

She had enjoyed living in this apartment. It was larger than the one she and her husband had lived in. She really hadn't fixed it up, or made it very personal because deep inside she really knew that one day she'd end this exile and just go home. It had really been Mike's idea to come here, not hers. She'd have ridden the waves back in Texas and let the seas calm a bit, but, as usual, Mike had no guts. He convinced her to run off to this place where she languished in hell. About the only thing good that had happened was Claudette showing up and helping her during the birth of her baby. Now, the old broker had thrown the doors back to Texas wide open, and she'd be damned if she was going to stand on pride and not go home! Still, she'd been comfortable here, until last night after the Doc had told her that she had to move out. He was so cool about it. He acted as if he hadn't really noticed she'd been there. He noticed her at night, but now she'd even lost that hold. This one had pride, unlike her husband who'd surrender all pride for a meal any day, just like his "Real Daddy!" The Doc had told her that he didn't want her "hanging" around his apartment while he was in Little Rock for the holidays. She was outraged at the very audacity of this southern trash to talk to her like that. She just retreated to the living room and listened to him rant. There was a big argument. There were loud words. He didn't hit her, but then, he never did. She liked that part about him. Her husband would slap her at the drop of a hat. He was cooler than that. He just made a decision and followed through with it. He was very angry with her, but then he did have a right. She *had* indeed slept with her husband while in Texas, and was indeed trying to

Cigar Box

put her life back together, but *she* was supposed to leave *Doc*, he wasn't supposed to throw her stuff on the porch! Horse shit! That was the part that really got her. He drove her infidelity home during the argument, and even though she never "owned up" to anything they finally called it a night with him in the bed and her and her son on the couch. He slammed the bedroom door. Then there was just the finality that comes with the end of every broken affair. June realized that no matter how "solid" a relationship is, or how many pillow promises are made, when there is no marriage vow there is no real bond. Yet, in her short life she'd come to realize that in her circumstance even the vows would not bind the restless spirit. In reality, she had been "fun" for the Doc as long as he was going to college. He had the continued support of his parent's money, and he had his salary at the local Wal-Mart. He didn't need June to help with any of his bills. He was in his first year of medical school, and his ego wouldn't allow him to live with a woman who took trips without him. And, to be honest, he'd begun to realize that this short blonde really did have connections he knew nothing about. Her silent arrogance put him in his place. Actually, she didn't mind. Her mind had been made up back in Texas. She was prepared to leave Memphis with its rednecks, mosquitoes, and humidity, and head as fast as she could *back* to that porch and her waiting glass of strawberry wine. She'd drink the wine until her eyes couldn't focus on the greens anymore, and then she'd sleep on the back porch of Claudette's house and wake to the maid scolding her for being a lush! *Si, mi amigo!* No worries here!

Her mind snapped back to the reality of the moment and she walked over to the couch to pick up her son. "Little Mike", as she called him, was asleep at the foot of the same couch that she'd slept on. Another pause. A seething reality sunk into her mind. Doc had put *him* on the couch, also. Even though he'd had his own room with "own bed" in it, the Doc had felt it necessary to have him sleep on the couch, too. His little life was going as rapidly downhill as hers was. Here was an heir to the fortunes of the Bend sleeping on a couch! He was as dirty as she was, but he was innocent. Just then, something gripped her. At what point did she stop using the word "innocent" to describe her own self? Then she realized that she'd left that innocence on a sandy riverbank. The sand. The west Texas sand! The sand itself had betrayed her like the will of God coming through to expose her sins to everyone. She'd come to realize that not all quicksand is wet; some is dry, but just as deadly! If only she'd been more careful that night. If only she'd not been caught up in the moment. The passion had overcome her common sense and her beauty had again trapped her. June had come to realize that in fact, she had never owned her beauty because it had owned her. Her destiny was drifting in the west Texas sand! The sand in Kuwait had been different. It was fine, like baby powder. You'd wake in the morning and it would be hanging in the air like a fog, but it was not a fog. And it was not like the sand of the Pecos. That sand would settle, and would announce your sins to the world like John the Baptist! West Texas sand was like that.

Cigar Box

She gently lifted her child and held him in her arms. He woke and began to complain a bit. She shook him playfully, "Hey, hey, little man. Don't you get up in a fuss? Hey." She reached out to him and touched his nose and said, "Noooooose."

The baby touched her nose and repeated after her, "Nooooose..." He was just beginning to mouth words that she said to him. He really couldn't form sentences, but he could repeat like crazy, in fact he was good at it. She studied his features. Did he look like Mike? She really couldn't tell. His little face had a lot of her features. He had the same mouth, the same ears, the same everything. Still, he had that particular look that secretly told her that Mike couldn't be the father. She held him up and studied his form a bit more. Shaking her head she had to admit that it was just too early to tell.

"Who *are* you, little man?" she asked out loud, but more to herself than to the child in her arms.

"Noooooose," the baby repeated back.

Just then, she heard the blare of a horn outside the apartment. Looking through the window down at the parking lot below she saw her friends Lois and Crystal waiting in Lois' little white Mazda. They were the friends she'd called the night before to get her clothes. She drew the curtain back and waved at them. They both waved back up at her. As she went through the apartment, she noticed for the first time that Doc had already gone. His car was not in the parking lot. She had so put him out of her mind that she hadn't even bothered to check to see if he were in his bedroom. She imagined that he must be nearby, however, because he'd been so adamant about her leaving his home before he drove to Little Rock. He probably didn't want the "good-bye" scene, and to be perfectly honest she could do without it herself. Last night had been enough. He tried to be cool, but in the end, she knew that she'd just "switched off" the Doc, just like any other man in her life that she was finished with. "Next!"

She went over to the dresser with her child on her left hip, and opened the top left drawer. Inside was some money, a few fives, ones and a twenty; all that was left of her last pay check. She'd left it in the drawer before her trip. Going to Claudette Montgomery's house did not entail any expense for June. The Doc had borrowed some of it leaving her only a little bit. She didn't think any less of him because of it, but she did make a note that in spite of his rambling on and on about how well off his family in Little Rock was, he sure got into that drawer and found that money. Deeper inside the drawer, where he couldn't have seen, was the old King Edward Cigar box she'd brought from Texas. When he took the money, he'd left it. She knew exactly where it was because she had pushed it to that position. It was so far back in the drawer that he didn't see it. She counted herself lucky. He could have just dumped it on the porch with all the rest of her things, spilling the memories of a lifetime all over the place. What was in the cigar box could not be replaced. Everything else could be, but not that. She gently let her hand run across it, and then picking it up she made sure the big, thick rubber band that secured it was in place. Looking at the cigar box for a moment she felt the slight sting of a tear come to her eye. "Ray." Her

Cigar Box

stepfather's name came to mind. She stroked the box as if it were something precious. Memories of an old barn, far away came to mind. Yes, she was very glad indeed that the Doc had not dumped the cigar box on the porch. There were memories of someone very dear to her lay within its tattered confines. The side was torn and the paper was peeling from it. She could close her eyes and still see Ray with this very same cigar box sitting on his lap in the barn back in west Texas. It was an old cigar box. In addition to the paper peeling from the side the lid was just barely attached, hence the rubber band needed to keep it all together. She made the rubber band form into a cross because one of the sides was coming loose and without the extra help the contents would spill out. It contained all that was Ray. All his love was in there. Everything that Ray was lay within the tattered confines of the box. It amazed her at how a man's entire life could be contained within the area of a simple cigar box. She closed it, and reseated the rubber band.

She went to the restroom and removed all of her personal items. There weren't many of them. When she thought about it she'd never really settled into Doc's apartment because in her mind it had always been "Doc's" apartment. She always knew inside that she was just passing through, and the more stuff she had in the apartment she harder it would be to gather everything up and leave, just as she was doing today. Then, suddenly, all the resentment rose within her and as an afterthought she took her lipstick and wrote on the mirror, "Merry Christmas Son of a Bitch!" Looking around briefly to make sure there was no part of her left here, she turned and left the apartment. It wasn't even a major decision to make; nothing at all like leaving the Bend. She could still remember that night. Grabbing the suitcases and sneaking out of town like a criminal. No, leaving this two-bit apartment wasn't anything like that. She didn't have any clothes here, so there was really nothing left to pack. There were no memories to pack either, just a sterile apartment where she once slept. With the eviction of her clothes, the apartment was the Doc's once again. It was totally his. Even the idea of June Montgomery was gone now. She'd have to stay with her friends for a few days, and then go through with her plans to go back to west Texas where she had always belonged. The Doc was her supervisor at work so she knew that her job wouldn't be worth a hill of beans now, and she'd be unemployed anyway, but then she wasn't really unemployed because she'd taken the "fast class" that Claudette had lined up for her, and renewed her real estate license in Texas during her trip. She'd gotten her real estate license the very moment she turned eighteen. Her renewal should have been at the end of the month of June because her birthday had been on June 21st, but she'd not done it and let her license lapse. She had to have Claudette arrange for her to take the necessary class and file the paperwork to renew the license. That had been the main order of business, and a principle reason for her trip to Texas. She *could* exist, just not here, that's all. Mike would swallow his tongue but no matter, Claudette would side with her because of the baby and the fact that Mike could never pass the state test and even get a real estate license! Walking down the steps in front of the

Cigar Box

apartment with her baby on her hip and the cigar box under her right arm June saw that Lois was driving the car with Crystal sitting in the front passenger's seat. She walked up to the car and asked Crystal, "Did you get all my stuff from Fat Daddy last night?"

"All but a few things. He kept a pair of jeans, and a pair of red boots. He put them back in his room. He said that Mike called from Texas and wanted to talk to you when he got back from there."

June bristled. In her conversation with Mike the night before she'd flown back to Memphis, he had considered her return to Texas, but then he turned and had rejected the idea. But, in typical "Mike" fashion he couldn't make a decision and hold to it, and now was holding her clothes ransom just so he could talk to her. Why? Mike had always been like that. In June's mind, she thought that he was trying to make sure he had a date over on Commerce Street back in her hometown, and if that date didn't work out then he'd take her back, at least temporarily. In the part of her mind that was still young and romantic she'd thought that she and Mike had began reconciliation that final night in Texas but now, with the kidnapping of her two favorite items of clothing, it was apparent that Mike had just slept with her because she was there, and no other reason! It began to occur to her that there were now two men who could apparently do without her. Was she slipping? Back in west Texas not long ago men and boys fell over themselves to gain her attention. To add insult to injury he'd kept the exact items that her sister in law, Angie had given her as a wedding gift. He had kept her pair of "501's" and red Justin boots. Angie had given her these so she'd look good on the River Walk in San Antonio during her honeymoon.

Memories of San Antonio flooded her mind. Somehow Ray was there! She felt that if she could go there again, back to the Alamo she'd find her stepfather's spirit. Somehow he would still be there. She recalled the night she and her husband had been there. The walk from the River Walk up to the Alamo wasn't that far. The building had an orange glow to it, almost surreal, that made it stand out among the more modern buildings in the downtown district. Sometimes the moonlight would make the Alamo see to bleed, and turn red. Mike hadn't understood a single thing she'd said that night. He just wanted to get her back to the hotel and get her clothes off.

Shaking these memories off, she opened the rear door of Lois' car. The car was small, with not much room inside. Far different from the cars and large trucks she'd become accustomed to in the Bend. She put Little Mike over against the driver's side of the rear seat. Looking at Lois she asked, "Didn't you bring the car seat?"

"No, we're just going a little ways and I couldn't find it. I think they lost it or something. I didn't see it last night. Forget it. Those things are such a pain. He's over two, isn't he?"

June looked back at the apartment, "But it was there the other day. I know it was. I saw it in the living room. Are you sure you didn't see it at Fat Daddy's place?"

"No. And that thing is so big! If it had been there I'd have seen it. Are you sure that the Doc didn't just

Cigar Box

throw it away? He'd do that to hurt you now, you know?"

"Yeah, forget it." She scratched at a bump on her neck, "God, I hate mosquitoes!"

"Get eat up last night?" Crystal asked, laughing.

"Yeah. I found out the big mosquitoes don't come and bite you. The big mosquitoes send the little mosquitoes to get you and bring you back to them. Memphis is one big mosquito nest! Elvis was an idiot for staying here!"

June couldn't hide her concern. She was very strict about the car seat. It was still on her mind. Had the Doc really dumped that too? It worried her. She'd have to buy a new one. It hadn't been in the apartment, but Mike's father hadn't given it to the girls either. Fat Daddy was an asshole, but he wouldn't have kept the car seat. He wouldn't hurt little Mike. There seemed to be something very wrong with the car seat being gone like this. Details like this troubled June. Actually, what really troubled her was the fact that it would be so easy to loose something at Mike's father's house. Maybe he hadn't noticed it. Entire sofas had been lost there! What chance did little Mike's car seat have? And her two friends just blowing off the whole thing really irritated her. These girls didn't have a baby so they didn't understand the gravity of the situation, but she was just too stressed and tired to worry, and besides, it *was* only a few blocks, and it *was* Christmas morning and she had enough problems to consider already. She slid Mike back to the middle and belted him in. The belt in the center fit better than the straps on either side of the rear seat, but no matter how much she tried to "snug" him the belts remained loose. Finally, she just shoved him as tightly as she could up against the rear of the seat.

"Nooooose…"

"Sit!"

She slid in and put her own belt on, sitting in the passenger's side of the rear seat. Closing the door and taking one last look at Doc's place, she placed her cigar box on the seat beside Little Mike. As the car pulled off, her eyes turned away and saw Crystal looking at her. "Mad?"

"Hell yeah, I'm mad. He dumps me like a whore just because I went home for Christmas. Throws my things on the porch, and looses my baby's car seat. Yeah, I'm mad. I'm really glad to be free of him."

Crystal casually watched the driveway go by and said, "Hey, he was a twerp anyway. Always talking about how much his family in Little Rock had. He thinks he's better than everybody else He is always looking down his nose at everybody else. You'd think that he doesn't know that *he's* working at Wal-Mart too!. I'm gonna quit soon. I can't stand working for him."

"I never liked him, June," Lois, who was driving now, joined in. "He just didn't strike me as your type."

The two girls were actually trying to make June feel better. Even though she *had* hoped for some measure of security from him, the Doc never could quite measure up to what she'd left in Texas. Not her marriage. Heavens no! At least the Doc *was* a man. Her husband, Mike was jealous of her relationship with the Doc but he was too cowardly to do anything about it. Still, she remembered the last night in Texas before

Cigar Box

flying back here. Mike seemed to be the old "Mike" she'd known years ago at Fat Eddie's catfish house. She considered that if Mike could just stay like that, her life would have been, would still be perfect! She was preparing to mend fences with Mike but then he "flip-flopped" on her and she realized that Mike was still Mike and Fat Daddy was still Fat Daddy. Still, all was not lost! She had an ace in the hole. She had a ready ally in her mother in law, Claudette. Claudette was not about to let go of her grandson, little Mike, and with that hold, June knew she would soon be a member of the Bend once again. Lois and Crystal had never known the status that June had enjoyed and in reality they never would! They had never seen the power wielded by Claudette. They had never been to a wedding reception where a drunken judge convened court right there in the living room. Her two friends in the car had never seen that world. They were just two Memphis hillbillies trying to make her feel better about her break up with her boyfriend. All three of these girls had worked the same shift. The two Memphis natives had the opportunity to date the Doc but he'd never taken an interest in either of them. However, when June came on the scene there was something about the little west Texas girl that caught his eye. She had beauty, and she had a form of "class," though it was a type the Doc had never seen before. It was a dry and sandy type of culture that made her know the right fork to use and then turn and drink whiskey from a Mason jar. She normally spoke with a California clip, but she had a soft Texas drawl that she turned on at will and would melt a heart with, and she had the passion of a true west Texas firecracker, and when that fire was blazing she'd keep it on high until the very last bit of it burned out, throwing all caution to the wind.

This diversity of culture was one of the problems between June and her boyfriend. The Doc did come from a good family, but they were nowhere near the wealth that was wielded by Claudette back in west Texas. Claudette had taken a patch of Texas sand near the only river for miles around and turned it into an exclusive resort for the rich and famous. Then, when that was done she took off to the Middle East and rebuilt entire nations from the ground up! She'd made even the hard-nosed Muslims bow and scrape, and June held the only grandson! The heir! The apple of the power broker's eye! Yes, she was beginning to realize that the problem between her and the Doc was just as much on her side as his! Even as weak as Mike was he was still richer than the Doc, and June knew that to get the grandson back in Texas Claudette would rope and tie Mike.

Crystal and June had been friends for almost two years now. They'd met at work and had even gotten matching rose tattoos on their ankles. June was going to have to stay with Crystal and her parents for a few days until she went home to Texas. Crystal's little sister looked after the baby for her when she worked. It wasn't bad there, but it would only be a stopping place for her on her way home. June knew with the way Crystal's father had looked at her she could stay as long as she liked. She'd seen that look before. She knew how to play him for a place to stay. She'd stay a bit, but the move back to the Bend was inevitable. It wasn't like a defeat. She had nothing to fear in Texas,

Cigar Box

and besides that, at least she would be around people she grew up with. Her own lawyer had stressed the futility of fighting her husband for divorce *and* custody of her child. Her Mother in law would allow the money that she deemed necessary to assure the outcome of any custody suit. June knew the old broker would win, but what the hell? She could win! All that would do is bring June back to west Texas, and the Bend. It would bring her home! She could try and fight, and go up against Claudette, but she'd just get crushed, and Mike would marry some prom queen, leaving her out of the loop. Just like her mother, fat, stupid and broke in a few years with everybody whispering behind her back. And to avoid that all she had to do was give in and go back to the Bend. Deep within her heart she knew that Claudette would take her back in to be near little Mike and that her husband would have to just "eat it," one spoonful at a time! June was a licensed Real Estate Agent, even at this young age. Part of the reason for the trip back to Texas was to take a class to renew that license. She knew that sitting in the little office in west Texas was far better than stocking shelves at a Wal-Mart in Memphis!

While these thoughts were racing through her mind, the car eased down the dirt driveway approaching Sherman Road. Little Mike squirmed in his loose-fitting seat belt, and June reached to settle him. The dirt of the driveway turned into the gravel of Sherman Road. The car left a cloud of red dust behind it as it rushed down the hill toward the highway.

"How'd Fat Daddy act last night?"

Wilbur Witt and Pamela Woodward

"Fat Daddy" was Mike's father. His "biological father." "Real Daddy!" This had been a big issue with her and her husband when they were dating. Both came from split families and to find "Real Daddy," had been very important to the both of them. Both had been led to disappointment, and June was beginning to understand why "Real Daddies" should remain the material of myth and memory. She couldn't have foreseen this on that day, long ago, when she and Mike had talked beside the cow pond back in Texas. "Real Daddies" seemed to hold all the mystery, and romance that the current husbands and stepfathers failed to provide.

Fat Daddy, Mikes Father, lived in a shack on the outskirts of town. The grass was never mowed. In fact, there was an old bathtub hidden out in the back yard. Talk was that a jealous husband had killed some woman there and that the previous owner of the house had thrown it out in the yard. In true southern white trash tradition, Fat Daddy had never moved it or taken it away. He just let the grass grow up and it sat there, hidden in the yard like a macabre grotto to the poor dead woman.

Fat Daddy's shack was a maze of old pizza boxes and candy wrappers. There was actually a room that no one could ever get into again, it being so full of trash. A large "Lazy Boy," recliner, that he called his 'cliner, was situated directly in front of the only new and well-kept item in the shack; his television set. The large chair was surrounded by the remnants of meals he'd known in the past. Pizza bits and chicken bones lay on the floor and Fat Daddy, oblivious to the smell, would sit there each night and fall asleep eating

Cigar Box

because he had become too fat to lie down and sleep anymore!

He would rise from the dead each morning and after turning off the television (which stayed on all night) he'd scurry down to work and not return until dusk where he would commence the same ritual again. Fat Daddy saw no reason to change. His world was intact and complete!

"Oh, he was ok. He really kinda enjoyed keeping some of your clothes. Like he knew it would tick you off."

"Just like him! He'd do that...keep my clothes! He did just what he knew would hurt me the most! He's hated me ever since I came to Tennessee! Guess I'm lucky he didn't keep my panties."

All three girls laughed about that one. Fat Daddy had a reputation of ogling the young girls. Everyone in the area knew it. He never molested any girls, but he was a sneak. When she'd stayed with him for a while she'd become accustomed to his "accidental" intrusions into the bathroom while she was there.

"Yeah, but I still think there's more to it than that," Crystal added as the car came near the intersection of Sherman Road and the highway leading into town, "he didn't want to let me take them because, like I said, I think Mike called and told him that he wanted to talk to you again. What did you two talk about down in Texas?"

"How great his momma is!" June stared out through the window. "That, and what a whore I am. I thought that men who sucked up to their mommas were supposed to be such good husbands. Wonder what happened to him." The other two girls laughed again.

Lois pressed the gas pedal and moved the speed up to about forty-five miles an hour. June watched the trees begin to rush by. Through the pines in the distance, she could just barely make out the Wal-Mart where she worked. Just then, a thought crossed her mind and she reached up and poked Lois with her finger, "Hey, run by Fat Daddy's, ok? He's not there right now, and I can get my clothes."

"You're not going to break in, are you?" Lois asked.

"Hey, the *wind* doesn't have to break into that place, why should I?"

Crystal looked straight ahead and said, "I don't think that's what we need to be doing right now, June. Maybe you need to talk to Mike about this. I think there are some unresolved issues here. He was holding on to a little bit of you when he kept the boots and jeans. He was really using the clothes just to get you to come back over."

"Then why didn't he say that in Texas? I'm not going to meet him in that shack.

Lois half turned, and continued to drive down the road, but she noticed that something was wrong in the back seat now. The baby was not fastened into his seatbelt anymore and June was just looking at her with a slight smile on her face.

"Where's the baby?" Lois asked, taking her attention away from the road. From her vantage point as driver, she could tell that the child was nowhere in the back seat, or even in the floorboard. "Where's the baby, June?" she raised her voice a bit more.

Cigar Box

With the smile still on her face, June simply said, "We're gonna teach the angels how to fly."

Sherman Road fed into a state highway with four lanes. At the point of intersection there was a curve in the highway so as to conceal any approaching vehicle as it rounded the bend until it was right upon the meeting point of the two roads. Lois gave a half glimpse to her right as she sped past the stop sign and drove right out into the four-lane highway. The passengers in the car could hear the sound of the tires go from the gravel road to the smooth sound of state asphalt. The cloud of red dust was left behind. An "S.U.V," a Ford Bronco, came suddenly into Lois's field of vision on her right as it rounded the curve. She saw the blur of motion in her peripheral vision and instinctively, her foot hit the brake causing the little car to skid to a stop. With the sudden stopping of the car the red cloud of dust that had been trailing behind it all the way down Sherman Road preceded and caught up with it, enveloping it as it sat idle in the highway. This was not the right thing to do because had she continued driving the whole incident would have simply been a near miss that they would talk about for days after, but by stopping Lois had set her small automobile up to be broad sided on June's side by the much larger, and heavier vehicle. June looked right at the approaching Bronco and saw the vehicle bear down on her. She knew that at the speed it was traveling, the collision would be deadly. She was amazed that she felt no fear. The size and speed of the oncoming vehicle made it so final that there was little left to do, so she just sat there and waited for what seemed like an eternity. It seemed as if time slowed for her but in reality she didn't even have time to take a last breath before the bumper touched the side of the Mazda.

As June waited for the sound of crunching metal that she knew she would surely hear, the strangest thing happened. The Bronco stopped; it just stopped! Frozen in a moment in time! No screaming tires, no crunching metal, not anything! One second it was coming at her and in the very next second it was sitting there as if it were parked. June looked out of her window and could observe the bumper actually touching the door of the car, but not so much as to even move the red dust still clinging from the trip down Sherman Road. She looked up at the people in the Bronco. The driver's eyes were wide, as were his wife's, and she could see that they had two children in the back, without *their* seat belts on, peering between the seats. They looked like very realistic dolls. June considered very seriously that she was dead. Perfectly amazed, she turned to tell Crystal about it, but noticed that she was frozen also, as was Lois. Lois was looking straight ahead, but Crystal was staring wide-eyed at the Bronco. Every one in the car except June was frozen in the same way as the people in the Bronco! The fear in Crystal's eyes was very clear, and June could see the reflection of the colliding vehicle in her eyes. She was beginning to "cross" herself, but had only made the very first motion of the sign of the cross. June leaned forward and looked directly into Lois' eyes. As she moved her hand in front of them she could tell that the reflection was there, but that neither she, nor Crystal could see anything! Yet there were still alive. Their skin was pliable. They were warm. She touched them and they were not stiff, or

Cigar Box

hard. It was as if time were a series of freeze frames of existence and that the world had been paused between two of these frames and all had just stopped. All but June! She looked down at little Mike. He was smiling and looking up at her. From his position, he could not see what was about to happen. She moved her hand in front of his eyes, and like her friends in the front seat, while she could see the reflection of it in his eyes she could tell that he could not actually see her at this time. Then, her eyes followed up to the driver's side window. To her surprise there was a tall thin man standing beside the car peering in at her. He was wearing a white tuxedo. He was a rather pleasant looking fellow. He had dark hair, with a clean shave. His eyes twinkled and he was smiling.

"Hello, June," he said. Would you mind if we have a talk?"

She felt a warm rush run the entire length and breadth of her body. This man was alive and moving, and could talk and see her. He didn't seem to be alarmed at all that everyone was frozen. He acted like he was on his way to a ball or something.

She stared at him. She was rarely at a loss for words but this was one of the times that she couldn't speak. "Hello," he repeated. "I've been waiting a long time for you, June. You might say I've been waiting here for you all of your life. Is that little Mike?"

"Yes! What's going on?" She forced the words out.

"A lot is going on. I've been put here at this intersection to do a job. How I do that job depends on you and I."

She turned back and looked at the S.U.V. "Why did it stop?"

"Oh, it'll start again, give it time. We only have a little time before it does. In my years here at this intersection I've figured out a few tricks, but I can't sustain this one for very long. That's why you and I have to talk. The impact will be terrible, and lots of people will die, but what happens, and who dies during that impact will depend on what you do."

He opened the door, and reaching inside he helped June out of the car.

"Oh, wait, I have to get Mike!"

"No, he'll be alright. He'll come out of that car, but how he does it will depend on you. If some people have their way he'll come out of that back seat dead! But I've been doing some thinking here at this old crossroads for the last twenty years. I think there is another option. He has to stay for now, but you have to come with me. We have a bit of traveling to do." He leaned over to help her out and as he did his hand brushed the child, causing a rash of sparks which made him pull back. He reached in once more, this time being careful not to touch the boy.

"Why did that happen?" she asked.

"He is protected. I can't touch him. The wreck was supposed to happen and I was here to witness it, and make sure everything went according to plan."

"And that plan was?"

"We'll get into that later. How much do you know about time and space?"

"I don't know very much. I'm not very educated."

"That doesn't matter. You don't have to understand it. I'll explain what you need to know. For

Cigar Box

now just understand that there are some who can manipulate time and space, and will do it to achieve their purpose. But I have learned a bit, too, and I can manipulate a few things myself."

Just then, she noticed that her usual jeans and shirt had been changed and she was wearing a long white gown. Her hair had been restored to its original length before she cut it. It was as if she had a new body.

"Why am I dressed like this?"

"The same reason I'm dressed like this. You and I don't make these choices. I was put here to wait for you a long time ago. I've been standing on this road for twenty years. I was standing here before you were born, and I was here before your son was born. There are plans and schemes in this world, and the people that plan and scheme want you, and your son dead. You and I are going to try to avoid that."

"Why do they want us dead? Why do they want my son dead?"

"Because of whom he is. He's not supposed to be, you know? He is a threat to someone very powerful, and very evil. He is afraid of your son. Your son is a dangerous young man. The circumstances of his birth hid him for a while, but in the time-space consortium he was revealed and now we have to move fast if he is to live and do what he is supposed to do. Moving back and forth in time and space has given the effects you have seen. Actually, you've been here before, if you understand these things, but you see it as only once. Why do you think you made that unusual statement you made just before the crash?"

"Which statement?"

"About teaching angels how to fly?"

"I don't know, but I know I needed to say it. It was as if I were expecting the crash. I knew it was going to happen."

"Indeed you did. That June knew, but you do not. When I am done with you then you will understand why you said that."

June looked back at her son, still frozen in the car. "Why can't I just take him out?"

The man looked at her, "June, the universe is a system of balance. It is a system of checks and balances. *One* of you will come out of that car, but not both. Someone very powerful, very skilled has placed us all here, and getting around what he has done is going to take a bit of planning. There must be a sacrifice today. You and I are going to work that out."

The man walked around the small car and approached the Bronco. He looked at the man and the family inside.

"He's a minister you know." He said this as if June were somehow supposed to know it.

"No, I didn't know. I don't know the man." She was still looking around, amazed at the world ground to a halt around her. In the distance she could see another approaching car, it too, frozen on the highway. Above her were birds, frozen in flight. Even a small bug on the ground was sitting there, not scurrying away from her but just staring out at the world through frozen bug eyes.

The man continued to talk, "He's going to die, and see that little girl in back; she's going to die, too."

"Why?" June asked.

The man grinned, "God's will. It's their time. He's been heading for this intersection all his life.

Cigar Box

Everything he has ever done is focused on this intersection. See, this thing we call life is a very complicated affair. We are all tangled up with each other in it. You've been heading for this crossroads, he's been heading here, and I've been waiting here for the whole bunch of you."

"What about his family. I mean, what about the lady, and the child that lives?"

"She'll marry again; move on. She brings her drinking problem out into the open after he dies and she'll blame it on this wreck, but actually it's been there all along. You see she's been living a lie." He crossed his arms across his chest when he said this and looked at June. The look in his eye told her that his last statement was intended especially for her.

June looked away from his gaze as he continued, "Just like a lot of people do."

This stung a bit. "You mean me, don't you?" she asked.

"I could be. But you are special."

"Why?"

He began to walk back around to the driver's side of the car that June had come from, "I don't know. I just know you are. We all have an essence about us, some more profound than others. Your essence is very profound." He leaned over and looked into the car at the little boy. "He's special. There are people who want this little boy to grow up very much. And there are people who don't want him to grow up. Like I said, what do you know about time and space?"

"And like I told you, I know nothing about that stuff."

"Well, let me give you a heads up. On this side, the eternal side, things are 'as one,' if you can understand that. If someone makes a plan and the situation changes that same someone can undo the plan, or alter it as if it were the same all the time. I was placed here because it was found after my death that someone pivotal would come along. The person was supposed to be a certain person, but due to an accident of conception it turned out completely different. So, instead of going on like a good ghost, I was put here to wait for that person to come down this road on this day, and make sure that the person did not survive this intersection. My death was a normal car crash at first, but due to this information the person placed me here for the time it took for you to come along with little Mike in the car."

"He placed you back here? Why?"

"Because some land was sold a very long time ago. Because the man that sold the land is a sort of Witch Doctor, who is very old, and if there is ever a male heir born in his direct line then he has to progress; move on; die. All these years he's made very sure that that didn't happen, but now little Mike has put a stone in his plans. Did you think you were born at Rio Casa by some accident?"

"Rio Casa?"

"Yes, the place you know as the Bend. That's the land that we're talking about. After my wreck, my sister went to that area and started that subdivision, but I'm getting ahead of myself. Just understand that I want you and your son to win this fight. If I gave you a certain choice right now you'd make the wrong one. I have to 'school' you a bit. Within you, June, there is

Cigar Box

a great spirit, but it's never been allowed to grow. I'm going to try to help you grow that spirit, but we don't have much time. Soon the shaman will come, and he's not going to be very pleased when he finds us gone! He never thought that would happen. He will try to find us, but before he does I have to show you some things, and you have to tell me some things, and then we will come back to this intersection and continue."

"Am I dead?"

"No, you are not dead. Actually, you're more alive now than you've ever been in your entire life. You've come down to this point you are at right now, but there is a bit more than just you at stake here now, though you are pivotal to this situation." The man looked back at the baby. In his eyes, June could see a great deal of love. Then he reached out and put his thumbs over her eyes. He pressed hard, hurting her, but when he took them away, and the blur dissipated she began to see a scene before her similar to a holographic image. It was as real as she was, and three-dimensional. Turning and glancing behind her, she saw that the Memphis scene was still there, and that this new image was a projection of a reality from another location. She saw Claudette pulling her car out into an intersection just outside of the Bend in Texas. Mike, and his older stepbrother, wife, and their baby girl were in the car with them. June knew that they must have been heading home from the store to finish Christmas dinner. Claudette was forever forgetting something at the store on Christmas, or any other holiday for that matter and having to rush off to pick something up. The image was alive and moving. She noted that they still had full motion, unlike the scene in Memphis, and she could even hear their conversation as if there were a great, cosmic set of speakers installed somewhere in the sky.

"Did you talk long with her before she left," Claudette asked.

"A little. The Doc is real mad about her even coming here. Dad called and said that the Doc had dumped all her things on his porch when he found out I was down here. She's gonna be hard put to find a bed to sleep in tonight."

The older woman looked with disgust at her son. "The Catter will find a place to sleep, rest assured!"

"I think she wants to come back to the Bend. She even talked with me about it the night before she left. I can't see her ever coming back here."

Claudette was fully aware of the conversation that she herself had had with June during her visit, irrespective of any "agreements" that had passed between June and Mike in the bedroom. The agreement between her and her daughter in law had been understood, and that was the only one that mattered! There was really no other reason to renew the real estate license unless she planned to use it and she couldn't very well use a Texas real estate license in Tennessee. June knew what she was going to do and the two had agreed upon this course of action. The broker decided to educate her son. "Mike," she said, "you heard what she said at breakfast. You know the deal. She wants to come home, and if you'd checked you'd have seen that June's clothes are still in the closet of the room you two slept in. Didn't you check?"

Cigar Box

He turned and looked surprised. "You'd let her live in your house? I thought you were just being nice. You'd let that slut come into your house after all she's done?"

His mother turned and told him, "She made *one* mistake Mike. And if you'd been a man she'd not have made *that* mistake. Of all of us here June is probably the only person who deserves to be in the Bend!"

"I won't come back mother! I'll stay in Tennessee. I can't live here if she's here. You know that."

She laughed. "You'll come back. Five minutes after June the Cat hits town you'll be here. Don't even *try* to be cool! I'll cut you off without a cent. Let your 'Real Da Da' support you for a while! You'll be back." She looked in her rear view mirror, "Buddy, you ok with that?"

The young man sitting in the rear seat next to the lovely Mexican girl said, "Yeah, mom, whatever you want. I just want this mess to clear up and let's go on." He patted his wife's hand and she smiled at him.

The car pulled through a green light at the intersection of the freeway and the access road. At that moment the daughter in law screamed, "Oh, my God!"

Claudette looked up to see a car rushing off the freeway coming directly toward the car. Then, she was frozen in time. The whole scene stopped. All the occupants of the car froze. Time froze. All eyes in the car were staring at the oncoming car, knowing the crash was unavoidable. Now the scene was just like the one on Memphis. There were two crashes, two identical sets of circumstances occurring at precisely the same time!

June winced and turned her face away from the scene before her, and the man in the tux put his arms around her shoulders and began to walk her away back toward the Mazda. She looked behind her for one last peek, but the image was now gone and then, in a moment of time, she was in an area she could only describe as "nothingness." Blue above her; blue below her; blue all around her. The scene from Memphis was beginning to fade. She felt slightly numbed. It was almost as if she were not in her body, yet she was. Then the area around her began to glow, and become white.

"Are they going to die?" June asked, glancing back at the fading Memphis scene.

"Depends."

"On what?"

"On what you decide.

She shook her head and stared blankly, "I really don't understand."

"You will, in time. You see, *they* won't live if *you* live. I see it in your eyes, June. Right now that's a simple choice because you are a survivor. My job is to take that instinct out of you. To do that we have to take a journey. There are a few rules on the trip we are about to take. One, you are not the same as your physical body. You have left that body. We exist on different planes. You share the same soul as your body, but it is more as if it is the same essence. You, June, are not the same as that June in the car. I'm leaving her in that car for the time being in case our friend comes along. He's going to be very upset when he finds you alive, but I need to buy time to make you understand what's at stake here, and understand what

Cigar Box

you need to do." She turned and for a moment she saw the Mazda still suspended in time and for the first time saw that in fact "June" was still sitting in the rear seat staring at the impending crash.

"Hey, this is really weird, ok," she said. "Is that me, or is this me?"

"You are you. Don't try to understand it. Let's do it this way. We'll give you a different name here. You'll be Veronica, ok?"

"Veronica?"

"Yes, Veronica. Whenever we discuss here," he pointed to June in the car, "we'll call her June, but between you and I, you will be Veronica."

"Veronica."

"Yes."

"Any particular reason for that name, or is it just an idea of yours?"

"I have my reasons. You'll come to know them in time."

"So I'm *Veronica*."

"Yes, and that over there," he pointed to the Mazda, "is June."

"Ok, I'm Veronica."

"Yes. Now, are you ready for a trip? I want you to tell me your story, and I will show you just why your son must survive this crash. You ready?"

"Sure, you first."

He extended his arm to her, "Care to go dancing?" As she watched in amazement, the "nothingness" began to form a scene around her. Then she was back to a few years before, in another place, another time. She had been transformed in the spirit back to her youth. She and her spirit guide walked into the dance hall unseen by anyone. She could see herself sitting at a table across the hall.

At The SPJST

The air was smoky in the dance hall situated out on the little desert highway in west Texas. Actually, it wasn't a dance hall at all, but an auction barn used by local ranchers, and sometimes used for science fairs, and such. On selected nights, the locals would come as far as seventy-five miles to attend the festivities, bringing their own bottle, and girl to dance and get drunk. It was said that Willie Nelson had once played here; and even gotten drunk here just like everyone else before he *was* Willie Nelson. This wasn't like a "club" in the larger towns. There were more fights, but then the boys would just dust off and go back in to drink more Lone Star Beer, and dance with the very girl they were fighting over in the first place. The main lure of the hall was the fact that it was out in the "back" and there was really no scrutiny over I. D. or age limits. Anyone could come, and so long as they didn't pull a gun no questions were asked, no arrests were made. Girls became women; cowboys became movie stars at the S. P. J. S. T!

The building was just a big huge metal building. The floor had been used for everything from "socials" to auctions. There were long cafeteria-style tables running the length and width of it, and just barely enough room to squeeze onto the improvised dance floor. The band was always too loud and badly mixed, but the crowd could hear the beat and that was all that was needed to two-step. The walls were lined with the trappings of whatever event the preceding week had held. All sorts of bottles and paper bags were on the tables. The people all brought their own "set-ups" and made their drinks right there at the table.

It was not that June didn't want to be here, she did! In west Texas this was about the most "happening" place one could find, but because her mother brought her she had to be slightly less than content. How could *anything* be cool if your *mother* brought you? No sixteen-year-old girl would be happy on a date with her *mother*. Her stepfather, Ray would have been with them, but he'd stayed home this particular night because of a persistent pain in his chest he attributed to the construction trade. He nailed shingles, and did dry wall work. He actually held a master plumbing license, but he would take any work he could find to support his family. He'd had these pains for a couple of years and was sure it was some kind of "sore muscle." June's mother, Barbara, was happy to sit at the table and watch. June was "hyper" enough for both of them. Always running out of time, always having to "do it now!" Even though she'd started the evening by not really wanting to be here, she fell very quickly into a mode of dance, and beer that the S.P.J.S.T. had plenty of.

Cigar Box

While she was sitting at her table, she noticed a young man "eyeing" her from the far corner of the room. Funny about the eyes; there is a definite soul contact when you look into someone's eyes. There is a surge, even if you really don't like the person, and June was sure she wouldn't like this guy. He was all decked out in his "cowboy" clothes. "He wouldn't make a scab on my daddy's butt," she laughed to herself as she watched him stroke his mustache because he thought it appeared "cool" to do so. Still, she had the need to know if she could pull him in. She looked right at him, her clear blue eyes piercing his until he picked up his beer and walked over. He had his left thumb tucked in behind his "rodeo" belt buckle. "Give me a break," June thought. Still she smiled.

"Hi."

"Hi."

"You here with anyone?"

"My mom." *How uncool! How uncool!* She thought. She looked over her shoulder at her mother who was trying to pretend she didn't notice the exchange.

He was dressed for a night out on the town. He had his Resistol cowboy hat, his Garth Brooks style shirt and brand-new "501" jeans. The Justin Ropers on his feet were almost mandatory. About the only thing that was really functional for a real cowboy would be the boots, and maybe the hat. The belt had a rodeo buckle that should have been *won* and not *bought*. You could no more buy a rodeo buckle than you could buy a purple heart, or a medal of honor. To be sure, there were real cowboys at the hall that night, but they were not dressed as well, and were more into the beer and the dance than flitting around displaying themselves like a proud peacock at the zoo. To this young man the western wear was more of a "theme" than a necessity. If he were in New York, he'd have been in a suit with equal ease.

"Wanna dance?"

"Nah, why don't you go get your beer and sit with us?" June wasn't much of a dancer. She knew a few steps, but she never really got into it. She preferred the edge of the crowd at the hall, and not the center of the dance floor. This ran contrary to her basic personality, which was gregarious by nature.

He wasn't about to say no to the invitation to sit, but he hesitated for a moment. Then he said, "Sure, gimme a minute." He walked back over to the other side of the room and picked up a twelve pack of beer that he'd been nursing for about an hour, and returned to June's side of the room. He moved in behind the long "cafeteria" table and sat beside June.

"You come here much?"

"Nah," she reached for one of his beers, "only when mom wants to."

The boy looked over at June's mother and touched his cowboy hat. She had the obvious look of an older woman trying to fit in, and smiled back at him. Her hair was tired, as were her eyes, and her face was bloated, and sagged with age. She had long ago lost the weight battle, but her choice of jeans proved she was in serious denial. June twisted open a beer, and put it to her lips. It was room temperature, but that didn't matter. In west Texas, room temperature could be cool. It was relative. She never liked beer anyway, but she needed to sip it for effect. She sat it on the table and let it sit there a moment, watching his eyes, and then took another swallow. Swallowing hard, she sat still for a moment, then stretching up her back she let out a low, slow belch.

"Oh, God, I'm sorry. Don't know why I drink this stuff. I don't like it."

The cowboy took the opportunity, "Hey, not bad manners, just good beer. Anyway, I got something else in the truck that won't make you belch," he whispered.

She cut her eyes to her mom, "Tell her you gotta go to the toilet," he whispered.

She smiled slyly, "Rock and roll."

"Yeah. I got a blue truck, in back," he motioned with his eyes.

He got up and made as if he needed to leave. June's mother assumed he was going to relieve himself because he left the beer on the table. June gave it a minute or two and told her mother, "Hey, I gotta go… you know."

"Ok, don't get lost, ok?"

She got up and eased through the crowd toward the ladies room. As she neared it, she became lost in the crowd so that her mother could not see where she was heading. Then, a little right instead of a left, and she was outside in the parking lot. The night air was warm. Texas warm. Night air in the summer is not cool in Texas, but almost hot! The steamy air had bugs floating all in it, and she could pick up the distant, and not so distant odors drifting aimlessly through the air. Around the corner of the tin building, she heard a real cowboy throwing up. She felt the excitement build. She knew what was waiting in the truck, and she wanted it. She wanted it bad enough to go there and let the cowboy think anything he wanted to think. She began to walk around to the rear of the hall. There it was. A blue truck was sitting in the parking lot. It was the kind of truck that a fool like the "cowboy" would have. It *had* to be a four-wheel drive, even though he never went into the desert, and it simply *must* have a "crew cab" in the rear, even though he'd never have a "crew" to ride in it. And, since this was the only blue truck with a stupid drugstore cowboy standing beside it, she knew it was the one.

She ran across the lot to the truck. He opened the door and she dove in.

"Ok, what 'cha got?" She rubbed her hands together.

He reached under the seat and brought out the joint she knew was there. "I got the best dope Mexico has to offer, my sweet!"

June eyed the cigarette. Then she licked her lips. Part of the reason was in expectation of the high, and the other, she knew was to excite him and make sure she got the joint.

"Hey, let's move the truck down by the river, ok? I don't want anyone to see us."

"Ok," he said, realizing that this was most likely a good move on his part. He didn't want to be caught in the parking lot of the S. P. J. S. T. hall smoking grass, and he wanted June alone, so it all worked out. He was a little nervous about taking his shiny new truck down onto the riverbank, but looking at June he figured it would be worth it. He started the truck and began to ease toward the edge of the lot, then onto the

Cigar Box

grass, then into the trees. He worked his way down an embankment to a long bridge that traversed the river near the dance hall. June could tell he was not experienced in four wheeling, but she hoped he could smoke dope better than he could drive on a riverbank. Stopping, he backed the pickup back a bit and when he turned off the motor, they could not be seen from the hall.

"Here," he said as he lit the joint. Blowing onto the lit end of it, he handed her the cigarette. She took it and drew in the smoke; all the way down. Closing her eyes, she let the lung full of dreams take hold. Yes, this was much better than warm beer. This was far beyond that. Her stepfather, Ray, had taught her this trick years ago. She was an old hand at smoking. She was far better than this phony baloney cowboy who only had one joint that most likely Juan Sanchez had rolled for him while he grossly overcharged him for the drug. He made no effort to take the joint from her, but let her smoke all she wanted. She took another draw, embarrassed that she'd been so greedy with it.

"I'm sorry, didn't mean to be a 'hawg." As the drug took effect on her she turned on her best Texas twang that made her even more fetching than she was, if that were possible. Her eyes began to draw into slits, reflecting the thin line of blue. She took another hit from the joint, drawing it deep within her lungs, letting her perfect breasts swell, exciting the cowboy all the more. She leaned back and handed him the smoke.

He took the joint, "Oh, you ain't no hog, hon, just lonely." He took the chance to put in that word and turn the conversation toward her feelings, but she was already taking the "ride," and didn't care what he said, so long as the joint was lit.

"I'm not lonely, just need excitement. You know what I mean?" She knew what that statement would do to him, and she wanted it to. She could hear him puff the joint eagerly. She knew a few well-placed words, the promise of love, would make this cowboy bark at the moon. June knew she was beautiful. This was her dance floor. She didn't need to have everyone glaring at her as she jumped around like a fool, so long as she could hold the undivided attention of one cowboy at a time. She knew what he thought. He thought that if she'd just smoke enough of that dope she'd let him make love to her. Well, *that* depended upon just how good this joint was! She leaned back against his chest and let him put his hand over her shoulder. He began to work it down. Slowly running across the firm mounds of her breasts. She didn't resist, and knew the feel of her body was driving him wild. She could actually hear his heart beat faster.

"How ya' feeling?" His voice was quivering.

She felt her pulse quicken. Within a few short breaths she relaxed and lay back to where she'd really been all of her life. As the cowboy had his way with her she stared at a streetlight in the distance, near the dance hall. She detached herself from her body and, closing her eyes, she ventured out from it, and away to a smoky land that she went often when reality crashed in. Then, she drifted back and when the entire episode was over she lay there with the cowboy panting for a minute, and then she sat up and began to look for her clothes. He reached down on the floorboard and gave the jeans to her. She wondered if this man knew that

Cigar Box

he'd just been with an underage girl. It didn't matter, because such things happened on this riverbank all the time. The real miracle was that they found a place to park at all!

"Hey, my mom'll be looking for me. I need to get back," she said between short gulps of air.

She made a last minute adjustment of her belt, and she checked her bra, dodging his parting kiss, quickly opened the door of the truck, scampered up the hill, and was across the lot, and back to the hall. June was laughing to herself thinking about him trying to figure out how to get that shiny new truck *back* up the embankment to the dance hall. She knew he was no four-wheeler. The cowboy was amazed at how agile she was. He was tired, and out of breath, and truly he didn't go back into the hall, because he *did* realize what he'd just done, and he wanted to just get out of there before anything was said to the fat woman he'd seen sitting at the table with June. It would be a long time before he would come back to the hall again.

Once back inside the hall, June went to the rest room, straightened up a bit more, and emerged. Glancing at the clock, she guessed she'd been gone about twenty minutes. When she came back to the table her mother was waiting, "Where you been?"

"Hey, in the bathroom, ok?"

"You were too long in the bathroom. Where's that boy at?"

June knew she had to admit, but she tried to cushion it by delaying a few moments. Then, "Ok, ok...I went outside with him a minute; just to talk, you know?"

June's mother wasn't angry about her having slipped out the back with the cowboy, and not even if she knew about the smoke because she, herself, did such things. She knew about Ray's little bag in the barn at his mother's place, and she didn't think it hurt anything. No, it wasn't anything like that. She was angry that June had gone there without *telling* her. It was a betrayal of trust. June's actions proved that there *was* a barrier between the two that she could not bridge no matter how hard she tried. The whole idea of bringing the girl here was to be able to be with her, and be her companion. It was an effort to be young again, if only for a little while. Also, there was a measure of safety. This was a friendly atmosphere, in spite of the occasional fight. The idea being that the hall was such that a young lady would be safe there, but how could she be safe if she slipped out the back with the first cowboy she met! Glancing at the table, she noticed that June had not even finished the beer he'd given her. In fact, the remains of the man's twelve-pack were still on the table. He had not returned. In her years in west Texas the older woman knew what all of this added up to, but she didn't want a big show of concern right now. Instead, she opted for the "motherly" route.

"You just gotta be careful, June. You gotta get to know people before you take off with 'em! Did you know that there's only three people ever been with me here?"

"Who?"

"Well, Ray, you know that, and Mr. Stillwell, he showed me this place, and then there's you. You are my best date." The fat lady smiled. She noticed

Cigar Box

something on June's jeans and asked, "Where did you get the sand on your jeans?"

June looked at the side of her jeans. There was a bit of river sand on them, obviously from when they had been on the floorboard of the truck. The cowboy had probably had some sand on his boots and it had been on the floorboard.

"I don't know," June tried to blow it off. "I guess they must've been dirty."

Her mother was not a fool. "You go down on the river with that cowboy?"

"I told you that, mom. Just for a talk. That's all."

"You're lying to me, June. I know you went outside, but that's river sand on them jeans. You went down to the river with him didn't you?"

June reached down and continued to brush off the jeans, but the very act of doing this was proving that there was a *lot* of sand on the jeans and her mother was watching the entire routine with a knowing eye.

"Ok," her mother finally said, "I know you are lying; you know you are lying, but we won't tell Ray about this. You just keep your little ass with me from now on. You need to go to the toilette from now on, I go with you."

June kept brushing the jeans and tried to ignore her mother.

On the other side of the mystic veil Veronica watched this entire holographic scene as if it were a movie she could step into, and out of at will. Her spirit guide let her watch. She could even taste the beer, smell the smoke, everything. It was like she was there, yet she wasn't. She felt the emotions. As she watched herself with the cowboy, she noticed that the

Wilbur Witt and Pamela Woodward

excitement began to return to her, even then. She walked around the dance hall. She remembered being there that night, and in places like it a lot of Saturday nights! She also remembered that this particular cowboy on this night was no exception, but the rule. June's passion would overwhelm her time, and time again. The man in the tux came up behind her and she turned to talk to him.

"You been right here all along?" She asked.

"Yes, that's my job, taking things in."

She felt a little embarrassed, "You seen what I did in that truck?"

"Yes, I saw it. If you are ashamed, why did you do it?"

"It felt good, that's why. Didn't you ever want to do something because it felt good?"

"You didn't love him though."

She looked at him with a wry smile, "Hey, I did for two minutes."

"Veronica, I'm not going to preach to you; that's *not* my job, but you are too young to have been this experienced. In fact, you ignored him during the act. June left her body and came here with us, though she doesn't know it just now."

Veronica was suddenly stunned, as a memory flooded back into her being that she really had lost for oh so long, and now it had returned. So many times this sort of thing would haunt her in life, and yet when she tried to remember where she'd gone, what she'd seen, it was gone, like a wisp of smoke!

"How do I do that?"

He looked at her, "Do what?"

"Leave my body, and then come back?"

Cigar Box

"It's a gift. You can't bring the memories with you when you go back to the physical world, but on this side you don't have that problem. You're seeing things as they are for the first time."

"What happens if I don't get back?"

"When such a gifted soul doesn't make it back one more person is found dead in their sleep, in their chair, in their home. Once the soul stays separated from the body for too long it chooses to stay on this side."

"Why?"

"Because that's God's will. You know about God's will?"

"Hey, mister, my mom took me to church every Sunday. She hauled me down to the Pentecostal Church and that preacher scared the piss out of me *every* Sunday. And I found out that if I was a good little girl that I'd get to go to heaven, but you know what else I found out?"

"What?"

"I found out that bad little girls get to go *everywhere* else!" She then noticed something in his hand, "What's that?"

"Chilidog! I love them. One of the benefits of this job." He ate the rest of the chilidog with one gulp, wiped his mouth and said, "Let's go. I have some questions for you."

*   *   *

Then, just as quickly, she was back in the "blue" room with no beginning, and no end. The man asked, "Why *did* you go there?"

"Go where?"

"Down by the river?"

She looked down at her feet. "I thought we just talked about that. My mother made me go."

The man raised her chin, "Your mom took you to a dance hall, but *you* made the choice to go down by the river, not her. *You* led the cowboy on. You know what was in your mind. You seduced *him*. He didn't seduce you! You see, you make your own decisions. You can blame anyone you want, but you and only you make those choices in life. You can put them off on other people, you can lie, you can reason, but just like that 'S.P.J.S.T.' is really a bar, *you* really wanted to *be* there in that truck on that riverbank!"

"She made me!"

"Did she make you go outside with the cowboy?"

Veronica was trapped within her own lie. She went with the cowboy for the thrill. True, she was using the methods she'd sharpened to a razor's edge to entice men, but it was ultimately her free will, and not her mother who went out that back door with the young man.

"Mom always wanted me to be the prettiest girl in town. She waved me around like a beauty queen ever since I can remember. My jeans were better, my hair was perfect, everything. It was almost as if she got a charge out of me. Do you think a woman can be like that, I mean as pretty as I am, and not go down by that riverbank?"

"Did you ever hear about self control?"

A shadow crossed her face, "There's a fire inside of me. I keep that fire burning on low, but every now and then it gets out of control. That fire just goes all over me, and I gotta just let it burn down."

Cigar Box

"Couldn't you have had 'fun' at your table. He gave you beer, and wanted to sit there with you. Why go out the door?"

She looked down again. The reality was coming home to her. Slowly she looked up and softly said, "I wanted *more*."

"More?"

"You know, the thrill. I felt like I wanted that fire to break out. I felt as if my whole life were trapped in this oily scum, and that if I went through that door with him that I'd feel clean and free for a little while."

"Did you?"

"No." She smiled a sheepish little smile, "After the fire goes down it really don't change anything. All you have left after the fire is gone is ashes."

She walked to what she thought was the edge of the room. She found that there was not an edge at all. She reached out a hand and the blue extended. She tried to "walk" a bit more, but walk didn't do justice to what was happening because she wasn't walking at all but existing in a series of moments, drifting along in the blue mists of eternity. It was so peaceful and she began to understand how a soul would eventually choose to stay here in this place of no return. For the first time in her life she was not conscious of ego, or self. Yet there seemed to be a "self" here, only it wasn't *her*, it was the *other*. This "other" seemed to permeate the entire existence of the beings that inhabited this side of the veil. While in life you intellectually knew about the other, here you felt it. You felt it as an abiding force, yet not a force, but something to be absorbed, or rather to absorb you. The "other" seemed to be just the other side of the blue mists but as she approached it kept going farther away. She felt like she could have walked forever. Stopping, she turned to look back. The spirit guide was still in the same proximity he'd been when she started walking. She actually hadn't gone anywhere!

"I didn't want sex. I wanted freedom. Being with him in that way didn't really give me what I wanted, but it came close, but you just can't quite touch it, you know?"

"Did you ever think that maybe your mother had those same feelings? Maybe she was trying to communicate some of them to you?"

She looked away again, and laughed dryly, "My mom; she got old, but she was still trying to…be *me*!"

"Could she ever be you? Could she have *ever* been you?"

"No. She lost it. She could never be me. She wasn't even a good grandma. After the baby was born, she never came to Memphis. She never wrote me. She never called. She just sat alone in that shack behind Fat Eddie's and got fatter, and all the time all she wanted was more party! She wanted more party. More party! She just knew if the men came to our table because of me, they'd notice her, too. Ray worked all the time. She was trying to go back. Thought if she tried hard enough she'd be sixteen again, and he'd notice her but it didn't happen that way, though. She never appreciated Ray. He wasn't like that. All she had to do was be herself, but she lost herself so long ago she could never find it again."

"Did you? Did you appreciate your stepfather?"

A film of tears came over June's eyes, "Appreciate? I loved him." She looked directly into

Cigar Box

the guide's eyes, "Ray was the only man I ever really loved!"

"Do you think that perhaps your mother felt the competition for Ray's attention?"

Veronica was shaken down to her core. In her mind's eye, a flash of a picture of her aging appeared before her. She remembered the pictures of her mom at her age. She was beautiful, too. She had in effect given up her life to raise the girl, who was the apple of her husband's eye, and now all she asked in return was to watch her have fun at the S.P.J.S.T. hall.

"Will I be at that table some day?"

He looked at her and replied, "No, you will never be at *that* table, but there is a table for you, just not that one. That's part of what I'm here for." There was a kind of finality in his words, with a gravity that made her blood run cold.

"I'll be one of those souls that gets lost and simply never makes it back?"

"No, it is important that you *do* make it back. You have work to do back at that intersection, but you have to learn some things about yourself before that. If I hadn't taken you on this journey you would never be able to make the right choices when the time comes."

Then he waved his hand and Veronica saw the scene appear before her again. Her mother was laughing, drinking her beer, and watching the people dance. She moved toward her and looked at her for the longest time. It became apparent that her mother could not see her. She watched her face. Slowly tears formed in her eyes and rolled down her lovely cheeks.

"Mom, I never realized. It's so awful to be old. It's so awful to know that you are not the center of the party. You robbed me of everything, my youth, my life, my dad, everything. Why couldn't you just put it down and be "mom?" You broke your neck trying to get into the Bend, and I just threw it away, doing the very things you taught me to do, and then, when I was of no more use to you, you never even called! And you know why I threw it away? I did it because I hated you! I hated you for what you did to me, to Ray, to everyone!"

She looked at her mother and saw a strange satisfaction in her face. It was a perverse satisfaction that she'd never noticed before. Only now did she realize where it was really coming from. She looked into the crowd and saw the people dancing. Her mother was enjoying the dance. Veronica could see herself sitting at the table miserable, even after the joint, and the trip outside, but her mother had the happiness of being the mother of the most beautiful girl at the hall! By being the mother of the seductress she was in fact the seductress herself. The beauty lived on in another generation. People were *still* captivated by the rare beauty that June had inherited from her. As long as that beauty was there, there would always be hope. For her mother, that hope was all that she had left.

Quietly, almost the volume of a human heartbeat June whispered, "I did it because I hate you. I did it because I hate you."

Her companion stepped up behind her, "Hate?"

"All the time I was in Memphis she never wrote or called. It was like once I left the Bend she had no more use for me. I suppose she was planning on dolling up my little sister to take my place."

Cigar Box

"Could she?"

"Ha! She is as ugly as a toad. She looks like Ray, God love him."

"Maybe an ugly duckling."

"Or maybe a big fat pig. She has absolutely no self control."

"You need to think about that; self control, that is."

She looked back at the man. "I suppose you never had fun. I guess you never did anything wrong."

He smiled and looked down, "No, you suppose wrong. Like you, there was a time when I was looking for *more* also. But you know, Veronica, suddenly your destiny comes upon you and you realize that there is actually very little you can do about it. The wrong turn on a country road, the wrong statement that you never get to correct, any number of things can come along and put that destiny on you. I've made mistakes. As a matter of fact that's part of what I'm doing here right now. There are more wrongs to right than that little fling you took under that bridge that night. You see God is wise. He always works things out in the end, but he uses us to help. You'll understand these things as we go along."

"Why do *you* think I went outside with the cowboy?"

"Because you thought you had all the time in the world, that's why. Have you ever noticed that you're always in a hurry, June?"

Her eyes narrowed and she said, "Yeah. Been that way all my life. Gotta do it *now*. Were you like that?"

"I was. I was until one night a man walked in front of my car, and suddenly I had all the time in eternity. He made sure of that. He made me realize that some

65

things may take an eternity to fix. You and I have to do some of that fixing, Veronica. It takes a little more work if we're going to save the whole thing."

"But you didn't save me any of that chilidog did you?"

The spirit guide laughed.

Back at the intersection Juan Sanchez stood staring at the frozen scene. The wreck should have already happened! Here were all of the participants but no Dreamwalker. He looked at the S.U.V. barely touching the red dust on the Mazda. Walking over he looked in at the little boy, still looking up, smiling at June who was staring at the oncoming truck. Then he walked back to the spot where the man in the tux had been standing. He was aware that the man was gone from the spot he'd been for so long, but he knew that he had not ascended to the light. But where had he gone? Juan was versed in these matters, but could it be that Dreamwalker had learned a thing or two during his imprisonment? Maybe? Maybe not!

He went back and looked into the Mazda again. Something about June's demeanor suddenly struck him. Having the knowledge of these things he knew that this was not June but a shell. The soul was gone, yet not ascended. He felt a terror grip his heart. Only certain souls could do this. He had miscalculated this soul, but then he had miscalculated the boy, too. Yet the boy's soul was still there. He could see the souls within all the others in the car, but not this one. This was a meat dummy left to fool him. Dreamwalker had fled and taken her with him, but where? He stared again at the boy, making sure the soul was still there. It was. Why had he taken June? In a moment of aggravation he tried to reach in and grab the little boy by the neck but the moment his hand got near to the boy's skin a blue flash came and he withdrew his hand in pain. He slammed his fist into the trunk of the car in exasperation. He tried once more, but got the same result. Looking around once again for the Dreamwalker Juan turned and walked back up the road a little way. Where had they gone? Juan knew that he was not just dealing with both sides of the spiritual veil but with time, also. He had to locate the true June, and her dream-walking companion and not just their images scattered throughout all the possible timelines that stretched in every possible direction from this point of reference. He knew that time not only went forward and back but sideways, too. Wherever the soul was that's where the true timeline was, and a soul so skilled could dance between these lines of time and leap like a gazelle at will. It would do him no good to locate one of the images that did not have the true soul within it. It would be like smashing mirrors in a carnival glass house, never finding your way to the very door you came in from. Yet this was his task, and Juan had been smashing these mirrors for over two hundred years. This wisp of a girl and her friend, Dreamwalker would not out fox him!

"Where are you, June Montgomery?" he screamed at her placid face, but there was no response. He knew there would not be any. He shook his head in exasperation, turned and disappeared in a puff of smoke.

Ray sat watching his old friend, Juan sit motionless. They were again in his barn smoking what Juan brought up from Mexico. Only now, Ray was beginning to not like what he was seeing. As Juan came to himself Ray was waiting on him.

"You talked this time."

"I did?"

"Yes," Ray continued, "and you talked about June. Why would you talk about June?"

Juan didn't know that he mumbled outside his experience, but he had to cover it. "Just crazy talk, that's all. It means nothing."

The two men called it a night, but unknown to Ray, Juan was beginning to see that his old friend was delving a trifle too much into his affairs, and he could clearly see that the day would come when he would have to take care of this problem.

At The Catfish House

June worked every Friday night at a local cafe known as Fat Eddie's Catfish Emporium, situated in the small Texas town where she was raised. She lived in one of the shacks behind the café that Fat Eddie rented to her mother. Her stepfather, Ray lived there with them. She'd hung around Fat Eddie's all her life and it was only natural for her to want to work there when she got up in her teens. Her earliest memories were sitting in a booth at the café, listening to the old men, and some young men, spin yarns about the various "going's on" of the little hamlet. She'd been too young to realize that her mother was probably the biggest story in years for the café, and that she herself was expected to live up to the family tradition. When she came of "age," which was actually about twelve, she began to help out in the place, and she evolved into a "Catfish girl" before she was much older. Even at that young age she was indeed fetching, and a delight to the people who ate there as she handed out the fish and fixings each Friday night. She had to go to school but Fat Eddie used her, and other pretty high school girls as weekend waitresses, and as "catfish girls" on Friday nights. It was "all you can eat" night with the fish, and the people sat there and gorged themselves. They would show up still dressed for the game. There was even a waiting room (outside in the parking lot) where the people would wait for their name to be called. June's was the prettiest "catfish girl." She wore a tuxedo, and a bright smile, and lugged the huge tray of catfish to all the tables to refill the plates of the waiting crowd. She would wear a baseball cap that had "Fat Eddie's" written on it. Her long blonde ponytail would lace through the back of the hat.

Michael also worked at the Emporium as a dishwasher. His mother didn't like him down there because of his status of living at the Bend, the most elegant area of the little town, but he wanted to be near June. He would go, and fetch the dishes at the tables and would look longingly at June as she placed new, hot fish upon the hungry cowboy's plates. Eddie dipped the fish in a special "hot sauce" that he concocted in the back of the greasy-spoon cafe. The "bite" that it gave the catfish made it a favorite of all the locals. It was especially good after the beer that was consumed under the stands at the game by the men who told their wives they had to go to the boy's room. Even at the catfish house, June was a vision! She had her long "pony-tail" hanging down her back. At sixteen, the men couldn't help but look longingly at the girl and imagine the woman she would become. She would struggle with the huge platter of catfish and bend over to give out the three extra pieces that Fat Eddie told all his "catfish girls" to give; no more than that because they would only eat three at a time. She'd

Cigar Box

never dropped her catfish platter. She would hand out all her fish and then scamper back to the kitchen with the other girls to get more. Fat Eddie would keep frying it up. He had special "cost cutting" methods, too. A big bowl of pinto beans was always served customers as they waited on the fish to come out. If the bowl came back to the kitchen with any beans left in it, Fat Eddie would just throw them back in the pot with the rest and warm them back up again!

Catfish night was the biggest night of the week in the little town. Catfish was the great equalizer. It was the night when the "have not's" living from week to week could sit down with the good citizens from the Bend and be on a semi-equal basis. During football season the catfish would be the victory celebration, and if the hometown team lost, well, no big deal. Fat Eddie would still "serve 'em up hot" with lots of tartar sauce! Michael fell in love with the little catfish girl. He made special note of every time she came back to the kitchen for more catfish.

June was attracted to Michael. Added to this the fact that she was beginning to understand the meaning of status and the idea of money. The fact that Michael lived at the Bend had originally meant very little to the teenage girl. The Bend had always been that area with the big houses sitting away from the main town. June had never known a time when it wasn't there. She was very familiar with the homes with their large terraces, and even airplane hangers and the golf course running through it. But all of that did not affect June as yet. She was a bit, but not all, taken by Mike. Yet, he had attracted her ever since she first saw him. She had a feeling for him that was not like the feeling she had for all the other cowboys she'd come across in her short, but eventful life. Her nickname, "the Catter," bore witness to her expertise with the gentlemen. Even at sixteen she was much more experienced than he, but she was drawn to him all the same. She'd known Mike all of her life. He was around two years old when Claudette relocated from Memphis. June was born that very year amid all the gossip surrounding her conception. She and Mike looked alike. They both had the same blonde hair and blue eyes. She and Michael had kissed, but nothing more. June was not innocent. Not by a damn sight! She had been to the golf course, but at night with many local boys. That and too many nights at the S. P. J. S. T had hardened the little catfish queen, but she adored Michael, and in that respect, she was pure, and he was pure until one night, out behind the shacks in a field. Michael had kissed her that evening, and June felt the fire rise within her, and there was a quickening of the heart that she was all too familiar with. Lying down on the Buffalo grass was the most natural thing in the world. She felt like she'd been waiting for this field all her life. She felt that this field of grass had been waiting just for her, for just this moment in time. There was a distant light, but this time she didn't go there, but stayed, and felt the rise of her passion. Michael was shy, but June knew what needed to be done, and she led him into maturity. He was clumsy, but she was not. In this respect, she was the elder, and he the child. June had been exposed to many things that a young girl should have put off until later, not necessarily as a bad thing, but just as a way of educating her to the ways of the world. It was only natural that the young

Cigar Box

girl would turn this knowledge toward securing the one relationship that she prized above all other relationships. Seducing Michael was almost too easy. In some societies people would pull back, be appalled, and say that this is wrong, but this wasn't just "anyplace," this was *Texas*! As they walked back to the shacks, she asked Michael how he felt.

"Oh, I don't know, just kinda good, I guess."

"Kinda good? That's all? Don't you feel, well, like you love me or something?"

"Yeah, sure. I just don't get into all that, you know? Sure I love you."

She was actually taken aback! She thought she had her hooks in deeper than that. He said it, but she was sure she couldn't see it in his eyes. Still, that didn't matter. She could hold him. Even at this tender age, June knew she could hold any man. No man could resist or even turn away for even a moment. Michael might wiggle on the hook, but he was still hooked! That was all that mattered! Men much older, and more experienced than he had melted under her gaze. Yet, she would have mercy on Mike because she needed him intact! She'd school him a bit.

*   *   *

The next day she walked over to his house about two miles away. She always followed the runway of the airstrip. She enjoyed looking at the private planes and imagined that one day she would fly in one of them all around the country just like Claudette, Mike's mother, making big deals and having dinner in far away exotic places. The cool fall air was a refreshing break from the oven-hot heat of summer. It put a spring in everyone's step and June was no exception. The cedar trees didn't turn colors like any tree that had good sense, but it was fall just the same. Her stepfather, Ray would hesitate before entering the Bend without an invitation, but June felt no such social constraints. To her the area was just the big houses "out there." Her mother had told her that the Bend was the old Stillwell Ranch, but she couldn't see any sign of the ranch now. If there had ever been cattle out there they were long gone now! Michael was still sleeping. She let herself in. Everyone in Michael's family knew June, and to look up and see her coming in, or even see her suddenly appear at the breakfast table was not an unusual occurrence at all. Michael's father, Bill, was just making coffee when she came in.

"Hey!"

"Oh, hi June. Mike's still asleep."

She got her cup down and put chocolate syrup in it while waiting for the coffee to drip. She dropped by so often that the maid had even assigned her a coffee cup. "Yeah, I know. He had a hard time last night at Fat Eddie's."

"Lot of catfish?"

"Yeah, then we walked and talked for about an hour. I knew he'd be wrung out today."

The older man got his cup down and the pot began to "grumble" as the last bit of coffee fell through the basket. June got up and poured her coffee and then his. Sitting back down she asked, "How do you know when you are in love?"

He looked into the sky blue eyes for a moment. "Are you in love?"

Cigar Box

She grinned and sipped the coffee, "Yah, recon that I am."

"That's how. You just know."

"Nah, I mean, how will I know when Michael is in love."

Something told Michael's dad that there was more to the "walk" she'd mentioned than a stroll around City Park. "You and Mike getting close? Well, I guess you can tell that Michael is in love if he stops eating."

She looked at him for a moment. June's eyes could never lie. She just nodded and sipped her coffee. "I wanna marry him."

He knew that she was only sixteen, but he also knew that this was the last thing she wanted to hear. It appeared that June was very passionately in love with Michael, or at least the idea of Michael, and she had "set her sights" for him more or less. The older man knew that this little lady was dead serious. This was a Texas girl who would get what she wanted. He laughed a bit to himself that Mike was caught and didn't even know it. June was in control of this situation; full control. She had roped Mike in the night before and never missed a beat. No remorse, no regret. It was just a thing that needed doing, and she did it. Young men were caught in Texas in this way all the time. Now to the little lady with her Social Services degree down at the county office building this would be horrible, but June understood life as it really was, and this was the way things were done! Yes, Michael was as hooked as he could be. He was a married man already and he didn't even know it.

"What about school?"

"Oh, I'll finish, some day. This is just more important. This is something I gotta do. You know what I mean? I'll just go into real estate like ya'll here. You don't gotta know anything to be in real estate."

He sipped the coffee, "Yeah, June, I know what you mean. Or you could be a lawyer. Now *they* really don't need to know anything to be in business."

She finished the cup and went over and picked up an apple from the window basket full of fruit. Turning she smiled and eased back to Michael's room. Slipping in she didn't wake him, but just stood there for the longest time looking at him. For a moment she seemed to drift off into fog in her mind. She felt a presence in the room besides herself and Michael, but she couldn't put her finger on it. Then her mouth opened and she began to speak; like speaking in tongues in church. To her great surprise the words just formed and came out of her mouth.

"Oh, my love. I have known you since before hereafter. I am this land, and this land is I. I will know you long after we are apart. My soul is your soul, and my heart is your heart. Where ever you may go, what ever you may be…I will follow thee."

She was frankly startled that she'd said such a thing. She didn't believe such nonsense, but she'd said it anyway. She'd said it in such a whisper that only the angels had heard, and even they weren't quite sure she'd said it. Then the second part of the ritual was upon her. She reached over and placed the apple by his head on the pillow.

In the same room, beyond the veil, Veronica asked, "How did I do that?"

"You stepped into her form."

Cigar Box

"I would have never said anything like that; why did I say it?"

Her spirit guide looked away, and then at her, "You spoke while in bilocation."

She looked back at the scene, at her form still standing there, and then faced the man again, "What is that?"

"You are existing in two dimensions, on two planes. Your "other self," the girl you see in the image is actually *you*. Remember, back in the car when I told you that your spirit name would be 'Veronica?' You have but one soul, though that soul may have many manifestations. That soul *is*, was, and will be. She can feel you are here, though she can't see you. Your thoughts are her thoughts. It's kind of like when a person is confirmed in the Catholic Church. They take on a confirmation name, a spirit name. That Spiritual side of them is as real as the flesh. This is not just a movie you are watching, Veronica this is life. In addition to that, God creates billions of realities, or time lines. We actually have the freedom to choose the time line best suited for us. That young lady there with that apple is just as alive as you are. She is not "locked" into anything. Now, add to that you are a highly developed soul, one with special dispensation. That is why I'm here. Your soul speaks at it knows to speak. When June spoke to Michael, it was actually *Veronica* that was speaking. Do you remember saying the words to your future husband?"

She looked down, and moved away a bit, "Yes. I remember. I just don't know why. It was like you said. It was almost like I felt *me* watching me."

His eyes filled with compassion, "Because you know your destiny Veronica. You and only you know both sides of the coin. You made a promise that you will fulfill."

"Could there be other '*Junes*' watching us now, from yet another dimension?"

"Could be. Only God knows that. He sits above the whole show and watches us all. He watches us choose the time line we want. Choose wisely, Veronica. There are many watching, and depending upon you."

A great sadness filled her heart, and she looked back at the bedroom. Mike was still sleeping with the apple by his head. The man continued, "He'll never have that depth of soul. He'll never appreciate these truths, even after he's dead ten thousand years, but you, you have known these things from the beginning of your existence."

"Why?"

"Because much is demanded of you, because much has been given to you. There are many things that you will make right if you choose the right path. Through you one will come which will right wrongs of centuries past. When you said you were of this land you spoke the truth. It's time for your first time and space lesson. While you were on earth you thought of time as one second after another. It was one time following another, endlessly, on and on. On this side time doesn't work that way. We are in the eternal *now*. You can't even imagine the eternal now. The man that's looking for us can, though. He travels through time and in between the spirit world and the earthly world with ease. He discovered your son's linage and

Cigar Box

came back through time to rearrange my death and position of my soul so that I could wait for you at that intersection. He left me in that Purgatory of a place, thinking that I'd agree with his little plan, but he never considered that I had a mind of my own. That's your first lesson in time and space. We have to stay on course. You have a choice to make, and before you can make that choice, I have to make you understand a lot of things."

She walked into the room and looked at herself. June was young and fresh, with a look of expectation in her eyes. She was amazed at this. She remembered her eyes that morning, before leaving Doc's apartment and how the age had shown through them, but this girl was happy, and yet there *was* an aura of destiny to her. It amused her at how she could see it so clearly from this perspective, and had never seen in from the other. That plane had always been there it seems, and she could have seen it had she only looked. She turned, and walked back through the door that only she and her spirit guide could see, and once again, she was with him.

"I loved him"

"Loved. Now after all that has happened?"

"After all that has happened."

"You said Ray was the only man you ever loved."

"Different love, different man."

"Now it's my turn to ask 'why?'"

She stepped away, "It's a story that you won't understand. It's a story of a mistake, a very big mistake, and if I could take it back, I would, but I can't. Now let *me* tell you something, Mr. Angel, or what ever you are; there are some doors that once you walk through you can't never walk back out again. There are some choices you should never make. There are some timelines God shouldn't have created. There are some mistakes that you make that leave a mark on you, and folks can't see it, but the mark is there all the same, and everyone knows it, even though they can't see it. And it don't matter how old you are when you make the mistake, or why you made it, you just make it all the same, and the mark is there; and the mark don't wash off. Not in the shower, not in the baptizin', not ever!"

"Tell me."

She looked down, "I'm a whore."

He reached and took her hand, "Veronica, the entire universe knows the mistake. Only you have a problem working it out. That's why I'm here." He raised her eyes to his and looked directly into the sky blue irises, "You must get through this. God demands it of you!"

She began to sob, "God demands it? God demands it? All my life God has demanded things of me! He sits on my shoulder like that angel you see in cartoons, just waiting for me to make a mistake so He can tell me I'm wrong. Well, I'm not wrong. I have a life. I HAVE a life!"

Just then, she realized he was looking even deeper into her soul. She straightened up, stunned, "I *had* a life. That's why we're here, isn't it? Why didn't the truck hit?"

"It will, give it time. You must grow a little bit before it does. Now, let me tell *you* something. I wasn't supposed to be able to leave that intersection when I did. I wasn't supposed to be able to freeze time

Cigar Box

like I did, but in twenty years even I can learn something. The plan is not going according to plan right now. I've taken you to teach you. You have a choice to make, and if I'd have let you make it right away, as it had been planned, the outcome would have been exactly as someone had predicted it would be, but I came up with a better idea."

Then he reached and pulled her head to his chest, "You still have your life, but you need to understand what you must do with it. Your life is very valuable. You are the center of this whole thing, and I think you're going to surprise some people. You have a life, and that life is beautiful!"

"No. No, Mr. Angel, I don't have a life. I haven't had a life since I made that mistake. You really don't understand, do you? Don't they give you 'angel' classes before they send you down here, or do you just not understand human nature? You never felt the fire."

He left his hand around her shoulder and said, "I understand human nature a lot more than you imagine, Veronica. I wasn't *sent* down here, I was *stuck* down here. I can't leave until I get this one thing right. I have been sealed here until I…" His voice trailed off.

"Until you what? What do you have to do?"

"I can't tell you."

"Oh, c'mon. Bullshit! You have something on your mind, now what is it?"

His face betrayed his feelings. "I was put at the intersection to make sure your son died."

"What? You want to kill my son?"

"Not kill! I could never do that. I was a witness, that's all. If he'd been strapped securely I was to make sure the seat belt was a little too loose. I was there to see this thing through, and if I did I would be set free of the Purgatory I'd been sealed to for all these years. All I had to do was just make sure that that car crash takes its natural course. Your father in law didn't loose the boy's car seat. It was taken. That was to make sure that he was not protected and that he would fly through the windshield."

"Why?"

"Like I told you. So I could ascend."

"By murder?"

"Not murder. Just making sure the right timeline is used."

"But why?"

"Like I've told you. He's the heir. If he lives this shaman fellow looses his power and his life."

"Well, why didn't you just do it? What happened?"

"It took me twenty years to figure out just how to do this thing. I froze the scene and got you out of the car because I have a solution, but I need your help."

"Well, tell me."

"That's the part I can't tell you; yet. I have to let you see some things because when I tell you what I have to tell you the choice will be the hardest one you've ever had to make, but if you make it right it will benefit all of us. It will help all of us but the shaman. He's not going to like it one bit."

"And he's looking for us?"

"Yes, and you really have to understand the psychology of this thing. I can't let June make this decision. Veronica has to make this particular choice."

"Oh, 'Doctor Angel,' now?"

"No, just someone stuck in the middle with you."

Cigar Box

"And I have to be the 'purified soul' to do this thing. This holy creature."

"In a manner of speaking, yes. I tend to call it an *evolved* state."

"And when I've evolved enough, we go back to Memphis, I climb back in that car and the show goes on."

"Yes, and hopefully you'll make the right choice. At least that's the way I've got it figured."

She pulled back from him. "Well figure this out; I committed adultery! I'm a little whore! Do you know what that is? So if you're waiting for some great help from me you're just shit out of luck!"

She folded her arms in front of her chest and stared at him.

"Want to talk about it?"

She turned quickly away, "No. No, no!" Shaking her head, she just walked a few paces and turned back around. "It'll be a while before I can talk about it. I can't believe I did what I did. I picked the very worse thing a woman can do and I destroyed two families with it. That's what I live with. That's what I did! I can't bring many things back. Lots of people I can't bring back." She wiped the tears away. "Ray!" June had this way of biting her lower lip and looking at a person indignantly when she was caught in a mistake as if to actually *challenge* them to say anything about her error." The man was amazed that he was actually disarmed by her look. He could see how this face could *really* launch a thousand ships, or make a boy do *man* things.

She took a breath and said, "We planned to get married, but they took Mike away from me. I got him back, but I really had to work at it."

"This is a good beginning, and I think you're on the right track. When you tell me your story then I'll be able to tell you what we need to do. I need to know your story, from your side of things. You have to relive some of these things. As you tell me the story, and we watch it, you'll evolve. Tell me about it," her spirit guide said.

"Come," she said, and walked to the golf course. "Let me tell you about the Bend."

Of the Land

Michael was nearing a turning point in his life. He had some big choices before him. He told his mother one day, "I don't know if I want a four-wheel drive truck or to just get married!" Claudette just stood there in her dyslexic perception of the world and tried to take in that statement. How does one compute such a statement? How does one understand, except to say that this is the ultimate link between the child and the man? Michael had always been his mother's pet. The other boys had taken a back seat to him. Buddy and Tommy, her stepsons had always been very close to their father, Claudette's second husband, Bill. Michael's younger brother George was too addicted to food to even worry about it. He stayed in his room and out of the way until dinner, when he would make a quick appearance, eat, and retreat back to his room again. The older sister, the adopted Angela had simply left for boarding school, and later went to college on the insurance money her father had left her to avoid the hassle of competing with Mike's hold on his mother. While the family became more and more dysfunctional, Claudette just *knew* that Michael would be *something* if she just propped him up enough.

The inevitable consequence of this was the obvious fact that Michael was not very mature. He couldn't put off personal pleasure for five minutes. He would regularly sneak into the kitchen of the big house and eat everything in sight. When all of the boys entered into puberty, *he* was the one most often in the bathroom with the door locked while the others complained to their parents about his behavior. Claudette's husband grew tired of explaining, and simply ignored the boy. Buddy whipped on him at every opportunity, and Tommy, while more sympathetic than Buddy, knew that Michael was extremely hedonistic.

He'd been carrying on his affair with June for a number of months now. He was addicted to her body all the while thinking he was mastering this relationship, but it reality it was June, herself, who orchestrated it. The driving force behind this was to "be" married, and not much more. Somehow, if the marriage occurred then everything would be all right; everything would work out. This is the dream of the little Texas girls that drift through high school, that somehow a marriage will come along that will make everything else make sense, but in point of fact it almost never does. Babies are born, divorces happen, boys leave their "wives" to "find" their teenage years they somehow "missed" and the babies grow up to be little Texas girls who think that somehow a marriage would make it all work out!

Michael had another woman in his life, Claudette. He had grown accustomed to her picking him up even

Cigar Box

before he fell. Mentally he was too young to be thinking about being married, but he was thinking about it. It was on his mind, and his momma could buy him anything he wanted. Now he wanted either a truck, or June; either "toy" would be acceptable. Enter into the mix June's mother, and stepfather, Ray. While her mother was not all that panicked by the advent of a wedding, Ray was a man who worked construction in the hot Texas sun every day, and would be more than happy to tear Michael's heart out over his little "angel!" June was everything to Ray. She was everything pure and good to him. There are some things worth killing for and probably the only thing that saved Michael's physical life was the fact that Ray stood in awe of Claudette all because she was in real estate and thus he perceived her as rich, which indeed she was. At his level anyone who did not collect a paycheck every Friday, and wasn't on welfare somehow had to be "rich." He was correct in assuming that Claudette could destroy his livelihood, which indeed she would have if her precious Michael were threatened!

Claudette, on the other hand had other ideas for him. She saw him finishing high school, and going on to college, perhaps in Austin. Destined to attend the University of Texas. After graduation, he would take the three real estate classes mandatory to sit for the state real estate exam, and then he'd move into the family real estate business where he would stay until he died. Of course, he'd marry some nice young lady from the Bend with equal education, and an equal interest in the family business.

Rays perception of Claudette's wealth was justified because Claudette *was* rich! Looking at her son that day she remembered when she'd first come to the little desert community from Tennessee. She had a high school education and little more than that. She'd left everything back in Memphis after the death of her brother. She'd filed for divorce and made her life in the little desert town just off the main road. She'd never really known what had drawn her to the town, or Texas at all for that matter, but she'd felt a compulsion to come. A vision she'd never revealed that told her how to get there. All this was seventeen years ago, when Michael was two and his younger brother was six months old. In the nearby towns, malls were sprouting, and communities growing. She went to work for a builder named Bill as a sales representative. It was a new career. New! Ha! She'd had no career before that. She'd been a factory worker in Tennessee. She'd worked two jobs to make ends meet while her worthless, fat, red-faced husband ate everything in sight. Bill introduced her to a completely different world. She had her own two sons, and her brother's daughter, Angie whom she'd adopted after her sister-in-law, the widow of her brother, had died of breast cancer. They lived in a mobile home out on the edge of town. Bill was divorced with two boys of his own, Buddy and Tommy. One thing led to another, and one day they went into the judge's office and got married during lunch.

She moved into Bill's old, dusty ranch-style home. Her husband was a builder, but he couldn't sell penicillin in a V. D. clinic. Claudette had that knack. A lifetime of "making do" had made her a natural at

Cigar Box

convincing people to take what she had to offer. Still, she needed to get her real estate license. Her new husband had his broker's license and as long as she sold only for this one builder, the laws of the state of Texas allowed her to do so, but to move into the areas that she wanted she had to have her license. This meant she had to pass the test for it, and that was the problem. Claudette couldn't read her own name! She was hopelessly dyslexic! She'd memorized her way thorough high school, actually returning again and again until she graduated at the tender age of twenty-one years. Her first husband had told her family that she was actually retarded because she couldn't read and the fact that she stumbled over her words as she spoke. Her speech was an endless array of slang and half words. She'd confuse words and once referred to condominiums as condoms! Her new husband read all the real estate books into a cassette tape and she'd listen to them in her car every day. Bill, being a broker himself, was very familiar with the real estate books and in addition to that he understood Claudette's way of thinking and more than that her understanding. He could explain the books as he read and this took her a long way toward eventually passing the real estate exam. Taking the three weekend courses were no big deal because a person who was comatose could probably pass them. For two days, they taught you the answers for the test on the third day. She had to take the state real estate test thirteen times in order to pass it. The letters danced across the page of the test document, and she eventually just took it so many times that she couldn't make any more mistakes.

Wilbur Witt and Pamela Woodward

She began to sell homes in the little town and she and her husband developed a fine business with a good reputation. The years rolled by and they built the business up as far as it could be built in the little desert community. They would frequently slip away to a spot out at the edge of town where the river took a turn that looked like a horseshoe. Like all west Texas rivers it had a sandy bottom and there were sand bars all over the place. They'd lay a pallet down, eat their chicken or sandwiches, and enjoy each other's company. The land belonged to an old rancher who no longer ranched it and had let it go considerably. The land had been in his family for generations, but he had lost interest since the death of his wife, and his housekeeper, June's mother, Barbara had moved out and got married. As they enjoyed lunch there over and over again Claudette began to notice that the ranch was in need of upkeep. All the cows were long gone and the ranch house was in extreme disrepair. Claudette was frankly amazed that anyone could still live in the house. She knew that old man Stillwell, the owner, could not be up on things as far as keeping up any financial obligations on the ranch if the physical condition of the house was this bad. One day Juan Sanchez came into the little real estate office and began asking questions about land in the area. During the conversation he asked if the Stillwell Ranch was for sale. Claudette checked around and told him that to her knowledge it was not for sale. Sanchez mentioned that he'd heard the taxes were stacking up on the place. The rancher didn't want to pay the taxes, and in fact had prepared to move out of the dilapidated old shack he used to call a ranch house before his wife died, and into an apartment in

Cigar Box

town to live out his days on his social security. The wheels began to turn in Claudette's head. In a flash of brilliance she realized that this was the reason she'd been drawn to the area in the first place! In a single moment of time the idea that was to become known of as the Bend formed itself in her mind. Sanchez had planted a seed that would blossom into a mighty oak.

 She knew how large the ranch was. It had been passed down for generations, and this old man was the sole heir to it now, having no children by his wife. Claudette discussed buying the place from the old man, but Bill told her the idea was not feasible because the sheer size of the track would place it in the two hundred thousand dollar mark and they could never secure financing on a parcel that large. It is hard to sell land in Texas if the buyer doesn't have ready capital, and though Bill and Claudette made a good living, they did not have that kind of money and besides, they weren't sure if Stillwell would even consider selling the family acreage to them. Combine that with the fact that Claudette had a plan, and it wasn't raising cattle and watching the grass grow. She was a Memphis girl, and try as she might that part of her wouldn't die. She knew that there was a big world outside of this sandy nowhere, and that if people had the seclusion that the area offered, combined with comfortable living, there just might be a future in west Texas after all! Claudette had been in real estate for a little while now, and she had seen the small, flat homes that the locals built. She had a vision of something more. A community of mansions, all nestled by the only river in the area, all resting comfortably under the Texas sun. She could stand on the sand after eating her lunch and look out at the Stillwell ranch and imagine all the buildings that would be there someday. If old man Stillwell had an inkling of this he'd go to someone else and try to do it on his own. That would put him back into the prime of life for sure!

Stillwell had seen her at the catfish house, but knew her only as "the real estate lady," and he, like everyone else in town, knew she was divorced! That stigma followed her down from Memphis. Being urban she hadn't thought it was such a bad thing but when she found herself in this simmered down environment she quickly discovered that a divorced woman was a bit under the covers so to speak in a place where gossip is the main pastime. By the time she found this out it was too late because the story was out. At any rate, she'd not be able to do business with Stillwell because of this lack of respect, and it was one that Bill couldn't get around. Bill and Claudette turned it over again, and again, and then the wheels in Claudette's head began to turn. She came up with a way to buy the ranch and never have to worry about Stillwell, or her divorce again!

Claudette had a friend, Chip, who worked as the county tax assessor collector and he had confirmed that the entire amount owed on the land was only thirteen hundred dollars. If the land were auctioned at the courthouse for taxes she could pick it up for that amount. There was no lien on the track, so the back taxes and county fees were all that she would have to pay. She was fully aware that the owner had two years after the fact to purchase his land back for that amount if he so chose to do so, but that didn't matter. She'd work around that. So long as she had that Sheriff's

Cigar Box

dead in her hand she could go with that. That would just give her two years to do the planning for the little project she had in mind. During this two years she just had to keep the entire project low key so that the old man didn't realize that his dilapidated old ranch was worth a bit more than he'd supposed.

A phone call was made. "Chip?"

"Yeah?"

"Listen, are you sure the Stillwell ranch is in arrears?"

"Yeah, but nobody wants it. I mean, old man Stillwell is just counting the days, if you know what I mean."

"Maybe I want it, Chip. What do I have to do?"

"Why don't you buy it?"

"I don't have the money right now, but I *do* have the tax money."

"Well you need to get with the lawyer. We hire a lawyer to do these things. It's gonna need notification, and a few things to protect you, you know?"

"Such as?"

"Well, we only give you a sheriff's deed. Now that's not a warranty deed in any sense of the word. You have to pay to make sure there are no problems with the land. Then Mr. Stillwell has two full years to come back and pay you the taxes, interest, and fees associated with the land, and just take it back. You understand, Claudette?"

"I know real estate law, Chip. Can you just get the thing auctioned?"

"Sure, no problem. I'll get right on it. But what are you going to do if old man Stillwell shows up and pays his taxes? He can just walk up to the courthouse

Wilbur Witt and Pamela Woodward

steps and pay me, and your plan goes down the crapper."

"Chip, I'm counting on you to make sure that doesn't happen."

"Now Claudette, I can't do anything illegal. You know that."

"I'm not *asking* you to do anything illegal. Just don't shout it from the rooftops, ok."

"Well, I gotta mail him a notice."

"So mail it."

"Isn't he living in town in an apartment?"

"Yeah, but mail it to his last *known* residence."

"That shack?"

"His ranch house."

"They'll just forward it."

"Put *do not forward* on the envelope! God! Do I have to tell you *everything*?"

"Now the big question; why should I do this?"

"Chip, do you still live in that little two bedroom house over on First and Hackberry?"

"You know I do."

"Well, if I pull off what I want you'll have a nice big home down on the river. Do you like the sound of that?"

"Claudette, I have never done anything like this."

"Chip, when you retire from working with the county, they're gonna give you a gold *plated* watch and you are going to go home to a two bedroom place that is only getting older, just like you! I can help you to a better way. Now, if you don't help me I'll just find another way and you'll be in that place forever. Chip, let's be friends."

"Claudette, I'm not mad, just a little scared."

Cigar Box

"Relax. That old man won't pay those taxes. He'll rock along and loose that place. If this ever comes to light you can cover your tracks easy enough. Just show that you mailed the letter and gave the old man a fair shake."

"I still don't see why you don't just ask him."

"I don't have that kind of money. Do I have to keep saying that? He'll want tons of money. If I thought I could just buy it I would. That old man's crazy. You know that. He still carries that old Colt Walker forty-four. C'mon. We're talking about old man Stillwell here! About the only thing he ever did that made sense was shaking up with Barbara that time."

"Ok, ok, but this really has to stay between us."

"Hey, no problem."

On the first Tuesday of the following month, on the north porch of the courthouse Chip came out and called out the conditions of the tax lien on the land. As usual, only a few people were there that day, and particularly *this* day because a "norther" had ripped through and the temperature was dropping to the teens with a nice wind to boot. Claudette wondered just *why* the sale had to be conducted on the north porch. When Chip had read his customary spiel, he asked if the owner was there, which of course he wasn't, and then he asked if anyone wanted to pay the taxes and receive title to the land. Claudette nodded and the deal was done right there. Claudette would buy the land that would become the coveted "Bend" for what she would later refer to as "milk money."

Her next step was a planning and waiting game. To her amazement Stillwell never contacted her proving that he'd never gone back to the old broken down ranch house and read his letter. She didn't make any waves and she was very quiet about what she planned lest she tip off the retired rancher spending his days at his apartment. She, and her husband drew up plans for streets in their own drafting room of their office downtown, but never let on just what their full intentions were. Indeed, they let the very fact that they had purchased it slip into antiquity. The sheriff's deed was logged in but no one noticed or even cared. The two years passed, and Claudette began her planning in earnest. She had been in west Texas about nine years now and had grown as patient as the lizards that crawled on the rocks down by the river. She commissioned a company in Houston to fly out and begin the project. The streets were designed to be wide, far more than was required, in anticipation of the private planes that would move about and leave from the private landing strip she designed. The quality of the streets was far better than what was in the little desert town. They needed to get the streets paved, and this was a considerable sum of money to be spent. Claudette met with the mayor and key members of the council and for the first time, behind closed doors, over bar-b-qued brisket and scotch, she let them in on what she proposed to do. She was designing a subdivision that would cater to retirees and quality buyers from all over the state, indeed from the entire country! But even the word "subdivision" didn't tell the enormity of the project. The Bend would dwarf the town it sprang from. The homes could be no smaller than three thousand square feet, and no home could be anything like any other home in the Bend. The lots would start at one acre, but she would entertain any idea as to size of a lot for a proposed home. The marketing would be statewide in the beginning, and then nationwide if need be. The landing strip would make it accessible to all areas of the nation, via the airport in El Paso. This "Bend" would be a hub of activity. The residents of the area would be true citizens of the world, free to fly and work and retreat back to the relative seclusion of west Texas.

The scotch was poured and the discussion began.

"How large will the area be Claudette?"

"We have proposed the entire Stillwell ranch to be used for this development. As you gentlemen know, it consists of over twenty-two hundred acres, mostly level, with the river flowing right through it and if the project fly's, we will of course, attempt to obtain other adjacent lands."

"How many homes," one of the councilmen asked?

"At least one hundred, no more than one fifty, I'm sure. Some buyers will go for the acre lot, but I'm after the home owner who wants five, or even seven acres, if need be to assure the space, and privacy this area can afford."

The mayor looked into his glass of scotch and then looked at Claudette, "And what will bring all these people to our fair city?"

She smiled at him. They knew there must be a card she wasn't showing. She didn't invite them for a meeting, and buy all this scotch for nothing. "That eighteen hole world class golf course you fine people are going to put running right through the middle of the neighborhood!"

More than one glass sat down quietly on the oak tables of the council chamber. "Now, Claudette, just why would we want to go and do something like that?"

"Because I'm going to give you the land to put it on. You are going to pay me in asphalt, not to mention the taxes on my homes will be through the roof with people rich enough to pay them!"

"City water? City sewer?"

"But, of course."

"And the layout of the streets?"

"The streets are to be forty feet wide"

They looked at each other. "Why so wide. I can see a little more, but forty feet?"

"To accommodate private planes."

"Private planes."

"Yes, some of my clients will have private planes, and the streets need to be wide enough to accommodate the trip to a little landing strip we'll have built at the edge of the subdivision."

"Do we need this?"

"Yes."

"Where are we going to get the kind of money to develop that course? Look at us. We're a small town in west Texas! We don't even have oil here!" The members of the council laughed.

"But you'll have the Bend!"

"The 'Bend?"

"That's the name of the subdivision. It'll be called the Bend, after the bend in the river where my husband and I have our lunch."

The men all milled a moment. Then the mayor said, "Claudette, you need to attract some interest in

Cigar Box

your little subdivision. You do *that*, and then come back, and we'll have this little chat again!"

She went out and began a statewide advertising campaign to sell "choice" lots at the Bend. The area was nice, the river adding more color than the surrounding semi desert area, but it was still just a dilapidated old ranch with a "gate" at the front six months later. Try as she might, Claudette simply could not generate interest in the land in any large circles. She was not interested in selling land to any of the local farmers and she was very aware that Stillwell was sitting back counting his days. She wondered if he understood just what had transpired. He had surprisingly taken the loss of the ranch well, and perhaps was more than slightly amused hat Claudette and Bill couldn't do any more with the land than he had done when he had it. Then, one afternoon a phone call came to her office from L. A.

A certain well-known retired talk-show host called her.

"Hello."

"Hello, did my agent tell you I'd be calling?"

"Yes, how can I help you?"

"Well, someone in my organization saw one of your ads when he was in Houston last week, and I would be interested it exploring the idea of putting a home in your 'Bend."

"Well, of course we'd be interested in accommodating you, Mr...

"Don't say my name over the phone. One of the main reasons I want to go there is for my privacy. I want to have at least one home that I can rest in without the press, or fans, or anyone bothering me.

That, and I like golf, and I want to have a home near enough to a world class course that will allow me to play undisturbed."

"Ok, I think we can do that. May I fly out to L. A. and talk with you more?"

"Yes."

Claudette seized on an idea. She flew out to L. A. and shot him a proposal that Don Corleone would have been proud of. She would be happy to build him his home. He looked at her proposed floor plans and said, "I want one of my people here in L. A. to help in design. I like the California style, I just don't like California right now."

She agreed and the architect was pulled into the mix and began drawing. Claudette was so impressed by the man's work that she invited him to submit several proposed floor plans to her and her husband to put forward to future homeowners in the Bend. This gave the area a decidedly different look from the usual west Texas fare. The Spanish tile type of roof and the stucco that graced so many California homes captivated Claudette's imagination. Then Claudette began to discuss with the star her problems with the city and her golf course. One of the problems she had was the design of the course. *Saying* you were going to have an eighteen-hole course was one thing, but *designing* it was altogether a different thing. She knew that it would take about two hundred acres to complete it, and she actually toyed with the idea of a thirty-six-hole course, but ruled it out for the more comfortable one.

"I think I can help you with that. I have a friend who, like me, is looking for a home away from the

Cigar Box

crowd. Let me call him and see if he can help you with those little logistics."

Right after that a certain well-known golf pro called Claudette and actually flew down to the little town to meet with her. They went out to the proposed subdivision and paced off all eighteen holes. The man was brilliant! He showed her how to conform the future course to accent the imaginary neighborhood that would build up around it. Choice lots could actually tee off from the back yard. He put in little things that he'd always wanted to have on a course. This course would be like no other course in the world, and one day it would host great golf tournaments with players from all over the country.

She went back to the city fathers and explained to them the caliber of buyer she was accruing in the Bend. They were impressed, but they still couldn't sell enough cows to build the golf course she envisioned. She flew back to L. A. Once there, she arranged a meeting with the talk show host, and the golf pro, and put a venture to them. She offered to build their homes at cost, if they would front the money needed by the city to develop the course.

"What do we get in return?"

"I will go to them and work out a plan that will be equitable for you."

She met with the city fathers one last time and explained the situation to them.

"I now have the money needed to build the course."

They all looked at her in amazement. "How?"

"I have arranged for a loan for the city to develop all eighteen holes."

"How much?"

She began to walk among them and lay documents on the table before them explaining the amount of money it would take to build a world class, eighteen hole golf course. They viewed the documents but no man in the room could put meaning to the words until the mayor asked, "How do we pay it back?"

Claudette sat. "The Bend will be the premier gated subdivision from San Angelo to Phoenix. People will covet it. People will come from far away to view it, and desire to live there. You men will be sitting on Camelot!"

"How do we pay the money back?" The mayor leaned back, crossed his arms and looked her right in the eye.

She drew in a breath, "On these two men," she shoved two new home contracts across the table to the mayor, "you will never charge *any* taxes of any kind, either now, or ever. These two homes are to be forever tax exempt!"

"Even state taxes?"

"The city will pick up the tab for so long as members of these men's families shall live within the walls of these two homes."

"What if they sell?"

"So long as it's family, taxes paid!"

One of the other council members spoke up, "But what if we only have these two homes? I mean, these two guys can build their big houses and then just be two guys with two big houses and a private golf course. This entire thing is based on other people buying into this and coming here to spend their money."

The mayor took that under consideration and looked toward Claudette, "What do you say to that?"

She thought for a moment, "Mr. Mayor, we have nothing in this area. No real agriculture, no oil, nothing! About the only thing we have to offer is a good climate. We, I think, are standing on the brink of a situation similar to the people in Branson, Missouri when they decided to become a little Nashville. Now they are the premier live entertainment center of the country."

The mayor thought again for a moment, "Claudette, you're from Memphis. I grew up here in this 'nowhere' as you call it. Can you give me some kind of assurance that you can do this thing?"

"Yes! I will sell this land!" Something about her demeanor put a form of electricity in the room.

The mayor leaned back and smiled, "I think it will work."

The rest of the council quickly agreed and scotch flowed, and the golf course at the Bend became a reality!

The logistics of the construction was left to Claudette's husband. He made the foundations happen. Using a floor plan from the L. A. architect, Bill constructed a large, well-endowed country club to compliment the course. He made the golf course become a reality, but Claudette was the power! She was the intellect that made the money flow from L. A. to west Texas, and her power of persuasion was what made the Bend *happen*!

June's stepfather hired on to the building project and was the hands on man in most of the construction. Bill had the "builder know how" but Ray actually

Wilbur Witt and Pamela Woodward

made the nails fly and the walls rise. During the entire phase of construction Ray was there. When the project wound down he went back to light plumbing and working around west Texas as if he'd never been to the Bend at all.

One buyer didn't make a big deal of his purchase, however. Juan Sanchez came back and met with Claudette in her little Real Estate office downtown one evening and paid her the first of four payments securing a lot near the river. He had a crop harvesting business and looked forward to building a house large enough to accommodate his entire family during the off-season. He didn't listen to his friend, Ray. He wasn't really impressed by the golf course, thinking it to be a nice view only. Still, Juan had other goals in mind. His main interest was in the land itself. His lot must be the one nearest the river. His front door must face east, toward the rising sun. His daughter worked in a local pub, but she was the daughter of his old age and he was more a grandfather to her than a father. No one really knew where Juan had come from, or who he really was. Some suspected he was a "wetback" that just hung around until the law got tired of deporting him and simply let him stay. He was surrounded by a tribe of Mexican people who looked at him with a combination of fear and respect.

Juan was a leader of his people. He was the spiritual father of his family. He had been so long that no one could really remember how long it had been. In hushed circles, only at night, they spoke of his power. Juan could leave his body and go to places far away. Juan could walk through walls. He would take the holy smoke into his lungs and sit transfixed for the

Cigar Box

longest time, returning with a start, and he would never tell anyone where he went, or what he had done. He had no sons. There were rumors that he'd had some, but that they had all been still born, leaving him only Sabrina, a daughter, as his heir. He confided in few, if any people. Ray was about the closest thing he had to being a friend.

But Claudette wasn't worried about all this because she now had another selling point. She used the remote location with its privacy option and the course with the country club and her "rock bottom" prices, which were roughly one third those in L. A. or Phoenix, or even Houston. Soon, she was getting calls from everyone from country music people to retiring postmasters about how they could purchase a track at the Bend. And, while no country music stars had moved into the Bend, Claudette came up with yet one more idea that was novel. She paid for and assisted the city in putting in a state of the art recording studio in the rear rooms of the country club, with a two-bedroom apartment, complete with kitchenette. When she made her frequent trips to Nashville she'd spread around the offer that any star who wished to develop a record, or album could book time and do so for *free* in the little recording studio at the Bend provided they would give one free Saturday night show at the country club in payment for said time. The idea brought name acts to the little desert town. The houses went up; the streets went in, and Claudette and Bill were on their way to becoming multi millionaires!

Then, about a year into the project the retired rancher came into her office one day. He knew that Claudette had purchased the land for back taxes, but he knew the statute dealing with the buy back of the property, and he was waiting for the land to be well developed until he made his move. Mr. Stillwell was crazy, but he was also an opportunist. He'd seen Claudette around town, and while he'd not pushed hard on her husband Bill, he thought he might just have an edge on this tall Tennessee woman.

"Claudette, you're doing a good bit of construction on my place."

She knew he'd be around. He was too tired to do anything with the land when he had it, and now that someone was doing something, he wanted his "share."

"My place? Seems to me that the deed has transferred to me and my husband, doesn't it?"

"Well, I been doing some checking, and I found out that I can buy back my land for the thirteen hundred dollars you paid in the back taxes. Now, I don't want to do that. I just want me a house out here with the rest of the fine folks you're roping in. You give me that and I'll end my days right here, and make no trouble for nobody."

She felt her anger rise, but she kept her temper. Claudette was respectful even when she was angry. She understood that this man thought that he had some kind of rights to the land, and in his heart he really thought he was being more than fair to her letting her off with just building him a house on the land that he had formally owned. But this was *her* land now! He gave up rights to it when he didn't pay his taxes, and the State of Texas was nice enough to give him two more years to raise the money to get it back. It wasn't her fault he didn't read the papers! If he hadn't been chasing teenage catfish girls down at Fat Eddie's he'd

Cigar Box

have paid more attention to business. Besides that, had he gone to Chip and paid the money, they would have deeded the land back to him, and Claudette and her husband would have just had to find another project to peddle. He didn't do that. He sat in his little apartment and watched Jeopardy until he smelled the asphalt being laid in the Bend, and now here he was with his hand out for his daily bread!

"Well, Mr. Stillwell, first of all the period of grace is two years. I believe it has been two and a *half* years since the land was auctioned. You have no claim." She shrugged and smiled, "Sorry."

He stared at her coolly from across the desk, "You mean to tell me you are developing a million dollar project on my land and I'm not even gonna get a brick?"

"Oh, no, you can have a brick. In fact, you can have a lot of bricks. Just go out and borrow the money and buy a lot from me and I'll build you a home here."

They both knew this was out of the question. He could not even raise the thirteen hundred dollars for the taxes, either then or now. He scraped by month after month on his Social Security check and ate on his food stamps.

"You robbed me!"

She leaned back, "Don't get dramatic! As the song says, 'This ain't Dallas!' You didn't do anything for the land, to the land or on the land. You let it go. How long did you have to go to rack up thirteen hundred dollars in back taxes on that ranch? And you didn't have the idea we had anyway. If you had you'd have approached me, or someone like me, and you would have been a full partner right now. No, you got what

Wilbur Witt and Pamela Woodward

you deserve. Now go back to your little apartment. I think 'All My Children' is coming on!"

He stood up suddenly and slamming his fists down on the heavy desk, tried to intimidate Claudette by towering over her and reducing her with his stare, but she just said, "Go home, old man." He turned and walked out of the office.

About a week later, he went to the bend of the river where Claudette and her husband had eaten their lunches so many times. He too, had picnicked there with his wife in his younger days. After his wife died, he'd brought another young lady to this spot, also. He had swum in the river with her back then. His father had left him the land. His grandfather had taken it from the Comanche, but he hadn't been like them. He'd been too ignorant, and lazy to work the land, and his wife had died, and the young lady who had stayed in the house with him had gone to a younger man. He did indeed spend his hours watching TV, and on Friday nights he'd go to catfish. When he'd owned the land he was at least "somebody," but a tall woman from Tennessee with a friend at the courthouse had taken his soul. Tears filled his eyes as he took out his old Colt Walker black powder "forty-four" from its case. Slowly, meticulously he took the powder flask and poured just the right amount of powder into one of the chambers. Then, adding a bit more. He put the conical shaped lead into the chamber. Pulling the leaver beneath the barrel, he pressed the bullet down onto the powder. Because of the extra powder, he had to take his pocketknife and trim the nose of the lead in order to make the cylinder turn freely. He didn't put the grease in the chamber because he only needed one shot and there would be no fear of back flash. Then, taking one last look at the bend in the river and the mansions rising up behind it, he put the Colt into his mouth and rode into his final sunset.

So was the history of the making of the Bend. Stolen from the Indians, then lost to laziness and stupidity, it had been baptized in blood and deceit. And right in the middle of it all was a small dark man called Juan Sanchez who began clearing his lot near the river to build his hacienda. Claudette's mind snapped back to the present. Stillwell had been dead over six years now. She had new issues in her life. Now Michael wanted to be married, and he really didn't care who the girl was. He had absolutely no common sense! She frankly wondered if she'd picked up the wrong baby at the hospital. How did he center in on June, she wondered. Fact was he had a couple of girl friends in the little town, though he wasn't as involved with them as he was with June. She was certainly the prettiest, but not the only girl in Mike's life. The difference in the two perspectives was that June was playing for "keeps" and Mike was playing the field. After he'd been initiated by June behind the catfish house he'd taken his truck around town, in particular to a little lady of seventeen over on Commerce Street. She was from a middle class family and knew how to keep her private life to herself. She was planning to go on to college, or the military and then college, and didn't want or need any problems with a passing affair with Mike to botch up her plans. Her father was the local deputy referred to affectionately as "Deputy Dawg" because he was so blamed ugly. This characteristic did not carry over to his daughter, however, and Mike was sneaking into her bedroom window at every opportunity.

What Mike, or Claudette didn't seem to realize was that June was in control of this situation, not them! At the tender age of sixteen, and just barely that, she was still quicker and more determined than most any girl in the little town. While the deputy's little girl was still playing high school games, June was playing big girl games. She set her sights and she went after what she wanted, and she always got what she wanted! Mike's mom may have been the big time real estate broker, but June was the small town operator.

Claudette stared at Mike in confusion. "Why do you *have* to be married? Aren't you happy with your truck?"

"Well, I love her. I need to be with her. I want her with me!"

"But all you have for a job is your dishwashing job at the catfish house, and you aren't even out of school yet! You're only seventeen. You'll be eighteen before you graduate. You need to wait on these things."

"Don't care. Gotta be with her!"

"Sounds like you been around her enough! A kiss or two behind Fat Eddie's, and you *gotta* be with her? When will you ever start thinking big, Mike?"

She just sat there and stared at him. He had about eight months to finish high school. She needed to keep him in school, but she knew that the attraction of this girl was very great. She added up the years and she was well aware that Mike was almost eighteen and June was just now sixteen. If he'd been catting around with her it was a legal issue that could blow up in his

Cigar Box

face, her face, everybody's face! She had to put him off so she told him that she'd give it some thought. What she did was to call her ex-husband in Tennessee. This rubbed her the wrong way, but it was the best place to send him to get his mind off June.

Calling her "ex" took a bit of preparation for Claudette. There had been no real contact between them for the last fourteen or fifteen years. He'd never paid a dime's child support, and he never contacted her. Mike actually didn't know how to get in touch with him, and had in fact forgotten all about him. She waited until one Sunday when her husband went to church. He went to Mass about once a month. Claudette, a Baptist, went to church on rare occasions, but watched the preachers on TV. She stayed home to "straighten up" the house, and try to catch up on any work she'd missed during the week. Michael didn't go with his stepfather because he was going to help her with the project. While Mike was out in the back putting up the yard chairs Claudette placed a call to Memphis. Ed was polite and listened to her dilemma.

"Michael wants to get married."

"He's only seventeen. He can't get married. He's still in school, ain't he?"

"Yeah, but it's this June girl. He thinks he's in love. She's quite a looker. She could melt the wax off of a Dixie cup at one hundred yards."

"Well, he ain't in love, he's in lust! What do you want me to do about it?"

Claudette formulated a plan with Ed, as much as she didn't even wish to speak with him. Together they would devise a method to remove Mike from Texas

Wilbur Witt and Pamela Woodward

and hide him in Tennessee away from the ideas he was formulating about marriage.

Later that very day, as she went through some old papers and things from a box, she let a piece of paper innocently fall to the floor. Michael reached down to pick it up, but she said, "Oh, don't mind that. Let me have it!" She made a grab for it, making a very big deal out of it so as to attract his attention to the paper.

Now, if you want a boy to get interested in something just tell him not to look at it. Mike picked the paper up and looked at the writing on it. An address, and a phone number on a page that he's not supposed to read will usually do the trick. "Who is it?"

She made a half hearted grab for it, "Oh, nothing. Let me have it!"

"No, who is it?"

She gave a long lingering "somber" look, and said, "It's your father's address and phone number. I never wanted you to see it 'cause I didn't want you to worry about him, that's all!"

Mike stood up and ran his fingers over the paper, yellowing with age. "He still there?"

"Yeah, he's still there. His mom and dad gave him the house he lives in. But you don't wanna call him. He don't care about you!"

Mike walked out of the room, carrying the paper with him. He left the house and went to the golf course. As he walked past the golf carts, he stared at the little piece of paper. All these years, and all this time he had never heard from his father. How long had she known where he was? What hadn't she told him? How could he know that his mother was

Cigar Box

counting on these very thoughts to work their way through Mike's mind? She wanted it to be just enough to work June *out* of his mind. He wandered around a bit and then the curiosity got the best of him and he took his cell phone and called the number. His father was nice and led him right into Claudette's trap.

By the time that Bill came back from church Mike had been on the phone with Ed for quite a while. The three of them met in the kitchen and Mike asked, "Would you mind very much if I went up to see my dad."

Bill was surprised, "What brought that up?"

"He found a paper with Ed's name on it. He went out and called him from his cell."

Bill didn't like Ed. He didn't need any help supporting the boys, but he had no respect for a man who deliberately lost contact with his children. "Well, I don't think that you should have any contact with him."

Mike took a defensive posture, "He's *my* dad! I can see him if I want!"

Bill's first instinct was to slap the wise cracking boy, but he held his temper. Like his sons, he knew that Michael had Claudette's full support. And, besides that, maybe this would get the little troublemaker out of the way for a little while. After years of disruption in his house the builder could see a small vacation might be good for the family. He knew deep down that Mike didn't have the fortitude to stay in Memphis for long. The soft life he'd had at the Bend would call him home, but the break would be nice.

"Well, you just do whatever you want, but don't think that we're going to support you while you're up there. Let ol' Ed feed you for a while."

Mike turned to Claudette, "Do I get a new truck before I leave?"

Bill left the room in disgust. He could see Mike tooling around Memphis in a brand new truck, which he would run into the dirt. By contrast, his son Buddy never asked for anything and in fact drove an old Chevy truck he had had the entire time he was in high school. Tommy just drove whatever he jumped into at the time. Only Mike had a personal truck.

A few days later, a few more phone calls were made, and the ex-husband, Ed, came to get Mike and take him to Tennessee. He was properly intimidated by the homes of the Bend. Claudette found it hard to imagine she'd ever been married to such a loaf of a man. He had gotten fatter, if that were possible, and had a beard that he thought made him look like Santa Clause. He looked like an inflated version of Mike. Soon the thrill of going somewhere different took over the idea of marriage, or a new truck, which was not purchased. Claudette was not going to provide Ed with a new truck to drive around in. Mike settled down in Tennessee. He went to high school there, rode horses there, and "cruised the strip" there. He forgot all about June. But June was not the type that would be easily forgotten. She began to plan, scheme actually, to get Mike back to Texas. Not knowing exactly where he was, or anything about the details of how he was suddenly spirited from her grasp, June was forced to wait until Mike contacted her.

Cigar Box

As soon as the "new" wore off of Memphis Mike began to miss June. The girls in Tennessee didn't have the ability that June had. They talked slow, and to Mike's way of thinking, they *were* slow! There was something about the little feisty west Texas girl that kept Mike thinking about her all the time. She became more beautiful in memory even than she was in life! She was certainly freer than the Memphis girls, who were actually more "big city" than Mike was ready for. They wanted to date, and spend time, and his style of a hot dog and two minutes in the back seat of a car guaranteed that the first date was always the last. The horses were fun, the girls were there, but life in the Bend was far better than living in a shack outside of Memphis. Mike was beginning to understand deep within his soul that he was indeed a spoiled brat. He began to miss the life he'd known, and the money. Borrowing Ed's old car was far different than driving around in a nice truck. He actually had to check his wallet when he went into a café to eat, and no one knew him. At the Bend, he was Claudette's son, Mike. Here he was Ed's son, and his father was not influential at all. When mixed with his lackluster personal style, the minute the girls saw just *where* he lived and met his father in all his chicken-dripping glory they split for higher ground.

Each morning he would rise as his father came in from his job at a local nursing home. He now worked the night shift, getting off about six in the morning, which gave him just enough time to get home and get Mike ready to go to school before he turned in for the day. In no time at all Mike did have a car of his own and stopped borrowing his father's. It wasn't much, but it got him around. He would cruise the "strip" and try to pick up girls, but he found that this was always a disappointment to him. He simply could not understand that he was also a disappointment to them too!

He began to grow during this time, and the world of adult relationships began to take their effect on his education. Since he hadn't settled on just one girl he had to constantly cruise for new game and his grades slipped as his nightlife became more important than anything else. Mike wasn't very concerned about school, anyway, but he had to come to the understanding that in this town he couldn't rely on who his mother was to get him by on anything, not even school. About that time, he began a late night habit of calling back to Texas to talk to June. This was the very opportunity that June had waited for! At first, he did it when he told his father he was going to "cruise," but later he did it from the house when his dad was at work. Then, in a moment of guilt about the bill he came to the realization of the collect call. June was more than happy to oblige him in this, and accepted every call. She led him through the paces of the stages of loneliness as only a Texas girl could muster. Before too long Mike could actually smell her baby powder perfume over the phone.

"Hey, it's me."

"Hi Mike. You know, I could almost feel you today. I was in school, and Jeremy, you know him, well, he asked me out for like Friday, but I told him, 'no,' because you might come in town and see me by then. I didn't let him think he could just come in like that."

Cigar Box

"I'll get him when I come back!"

"Oh, could you just talk to me a while. I'm laying here on my bed and when you talk to me I can really feel you touching me."

"Really? Where?"

"Special places. I've got my pink gown on and it's *so* hot here, I just want to take it off, you know?"

Mike's heart was beating like a sledgehammer. As the sweat poured from his forehead, and his hands trembled on the phone, June was actually reclining on the living room couch, fully clothed and eating popcorn while watching an old movie on TV. She put the phone on the back of the couch so she could just make out when he stopped talking. She knew him so well she'd give him a moment alone.

Between short, gasping breaths Mike said, "I gotta get back down there, June. I can't see my life without you."

Statements like this proved to June that the hook was in, and it was in deep. Mike was repeatedly saying phrases like, "when I come back," not even bothering to say, "If." It was a done deal as far as he was concerned, and that's exactly what June wanted him to feel. Slowly but surely those Tennessee hills looked less, and less inviting, and Mike began to find little things wrong with his life in that state.

As the calls progressed he knew he had to get Claudette to agree for him to come back. Over the last couple of months he'd figured out that it really wasn't *his* idea to come to Memphis, that in point of fact he'd been duped to remove him from June. Knowing this, he quickly figured that he had to turn Claudette's thoughts toward bringing him back home. He knew his mother well enough to know that if she'd schemed up a way to get him up to Tennessee that it would take a fair amount of talk to get her to let him come home before he got out of high school.

"The mosquitoes are killing me. I can't take it. Can't sleep up here." It was one complaint after another on the phone to his mother, who was beginning to miss him a little bit. Claudette had visions of Mike being a great real estate agent. She saw him heading up the family business and all the others falling in behind him just hanging on to every pearl of wisdom that dropped from his lips. Still, she knew that he had to graduate, and she knew that June was waiting in the wings.

"You've got to stay for graduation, Mike. You've only got four more months to go."

"I don't *want* to stay for graduation, mom. I want to come *home!*"

She wanted him to finish school and possibly come home after that. After all, that was the whole idea of his going to Tennessee in the first place was to finish high school. If he wanted to be with June after that, it would work out maybe, but not as a drop out. Ed didn't really care. He had never really cared. The only reason he'd allowed Mike to even come to Tennessee was that he thought that it would get him into the bank account a bit. He was a huge insult to Claudette. Not only did he never support his own children in any way, he would now leap at every available opportunity to have *her* pay him for any thing he might do for his own son while the boy was residing there. The boy was a burden on him. He'd been free of this task since the divorce, and didn't like the idea of anyone

Cigar Box

intruding upon his "space." Claudette had been deliciously free of this slug until Mike had said he wanted to marry June, and her life was fine without him. He was even more of a deadbeat as an ex husband! It didn't surprise her. He would call her (collect) and tell her how miserable Mike was up in Tennessee, and how he needed to be with her. "Typical," she thought. "He never was any good at all, and now he can't even to this one little favor for four more months!" She became angry with Mike forever starting this entire mess, but even more angry with herself for contacting Ed in the first place. She had secretly hoped that one day she'd just hear from someone that he'd been found bloated and dead in his little shack and that would be the sordid end of Ed!

Around February, it all came to a head. Having exhausted all other tricks and moves June confided in her mother one afternoon.

"Mom, I gotta talk to you."

"What about dear. What's on your mind?"

"Well, it's me and Michael. We, uh, we been, uh, well, *together*."

"Are you telling me you're pregnant?"

"Well, I don't know."

"He's been up there in Tennessee for a long time. Why you telling me this now?"

"I'm spotting now. Mom, I'm scared. I ain't ever been this way before."

Barbara was being cool about the whole thing, but inside she was scheming. If June had been with Michael in that way, it gave her a hold on the prize of all prizes. Not only to marry into "a" family at the Bend, but to marry into "the" family at the Bend! She knew that Mike was seventeen and June was sixteen, and all in all that didn't look too bad, but soon, when he turned eighteen, things would be a tad different. For the few months that June was sixteen, and Mike was eighteen, Mike would actually be messing with a minor and he'd be an adult. That would give Barbara the advantage she needed to pry her daughter into the Bend! She wasn't actually concerned about any misgivings concerning June's chastity, which she was sure had been left on some sand bar down at the river a long time ago, but she could put up the front that she was very outraged, and besides that, the judge wouldn't care at all about June's past, or present. She was sixteen years old! That was all that counted! She really didn't want Mike to be in any trouble, but she did want him sufficiently scared enough to marry June. She knew that June couldn't be pregnant by Mike, but she could string along the statutory rape thing just enough to put the fear of God in him and his family. It was an old Texas trick. Teenage girl comes up saying she's been with someone. The families get together to work it out under the ever-present shadow of the law, and they come to the brilliant conclusion that the couple needs to just get married to "make it all right!"

Barbara viewed the Bend with envy. Years ago she had slept on the very same ground that Claudette's home rested on now. Her jeans were tighter back then, and her blood ran hotter. She followed her lust instead of her mind and lost what little hold she would ever have on the Stillwell ranch. She could not see that Claudette's business savvy had manufactured the myth that was the Bend. She, and she alone had sold this myth to the councilmen that day long ago. In point of

Cigar Box

fact the Bend was whatever it became in the mind of man. All Barbara could see was what the area had become, and she actually hated Claudette for it! To her it was as if there were some magical seed somewhere on the ranch that later took root and became the enormous subdivision with all the wealth, and power. But now God, in His wisdom, had placed the Bend within her reach! And she would take that shot.

She had a love affair with old man Stillwell during his late wife's illness. With the old lady in her bed dying, the voluptuous Barbara would meet Mr. Stillwell in one of the far rooms and fill his every need. After the lady of the house died Barbara hung with the older man for a while, but when Ray came back from prison she'd found herself slipping off with him to scratch the itch that the older man just couldn't seem to help her with, and in time her lust clouded her ambition and the entire thing blew up in her face. Only problem was at the time of the breakup she was already with child. A child she would name June, for the month she was born. Inside, Barbara knew whose child it was, and by then Stillwell was so mad about it he wouldn't even talk to her. Combine that with just a little bit of guilt over how he'd carried on with his maid while Mrs. Stillwell died, and you have one very bitter old man!

Over fifteen years of living in the shacks behind Fat Eddies had prepared Barbara for the eventuality of getting a chance, any chance, to break out and get a piece of the proverbial pie. That was one reason she paraded June around like she did. Inside she knew that her beauty had fled, but June still had it, and that beauty would snare someone someday that would put her where she felt like she deserved to be. The affair with Stillwell was forgotten, or at least not spoken of in open company, and time and tears went by. Little June grew and knew that this man, Ray, was not her actual father. Barbara, not wanting to tell the little girl of her fling out at the Stillwell ranch, concocted a story about a "gambler" who came through town and romanced her. She told little June that the man was a big time dealer in Vegas, and that he swore to come back and get them all and take them up there some day. With enough repeating the story became carved in stone, and June accepted it as the truth.

June, in all honesty, didn't entirely create the reputation she had. Barbara in her younger days was the "spittin' image" of June, and her carrying on with the old man and the "dealer," made many a lively conversation around the little desert community over the years. As Barbara's beauty faded, little June came along and the reputation naturally attached itself to her, giving her looks a "timeless" capacity that men, both young and old enjoyed as they watched little June serve catfish on Friday nights.

She knew that her daughter had been carrying on with Mike, but to be honest she hadn't really thought that Mike was "man" enough to have an affair with her little June. She viewed him as slightly effeminate to say the least. Now, that view would actually assist her in achieving her goal. Mike was a born coward; hell everybody in town knew that. Buddy actually got thrown into jail once in high school for fighting to take up for Mike who was too chicken to defend himself. If she could raise the specter of deputy Dawg before the

Cigar Box

trembling boy's eyes he'd do anything she asked. And, besides that, he'd get to marry June, who in her opinion was the best looking girl in town, if not the county, if not the state of Texas, even if she was only sixteen!

The phone rang at the little real estate office in town.

"Hello.'

"Hello, this is Barbara, June's mother. I've been talking to June, and I think you and I should have a little chat."

"What about?" Claudette was being cool. She knew perfectly well what this call was about! It could only be about one thing. The two women didn't run anywhere *near* the same circles, and the only reason a "have not" called a "have" was to "get!"

"Well, June tells me that they've been intimate. I think that Mike is just a little too mature to be carrying on with a sixteen year old girl, don't you think?"

"Well, I don't think anything. He knows better, and he'll suffer the consequences. Well, you've told me, now what do you plan to do about it?"

"I just think we need to get together and talk this over. We need to see if these two kids really love each other, or what."

"They are not old enough to *love* each other Barbara!" Claudette felt her temper rise, but then she calmed down and asked, "Would you like to meet at the catfish house?"

"Just me and you, Claudette. I'm not telling Ray. He'll go nuts, and I don't need that right now."

Claudette knew that Ray would not "go nuts," but she'd rather meet without all the cussing and table banging. Her husband was the biggest builder in this part of the state with the most connections. Ray wouldn't destroy that income base over this, and besides, June being a part of such a family would actually benefit him. Claudette knew that Ray wasn't as mercenary as Barbara, but she also knew that he really did want the best for his little girl, and to be perfectly honest a life at the Bend just beat the hell out of life in the shacks behind Fat Eddie's!

Ever since Mike began his campaign to return to west Texas Claudette had been waiting for this news. She knew that Mike had been alone with June, and the whole problem of marriage or new truck had gotten him to Tennessee in the first place. Mike was seventeen, and in Texas that was an adult. Depending on the Judge (And Claudette owned them all) he could be charged with God knows what in this mess, and it would take a fair amount of "lawyering" and money to untie the knot! Mike's stepfather, Bill, was another matter. He had always suspected Mike as being "low slung" in morals, and though he actually liked the little blonde from the other side of the tracks the most alluring thing about her was that after she popped in for coffee she went *back* to the other side of the tracks! He didn't shout, but his opinion was firm.

"He took off out of here because he knew he was in trouble. So now, we have your ex-husband on the tit, and June about to move into my house. Do you think she's really pregnant?"

"I don't know. No, she can't be. Not by Mike anyway. He's been gone five months. You know her reputation out on the flat. We don't know how many cowboys she's been with. But we see her every Friday

Cigar Box

night at the catfish house, and she don't look like she's swelling up none."

"She's a small girl. I knew a kid once when I worked at the college who got pregnant. She was so small that no one knew she was pregnant until she just didn't come to work for a week in the snack bar and showed up with a baby. I honestly thought she must have carried it in her pocket. June could be that way. You never know!"

"I don't think so. I think Barbara would have pulled that rabbit right out of the hat. I don't think she has the smarts to hold anything back."

"She's not smart, but she's trash. Trash makes up for smart any day of the week."

Claudette took offence at this remark. "I was raised up on Woodward Street in Memphis. Before that I was raised on a sand bar out in the Mississippi. Am I trash, too?"

He looked at her and smiled. "You and I are no different from them, hon. I was raised up in Briggs in a little house that just barely had a floor. But look around you. Do you see all we got? We are trash, too. But we are rich trash! Barbara's attacking the only way she knows how. Heck, I don't fault her. She's just trying to survive. Make the best for her kid, that's all. Can't hold that against her. Still, I don't want to just hand over my pile to someone like her."

"We can't just let them waltz in here and take all we got."

"True. See, that's trash for you, and Barbara's not expecting that. She thinks we'll be all righteous and scared, when really it don't mean nothing. She's just trying to marry off one of her kids. In a way, we're lucky. Have you seen June's little sister. 'Moooooooooo!' I'm just glad Mike didn't get involved with her." He laughed, but Claudette didn't see what was so funny.

He knew that Barbara would not actually put Mike in jail. That was not the plan at all, because she wouldn't get what she really wanted out of them. She wanted position, stature, and security for June, and Mike sitting in the county jail would not provide any of those things. Not to mention that the lawyers would come out, and the trial would be very bad publicity for June and family.

He thought a bit more, "Isn't he involved with that other girl over on Commerce Street?"

"Oh, God! I don't even want to think about that right now. That's just what we need is to have that come crawling out of a sewer and bite us in the ass with this going on."

"Sewer? Are you insinuating that *she's* trash, too? Wow, a whole town full of trash. Isn't that the deputy's daughter?"

"Oh God! Let's don't open that can of worms. Deputy Dog'll kill Mike!"

"Hey, I figure he'd be glad to get rid of that ugly little girl. Remember them big ears she had in the sixth grade? They'd hold up her baseball cap"

"No, that was Anna, who dated Buddy, and it was not the sixth it was the ninth."

"Yeah, you're right. You know, with all the ugly girls in this town, no wonder June looks so good to Mike!"

"Not funny!"

Cigar Box

"Yeah, it is. Mike got himself into this. All he has to do is stay in Tennessee and he'll never have a problem. Barbara'll just find another mark and marry her little girl off to him."

"What if he loves her?"

The man looked amazed. "Love? You honestly think he is capable of such a thing. I believe he wanted a new truck not six months ago. Threw the biggest fit in the world for it. Now that's maturity. I can just hear you and him talking that one over. 'Oh, mom, I want a truck; no, make that a wife. A truck, or a fuck." He smiled contentedly to himself at the little rhyme he'd come up with but Claudette didn't think it was so funny.

"Do you have to talk like that around me? I hate that! You know I hate that."

"But, it's the truth."

"I'll admit he's a bit childish."

He stared at her. "A bit?"

"Well, maybe a lot. But that's not the problem here. I know he's coming back, and he'll want to be with June."

"Oh, he'll come back. That's in the cards. That boy always wants to be somewhere he's not. When he's here, he'll want to be there. Then back again."

"Can we leave the subject?"

"No! I'm sick and tired of every time Mike's little world turns around we all have to put our lives on hold."

"That's not true."

"It is true and you know it. My boys paid all these years. Every time Mike sneezed, they paid. Your precious Mike got what ever he wanted."

Wilbur Witt and Pamela Woodward

Claudette put her head in her hands, "Stop it! I just want him to be happy."

Bill pulled her hands away from her face, "Why can't we all be happy just this once? Why do we all have to play Mike's little game?"

Claudette didn't answer. She walked out through the French doors at the rear of the house and sat in a lawn chair, staring at the greens that she had built with her own intellect and sweat. How had Mike screwed up like this? She wondered how bad it would be having him marry the little blonde. She wasn't bad looking, and she did come over to the house a lot. Claudette didn't dislike the girl. She was just against being blackmailed. Bill came out on the porch.

"I'm sorry. I know this is hard for you."

"Bill, I know he screwed up. I'm as mad about it as you are. We just gotta get through this thing the best way we can." She reached up and held his hand.

"I think you need a sandwich down at the bend."

"I used to know a man who'd take me there."

"I still can."

They left the conversation at this point. Meanwhile, back up in Tennessee, Mike was causing as much trouble for his father as he could. The fat man's wits were already failing him. Unknown to him diabetes was creeping into his blood and in a few short years he'd be *in* the nursing home instead of *working* there. He had never wanted the responsibility of children and Mike was a well-grown child now! Mike made sure that he kept him up after he got home from school at three in the afternoon. Over the period of weeks, the loss of sleep began to tell on the man. He was used to sleeping until he decided to get out of bed.

Cigar Box

If he slept all day and had to rush to work in the early evening, so be it. There was no problem there at all. He could always raid the kitchen at the nursing home. He ate one big meal a day, and if that meal was at the home that was perfectly fine with him. Mike threw a wrench into this life style. The constant care needed to provide him his needs wore the older man down and soon he was eagerly waiting for any reason to get him back to Texas, if for no other reason other than to get a good night's sleep.

Now, enter into this mix June's stepfather, Ray. He was genuinely upset when he heard what had been going on. In a life of low means and rough times, June had been the one ray of sunshine that had shone on this man his whole life. He'd married Barbara just five months after June was born. He'd lived with her in the shack that she ended up in after she and old man Stillwell had their little falling out. June had never known any other man as her father, and he lavished on her more than he did his own daughter by Barbara of some years later. June was his angel, and Mike had defiled her! Never mind the fact that June had initiated the meetings all by herself. Forget about all the Saturday nights at the SPJST! He didn't want to hear that, and he *wouldn't* hear about any "marriage!" Still, Huntsville prison had taken its toll on the little man. He'd been hurt there, and he was determined never to go back again. Deep in his heart he knew that he'd never do anything to cause his old school chum, deputy Dawg, to have to arrest him again.

Ray had been a good man up until he found drugs. The drugs led him down a road to stealing and worse and it all ended one night when he ran out of money

Wilbur Witt and Pamela Woodward

for the white powder the marijuana had led him to. In a fit he ran into a gas station and tried to grab money from the till. The man behind the counter had hit him with a ready baseball bat and Ray, dazed, stumbled back to his truck. He hadn't driven very far when the deputy pulled him over. By this time Ray was "all in."

"I gotta take you in, Ray," the deputy had said.

All Ray could reply was, "Johnny, I think you really should."

He got six years, and did them without parole. When he came out and drifted back to west Texas he'd left his pride in Huntsville. He hung out at his mother's ranch for a while, meeting with Juan in the barn as often as he could. Then he met Barbara, and as bad as she was, she was a tad better than what he'd left behind. She'd been carrying on with the old man, and there was a rumor about her and some drifter who had come through town right before Ray got back. Some people could remember the drifter, and some did not. In point of fact, he was only in town for a few days, ran into trouble at one of the private poker games that flourished in the area, and left quietly before he got hurt. They began to sneak around and before long Barbara was with Ray and they were both in the shack behind Fat Eddie's. Then, in a short while she had June. A few years later the little sister came along, and this one *was* Ray's, but the lovely June was always his favorite. For everything sour in his life, his little June was the sugar in his day. He did indeed want the best for June!

By this time, Mike was rolling full tilt to get back to Texas. The more he thought about June the more control the memory had on him. He began daily phone

Cigar Box

calls to his mother, and nightly calls to June. Soon all hope was abandoned and he was on his way home again! His father drove him down and was more than just a little vocal about this whole mess.

"Just wants to be somewhere he's not!"

"He thinks he's in love," his mother said.

"Well, we'll see just how in love he is in a year or two. Hope he graduates high school!"

Claudette walked out to his truck as he was leaving.

"Uh, Claudette, You got a fifty you can spot me 'till I get back to Memphis?"

"Gas?"

"Yeah, that kid tapped me out on the way down."

As she reached in her jeans to retrieve the money she said, "You've been tapped out all your life, Ed!"

He looked at the big house and then he looked back at Claudette. Her teeth were fixed, her hair was done, and her weight was under control. It was to him as if he were looking at a stranger. He wondered if she were actually the same woman who left Tennessee so many years ago.

"I wish we could have worked it out."

Claudette stared in amazement at Ed. "Worked it out? Are you insane? Do you remember how you spent the money I saved to get pavement on our driveway just so we could get propane to that little trailer you put me in? You bought a horse Ed! I froze out there while you rode that silly-ass horse."

"He died."

"Good! You probably ate him!"

"You sure have a sharp tongue now."

"Yeah, but at least I didn't call you retarded while your brother was laying there dying, now did I?"

"He was gonna die anyway. You know that."

She shook her head, "Just take your fifty dollars and go."

"Claudette…"

"Just go!"

Mike knew better than to try to see June right off the bat. Her stepfather was waiting and he wasn't being very diplomatic about it either. Ray's reputation would keep Mike away for a while. Actually Ray was dodging Mike, hoping that there would be no incident, but it all came to a head one day at Fat Eddie's.

Mike, and his stepfather were having breakfast at a table when Ray came in to have coffee before he went to his construction site. Right away Mike saw him and fear rushed through his body. He froze and looked down at his plate. Bill saw the man come in also, but made no note of it. Slowly he walked past them, and then turned. Looking Mike dead in the eye he said, "If I ever catch you talking to my daughter again I'll stomp your guts out!" It was threat enough to scare Mike, and it had all that Texas flair that made Ray look like an offended father.

He then went and sat at a table. When he took off his cap, Bill couldn't help but notice that he was bald! Then he looked at the general build of the man. Small, yes, and wiry, but small nonetheless! He went over to sit at the table. Ray seemed to have shrunk since he'd been building homes in the Bend. Bill knew that he couldn't let this slight go unanswered, but he didn't want a big incident.

"You better just move along," the bald man said.

Cigar Box

"Well, what if I just don't feel like moving along. You see, I want to know why you said that while I was eating my breakfast."

Ray looked at him. He'd never had anyone sit at his table, look him in the face, and question him like that. But this man wasn't backing off one little bit! He decided to give an answer.

"After what he did to her, I don't want him talking to her anymore."

"What did he do?"

"I *said* I don't want to talk about it!"

And I *asked* what he did!" Leaning forward, he said in a quiet voice, "I don't care about your little record, I want to know why you just disrupted my breakfast! If you ever do that again I'll personally see to it that you never drive another nail in this county, convict! Ray, we don't need this kind of trouble." Bill was suddenly ashamed that he'd been so hard on Ray. Ray was only mad at Mike for being Mike, the very same thing Bill was mad at Mike for. He couldn't blame him for that.

Ray got up, put his hat on his little baldhead, and left. Bill went back to his table and told Mike, "I strongly suggest you dodge him. He *is* the kind of guy who will hurt you!"

"Why didn't he hurt you?"

"He's not mad at me, he's mad at you Stay away from him. I don't feel that Ray really wants any trouble, but if you push him you won't be able to take the ass-beating he'll give you."

They ate their eggs in silence and left.

On the way home Bill talked to Mike. "What do you plan to do about that little girl?"

Wilbur Witt and Pamela Woodward

"Well, I wanna marry her."

"Don't you think at 17 you're just a bit too young to marry anyone? You need to graduate first."

Mike stared out of the window and didn't say a word. That was his way of ignoring the situation. He wanted to marry June, and he wanted to marry her this afternoon if he could. Or get a new truck! This problem would involve more than one breakfast at Fat Eddie's. It would involve a meeting of the minds.

Bill looked at him staring out the window, "You gonna answer me?"

Mike just continued to stare. Bill reached over and took him by the hair on the back of his head and drove his face into the glass he'd been staring through."

As his head came bounding back Mike yelled, "What the hell'd you do that for?"

"Cause you didn't answer me. And don't think that running to your mom crying will help. You're about to ruin that little girl's life and for what? So you can get laid!"

"I told you I love her."

"You don't love anybody kid. You love yourself. Forget it. You spoiled little bastard. You got your mind made up. I couldn't stop it all these years, what makes me think I can stop it now."

They rode the rest of the way to the Bend in silence. When they got home Mike ran back to his room.

"What's wrong with him?" Claudette asked.

"We saw Ray down at Fat Eddie's."

"What did he say?"

Cigar Box

Bill looked at her surprised, "What the hell do you *think* he said? He told Mike to stay away from his sixteen year old daughter."

"Did you take up for Mike?"

"Hell yes! I embarrassed that poor beat up little ex con in front of all his friends. Now, are you happy?"

"No. I've been on the phone to Barbara. She wants to meet next week sometime. I think she's going to make the big push to get us to let June marry Mike."

"Surely she's not that crass."

"Why hell yeah she is. Oh, she'll be all offended, but the main thing is to get her trashy ass back on this property."

"Like I said, a whole town full of trash."

"I don't even want to start that conversation again. Let's just worry about one thing at a time."

Bill went and sat on the back porch, looking at the greens. He'd built this with his ability, bare hands and guts. It only goes to follow that there would always be someone out there that would want to try and horn in on it. The "tracks" are not a barrier so much as an invitation. The tracks were an invitation to every one of those mother's sons out there who wanted a piece of the good life. West Texas had always been the hardest part of a very hard state. Bill expected them to come, but he wasn't going to just sit there and hand it all over. Not by a damn sight! Still, he would wait and see what the meeting of the mothers brought. He wouldn't step in just yet.

* * *

Wilbur Witt and Pamela Woodward

The mothers met at Fat Eddies the following Wednesday about noon. They sat in the back of the café and ordered the "special" which was always meat, two veggies, a salad, tea and bread. Fat Eddie would brag that he didn't have an "all you can eat" bar because if his lunch didn't fill you up he'd bring you more out to eat. They ate their salads in silence and then Barbara spoke.

"Look, these things happen. God knows June is wild as a cat, but she is just sixteen, and your son."

"Don't tell me about *my* son Barbara! *My* son still wanted a truck for Christmas. Your little girl is not a little girl. Everyone in this town knows how she gets around!"

Barbara was not a coward and would have slapped Claudette, except that the real estate lady still had something she wanted. She was smart enough to hold her temper. June *was* wild, that was no lie. She *did* get around, and that was no lie either. Still, the object of this meeting was to work out the wedding. They both knew why they were here. She agreed that Mike needed time to graduate, but just as soon as possible after he walked across that stage down at the high school gym, he needed to walk down the isle down at the church! She decided on a verbal attack as opposed to a brawl.

"Don't you look down your nose at *me* Miss High Falutin' *divorced* real estate lady. Your little spoiled wimpy son runs around messin' with little girls and gets caught, and I want to give him a decent way out. I wonder how he'd do in the county jail? Wonder how them little shorts with the pockets in them would do in there. What do you think?"

Cigar Box

Claudette was surprised at the bitterness in the woman, but she knew the determination, too! This woman meant to marry into her family by any means possible. The reference to Mike's shorts was recalling a time when he ran around the golf course with tailored shorts with fancy pockets. His stepbrothers wore jeans, but Mike always had to look his best. Apparently Barbara, just like practically everyone else in town, thought Mike just looked silly. Imagine, a west Texas kid with such a get up!

"Ok, calm down. We'll talk it over more. Let's just agree to let them see each other for now."

June's mother leaned near to Mike's mom, "Don't let Ray know. He gets crazy about June. He's already mad at Mike. Let's let that pot cool just a bit, and we'll bring them out of the closet at little at a time. Is Mike coming back to work down here?"

"No, I don't think that will be wise. He's going to work on a construction crew on the weekends. My husband is trying to interest him more in the builder trade."

"Good! Just keep it cool."

"Ok. Look, we'll be here Friday. Buddy will be in town visiting and wants to do the catfish thing. Do you think Ray will be here? Maybe if he saw us it might take the edge off just a bit."

"Yeah, we'll try that. How long is your son in town for?"

"A week. He'll leave Wednesday."

"Ok, see you then." They finished their lunch and left. Claudette would never have met with the likes of this woman under any other conditions, and the idea of this "lady" being in her family in any way was repugnant to her. It had hurt when Barbara threw up the divorce to her, but she'd been called worse things so she looked over it. Barbara was just making sure that Claudette knew that as low as she may have thought Barbara was, she was *not* divorced! Anyway, Buddy was coming to town, and that would be something nice to look forward to. Buddy had graduated high school and took off to work in Houston. He took night courses and liked the big city life, but he also liked to come home now and again and he especially liked to do the ritual of "eating the cat," with his family. Claudette realized that she wanted to keep the problem between Ray, and Mike quiet. Buddy was rough hewn like his father and he was the type to pull Ray up and slap him in spite of his so-called reputation.

As the weekend approached, Claudette began to make plans to have June drop by and see them. She knew that he'd have to watch out for Ray, but that was no matter because Barbara was firmly on the side of June seeing Michael at any opportunity that could be arranged. They planned to eat out on Friday night because Ray would be there with everybody else eating catfish. True to her agreement with Barbara, Claudette steered the family toward the traditional catfish dinner. June and Mike made other plans, however. June had been calling Mike at a mutual friend's house all week and they had set up a meeting. Late Thursday night June slipped out of her bedroom in the shacks behind the Catfish house and sneaked to City Park, where Michael was waiting near the duck pond. After making sure they weren't followed, they kissed and talked.

Cigar Box

"I can't go on without you," June began.

"We'll be together soon, I promise," Michael said, trying to appear "grown up" and in "control."

She wrapped her arms around him and held him for the longest time. "I miss you more and more every day."

All that was on Michael's mind was physical, but he played the game anyway. He had chosen a part of City Park far enough away from the main road so as to assure privacy, but he didn't see the two forms watching from a nearby tree.

Veronica watched June begin to kiss and hold Michael in the distance. Her spirit guide with her let her watch for a few minutes and then asked, "Did you know what he wanted when you went there?"

Without looking away from the scene she answered, "Sure, I knew what he wanted. What does any man want? I knew he'd be there. All I had to do was make a promise and he'd be there. Sex will lure and hold a man every time!"

"Why didn't it hold him to you in Tennessee?"

She turned to look at the man. "I thought you were supposed to be an angel. What's an angel doing worrying about sex for?"

"I never told you I was an angel. I told you there were things we had to talk about!"

"My, aren't we splitting hairs here."

"Not splitting hairs, I'm just letting you understand that surprisingly, I may be in the same boat as you. I have things that I have to work out, too. I just have a few miles on you, that's all. Both of us were put at that intersection. You for your reasons, and me for mine."

She turned back to the scene. "What broke us up in Tennessee happened in Texas. Like I told you, some things are real bad, and it ain't easy to get around them. Mike couldn't get around something I did."

"Then you've got to understand why you did it."

Veronica looked at him with a puzzled stare. "I did it because I had done things like that all my life! I didn't expect to get caught, and when I did get caught I didn't expect them to all go on like they did about it."

"Two sets of standards?"

"No, a set of standards I inherited. Look, Doctor Angel, I just played out the role they gave me. Mike and other men wanted the pretty little blonde and I was there. I was their toy as much as they were mine. I think about the only one who took me serious, as funny as it may sound, was Claudette, and dad."

"Ray?"

"Yeah. I seemed to fill a need in him, and not a bad one. It was like I replaced something he'd lost. I pushed him away for a while, but I never felt him push me away."

"You look happy enough there," he said looking at the couple in the distance.

"We were happy there. It took a lot to break that happiness up, but believe me, if you work on it, you can break it up. I broke it up real good."

"How?"

"Just trying to have it all, Dr. Angel. Just trying to have it all."

Within a few minutes, her alter ego was coming out of the trees, adjusting her jeans and blouse and scampering back to the shacks behind the Catfish

Cigar Box

house. Michael sat in the oaks of City Park convinced that he was totally in love.

Juan drew the smoke deep within his lungs and let the drug take hold of him. Slowly his mind relaxed into oblivion and he became glassy eyed. Then the soft spot in his head from his infancy opened up and a single dove emerged and flew up into the night air. Flying this way and that the dove looked for signs of someone who would be recognizable only to it. Someone who was pure soul, yet was not dead yet. Within a moment or two it spied the young June coming out of the bushes and it descended on her. Unseen in the nearby brush, Dreamwalker pulled Veronica back near him.

"Be still! Don't let him see you."

"Who?" her eyes searched the night sky.

"That dove. That's the shaman. He's trying to find us. He can't see you very easily."

"What if he finds us?"

"He will try to force us back to the accident scene and continue the accident. It is not good that we do that right at this time. You have to learn some things, see some things before we go back."

They watched as the dove discovered that the young June was not what it was seeking and turned, flying back to the body of Juan, still sitting in his home. It returned to his body and he came back from the realm of the unseen, a bit angry that he had not found what he sought. By doing this he had crossed not one, but two barriers. The first barrier being the obvious one of leaving his body and searching such as he did, but the other was the barrier of time. Juan had crossed over the barrier of time and actually gone back looking for the Dreamwalker and his consort. Juan knew they were somewhere, but just where in time had not been made clear to him. It was not like searching in one era which to be honest is rather two dimensional, but searching across time took some doing. That took some real savvy.

If he could locate the Dreamwalker he had spiritual power over him that could force him back to the accident scene, and his newfound friend with him, but if he could not find him then he would have to just wait and see just what the spirit had up his tuxedoed sleeve.

Catfish Nights

    A wedding of epic magnitude can be a healing event or it can be a destructive thing. Such a wedding was in the works that Friday night at Fat Eddie's Catfish Emporium. Claudette was only playing for time, trying to let the steam off of the little relationship between Mike and June, but Barbara was preceding full tilt toward Mike's eighteenth birthday. The whole town knew about it. Mike's older brother, Buddy was in town, and he wanted catfish, also. He hadn't seen June in the last two years, least ways not that he could remember, so the opportunity was being taken to reacquaint them at this particular Friday night. After graduation, he had gone to work in Houston. He was a diesel mechanic and the demand was very good there with the shipping trade. He would make a trip up to the little town about three, or four times a year, but up until now June was just one more high school girl that Mike knew. He and Mike were stepbrothers, his father being a builder, and Claudette his stepmother. Before the marriage, he had been the oldest son, but with the advent of Mike there were actually *two* oldest sons now, Buddy being more than a year older than Mike. The adopted Angie didn't come into play because she was a girl, and the boys didn't mind her much. She kept off to herself for the most part and when she did say anything it was largely ignored. Then there was the youngest brother who was very fat, slightly retarded and addicted to food. Tommy took care of this stepbrother and saw that he looked good at all public gatherings. But Buddy and Mike were at opposite ends of the Texas universe. The rivalry between the two was non-stop, bordering on a genuine hate. Each boy would do anything they could devise to hurt the other. The parents hoped that as they grew older this would wane. It did not. The animosity spilled over into Bill and Claudette's marriage on more than one occasion. Bill had come to suspect that there was something genetically wrong with Mike.

The town had been buzzing about the affair between Mike and June for some time now. Ray was observed that Saturday morning in the verbal altercation between himself and Bill, and though Bill had tried to graciously pull back so as not to embarrass the little man it had not worked very well, and it was common knowledge that the situation was a genuine power play between the two families.

And the situation was very simple. In Texas a seventeen year old could be certified as an adult. A judge could view Mike's liaison with June as statutory rape! When he became eighteen, and *if* he kept seeing June, which there was really no doubt that he would, Mike could very well end up in a situation of criminal proportions and end up hauled into court and go to jail! This was the thing that Claudette was fighting against,

Cigar Box

however Bill thought the boy most likely deserved it. He had never approved of what Mike was doing, and he knew about the girl over on Commerce Street, the daughter of the deputy. To Bill's way of thinking it was high time that Mike got "jacked" for his shenanigans. His sons never got caught up in this kind of stuff, and Mike seemed to be forever in the middle of it.

In the middle of this supercharged political situation two pickup trucks and a car were loaded for Fat Eddie's that Friday night. They all arrived at the same time and parked in the rear. Fat Eddie had a golf cart to bring patrons around to the front of the establishment. All the employees except the cooks wore tuxedos on Friday night. The golf cart driver had one, too, and she (that's right "she") would pick up the people six at a time, and with great ceremony, bring them around to the front parking lot from the back parking lot.

The waiting room, if it could be called that, was a sitting area in the parking lot. Eddy had bought some five dollar chairs at Wal Mart and set them all around the front lot so the elite could enter their names and wait until they were called to dine upon the ultimate in red neck cuisine. There was even a piece of art on the front window of two catfish in a formal gown and a tux walking into a door. The gentleman fish was asking, "Where to you want to be on Friday night toots," to which the lady catfish replies, "I wouldn't *think* of going anywhere but *Fat Eddie's Catfish Emporium!*"

The patrons would sit and chat in the parking lot under the warm Texas dusk. Everyone who was *anyone* was there. Lawyers, Judges, police, schoolteachers, and even the local vagabonds, and riff raff came, for all were equal and welcome at Fat Eddie's Catfish Emporium. Fat Eddie himself was the chief cook in the kitchen. The hot grease, (exactly 475 degrees) was kept at the ready. Fat Eddie had a trick he used to see if the grease was just right. He'd put a big ol' kitchen match in it, and when it hit 475, boom; that match would go off like a sparkler! Eddie mixed up a special batch of his secret hot batter that gave the catfish a "special" bite. And, to boot, these were only farm-raised catfish. They had been well fed and kept happy all of their lives!

Every Friday night had to have a main topic of conversation. The football team *never* won, so it had to be something else. An affair was usually good food for thought. There was very little to do in the little community except drink and fornicate so there was always a good supply of gossip in that area. Sometimes a murder, but the police in this town never caught anyone but drunks, so unless the killer was a drunk it usually went unsolved, and that wouldn't make good conversation. This Friday, however, there was really a story circulating! June the cat was trying to marry Mike because they had been slipping off to City Park! The couple had thought that their little liaisons were secret, but to be honest there was an alley cat in the back of Fat Eddie's, and even that alley cat knew all about their shenanigans!

Mike was startled to find Ray was already seated and consuming his third plate of fish when they arrived. June made sure that her stepfather had all the fish he wanted. He looked up from the plate as they walked in, but did a head count, and quickly looked

Cigar Box

back down at his fish. June's honor didn't rank *that* much fight. He had made the decision in his life never to go back to jail. Ray had learned to use his head for these types of fights. In addition to that, Angie was with them, just down from Dallas where she was a chiropractor. He noticed Buddy also. Buddy had a reputation from high school of being just a little left of center. He'd once stormed off a roof he was working on to knock out a man who had insulted him from a car. The combination of respectability, and Buddy put him on notice.

They positioned themselves in line and waited the call to eat. When it came, they were seated in the same dining room as Ray. Fat Eddie's had *three* different rooms in which the famished were served. The waitress came over with menus, but the family all just raised their hands and said, "Tea, catfish." Even Doctor Angie ordered the fish. First, however they had to "eat the bean." The cafe served a big Mexican bowl of pinto beans with Tabasco on the side for the so inclined, and lots of onions. By the time they had finished the beans the fish arrived. Four steaming pieces of catfish, a little plastic cup of the absolute worse Cole slaw you *ever* put in your mouth, two hush puppies (and not the kind momma used to make, but the little round ones they got out of Austin,) and French fries. There was ketchup, and tartar sauce to season the fish, or the Tabasco that was left on the table from the beans. Fat Eddie had a cost cutting measure also. When the bean bowl was taken back to the kitchen, he would pour the uneaten beans back into the big pot.

Wilbur Witt and Pamela Woodward

They began to eat and look around at the crowd. As usual, the people sat in groups, all chatting, and trying not to look at the table where the Montgomerys were all sitting, and the waitress had to push two long tables together to accommodate all the family. Claudette actually hated catfish, having had to eat too much "mud-cat" in her life on the Mississippi, but ate to fulfill the ritual. (And people wonder where religious rituals come from, and how they get so entrenched!) Then came the "seconds." This is the part that June played in. She came around with her "tux" on and her platter of hot catfish steaming. On the edge of the platter were refill portions of slaw, fries and puppies if the patron so desired, but very few were stupid enough to take any more of them and usually opted for the "cat." June's nickname "June the Cat," had stemmed *not* from an old Tennessee Williams name, but actually referring to her service at the Emporium.

Buddy had never seen her this well grown, and up close like this. She leaned over him and refilled his plate and his reaction brought a jest from Angie of, "Careful little brother! That one's taken. I believe Mike has her in *his* corral." He smiled sheepishly and went back to eating the catfish June had just put on his plate. Still, he couldn't take his eyes off her as she walked away from the table and filled other plates, including her stepfather's at the table directly across from theirs. She had filled out perfectly. As she bent over to fill the plates Buddy was captivated by her legs, and form.

Barbara showed up late and went right to Mike's table and said hello to the group. "Mike, are you

Cigar Box

gonna come out and see June tomorrow? We'll be out at Ray's mom's ranch, and she'd love to see you."

Mike was stunned, but he glanced over at Ray and the bald headed man was not looking very aggressive right then. Michael correctly deduced that there must be more going on behind the scenes than even he knew about. He didn't really know what to say, but he looked at his mother, who said, "Hey, you're a man now. You go and meet little girls at City Park. You have to make these decisions!"

He could feel his face getting red. He'd thought that those meetings were hidden. Never mind that they were in the only real lover's lane in town, and that the whole town was watching him anyway. He thought all but him and June retired at 7:30 sharp!

"You know about that?" He looked a bit astonished.

Tommy, his younger brother looked up from his plate, "You wanna buy pictures, Mike?"

Mike looked down at his plate. Barbara moved in for the kill. "Look, kid, you wanna see my daughter you're gonna have to do it in the light of day. You're gonna have to face Ray; he may kick your butt, but you are gonna have to face him, and you're gonna have to do the right thing."

"I love her."

"Yeah, I'm sure you do. Still, you gotta come out and do the right thing." She leaned down, "Look kid, if Ray sees you a lot then he'll get used to you, ok. Just do it my way."

All this time Claudette sat silently and let Barbara do her bit. She was actually upset, but she didn't want an incident and she didn't want him to go to the jail either. Like Barbara, she knew that June wasn't pregnant, so she'd just wait until Mike lost interest in her and moved along to another girl. That shouldn't take long. Mike never seemed to stick with anything very long, and this shouldn't be any exception to the rule.

Buddy watched June for the rest of the dinner. The poise, the heart shaped lips, the long blonde hair going through the little "Catfish" cap, all served as a lure for the boy. He and Mike had never really gotten along, and this gave him one more reason to be upset with him. As pointed out before, these two had a rivalry that went far and above the normal ones between brothers. Buddy's mother had died of cancer about the same time rancher Stillwell's wife had succumbed to the illness. When his father had married Claudette, he had looked to his adopted sister Angie as a role model and the older girl had been a good one, in spite of being Claudette's adopted niece. Mike was spoiled, and Buddy was the classic older child. The two never mixed. Mike could never do anything right. Combine that with the fact that Buddy was a fighter, and Mike was not, and you have the mix for a perfect hate club.

June went from table to table giving out fish. Ray watched without letting them know he was watching. Barbara went over to sit with him. June didn't have to take her order because she knew what her mother would want. She would want the same as everybody else, catfish. June signaled a dishwasher who brought a plate and she filled it directly from the tray, which was basically against the rule, but it was overlooked for June.

Cigar Box

    This setting was almost "hallowed ground," and no one would start a fight, or even a heavy discussion here for fear that the catfish night would end. There were never any cops called to Fat Eddies, mainly because they were all there eating anyway. Finally, though, Mike's stepfather and mother went over and sat at Barbara and Ray's table. Before anyone could speak, however, Ray said, "I don't want to talk about it. It has me really upset!"

    Mike's stepfather nodded, "Us too. I think these kids are out of control…"

    "Yours a little more than mine! She's sixteen!"

    "I know that, but look at it this way, she's only one year younger than Mike. It's not like he's in his thirties."

    "Good thing, too, else I'd have him in jail!"

    This was just a bluff. Nobody was going to jail over this matter unless the two men got in a fight right there in the café. Ray was putting on a good show to let everyone know he had good morals, no doubt taught to him in prison. Just then, June came over with some more fish.

    "Ya'll want me to bring some plates over here?"

    "No, hon," Bill said, "we're just about finished."

    "What ya'll got on your minds over here?"

    The four adults looked at the girl as if she was crazy. What did she *think* they had on their minds? June just stared back at them. "I'm gonna marry Mike. That's all there is to it. If ya'll don't like it ya'll can just jump up, but I'm gonna marry Mike. Now, if ya'll can't get together on where and how, we'll just run off to Mexico."

    "Won't be legal," her stepfather said.

"Who said I'd be comin' back?"

Barbara spoke up, "Oh, honey, you don't wanna do nothing like that. Mexico? You'd be down there with all them Mexicans? They sell girls like you down there. We'll work this out. You and Mike can see each other. I think this whole thing's done got out of control."

June leaned back, resting her catfish platter on her hip, "You mean that?"

"Sure, baby! Sure, I mean that. You can go and see Mike, and I'm sure he will be able to come out to Mommaw's ranch, huh Ray?"

Claudette said, "June, you been coming over to our house for Christmas since, God, since I don't know how long. We ain't gonna stop that, now are we. Don't you even *think* about no Mexico, you hear. We love you. We don't want you down there getting all kidnapped, ok?"

"Ok, but I wanna be able to see Mike!"

All the adults nodded consent, surprising all at the table, but not the people in the restaurant, because that's what this meeting was all about. It was not about so much *if* June and Mike would be together, as when, and how. The only person who seemed disappointed by this event was Buddy, sitting at the end of the table his father and stepmother had just left. His sister Angie noticed his face and asked, "Something on your mind, Bud?"

"No, fish just not sitting right, that's all."

Angie was wise beyond her years. She looked at Buddy, and then at June, still basking in her glory in her victory at being able to see Mike. She couldn't

Cigar Box

help but notice that June kept giving glances over to the table where she and Buddy were sitting.

Veronica and her guide sat in the corner of Eddie's Catfish House and watched all of this transpire with no comment. Then the man spoke, "Did you have an interest in Bud at this early date?"

She looked over across the café to where Buddy was sitting, "I was drawn to him. I liked the way he looked. I wouldn't really call it an interest."

"He has an interest in you. Don't you think you should date one brother at a time?"

It was the first time he'd really asked her a loaded question. June showed her savvy, though, "How do you know I dated two brothers? I thought you were a neutral angel."

He smiled sheepishly, "I didn't check my brain in when I had my car crash, and I am a man *not* an angel. I keep telling you that, Veronica. I can see what's in your eyes. You love the 'kill;' to know you can bend a man your way; make him do what you want him to do."

He watched as the perfect lips formed a little smile on the ends of her mouth. The sky blue eyes twinkled. He could virtually *feel* her intellect taking control of this situation. She wasn't shamed at all by his insinuation. Indeed, she accepted his judgment of her actions, but she was like a cougar, killing a deer. She felt no remorse, for the cougar must survive.

"Is it sin, if you don't *know* it is sin?"
"But you know."
"Do I?"

Her stare went cold. She rose and walked to the door. He went behind her. She passed June at sixteen years of age giving out more catfish to the hungry cowboys. The spirit guide reached and picked a piece of catfish from the platter. June did not see him, but kept handing the fish out to the people. They walked into the parking lot.

She went over by the blinking neon light reminding passing motorists that Fat Eddie's was open, open, open. He came behind her still chewing his piece of fish.

"You don't have to be so hard on me. There are things you should be nice about, and keep to yourself. You never lived in west Texas, Dr. Angel."

"Veronica, there are some things you are going to *have* to understand, if we are going to get through this thing. There is no sin that is unforgivable, but you have to know you did it. You are sitting in eternity laughing at men who fall in love with you, and using them."

Her eyes flared, "Do you see them in there? Do you see all that money and power? Look at me! I'm one girl, and a small one at that! You think I should pity them for letting the little head get harder than the big one?"

He was surprised at her stooping to such slang, but it revealed a part of her that he hadn't seen, and perhaps he needed to now. She very rarely bared her teeth and claws, but for a brief moment she did here and now. He was reminded of a tiger that slips silently up on its prey, making no noise until the final rush, and death!

"You should know right from wrong."

"Well, 'Doctor Angel,' I guess I'll just have to work on that, huh?"

Cigar Box

"I told you I'm not an angel."

"And I should have told you never to eat the catfish here; I don't."

*   *   *

The next morning Mike rose early and got dressed. Walking into the living area of the big house he noticed Buddy sleeping on the couch with only his boots off. After catfish he'd gone to a local bar and closed it down with friends, drinking lots of beer and shooting pool and making conversation with the bar maid, Sabrina, whom he'd gone to high school with. Mike went to the kitchen where his stepfather was already having coffee. He wasn't going to drive his new truck to the ranch so he asked Bill to drive him there.

"Where you wanna go?"

"June's grand maw's house. Remember, Barbara said they wanted me to start coming out to see June there?"

The older man eyed Mike for a minute, "You better watch out about going out there. Ray'll drag you out to the hills and skin you!"

"No, I think It's gonna be ok. He's gonna like me in the end."

His stepfather chuckled, "You're just hot on the trail of that little girl."

Mike got all defensive and half yelled, "She's not a little girl, and I don't like you saying that!"

His stepfather was not taken aback by this outburst. He just figured it was Mike's time to "jump" because that's what all the other boys had already done. They

Wilbur Witt and Pamela Woodward

had all tried out the old man except the youngest who was too fat and slow to jump on anyone, or anything but a pork chop. "Oh, you a man now? How's your head feeling?"

Realizing he was setting the stage for a major altercation, which he wasn't ready for, at least not just yet, Mike backed off and said, "I'm just nervous about going out there, dad, and I let it get to me."

"Why don't you just date that girl you been seeing across town? The one you been sneaking in the back window on?"

Mike went at least two shades paler. "What are you talking about?"

"Deputy Dog's ugly little girl. You know, the one with the big ears."

"That was Anna dad!"

"Oh, yeah, your mother reminded me of that, too. Anyway, you have been sneaking in her window every night when the Deputy's on patrol. Why don't you marry her?"

"I…don't…love…her!"

Mike was starting to grit his teeth, but he controlled himself because he could tell that his stepfather was fishing for a fight, and his head *was* still sore. The old man really had a laugh out of all this, but then it was getting on his nerves too. About that time Buddy roused and walked into the kitchen.

"Dad, is there coffee?"

"Right over there," the older man pointed to the pot sitting about half full.

Buddy got a cup and poured it and began to drink without any sugar or cream. "You screwing Anna, Mike?"

Cigar Box

"I may see her from time to time but it's not serious." Mike didn't dare show any anger at Buddy, who was obviously working off the night before. He couldn't lie to him both because Mike's roaming was the talk of the night at Sabrina's bar among people their age and Buddy had been completely filled in on all the details. He also had been filled in on all the details about June the Cat, too, but he didn't bring it up because he didn't want his dad to jump in the middle of that kind of argument so early in the morning.

"Dad, do I get the ride or not?"

"Sure, I'll take you, but you tell Ray *not* to shoot until I get my truck off the property!"

Ray was working in his mother's barn with the little truck rolled up. He was a wiry man who constantly wore a floppy felt cowboy hat, even in the summer when everyone else wore straw. He never wore a baseball cap, or any other, just one hat that he'd apparently had since he was very young. He had a thinning beard and those crazy eyes you see on movies about hillbillies hiding in the woods making bar-b-cue out of tourists.

He walked out of the barn with an axe over his shoulder. He walked slowly to the truck and looked at Mike. Mike sat straight up and slowly began to sweat. Talking back to Ray at Fat Eddie's was one thing, but he was out in the desert now and Ray could just about get away with anything out here. But, that's what made him civilized, too. He had control now.

"Well, just get out! You can't see her if you're a sitting in a truck. I ain't gonna kill you right out."

Mike let out two lungs and a half of air. He opened the door and stepped out onto the sandy soil that Ray called his drive way. The man with the axe looked at Mike's stepfather and, without Mike seeing, winked, and said, "Where you want me to send the body?"

"You can just keep it out here if you want."

They both laughed and Ray put his arm around Mike and led him toward the house. Bill backed the truck into a field and drove off the land. Ray's mother owned eighty acres of land about ten miles from the little town. Now, if one understands that the town itself was in the "middle of nowhere" then it can really be understood that the farm was *really* nowhere. She'd inherited it from her dead husband's estate. Land isn't very valuable in Texas unless it's in Dallas, or Houston, or somewhere like that. Other than that, it is generally "dirt" cheap. The farm had produced nothing but Ray. They ran a few cows on it, and some goats, but it actually did not sustain life of any kind as far as making any produce for market, but that was typical for this part of the country. The ownership of land was a pride thing, and not an economic thing. There was a vague "value" to the ownership of the land. Something you really couldn't put your finger on, but it was real nonetheless. This ownership put Ray's mother in a slot of society that was peculiar to Texas. Sheriff's would even step lightly before driving out into the desert to arrest such a person, and the law didn't always stand on the side of the deputy who transgressed this understanding. You must really ask yourself, did the Branch Davidians really break the "law" or were they just shooting some Yankee trespassers who came onto their land?

Ray lived, and had lived in the shack behind Fat Eddie's for quite some time now, but he would still

Cigar Box

come out and help his mother keep the place up that had been his father's. His mother had never approved of Barbara, and tolerated her only on occasion, never allowing herself to be given a daily dose of being around her son's wife. She'd accepted June with the same affection as she granted June's little sister who was, after all, her maternal grand daughter. She's given the young lady tips down through the years, but she never had approved of Barbara's raising of the child. She knew full well the secrets that the foundations of the Bend sat on top of, and she didn't like what Barbara had done in her past.

Yet, with all of this Ray really wanted to have his little stepdaughter live in town at the "Bend" with "quality" people. June was the apple of his eye. With his having growing up in west Texas, he understood the way things really were, and he didn't want her to end up looking like his mother at fifty years old. He wanted her to look like Claudette. He wanted her to have all those things he saw in the homes he put sheet rock and roofs on when he worked his day job in construction. His show of force back at Fat Eddie's place wasn't so much that he didn't want Mike to *ever* be with June, as he wanted to seal the relationship in stone. If he had to scare this wimpy kid to get his little girl into the Bend then that's what he'd have to do. Mike was in no real danger. Ray would never hit, or harm a man, or boy, who wasn't trying to hit or harm him first. He wasn't an animal. He loved to read. He read Stephen King's works all the time, and he liked western novels. He'd been in construction for a number of years, to the point of getting a master plumber's license. He'd do a little light plumbing here

Wilbur Witt and Pamela Woodward

and there, but sheet rock was the work he really loved. And, he was good at his trade. People take for granted the craftsmen who build their fancy homes. The molding, the pipes, and all that goes with a beautiful home always comes from the hands of a man like Ray. He was beginning a contracting business that would take him around the state rebuilding apartment complexes. This was one more reason he didn't want to make enemies in the Bend. A lot of his initial funding may just very well come from Claudette herself! The Bend was filled up, all but the one house that Juan Sanchez had been building. Politics were rumbling over on that deal; politics that Ray didn't understand, nor did he care to understand. All the good construction money the Bend had generated was long spent. He was a hard working man who genuinely tried to treat everyone fairly, and all he wanted out of Mike was to move his little girl into the Bend; the place that his own hands had built!

Juan would make occasional visits to the ranch to see Ray, and they'd go out to the barn to talk, and sample what Juan had brought back from the "valley" down on the Rio Grande. Juan generally kept all in the area that were so inclined supplied with the Bend, and Ray had warned him that it may be an uphill drive for him to finish it.

They walked into the house. The home was the usual Texas ranch style home with the moderate living room and a big kitchen. (Cause that's where everyone stays anyway!) There were stairs going up to rooms in the attic, and a "Florida" room on the back for hot summer days. Ray's mother was in the kitchen

Cigar Box

making lunch when the two walked into the home. Mike looked around for June, but didn't see her.

"She went into town with her mom," Ray said without having to be asked.

Mike rolled his eyes. He had an obnoxious way of rolling them where they ended up looking down and to the right. Ray picked up on this at once and told him, "You wanna see June you gotta play by my rules. She had to go into town with her Ma to get some things. She'll be back. You ain't getting her alone out here anyway, so you might as well relax. Turning to his mother he said, "Mom, we're goin' back to the barn, ok?"

The small, white-haired woman turned and said, "I'll yell out the door at ya when it's done."

Ray nodded to her and pointed toward the door for Mike to lead. Mike eased out the door and started walking for the barn. He began to get scared. Sure, Ray was nice while his step dad was here, but how nice would he be now that he was out here alone. Behind him Ray was enjoying seeing him sweat. He didn't mean the lad any harm, and figured that it would be good for him to get to know the boy.

They entered the barn through the big double doors at one end. There was hay on the floor, but none in the loft. This barn wasn't used for that.

"C'mere," Ray called as he walked to the back of the building. He reached behind a bale of hay and pulled out a King Edward cigar box. It was held together with an old rubber bank. Removing the rubber band, and opening the top so that Mike could not see the contents of the box, he drew out a sandwich bag of marijuana and some rolling papers. "Old Juan gets me this stuff whenever he's down near Mexico. Say's it's special! Big medicine! He's an Indian you know. At least he *claims* he is. Hell, all them 'Meskins' say they're Indians, I don't know." He laughed, and sat on an old wooden chair and began to roll a cigarette. Mike stood there and looked nervous. When he finished rolling he stuck it into his mouth all the way and sealed it. Then he lit it, took a hit and handed it to Mike. "Here."

The boy looked edgy. Ray looked at him and said, "You can sneak around with a sixteen year old girl over in City Park, but you can't smoke a joint with her dad, huh? Listen, the next time you're jacking off and thinking about my little girl just reach around and put your thumb up your ass. I can tell you, if you like that feeling you're heading for a place where they'll make you feel like that all the time. Now, take this joint!"

Nervously Mike took the cigarette. He put it to his lips and drew some of the smoke into his mouth. Then he let it out, but didn't inhale. He started to hand it back to Ray when he heard a car in the drive. Turning he saw Barbara and June coming down the lane. The car rolled up and June got out with her mother. They both started walking into the house, but Ray called out, "June, come out here, hon. The barn!"

She turned and ran for the barn. She was dressed in nice jeans and a pretty flannel top. She came into the barn and walked over to where they were. Mike looked at Ray as if to ask if he were going to get rid of the joint. Ray smiled, handed it to June and said, "Why don't you show this idiot how to hit a joint, hon?"

Cigar Box

June took the cigarette and put it to her lips. She perfectly inhaled the smoke right down into her lungs, and held it there. After a second or two she let out little puffs, one at a time, and then all of the smoke. Smiling, she gave it to Mike. He took the smoke and put it to his lips. June said, "Just draw it right down. C'mon, it won't make you crazy, just suck it." She winked.

He did as she asked and felt the smoke come into his mouth, and then down to his lungs. His lungs began to feel "fuzzy" as the smoke rested there, but before the first half second he coughed violently and all of it came out."

"It's ok, here, try again," Ray said. He took a second puff, and this time it went down better and he held a bit longer. He let it out. The drug began to take hold, but not in a strong way. It felt light, easy, not harsh. Then he began to get sick. Ray noticed this and told him, "Don't puke in the barn, go 'round there and puke."

Mike went outside and threw up against the wall. When he came back inside the barn Ray told him, "It don't make you sick, it just makes you feel that way." He and June both laughed at the statement. June took the joint and took another hit from it. She closed her bright blue eyes and smiled as the smoke drifted between her perfect teeth. Ray took another hit and killed the joint. He put the remainder back into the cigar box, replaced the rubber band and hid it back behind the hay. He looked at June and said, "You two wanna take a walk over by the cattle tank it's ok, but don't be outta sight too long, ok?" Looking at Mike with a half grin, "I'd have to kill you!"

Wilbur Witt and Pamela Woodward

"Ok, Pa," she said, and took Mike's hand to lead him away. They walked over the rise and she took him to a little man made pond surrounded by an embankment. She sat and pulled him down to the ground with her. He started to kiss her, but she pecked his cheek and said, "No, not here. Pa'll be coming over that hill and see us. He'll beat your butt good you messin' with me out here. You like the joint?"

"I didn't know you did dope."

"Well, I don't 'do dope,' I just smoke a little grass. How'd it make you feel?"

"Wow, like, two beers. I feel, real good."

She laughed, "You ain't a good liar, Mike. You didn't smoke enough to make you feel much. Next time you'll do better. How'd Pa treat you before I got here?"

"He did ok."

"Thought he was gonna kick your ass, huh?"

"No, I wasn't worried."

"Liar! Everyone in town's scared of my Pa. He's been in prison."

"Well, ok, maybe I was a little. But I love you, and it's worth the risk."

She smiled and leaned back on the Johnson grass on the embankment. "My real Pa's in Las Vegas."

"Really? You ever meet him?"

"Nah. He left before I was born. They never got married. She told me he came to town and was runnin' card games all over the county. He was so good he decided to go to Vegas. He's rich there, I bet! Ray's my mom's first husband. Boyfriends don't' count. Your mom's divorced, ain't she?"

Cigar Box

"Yeah. My Real Daddy lives in Tennessee. You know that. I just got back from there!"

"I know, but your mom's divorced. Ray says that's like drinking a beer every day and then they shut down the brewery. The Bible says that if a man marries a divorced man he lies down in adultery. My mom's always telling me that no matter how bad we seem at least we ain't divorced."

Mike's face turned red, but he tried not to show it. His mom's divorce was an embarrassment in the little town. He didn't like to talk about it, and June was dragging it all out in the open, even if it was just around a bunch of cows and goats.

"Some day I'm gonna go and see him in Vegas, though. I know he loves me, and he'll take care of me. I don't like it here."

"Why don't you live out here instead of the shacks behind Fat Eddie's?"

"Grandma don't like mom. Says she's a whore. She really don't like her to come out here at all, but she lets her come out on Saturdays because Ray wants to see his mom. She needs him out here to keep this rat trap of a farm fixed up."

"Fat Eddie is talking about tearing down the shacks so he can have a bigger parking lot for catfish night. Did you know that?"

"We heard. Guess we'll have to move out here then. But one day I'll be married, and I'll leave here, and the shacks, and go to Vegas where I belong!" She was lying. She planned to go no farther than the Bend. She wanted to meet the man her mother had told her about, but she had no intention of living in Vegas.

"How's Buddy doing?" she suddenly asked.

"Oh, he's fine. He's sleeping it off on the couch this morning. He ended up at Sabrina's bar last night and drug in late."

"He and Sabrina getting' it on?"

"I don't know. Maybe. Anyway, she's a Mexican girl. You know how that goes."

"What does her being a Mexican have to do with anything?"

Mike was in a corner. In his arrogance of being a member of the Bend he'd started to insinuate that the little Mexican Bar-hop was somehow less chaste than an Anglo girl, but then he realized that it was a very small distance from the trailer park where Sabrina lived to the shacks behind Fat Eddie's.

"Oh, I don't know. Buddy say's she's Catholic, and I think that's real important to him. You know, him and Tommy are Catholic."

June eyed him, "Oh, yeah, that's probably it. Catholics don't get divorces you know. Did you ever stop to think that Buddy and Tommy don't really think your mom is married to their dad? That means that you ain't really any kind of brother; I mean like real brothers. Like for instance, if you and I should break up, and I was to date Buddy it wouldn't be all that bad. That kind of thing."

Mike was a little shook, but it was true. It wasn't like they were real brothers. Still he'd never considered the possibility of little June dating Buddy. That seemed very remote and distant right now. Yet it seemed as if a seed had been planted.

"You ever think of Buddy in that way," he asked?

Cigar Box

June looked at Mike. She *had* him! Nothing makes a fish bite like taking the bait away a little bit. She could almost hear the pleading in his voice.

"No. Not really. I never think of him like that," she said and let the subject pass.

They passed the rest of the afternoon walking around the tank and talking about life and family, and "getting out." Then they heard Ray's mother call them all in for supper. The little family gathered around the old woman's table to eat brisket, beans, and corn bread. She'd marinated the meat and smoked it the night before, finishing with it in a broiler she had set up in the Florida room. She had cut it long ways to divide the "two briskets" that it contained. One was fat and coarse, and the other was leaner, and the grain of the meat ran across the top piece. There was very little conversation at the table. As soon as the meal was over, they loaded up and took Mike back to town.

He stayed off to himself most of that night, not talking with his brothers or mother, but Sunday morning he cornered his mother in the kitchen. "Why did you divorce my Real Daddy?"

She was surprised by the words "Real Daddy," but asked back, "Why do you want to know?"

"Well, he *is* my Real Daddy, and I just wanted to know why you divorced him. June's mom isn't divorced."

The woman could feel the hair rise on the back of her neck. This was the ever-present threat in the town. Divorced women still had a mark on them. "Your so called 'Real Daddy' was too stupid to make a living and too lazy to do anything about it."

"June's Real Daddy lives in Las Vegas."

"Well that's no big recommendation. He wasn't no 'count here, and he's probably no 'count there. What's he do, deal cards there?" Claudette feigned disinterest. She knew all about the gambler and the story that Barbara wove around him to hide her history with old man Stillwell.

Mike got defensive and raised his voice, "I don't want you talking about her family like that. He works at a job, that's what he does. Anyway, he's her Real Daddy, just like my Real Daddy."

She glared at the boy, "Do you know how much child support your 'Real Daddy' owes you? Over forty thousand dollars!"

"It's not his job to pay that when you got remarried."

"Oh, he don't have any obligation to his own kids? I never pushed it 'cause he's so worthless, but he still owes it. How many Christmas cards have you seen from him?"

"He didn't know where we lived."

"Wrong! My Grandma *never* moved! She lived right there with the same address and the same phone all the time we've been here in Texas. He found that house when we were married and he wanted to eat! Then, when she got down, and we moved her out here, he still knew how to contact her relatives in Tennessee, and I'm *only* the biggest Realtor in west Texas. HELLO! He can't find the phone number to send a card, or a dollar?"

Mike began to look down and to the right. She slapped him. "Don't you pull that stuff on me! You look at me when I'm talking to you. So that's what you been doing out there on that farm. You and June

Cigar Box

talking about your 'real daddies? Well, I hope the both of you get to live with your 'real daddies!"

"It would be better than here," he said rubbing his face, "Up there in Tennessee I get to do what I want."

"Seems like you're doing what you want down here, young man. You seem to get over to City Park often enough! Up there you'd be in jail!"

Mike's eyes flared, but he backed off as his stepfather walked into the room. "What's going on here," he asked, as he got a Coke out of the refrigerator?

"Mike's worried about his 'Real Daddy," his wife answered, and crossed her arms, staring at Mike.

The man looked at Mike as he opened the Coke. Taking a large gulp from it, he reached up in the cabinet and took out a bottle of whiskey with an auto-jigger on top. Holding it up he let the device dispense a shot of whiskey into the coke bottle. Placing the bottle back in its spot, he turned to the issue at hand. This had not really been a problem until Mike's recent trip to Tennessee, but now "Real Daddy" was showing himself to be a "real pain." The man sat on a stool at the island in the kitchen. He really didn't know much about "Real Daddy," nor did he "really" want to, but this was a problem that he felt must be addressed.

"Why don't you just count all that child support he's sent over the years?"

"Money don't buy everything!"

"True, but I don't see you selling off your weight set, or your golf clubs, now do I?"

"All I'm saying is that he *is* my Real Daddy, and I'd like to know why mom had to divorce him."

Wilbur Witt and Pamela Woodward

The stepfather actually became angry, but didn't let Mike know it. He knew that "Real Daddy" was an irresponsible boob, but he couldn't just come out and say that. He had to prove "Real Daddy" wrong. What he didn't know was that another agenda was at work here. Mike didn't want this issue resolved because he needed the "Real Daddy" argument to escalate so that he could put it before June because she also had a "Real Daddy."

"You both don't understand!" And with that, Mike left through the front door, slamming it behind him as he went.

"Now what do you suppose brought that on?" the man asked.

"I don't know, but I think it began out there at June's grandmother's farm. He came back all weird. I have no intention of showing any respect to his so called 'Real Daddy!'"

Bill smiled and went back into the study to watch TV for the rest of the day.

The days turned into weeks, and Mike and June continued their "cow tank" discussions, always picking up where the last one left off. The little chats seemed to always center on "real daddies," and such. They never noticed the two entities listening in on every one of their meetings. Graduation day came and went, and Claudette got her one small victory in that he did get to walk across the stage at the football stadium and receive his diploma. June was there, with them in the stands that night, and then they all went out to eat catfish. Fat Eddie gave her the night off that one time because she was Mike's guest, and she got to be served. She didn't eat the catfish though, opting for the baby back ribs instead.

Veronica and her spirit guide talked one afternoon.

"Why did you want to see your biological father so badly?"

She sat on the grass watching Mike and June talking. "It wasn't so much him as it was just wanting to leave this place."

"You just wanted to leave."

She lay back on the grass, and took a piece of it, put it into her mouth and chewed on it. "Not like for always, just for now, ya know? There's a big exciting world out there, and I wanted to see at least something outside the county. You know I used to get so excited about going down to Austin, like that was a big deal. When I went on my honeymoon in San Antone, I took my very first escalator ride in a department store. Can you imagine such a little hayseed as that? Never even seen an escalator!"

"Did you love Mike?"

She looked sideways at him. He could tell that even now, in eternity, she was a fetching woman. Veronica studied his eyes determining just what kind of answer to give him. Then she simply said, "Ya, at first. Not like Ray."

"Not now?"

She sat up and looked at the couple sitting across the pond. "You see that little girl over there, Doctor Angel? Now look at me. She isn't anywhere near what I am now. She has no mileage. That girl over there would be happy if he took her over to the county fair for sausage on a stick and a beer." She looked him in the eye, "But I'm not!"

She got up and walked around the pond to where the couple was sitting. She knelt down and looked June right in the face. "Look at all that baby fat! You see that. This kid's been eating nothing but Bubba burgers and fries her whole life. Her heart's going to give out."

She caught a glance of the man's eyes as he looked down. "She's not going to make it that long, is she?"

"I don't know Veronica. That's all up to you."

"I wanted to find my real father so I would know who I really was! Is that so hard to understand?"

"Well, do you know who you really are?"

"I do now. I'm a bastard!"

Barbara was beginning to get a little fed up with this cat and mouse game that Mike's parents had lured her into. She was beginning to understand that all they were really trying to do was keep everything cool until Mike found another girl in the little town to capture his attentions. This would not go along with her plans at all. June was going to live at the Bend, and that was that. It was time to pull out the big guns. She knew that in April, right before graduation in May, Mike turned eighteen. That fact put him in a slightly different legal status with the sixteen-year-old June. It was time to make use of that little legality.

The phone rang one Monday afternoon at Claudette's office.

"Hello."

"Hello, this is Barbara. We need to have lunch again."

"Oh, I thought everything was going along just fine. What's wrong?"

Cigar Box

"Please just meet me at Fat Eddie's for lunch and I'll tell you."

To be perfectly honest, Mike's mom knew that this was the big push. She'd been expecting it for some time, in fact since Mike's birthday. Her only question was how hard a push it was going to be, and could she fend off the blow this one more time? She arrived at Fat Eddie's at 11:45 that morning trying to be early, but Barbara was already there.

"What seems to be the problem," she asked as she eased into the booth. The waitress came over and she looked up, "What's on the special?"

"Grilled chicken on a bed of rice."

"Um, ok, then that, green beans and a salad with ranch. Tea."

The waitress wrote down the order and went to the kitchen Then Mike's mom asked again, "What's going on?"

Barbara did her best to look outraged. "Mike has been sleeping with June all this time!"

"And you didn't know that?"

Barbara looked at her hard, "I never really dreamed."

"Oh, don't tell me that! Don't sit there and act like that. Now the last time we were here you went on, and on about it. We both know the score here, and I don't want to hear anymore about my divorce."

The fat woman leaned back. Mike's mom went on, "You want your little girl to marry Mike and move into the Bend. That's what this is really all about. And Mike is stupid enough to fall for this so you have me. Lets dispense with all the talk about the cops, and lawyers, and all that, and just get down to the bottom

Wilbur Witt and Pamela Woodward

dollar, and that's what this is all about, dollars! You get your little Miss Precious blood tested and we'll get Mike's, and we'll have a wedding on our porch. You want a wedding at the Bend. That's what you want, isn't it."

"They love each other."

"Oh, give me a break!" Then Claudette's eyes narrowed. "I left Tennessee to get away from this filth! They pulled the plug on my brother and then Mike's 'reeeeeeal da da' was playing strip poker with my little sister! I divorced that bum and came to Texas. I won't see my son drug down into that garbage heap like I was. Your little girl will be under my eye all the time. She *will* be a lady of the Bend! She will raise herself up. If she doesn't I give you my solemn word, I will destroy the whole bunch of you desert rats, including that ex-convict husband of yours, and you'll never work in this town again. He's after me to finance his next little venture, so you will do as I say. Now, you've pulled your bluff, you've got what you want. I don't have to sit here and eat and look at you!"

With that she rose, laid a five-dollar bill on the table and walked out the door. She drove across town while dialing her cell phone.

"Hello," her husband's voice came over the phone.

"Hon, Barbara just gave Mike a birthday present. We have a wedding to go to."

"I'll meet you at the Daisy, hon."

Wedding Bells in the Bend

"Dish" Bob sat back and answered his phone. He worked full time as a used car salesman, and part time as a minister of the gospel, saving souls wherever he found them. He had drifted into west Texas from a very mysterious past and insinuated himself upon the local scene in the Bend and the little town that hosted the click. He was a well-rounded man standing every bit of five feet tall and weighing just over three hundred pounds. He had a passion for young women and sweet wine. He had memorized the Bible years ago and one did not want to get into a debate with him on that subject. He got the nick name "Dish" Bob from his Louisiana drawl when he answered his phone with a, "Dish Bob, kin ah hep yew?" He really didn't have a thick accent, but he found that it helped sales and it had hung him with the nickname "Dish" Bob. He had an easy manner, and honestly did know his bible front to back. He was as much of a theologian as this little sleepy desert town would ever know or need. He had drifted into the little town a few years back, no one could remember exactly when, and become ingratiated to the locals by performing whatever service was needed at the time. He had no formal church, preferring to borrow from whatever ministry he felt close to at any given moment. He was somewhat of a mystery. No one really knew where he'd been, or where he'd come from. To be perfectly honest he was too "street wise" to be in this little village, but he was smart enough to know that he could live comfortably here. He acted as if he were safe there. As if he'd left some things somewhere he'd like to forget. He'd popped up when the Bend was well developed, and quickly became a local fixture as if he'd been there all along. The little town was full of people like that. No one was *from* there. Everyone seemed to have just *moved* there. He was the preacher everyone ran to when they needed a quick wedding with no questions asked. He also was very good at putting people down and blessing them onto heaven without counting individual sins with a heavy hand. His weddings were a fixture in the little town. He'd give the young couple a little lecture, and then he'd do his duty, and collect the twenty-five dollars that was customary to give a preacher in the town for such an event.

"Dish Bob, kin ah hep yew?"

Claudette's voice came over the phone, "Bob, we need a bit of marrying over to the Bend. Mike's marrying June the Cat."

At the sound of Claudette's voice he dropped the accent, "Praise the Lord! Young love in flower. Isn't it amazing how God's creation renews itself repeatedly?"

Cigar Box

"I don't know nothing about that, but we need to get them married on Saturday."

"Might I inquire as to the nature of the expediency of the proceedings?"

"She ain't pregnant if that's what you're driving at. Barbara's threatening to put Mike in jail if he don't marry her."

"Oh, my. Two young lovers torn from each other's arms much as Romeo and Juliet. We certainly can't have the young man trapped within the walls of Huntsville prison. By all means, I say, by all means we will convey the rites of holy matrimony to the couple at your convenience."

"We will need your services on Saturday."

"*This* Saturday? I mean, here it is Tuesday, and that barely gives you time for the blood tests, and, if I may be delicate here, there is the issue of the lady's age. She is *sixteen* is she not?"

"She's fifteen or sixteen, I don't know for sure. She's running 'round the SPJST halls ain't she? She's old enough, and Barbara's gonna sign for her. Can you make it? I'll pay you a thousand dollars."

"Most assuredly. Might I inquire as to where the reception will take place?"

"Same porch you're gonna marry them on. Food and drink will be provided."

"Ah, dinner in the Bend. I *do* so love a good plate of Prime Rib, and what will the beverage be?"

"Beer, Whiskey and tea."

"Ah, sister, I knew we were of a kindred spirit. I will surely be there to place the Lord's blessings on the proceedings."

Wilbur Witt and Pamela Woodward

Anyone who was *anyone* in the little town went to a flower shop known as the "Daisy" to get fixings for a wedding. Since this was to be a wedding at the Bend, it had to be top flight. No social event at the Bend could be under done, even a rush job like this one. There must be too much food, too much drink and too many people to turn out and show the town exactly what it meant to live in the Bend! The police who patrolled the area would even drop by, as would the ever-present Deputy Dog who would always be willing to eat at least one plate full of everything.

The proprietor of the Daisy would handle all the floral, and decorative arrangements. Only the best bows, the best ribbons, and the best flowers were to be used for *anyone* prestigious enough to recite their vows in the Bend! Normally the father of the bride would be in charge of all of this, along with the bill, but the very fact that the wedding involved a citizen of the Bend cancelled all social norm. Ray would be *allowed* to come to the wedding; indeed, he should have been *honored* that he would be allowed to be there at his stepdaughter's wedding! He had built most of the houses in the Bend, but the minute they were done, like anyone else in the little town that didn't live there, he knew that he was "out of place" among the wealthy and well positioned.

"I think that June should have a bouquet of cascading fresh flowers of stargazer lilies, white roses and assorted greenery," the owner of the flower shop said.

"How about the little champagne roses," Claudette inquired.

Cigar Box

"Oh, no, no, too small, too withdrawn. We're dealing with June the Cat here, you know. Everyone who is *anyone* will be expecting more than the usual. You do understand that this will not be your average wedding at the Bend, don't you?"

"What about the house?"

The old lady considered for a moment, and then said, "White silk roses all over the place, from one end of the house to the other, nothing but white silk roses. Her theme must be white."

"We *are* dealing with June the Cat."

The flower peddler smiled a knowing smile and said, "If we don't give her dignity who will? Her *first* wedding *should* be white, don't you think?"

Claudette smiled and continued to look at flowers. All the ribbons were decided on, and all the other "pretties" that would adorn the house. The old lady came over to the home and measured all the distances needed to make the decorations. It was decided that the French doors would be open and framed by an arch of flowers so that the couple could be viewed under the flowers in the arch as they came back in from the altar, which was a table that normally resided behind one of the white silk couches in the living room.

Across town, June was being ferried to the local doctor to get her blood test. She hated that part. It was almost not worth getting married if she had to go through all of that.

"Oooooooch!"

"Easy, June, it'll only take a minute."

"Why don't you just stick it in my butt? That's where you put all the other needles!"

The old general practitioner smiled and said, "Cause I'm looking for blood Cat, not fat."

Her blue eyes flashed, "I'm not fat! Mom, is my butt fat?"

"Your butt is perfect June. Anyone in town can tell you that. Now quit squawking and give the Doc your arm, will you. We gotta pick you out a wedding gown."

"You getting married over to the church," the doctor asked.

"Heck no! I'm getting married in the Bend!"

He smiled to himself trying not to appear cynical. He remembered June when she was just a baby, and now she was heading for the Bend to be married. He had delivered her and knew her entire history. He finished her examination and she left to meet with Claudette and go to the woman who made the gowns.

"Now you know we ain't gonna have time for no custom made gown, June. Heck doc's just barely got time to get them blood tests back. I hope Mike got his done."

"What kinda gown am I gonna get, mom?"

"Well get something nice, but something that's made up already. Let us worry about them things. You just get yourself settled, ok?"

When they arrived at the seamstress's shop Claudette was already there talking to the lady. June and her mother entered the store and were motioned to the back by an employee.

"June, just stand here and let the lady look you over," Claudette said.

Barbara asked, "What are we going to do here?"

Cigar Box

Looking very cool and collected Claudette replied, "Why Barbara, we're about to put a wedding gown together. A young lady to be married in the Bend must have a gown that has not been worn by anyone else. Anything else is simply not acceptable."

"Do we have time?"

"Absolutely! No wedding at the Bend has ever had a "rack" gown. June will be in a custom gown, just like all the other young ladies of the Bend!" Claudette let her hands flow over June's perfect body, checking out the width of the shoulders, hips and so forth, and she was amazed by the simple grace and downright beauty of the young lady who had been raised in the shacks behind Fat Eddie's Catfish Emporium.

As Claudette sized her up June felt her heart swell with pride. She had never been treated in such a way by anyone, especially not the rich and powerful Claudette Montgomery. It made her feel as if she had worth now. She felt like she was being elevated above her mother onto a plane of existence she'd only dreamed of before. The lady wrapped the tape around her again, and again. Claudette was frankly surprised by how well developed she really was. She was perfect! From her toe to her nose, there was not a flaw. Perfection in the flesh! She was a perfect woman, not girl, but woman. Claudette could not believe that this young girl had grown up in the shacks behind Fat Eddies. She was a true flower in the desert. The clear blue eyes, the perfect teeth, the sculptured lines of her body, all blended to give the effect of a stunningly beautiful girl. The broker recalled seeing a statue once in Nashville, at the Parthenon in the park of a young girl, much as June, frozen, timeless in beauty

Wilbur Witt and Pamela Woodward

for over two thousand years. In June this beauty was recreated and brought to perfection. As there eyes met, Claudette began to think that perhaps, just perhaps, June the Cat deserved to be in the Bend. Maybe some people of quality were accidentally born outside the society they belonged within, and it just took a little time to bring them to the point they should rightfully be.

"When will it be ready?" Claudette finally broke away from the spell of June's radiance to ask.

"Tomorrow night we should be ready for her to come and try it on. I'll work through tonight, and then tomorrow, and it'll be ready then."

"It should be hanging in my closet by Friday for sure?"

"Most assuredly!"

They walked out into the parking lot. June asked, "The gown is going to your house?"

"Yes, you'll get dressed there. I don't want to take any chances with it. I want you to walk out in it, and onto the porch where Dish Bob will be standing. Mike will be there by then. I don't want the gown to tear, get dirty, or anything like that."

"What's Mike gonna wear?"

Claudette paused, "He'll wear a white tuxedo. My late brother, his uncle Mike wore one at his wedding, and we buried him in it back in Tennessee."

June looked at her mother expecting some reply, but none was forthcoming. Barbara had what she wanted. She wasn't going to get into any squabbles now as her dream for her daughter was being realized. This woman was actually putting out money on June to

Cigar Box

make her look great on her wedding day. That was enough for Barbara!

Mike was at the local department store and western wear shop being fitted for his tuxedo. It wasn't his first tuxedo, but it would be a special one. His mother had insisted on this one being white. He didn't argue with her because he was getting what he wanted, the same as Barbara. All in all, the entire wedding was coming together quite well. As the man stretched his yellow tape around Mike, he dreamed of his wedding night. June was a vision, and the fact that he'd been with her didn't seem to matter. To be able to be with her forever, every night was beyond his wildest dreams.

*   *   *

Across town, Fat Eddie put down his telephone and turned to his wife. "They want us to make the cake for the wedding over at the Bend Saturday. What kind of cake do you think would be right?"

"Three tier, bride and groom on top. Just make it big. They like everything big over in the bend, you know."

He began to fetch the big round cake pans and the square pan for the groom's cake. "They want a spread of prime rib, too. We gotta go and get some. I wish they'd just settle with a Mexican spread like everyone else does."

"Wouldn't be the Bend without the prime rib. You know that. You just stay off the beer until the reception is mostly done. Don't need you drunk over there, you know?"

"I wonder if she's gonna still work on catfish night?"

His wife looked at him with amazement. "A girl from the Bend. Work as a catfish girl? Get a life Eddie!"

"Mike works here."

"Mike works here because June works here. Once he has June, you'll loose your little catfish girl. Get ready for it!"

Eddie went to his pantry to fetch the ingredients for the cake.

Buddy dropped into the local pub to have a beer. The place had been a Mexican Restaurant, but after a while, the beer sold more than the tacos so now the only Mexican food in the place was the nachos that graced the table while you drank beer. His mother had called him and he'd driven all the way down to be at the wedding. This afternoon his mind was troubled, though, and a few beers would ease it a bit. The little bar was actually dirty, and the food would make you sick, but that didn't matter because no one ever really came there to eat anyway. They went there to sit at the tall tables and play video games, drinking piss warm beer and telling lies. Anyone who was stupid enough to eat there deserved what they got.

"Miller," he said as he sat in the booth.

The young girl took his order and returned with the chips, sauce, and beer. He sipped the glass and ate a chip. She watched him and since it was not a very busy afternoon, she came back to talk a minute. Her name was Sabrina, and she'd known Buddy all of his life. In high school the lines between Mexican and Anglo had been heavy and black, but they had become

Cigar Box

light and gray of late and her heart warmed to the boy she'd loved all of her life.

"How's it going, Buddy? You in town for the wedding over to the Bend?"

"Oh, yeah. Wouldn't wanna miss that crock of shit! Not every day you see a sixteen year old girl get married on your momma's back porch."

The waitress smiled. She was thin, but not too thin. Her jeans fit well, and she had on a little Mexican top that accented the slight figure that she had. Her hair was dark, and very tightly curled, falling to her shoulders. In all of her years in high school with Buddy, and knew his moods. She knew a lot more about him than that. They had been on the school newspaper when they were seniors, and more than one time they had cleared the drafting table off and fell into each other's arms. Then, after graduation, they'd drifted apart. The little west Texas town had exactly two kinds of people in it. There were those who stayed, and those who left. She was one of those who stayed, and Buddy was one of those who would never be home no matter how far he went. Still, inside he was coming to the slow realization that just perhaps "home" was more than the Bend, and as close as this young lady's heart. She never pushed him toward any choice. She was just always "there."

"Yeah, but *this* sixteen year old is the Catter!"

"You know, I get the impression that little girl was born fully developed. I can't remember a single time she didn't look like Tanya Tucker."

The waitress sat in the booth opposite Buddy, and studied his face. "You're taken with June, ain't you?"

He looked up from the beer, "What in the world makes you think that?"

"Oh, a woman knows. Hey, it's not so bad. Mike's like seventeen, eighteen, huh. June's sixteen, but you Buddy, you and me, we're twenty-one! When we were in high school she was like eleven!"

He smiled, "Yeah, and she looked just like she does now."

"Well, your brother…"

"Step!"

"You're *step* brother is close to her age, and they've known each other a long time." Her finger eased across the table and played with his hand that was on the beer glass. "Why don't you try someone who's more your age, and type?"

He let his other hand lay gently on hers. "Sabrina, I don't let that bother me. I don't like Mike anyway. You know that. June is an angel, but she deserves more than him."

"Well, she probably does deserve better, I'll give you that, and you are right; June the Cat is not an angel by any stretch of the imagination!"

The woman who owned the bar came in and Sabrina got up and began wiping the table as if she had been there all along working. Leaning over, "Where you going tonight?"

"Home. Over to Momma's. Where else? What you got in mind?"

"I live over on Cactus Drive now. Not much of a trailer, but I got beer, and a VCR. If you wanna?"

"I'll drop by after I pay my respects, ok?"

She winked and went to refill his glass.

Cigar Box

Sabrina Sanchez was thought of as "Mexican," but her real heritage was Comanche. The land of the Bend had been her people's land until the last century when the ancestor's of John Stillwell had suddenly turned up on it and the Comanche were all moved off after being sold out by an old Witch Doctor who vanished into history. Now the Indian face was so rare in west Texas that any dark skin that wasn't Negro was regarded simply as Mexican. But Sabrina's father had never let her forget that she was not a Mexican but a descendant of a proud race.

Buddy sat there and drank beer until he could no longer feel his lips. He was looking for direction and would not find any answers tonight, only a headache in the morning. Events were swirling around him so fast that the beer could not slow it down. As he looked over at the bar he thought that perhaps somewhere in Sabrina's arms tonight the rush in his head would subside somewhat and for a little while he would just be the Buddy that he'd been before Mike came along!

*   *   *

The week wound down to Saturday with the entire town waiting to see the outcome of the marriage of June and Mike. Old ladies gossiped, teenaged boys lusted, and Claudette and Barbara became bitter enemies. Barbara was pushy. She always had been and would be forever. She had no class. She was a liar and a manipulator and she didn't have the money to manipulate so she was just obnoxious! Claudette had come from a similar background, and didn't want Barbara to get one bean from her plate that wasn't given to her willingly. The difference was that Claudette did have a sense of grace and dignity. Life had a spiritual meaning for her, and that had deepened since the death of her brother back in Memphis all those years ago on Christmas day. This was not a union of two great families; it was blackmail, plain and simple. Mike was marrying June to take the gun out of Barbara's hand. Now it would be dishonest to say that Claudette did not have plans to dispose of June once the vows were read. After a divorce, Barbara would have no hold on Mike anymore, and she could take her little daughter back to the shacks behind Fat Eddie's before the ink was good and dry on her divorce papers!

Barbara, on the other hand did not intend to let something like this happen. She knew the game. She also knew June. June *would* be pregnant, if she wasn't already, and that baby would seal the union, because that particular baby would be the first grandchild, and that baby would be a citizen of the Bend, born and true! She'd let Claudette play her little society game because she knew that while she could toss June back across the tracks that a baby would be far more difficult to get rid of. That would be the first grandchild and all the bullshit and excuses would not erase that! There was a history behind this mental attitude.

Years before Barbara had slept in the Bend, before it was the Bend. John Stillwell's wife was dying of breast cancer, and he hired the then young and fetching Barbara to take care of his house, and tend to the lady during her final days. Barbara had a room up in the loft of the old house. Days passed and one night Stillwell went to bid her good night and his passion

Cigar Box

overcame him. He fell into the arms of the eager young woman, and stayed there most of the night.

Mrs. Stillwell eventually died, and the old man found that he could not keep the attentions of the girl. A young man fresh out of prison caught her eye. Ray married Barbara a few months after June was born. Even though Barbara knew who June's father was, she told the girl as she grew that a gambler who'd come through the dusty little town was her father to keep the sparks between Ray and Mr. Stillwell at a cool limit. Barbara actually breathed a sigh of relief when Stillwell committed suicide that sunny afternoon at the bend of the river where she swam naked with him so many years before. Barbara found it poetic that the house that June would move into was actually on the very site that she'd been conceived. She found it amazing that no one in town had ever told June who her true father really was!

*   *   *

The Daisy was decorating the house, and the cake was in the oven. The blood tests arrived, and to no one's surprise both June, and Mike had a clean bill of heath. Thursday night the seamstress called and the ladies, June, Barbara, and Claudette went to have the final fitting done. When they entered the shop, it was on a display mannequin. It was all white. There was a modest train behind it, not Princess Diana's, but a nice train for Texas. As June began to put it on, Claudette was amazed again at how lovely she truly was, and how small. She was so small. She slipped it on and stood up while the seamstress buttoned the back.

Wilbur Witt and Pamela Woodward

Claudette noticed that her stomach was flat. No sign of any bulge at all. Then, the lady came and put the veil on her blonde head. A real blonde! No dye had ever touched that hair! June looked at them. The crystal blue eyes penetrated all in the room. No bride was ever more beautiful. And June was not pretty in a dusty, Texas sort of way, but in a classic way. She *was* a goddess! She *was* the girl at the Parthenon!

She looked right at Claudette and whispered, "Thank you." It was in direct opposition to her mother and everything she had stood for. June was not back at the SPJST hall and she was not down in the bushes with some horny cowboy smoking a joint. She was a member of the Bend now and Claudette had brought her here. At this moment June the Cat became June Montgomery! At this moment she left her past behind.

For a moment, Claudette felt the innermost twinge of sadness. She felt as if she were looking at something that was so precious, so lovely, that God would not allow it to stay. She knew in her heart that there had never been, nor would there ever be, such a creature in this little desert town again. Her beauty was indeed timeless.

She drew a breath and told the proprietor, "Have it delivered to the Bend, will you?" She looked back at June and the two realized the import of the statement. This dress, this woman, was not coming out of the shacks behind Fat Eddie's. This dress was going to the Bend, and this lady was walking onto a porch at the Bend to be married! No Justice of the Peace would hand her a box of soap and shoo her out of his office; she was to have a *reception*! And at the same time, the bride would be a debutante! She knew that such an

Cigar Box

event could not occur and not change this girl. She *would* be of the Bend. She *would*! The two thousand year old statue had come to life!

*   *   *

Later that evening Veronica and her spiritual escort sat on a bench at the fourth hole of the golf course at the Bend. The stars were very bright indeed that night. She looked out across the little pond and sighed. "Ever live like this 'Dr. Angel?"

"No. I worked all my life. I knew no privilege, no circumstance."

"Well let me tell you. People come in breeds, like dogs. Some are pure bred, some are mutts." She rested her elbows on her knees and put her chin in her hands. Then, cocking her head at him she said, "I'm a mutt!" Pointing to the houses in the Bend just beyond the golf course she said, "Those people over there who own those houses work very hard to keep mutts like me out. Look at them houses. You see them houses."

The spirit nodded.

"Well, you see that high fence around them?"

He looked and replied, "No, none. Very few fences in fact. Seems like a secure place to live."

She laughed, "Well it is secure, Dr. Angel, but there's a fence around that place that you can't see and you're a ghost! Mutts like me try to jump that fence all the time, and very few make it." She looked at him and grinned, *"I made it!"*

"But you didn't stay there."

Wilbur Witt and Pamela Woodward

"A mutt is a mutt, is a mutt. I jumped the fence, but the mutt part of my life followed me. It's such a shame. I had it all, and wanted more!"

"But didn't you have it all?"

She looked at him and smiled a wry smile. She was amazed at how naive he really was. For all of his spiritual "wisdom" he really hadn't learned anything. She began to see why he needed *her*. "When you build a fence, like the one we're talking about, how many nails do you put in the top of each board?"

"I don't know, one, maybe two."

"Well, some people think one's enough, but I've always been a 'two-nail' person myself. Never leave to chance what you can insure." She shook her head. "You know, for high bred people they sure are dumb! In a lot of ways you're dumb, Doctor Angel."

Ignoring the insult he asked, "Did you put two nails in your fence, Veronica?"

"I sure did. I nailed it good and tight, or at least I thought it was good and tight."

"Did your nails come out Veronica?"

"Yeah, sure did."

"What happened then?"

"Another mutt jumped the fence in my place." She walked down by the pond and dipped her fingers into the water. "It gets hot in west Texas, Dr. Angel. You know that?"

"Hotter all the time."

Veronica smiled, "Yeah, and all the Yankees living over there say every year it's the end of the world; it's the end of the world, but you know what?

"What?"

Cigar Box

"When you try to nail that fence the wrong way; that's the end of the world."

"If I had blood it would run cold, Veronica."

"It should." She continued to play in the water.

*   *   *

Saturday morning dawned bright and clear. The house at the Bend was prepared for the upcoming event. The last touches were added as the owner of the Daisy placed votive candles along the privacy fence to illuminate the guests that evening. All business, real estate, drinking, everything was put on hold. Dish Bob arrived about ten in the morning. Mike's stepfather was making coffee as the doorbell rang. He went to let the preacher in. Bob greeted him warmly at the door. Coffee was poured and the pair went to the rear of the house, through the French doors to examine the set up.

"Now, this little table is gonna be the altar, am I correct?"

"Yes. They'll stand right here and recite the vows and then turn and walk back through there," he pointed to the French doors, "and we'll commence with the party, I mean reception."

"And how many do you recon will be in attendance?"

"I don't know. We sent some invitations, but this is a 'Bend' happening, so most of the area will show at one time or another. The French doors will be left open so the guests can mingle out onto the lawn. We'll keep the golf carts ready for those who want to cruise the course at night."

"Accommodations?"

Wilbur Witt and Pamela Woodward

"Oh, yeah! We'll keep the back bedrooms ready for those who want to stay over 'till Sunday, and there is the apartment up at the country club, too. Hey, why don't you stay over and preach on Sunday right here?"

The preacher smiled, "Well, I gotta be over at the mission Sunday morning, but I recon I could give a few moments of prayer. Considering the style of this reception I would want to hang around a bit to help a few souls, if you know what I mean?"

The other man smiled. He knew that Dish Bob would occupy one of the rooms. They always had a room ready for him. "Prophet's room" it was known as. All the needs provided, down to a little bible on the night stand for him to read. Claudette always had a Bible, and bell and a small candle for him when he stayed over. Usually, when there was such a big "do" in the Bend people would drink and eat too much, and it was customary to let them "sleep over."

At noon the refreshments began to arrive. Kegs of beer set up on the lawn, in the shade, hundreds of tacos, burritos, sandwiches, and all the "fixings" it took to throw a proper wedding at the Bend. What was normally considered the dining room table was covered with all manner of liquors, so that no taste was left unattended. Claudette had placed various lemons and limes in the refrigerator waiting to be cut and sucked at the opportune moment!

The fare of the day was prime rib, but the staple was smoked brisket. Mike's stepfather, and Tommy had all sat up most of the night, drinking beer, and smoking briskets on the two big barrel smokers in the back yard. They had the firebox off to the side of each of them so the meat never touched fire, but only had

Cigar Box

smoke drift over them all night. One had hickory because Mike's mom loved the taste of it having been raised in Tennessee, but the other was Mesquite, a true Texas flavor unique to the area. All the pieces of meat were saturated with Italian dressing and then the cheapest bar b que sauce that could be found. The following morning the briskets were finished by putting them in the ovens to make sure the internal temperatures were just right. The kitchen in the big house was very large. There were actually four ovens and a six-burning gas stove. Pots hung from the ceiling all around, and there was a huge, "butcher-block" island in the center of the room. They would be sliced to use all parts, both the lean and fat to make various sandwiches, plates, and just snacks that would grace the reception. Much more brisket would be eaten than prime rib. Brisket is just about the sorriest piece of meat you can legally feed to a human being in the United States, but it stands to reason that any state that makes a sport out of eating jalapenos would make a cut of meat such as brisket a prime cut! Keeping the smokers at exactly two hundred degrees was in fact an art. The charcoal increased heat, while the soaked wood increased flavor, and the balance must be maintained between the two if one was to have a successful meal.

    Dish Bob reached over and sampled a deviled egg as he continued to talk. "I need to consult with the couple before we perform the ceremony."

    "No problem. We'll get them in the back bedroom for you."

    "They'll get there soon enough. I would like to take them onto the porch."

Mike's stepfather added, "Oh, no. They're going to San Antone for the honeymoon. River Walk Marriott! Can't be no other place."

The preacher smiled, "You do have style!"

"Oh, yes. They'll stay there, and eat at the Casa Rio, Lone Star, and all the best places. June's never been there, you know?"

"Oh, I didn't know that."

"She's really never been much out of the county. That'll be her first time out like that. We were all gonna go, but we'll just let them. You know, give 'em privacy."

The preacher nodded. He rose and walked around the home a bit. He was familiar with the house, having been there many times. It was the typical ranch style home with the huge living room and even larger kitchen. There was a formal dining area, and a big master bedroom with several smaller bedrooms. Then, there was an equally large upper floor that overlooked the golf course. When the boys had all been home the home was full but now that they, and Dr. Angie were gone, it was very large and empty.

The lady from the Daisy arrived and began to make final preparations. About three that afternoon June came over with her mother. Barbara dropped her off and went back to her home to ready herself for the event. She walked into the house as if she'd never been there before. Indeed this time except for a trip to San Antonio, she would not be going home. She would not be going back to the shack behind Fat Eddie's. She would live here, at the Bend. For a moment the weight of it overcame her. She sat at the huge formal table and considered what she was about

Cigar Box

to do. At this moment she truly loved Mike for having brought her to this point. The rich woods of the room, the paintings, even the little things made her stop and think. She'd come here a thousand times in her life, and yet she'd never *been* here. Her mother would never *live* at the Bend. Just then she felt a presence behind her. It was Mike's mom.

"Taking it all in, hon?"

She turned to see her, and said, "It's all so grand. I never really looked at it all. Where did you learn all this?"

The older woman sat and smiled. When I was living in Tennessee I used to watch "Dallas" on TV every chance I got. I looked at all them fancy things on that show, and I studied them. One day I knew I was gonna have them."

June looked down, "I'm too stupid to do that. I could never be a real estate broker, like you."

Claudette looked her directly in the eyes. "June, I had to take that stupid test thirteen times! Did you know that? Thirteen times to get my license. Now I got it. You can do it." She took June by the hand and led her to the fireplace. On it was a brass plate with an inscription. "Read it," she told June.

The young woman leaned and looked at the plate and read, "Rise above every obstacle. Teach the angels how to fly." She looked at the older lady. "Where'd you get that?"

"The saying, or the plate?"

"The saying."

"My brother Mike told it to me when we were little kids playing on the Mississippi. He always said that man was created to judge the angels, and that it was really our job to teach them how to fly. That's my motto. Never look up to anyone, or anything. Man was made to teach the angels how to fly. You learn to fly, and then you teach them."

"Do you ever see him anymore?"

"Who?"

"Your brother."

"No, he's dead. He was killed in a car crash on Christmas day years ago. That's when I decided to move here to Texas. Senseless, really. He didn't need to die like that."

"I'm sorry. I didn't mean to bring it up."

"Ain't your fault. Ain't nobody's fault; just is! People die all the time. Some just affect us more than others, that's all."

"I'll bet he was a lot like you. Strong, and kind. I could never be like you."

Suddenly she didn't want to crush June. She knew her to be just as she must have been at some point back in Memphis. She was a girl just trying to carve a place in the world. She took her out to the porch. The maid, and the cleaning woman were working, and June and Claudette sat in the lawn chairs and talked.

"June, I grew up poor, back in Memphis. I was so poor, heck; I thought the folks on welfare had government jobs 'cause they always had a check! I remember one time when this local fat cat's son asked me to sleep with him. I told him, 'No!' He asked me why. He would pay me; make my life easier, what ever I wanted. I still remember him saying, 'Who's gonna know?' I told him, 'The Lord will know!' I ran outta there and never went back. You know what the Lord gave me for that?"

Cigar Box

"No."

"Nothing! Lost my job, went hungry. Had to marry Mike's no account father! Took me seven years to shed that worthless piece of nothing! What do you feel, June? I mean what do you *really* feel?"

June felt nervous, but wanted to give the right answer. "Well, all I know is that I love Mike."

The older woman began to laugh. "Love? You *love* Mike? Child, you're too young to know what love is. You're telling me that you love *him?* You get rich, and then you'll have time to love."

"Do you love your husband?"

Mike's mom looked sly, just like June when she was hiding something, and replied, "Sometimes. I loved him a lot when we used to go down by the river and have our picnics. That was before that darn fool Stillwell blew his head off right on the very spot I used to eat." Her eyes narrowed, "It don't pay to totally love *any* man! Don't think you'll get in my good graces by feeding me what you *think* I want to hear. You show me you are smart, and that'll go much farther down the road with me than all the little con games in the world! And don't you love Mike! He's got a lot of growing to do. You be smart like the fox."

They walked out to the fence and looked over it to the golf course. The older woman asked, "How old are you, really?"

"I'm almost seventeen."

"Sixteen!"

"Yes."

"You pregnant?"

June looked at her. She was tempted to act like a little girl whose feelings were hurt, but looking into the

199

woman's eyes she knew that wouldn't fly so she simply answered, "No. I had my period last week."

"Good. I hate pregnant brides. We're in the chute on this thing."

"What do you mean?" June had never heard the phrase before.

"like a bull rider, sittin' on a bull. They sit there for a minute or so and they're in the chute. No matter what they think, or feel, that's not gonna stop that gate from flying open and that bull goin' crazy! It don't matter if you're pregnant or not, me and you, well we're about to ride this bull! Only with Mike I can guarantee you it's more bull*shit* than bull!"

June laughed. "I'll try."

"That's all you can do child, but it'll be easier to teach them angels how to fly."

They turned and went back into the house. Mike was coming in just as they walked through the French doors. June ran up and hugged him. He felt strangely different to her after the conversation in the back yard. He put his arm around her and walked over to his mother, "Well, how's it going?"

"Going good. You pick up the tux?"

"Yeah. Hey, how come I gotta wear white?"

"Because it's a white wedding, and that's what my brother, Mike wore to *his* wedding."

"Just asking. I thought it was supposed to be black."

His mother looked at him, "It'll be pink if I say it will. Take it to the back closet. I don't want any stains on it before the ceremony."

Buddy walked in about that time, and his mother asked, "Where you been?"

Cigar Box

"Went into town to play pool last night and stayed over at a friends. I told you I'd get here, didn't I?"

"Well, your sister's on her way down from Dallas. You need to get with her and make sure Fat Eddie gets the cake over here on time, ok?"

"Fat Eddie will be here. He won't miss a party."

A stare from his mother sent him out of the front door.

Fat Eddie arrived with the cake about two in the afternoon. It was a three-tiered thing with the little bride and groom on top. He also brought the groom's cake, which was small and square. It was set on the formal dining table. June came in and inspected it for the longest time, looking at the various levels, and the little dolls on top. Then Mike's grandmother arrived to help her prepare for the wedding. She lived in an apartment in town provided for her by Claudette. After the death of her son she had existed poorly in Tennessee until Claudette had sent for her and set her up in her own place. She stayed mainly off to herself, but would come out for an occasional wedding, or funeral if the need should arise. Other people were coming in all the time. The wedding itself was going to be at 6:00 sharp, but the reception seemed to already be starting. The kegs were tapped early in the evening, and Tommy was the first to draw a glass of beer. He began to guzzle, but his girl friend kept him at a civilized level until the actual reception began.

At five June retired to the master bedroom to be fitted into the gown. Mike went to the back to put on the tux he'd rented. Mike's grandmother came in and helped June. The gown slid onto her form smoothly. She was perfect! The older woman, like Claudette was amazed at the perfection in this young lady. Tommy's girl friend, Christina, came in toward the last to help. June reached over and opened a box. Retrieving a bolt of cloth from it she handed it to Christina.

"Here, this is for *your* wedding."

Christina took the cloth and thanked her.

June stayed in the back of the room until Dish Bob came in to give her instructions as to how the ceremony was to proceed.

"Now, when they come in, you follow the group to the porch. Mike and I will be standing out under the roof. I'll be behind the coffee table, and you in front, ok?"

"Ok."

"Fine. Now, you'll do just fine. Just be calm and repeat all that I say, ok?"

"Ok."

The preacher looked June in the eye. "This is a big step for a girl. How do you feel?"

"You just tell me what to say, and we'll get to the other side of this, ok?"

"Ok. You'll be fine."

A couple of her friends from high school were there as maids of honor. They all giggled like little girls, which indeed they were, as the whole thing proceeded. Then, there they were, all alone in the master bedroom, in the big house at the Bend. June had made it. She'd jumped the fence. She was in the Bend! Then, a woman came in to tell them to get ready.

"Now, there's gonna be some music. Ray's gonna come in to get you, June."

Cigar Box

This surprised her. She didn't see Ray arrive. Just then he came through the door. He was dressed in a suit, with his hair neat, missing his ever-present cowboy hat, and wearing low quarter shoes.

"You ready, princess?"

She looked at him and said, "Yeah, I guess, if you are."

Ray took her hand and said, "I'll never be ready to walk you out that door. In my life nothing has ever been nice, or easy. I thank God every day that He gave me you, June. I always thought that I had more time, but I guess the prettiest flower on the hill always gets picked first, now doesn't it?"

"How's it feel to be in the Bend daddy?"

"Heck, been here before."

"Yeah, but how does it feel to be here as a guest?"

Ray's eyes squinted as he smiled and he said, "Heck, hon, these people are just like anyone else. They ain't no different. We are all the same. I don't really look down on them, or hold it against them 'cause they are rich. They can't help it."

They both laughed. Then he gave her his arm with much dignity and led her through the French doors in the master bedroom to the porch. The music was playing, but she didn't hear it. Mike was standing there in his white tuxedo with Tommy slightly drunk on the side. Claudette was just off the porch. She looked around at the people. There must have been two hundred, and they were all looking at her. They were all looking at June the Cat. She deliberately looked down at her shoes and took steps toward the altar/coffee table. Dish Bob was holding his bible in his right hand as he reached for her with his left. Then, there she was standing before the altar, in the Bend, beside Mike, with the whole town looking on.

"Dearly beloved, we are gathered here, in the sight of God to unite this man, and this woman in holy matrimony."

The crowd hushed and relaxed.

"In as much as a man must leave his father, and mother, and cleave unto his wife, this man has chosen to leave his father and mother and unite with this woman in the bonds of love, and marriage. Michael, do you take this woman to have and to hold, in sickness and in health, for richer or for poorer, to be your lawful wedded wife?"

"I do."

"June, do you take this man, to have and to hold, in sickness and in health, for richer or for poorer, to be your lawful wedded husband?"

"I do."

She heard the words, but they seemed distant to her. They seemed as if spoken through a veil; a veil she could not see, yet it was there, as real as that fence she'd just jumped. Dish Bob went on, and on about the fidelity of marriage, but she didn't hear. She was amazed at how this was a lot like an execution. It seemed to move slowly until the rifles went off, and then it was done!

"And so, by the power vested in me by the state of Texas I now pronounce you man, and wife. What God has joined together let no man put asunder!" You may kiss the bride."

At this point Mike did not kiss her, instead he said, "June, I pledge my undying love to you for ever and

Cigar Box

ever. I will defend you against all others, and I will lay down my life for you. You are the love of my life."

The people were stunned that such a declaration of love could come out of Mike. June, stood back and looked at him, but he pulled her to him and kissed her. Tommy stood there gapping at the whole scene, wondering when it would end so he could get back to the beer keg. And then, just as quickly as the wedding had begun, it ended, and the reception began.

The kegs having already been tapped, and the liquor was out, the only thing left to do was break out all the food. There were no formal plates other than the plates Claudette had made with their pictures on them for wedding cake. There were the paper plates that grace most back yard cookouts, which was what this thing really was anyway. The prime rib was cut and served by Fat Eddie himself, but as soon as that formality was finished the brisket was pulled out of the ovens and the real eating, and drinking began in earnest.

June slipped into the master bedroom and put on some jeans and a nice top and rejoined the party as fast as she could. Mike stood around in his tux. Tommy stood near the beer keg in *his* tux. Christina looked disgusted. There had been placed several cafeteria-style tables in the yard, with metal folding chairs for the guests to sit and eat and drink. Soon all were talking in various little groups about this or that. As soon as Fat Eddie had served the last piece of prime rib he went to the kitchen and fetched a mason jar. Returning to the beer keg area he filled it and began to drink beer with the rest.

Mike's aunt, his stepfather's sister in law was there. She was a scorching blonde beauty, but nowhere near June in rank, but her entire desire was to hold everyone's attention for as long as she could. Someone was always trying to "rape" her, or "couldn't keep their hands off her." She slid up to the liquor in the kitchen and began to drink Black Velvet and coke until her eyes turned red. Then she eased back to the guest restroom and soon, right on cue, a scream was heard from that area.

Everyone raced to the room to find Luke Schultz, a local construction worker friend of Ray's, staring in amazement as the woman trembled and wept and cried, "He just clutched me! He just clutched me!"

Deputy Dog came out of the crowd and put his arm around her and said, "Now now, little lady, just calm down." The old deputy knew this woman *and* her game. He looked around the crowd and spotted Judge Potter refilling his glass in the back yard. "Somebody go get the judge." A boy about fifteen ran out to the judge and told him Deputy Dog needed him.

"How can I be of assistance," the judge asked as he came into the restroom.

"Well, your honor," the deputy began, "Luke here seems to have 'clutched' Rhonda, and she's beside herself with fear. I suspect charges will be filed."

The Judge, who by the way was into his *fourth* mason jar of beer looked sternly at the woman and asked, "Is this true? Has this happened?"

Through her tears she cried, "Yes. I was just trying to relieve myself, and he came through that door and tried, "she lost control for a moment, "tried to touch my private parts!"

Cigar Box

The judge looked at Luke sternly. "Rhonda, cover yourself! Young man, do you know how serious this offense is?"

The boy was shaking visibly. "Your honor, I was just trying to take a pee, and here she was on the toilette. I didn't mean no harm. I was trying to get out of the room." Actually he was lying. Rhonda had a way of making sure that she displayed herself at every opportune moment, and had opened the door slightly when she heard the young cowboy approaching.

"Silence! Madam, will you prefer the charge?"

"Yes, your honor. I will."

The judge turned to the lad. "Court is hereby convened. You stand accused of molesting Rhonda here. What do you plead?"

The boy was positively white. "Hey, ain't I gonna get a lawyer or nothing?"

The judge snapped his fingers and cried, "Thomas! Come over here." A young lawyer in the back of the now gathering crowd came forward. He too had his mason jar full of beer. "Thomas, you are hereby appointed as this young man's council. Plead him!"

The young lawyer looked at the boy, and then at Rhonda still zipping up her jeans, and said, "In light of the evidence I suggest you plead guilty and throw yourself on the mercy of the court, son."

The boy looked at all the people standing around and bowing his head he said, "Ok, I'm guilty. But I only wanted to look at her."

"Done," the old judge cried. This court finds you guilty of looking at Rhonda here while she sat on the privy. Rhonda, before the court imposes sentence did he hurt you?"

"Well, no, not actually. He really didn't 'clutch' me, just kinda fell into me."

"Ok, then. This court finds you guilty of 'clutching without a license,' and hereby sentences you to ten hours of community service, that service consisting of serving drinks at this here reception. Now both of you get out of this bathroom, I gotta take a piss!"

With the legal proceedings out of the way the crowd retired to the back yard once again. Claudette asked Deputy Dog what the problem was in the house, having not gone in herself and he told her, "Oh, Rhonda got molested again." They both laughed. The young man under sentence eased over to the beer keg and began to fill glasses, the judge's first. Ray came up and made like he was going to hit the boy but leaned over and asked very quietly, "Well, was she a real blonde?"

The lad looked around for Rhonda and said, "No."

Both laughed and the beer flowed. Soon Tommy was sitting beside Mike crying like a baby. "I love you. You are the best brother I ever had. I never thought you'd do this to me. Oh, Mike, what are we gonna do now?"

"Mike was feeling his beer by this time and he, too, began to cry. Buddy saw all of this from the other side of the yard and just shook his head. The waitress from the bar was there with him. She would never come to the Bend on any other occasion, even though her father, Juan, was building a home there, but her dark beauty let her blend in well with the people there. Buddy watched her move among the people and frankly wondered just why he'd never really pursued this lady more earnestly. She was typical of the

Cigar Box

working class people in the little town. Her father had picked oranges in the "Valley" of South Texas, and they had settled here when she was five years old. He had now expanded his business to include several harvest machines and he worked his circuit all the way from the lower part of Texas up into Nebraska before circling back to the little west Texas town to ride out the winter. Her natural curl to her hair, and her little button nose made her very cute, but not the beauty that June had. She was not as developed as June, even though she was considerably older, but she was friendly and laughed readily, making everyone in her little circle of beer drinkers (most of whom she knew from her job in the pub) smile and relax.

Not noticed by the others, Ray went back into the house and let himself into Claudette's private office. He had asked her earlier for a private talk about a venture he was considering.

"Ok, What's the deal," the broker said.

"Well, Claudette, work's just about petered out here in the Bend, if you know what I mean."

"Yeah, getting' tight, I'll admit, but what do you need from me?"

The sheet-rocker sat in one of the big leather chairs. "Well, I got this here idea. There are apartment complexes around Texas that need to be built up and fixed up, and I want to come up with a company to do it. I'll let you in for half."

Claudette looked at him and didn't laugh. She developed estates, and built dreams for stars, but she understood that to Ray his dream was just as big as hers, and her Memphis roots would not let her look down her nose at him even for a minute. Still, she didn't want to be a partner with an ex-convict. He was a good man; she knew that, and she didn't want him to be hurt. "Ray, I don't want to own your business. Let me make you a loan, ok?"

"A loan?"

"Yeah. I mean, we're family now, right? What do you need to get started?"

He thought a moment, "Well, a compressor. I know I need that. I got a truck, so I'm ok there. Some attachments. That'll do it."

"How much?"

He figured on a little pad for a minute, "About ten thousand."

She thought he was being a little soft with his bid, but she didn't let it show. "Will that do it? Why don't we give you a running start and give you fifty?"

Ray was taken aback. "I...I don't know if..."

"Tell me about your idea."

He fidgeted a bit and then began, "Well, I can get contracts to renovate broken down apartment complexes. See, you take these places they would tear down and you got the shell, and you just outfit 'em ever how the owner wants, and you do it so cheap that they can't rebuild it for that."

"How bad of shape are they in?"

"Well, depends on the building. Some ain't so bad, just fix up, paint up, but some; man, they look like a war zone, but if a man could fix 'em then he'd have a good piece of property, and the rentals could come in again. You understand, Miss Claudette?"

She nodded, "Yeah. Me and my husband have always been into new sales."

Cigar Box

"Yeah, but them 'new' sales is runnin' out here lately."

"Tell me about it. We made good off this mess, but it's becoming apparent that we're gonna have to flush a new bird soon or we are gonna have to scout a bit. Tell me something, Ray; why do you insist on these building projects when you have a master plumber's license?"

"Well, I don't like plumbing. I only got that dumb license because my paw told me I had to have some kind of license. I'd been working with him a lot most of my life and plumbing seemed to just be the natural way to go, but Miss Claudette, plumbing is just plumb nasty. You ever hear the story about the plumber who dropped fifty cents in a plugged toilet?"

She shook her head and Ray continued, "Well he goes to digging in his pockets and pulling out dollars and dimes and such, and dumping them into the John. The lady who hired him asked him what the hell he was doing and he tells her, 'If you think I'm a gonna reach down into that for just fifty cents you are crazy!'"

The broker laughed and Ray said, "You sure you don't want to be a partner in this?"

"Nah, that's *your* bird. I'll find bigger fish to fry. I'll remember you when I do. Do you have a crew?"

"I will have. Just as many out of work around here as me. Finding a crew won't be no problem."

"Will the fifty be enough?"

"Yeah, that'll get me going. I can pay…"

"Don't worry about it. Just pay as you can. Go out and get all the contracts you can get, ok?"

He looked at the powerful woman across the expensive desk, but did not hold her in contempt. She was just like him. Same background; same spirit. Ray knew he'd never be like her, but he appreciated the fact that they came from the same mold. Years ago, before Claudette *was* Claudette, there had been a brief moment, but the two ships passed too quickly in the night, and destiny took over for the both of them. Claudette wondered how Ray put up with Barbara. He was actually a sensitive man. He was a good man with many good qualities. How he retired to that shack behind Fat Eddie's was beyond her! With the right marriage, and the right chance, Ray would easily have been a great builder, and here he was begging for lunch money on his daughter's wedding day.

"I don't know how to thank you Claudette."

"Just keep me posted as to how your idea works." She rose and shook his hand. He didn't expect the check right then, knowing that she would handle all the details after the wedding.

Meanwhile Dish Bob was drinking wine in the kitchen from a paper cup. He didn't mind people see him drink, but he didn't make an exhibition of it. He had just about finished off an entire box of wine before he moved to the beer keg in the yard. Since Mike's stepfather was Catholic, the local priest was there also enjoying the food and drink. Dish Bob eased over to the man and shook his hand. They knew each other, and didn't bother to even discuss religion at a gathering like this one. The only thing the priest asked him was, "How many sixteen year old girls do you marry in a year, Reverend?"

Dish Bob smiled and looked over at June, sitting at a table with a group of people. She was drinking

Cigar Box

strawberry wine and laughing and talking. "You see her over there, Rev?"

The priest nodded.

"Well she just married a legacy, my friend. Hope she can live up to it." He turned to leave, but then looked back at the priest and said, "I believe Mary was fourteen when she was married to Joseph." The old priest smiled and walked off.

June was sitting at her table drinking wine with several people. They were mainly people from the Bend who wanted to get to know this newest member of their very elite club. The conversation turned from one subject to the next until it settled on the fact that no one was *from* the Bend, everyone having bought into the development when it was founded some years ago.

"I came here from Phoenix," one older man offered. "Retired out there, but the price here invited me, and it's close to everything. I like it."

"I came here on a job doing a shopping mall. Found this place and was real taken by it. Quiet here, and the police have respect, you know?"

One man asked June, "Didn't you grow up here in town?"

She was smart enough to know they were evaluating her. It was no secret where she'd grown up; she'd grown up in the shacks behind Fat Eddie's, but she was married into the Bend now. "I lived in town all my life," she said. "I've always wanted to be right here. The Bend is my dream."

This made the old men glow with pride, to know that their little subdivision was so coveted by this beautiful young lady. June took another sip of her strawberry wine and looked across the table at a woman of about thirty years who was sipping dark red wine and staring right at her. Trying to be in tune with the conversation she leaned forward and in her best west Texas drawl she asked, "Where ya'll from?"

The woman looked at the young girl with utter contempt and replied, "I'm from somewhere that people do *not* end sentences with prepositions!"

June was taken aback. Her feelings were actually hurt. She couldn't understand just why this woman would act like that, but she was also June the Cat. She sized the socialite up physically and saw that basically she was no match. Her age, her slender arms, her frame told June she was a pampered pretty of some fat cat in the Bend.

"Well," she said, leaning forward and getting about an inch from the woman's nose, "pardon me! Where ya'll from…bitch?"

It was a moment of truth for the socialite. She had to swing, or walk away, but before blood could be drawn Claudette intervened.

"Pat, I see you've met my newest member of the family."

Both women broke their stare to look up and see Claudette standing there over them. "She's feisty, isn't she?"

"Yes, she is," the older woman said, without actually looking away from June, who was leaning back sipping her wine through a grin.

The music began to play a bit louder and people began to get up and dance on the little temporary dance floor that had been placed in the center of the back

Cigar Box

yard. Mike's stepfather came over and took June by the hand.

"I never miss an opportunity to dance with so lovely a lady. Might I have this dance?"

She broke her gaze from the lady across the table and, looking up at him said, "Certainly sir." She rose and walked to the dance floor with him. The music was slow country, and invited him to hold her close. She leaned into him and followed his every move. People began to leave the dance floor and let the couple dance alone. She tucked her head beneath his chin, and in the dim light of early evening he noticed a slight tear beginning to roll down her cheek.

"Don't ever let them see you cry Cat."

She looked up at him and winked. She used his shirt to wipe the tear without the guests noticing it. The party drifted on and on until mid evening. The beer flowed, the brisket was eaten, and arguments flared, and went away. All of the forbidden topics were discussed. Politics, women, religion. The priest left early, and Dish Bob sat on the porch sipping beer.

Then Tommy appeared on the porch, "Hey, preacher, you up for a little deer hunting?"

The plump man looked at the lad, "Deer hunting? Where?"

"The golf course. There's a bunch of us got our golf carts out and we're gonna go and knock some deers in the head. They are all over the greens."

The preacher rose and followed Tommy to the front of the house where he found about ten men and boys and five golf carts waiting.

"Now I think a one wood is the best. Pop's 'em 'long side the head and boom! They are gone!"

"I use a six iron myself. Ah, Dish Bob, you got a set of clubs with you."

"Why no brother, I don't. Might I borrow one?"

Buddy stepped up and said, "Here Dish, use this three wood. It's good for beginners."

The reverend took the golf club and balanced it making a practice swing, but Buddy took it back and, holding it like a baseball bat said, "No, like this." He swung at the air. "Try to clip 'em right behind the ear, if you can!"

Taking the club back again he asked, "Might I inquire what we are about to do?"

"We're going deer hunting preacher. This time of year, at night, them critters go out there and eat all the grass off the greens. We get out there in our carts and try to knock a few of 'em in the head. You up for the sport?"

"What about the law?"

"Well, preacher, we're bringing the law along with us. We got the judge right over there in cart number one." He pointed to the inebriated jurist in the front golf cart.

At that they all climbed in and proceeded down the road to the little concrete driveway that led to the course. Within moments Dish Bob saw that sure enough there were deer all over the place; all munching down on the best turf in the area.

"Get him!" One of the carts commenced to chase a deer across the green. The deer easily outran the drunken men in their golf carts. They had grown so used to the smell of humans that once the cart had missed it's mark the deer would simply stop, and continue to eat their favorite green, until the next cart

Cigar Box

came along. They were all whooping and hollering and swinging clubs until a bright red and blue light brought them to their senses.

"Ya'll just get them carts back up to the house, or I'm gonna haul you all in," Deputy Dog's voice boomed over his P. A. system from the car.

Just then he noticed the judge leaning back to get a beer from a box in his cart. The deputy got out of his car and ran to the judge, "Oh, your honor, I didn't see you."

The old judge looked up at him and said, "I just imagine you didn't. Is that boy Luke still serving drinks at the house?"

"Your honor, I believe he has gone."

"No matter. He's in contempt of court." Then the judge yelled, "Ya'll round 'em up and take 'em to the house. I'll ride with you deputy."

"Me too," Mike's stepfather added. Just as the men were about to get into the car Dish Bob was trying to get the cart he was left with in forward gear. It lurched forward a bit, stopped, and lurched again, throwing the round preacher onto the ground. The deputy ran over to him, "Dish Bob, are you ok?"

In a drunken drawl the minister burped, "I have been stricken, even as the Philistines!" He got off the ground, remounted his cart and preceded to the house, with the other carts in single file behind him and the Sheriff's car, lights going, behind them all.

At two that morning the party had all but died. June went to get her luggage that she'd brought from the shacks that had been left in the formal dining room. To her surprise she found it gone!

"Has anyone seen my things," she whispered?

"I took them to town. Gave them to the church," Angie's voice came from behind her.

"All my clothes?"

"You don't need them anymore. In your room, you'll find a new wardrobe, and all of your drawers are full. There is new lingerie in the dresser, and you'll even find a new toothbrush, and make up in the bath. Forget about your past in the shacks. You are one of us now."

Mike came out of the rear of the house. "We gotta get! We need to get to San Antonio. Mom's made all the arrangements for us."

June went with him out to the car and got in. The taillights disappeared into the night. Standing beside a crepe myrtle tree Buddy sipped a beer and watched as they drove away.

Honeymoons, Travels, and "Real Daddies"

The newlyweds sped towards San Antonio all during the night, and neared the old town about eleven o'clock the next day. They came down Interstate 10 and entered the city from the western side. Taking the Broadway Street exit, Mike piloted his car to the Marriott on the River Walk. This hotel positioned itself on the walkway in the center of downtown with a commanding view of both the walk, and the city. It was literally a stone's throw from the Alamo, and even had helicopter service to the San Antonio airport.

This was June's very first trip to any city of size. She'd seen El Paso once, but only to pass through it for gasoline with Ray, on their way back from one of his repair jobs that he'd contracted in New Mexico. This was the first time she had actually set foot into a metropolis. The hotel overwhelmed her and in her darling accent she gasped and looked at the lobby and exclaimed, "Oh, Mike, My Ah's just can't behold it all!"

If June was beautiful as a girl, she was enchanting as a wife. She seemed to have relaxed a bit, even gaining a little height as she walked, holding herself up proudly because now she was a citizen of the Bend, with all of its rank and privilege. She really didn't understand credit cards, but Mike gave her money, which she stuffed into the pocket of her jeans. Angie had given her the jeans. They were "501's." To compliment them Angie had given her a pair of red Justin boots. June had never owned a pair of "501's," and had only seen Justin's in store windows, and now she owned a pair of each! When she took the boots from the box in her room at the hotel she put the leather up to her face and just inhaled for the longest time. Then, she slipped them onto her tiny feet. Angie had gotten it just right! She'd fitted June's clothes and boots as if she'd been shopping for herself! It totally amazed June how she'd done that.

She and Mike stayed in the room until about six in the evening, and then ventured out to see the "Walk." The River Walk in San Antonio is truly a romantic spot. It's old world flavor, combined with the big city rush above produced an effect equaled nowhere in the world. Mike took her down to the Casa Rio, where he had eaten many times before; where his mother had eaten with his stepfather, and his stepfather's mother had eaten in 1939 to commemorate her high school graduation. They sat out on the river at a table. No one who is anyone eats inside the café. As they ate their chips and dip the ever-present pigeons came and bummed chips from them, and the fed the birds in spite of the warning of signs around the café about feeding the birds.

The meal consisted of the usual Mexican fare. Actually, the food at the Casa Rio is standard Mexican,

Cigar Box

with no surprises, but the atmosphere of the River Walk makes it special. June knew her Mexican food, and devoured all the enchiladas, tortillas, and tamales with zest, gulping her iced tea like a field hand while Mike watched in mild amusement. Then two mariachis came to the table.

"Would you like to hear something?"

June looked up in surprise, "You mean you play in right here, on those fat guitars?"

The old Mexican laughed at the little country girl, and replied, "Si, Senorita. We play for you. Whatever you want to hear."

"I don't know any Mexican songs, but I just got married, so could you play a newlywed song?"

The old man looked in amazement, "You are a senora? Si, Si, we'll play a nice wedding song for you."

They played a romantic ballad, all in Spanish for the pair as June glowed. When the song was finished, Mike whispered into her ear, "Pay them."

She turned, "Pay them?"

"Pay them. Give them some money. This is what they do for a living."

"Oh, ok." She reached into her jean pocket and pulled out a five-dollar bill and handed it to the oldest man.

"Gracias," he said and then, tipping his hat to the lady he turned and left, going to find another table audience to perform for.

June watched as they moved away from her table. "Mike, I never thought life could be this nice. I must be dreaming."

Mike took her hand, "No, June, I'm the one who's dreaming. I'm with an angel, and I never want to wake up."

She looked surprised, "You really love me!" It was not a question, but a statement of something she'd only just discovered."

Mike looked at her in utter amazement, "Of course I love you. What made you think I didn't love you?"

"Mike, no one's ever loved me. I've always felt that no one cared. When I married you, I did it because I loved you, but I really didn't expect you to really love me back."

Mike was just discovering the complexity of his new bride. June hid behind a wall of insecurity, and it all stemmed from a myth she called "Real Daddy," who drifted in and out of memory. He was a man, larger than life, faceless and mysterious. It wasn't that she didn't like Ray, but she looked nothing like him, and he was more like a friend than a father. He was a good friend, but a friend nonetheless. Her real father, on the other hand, had acquired the stuff that legends are made of. She knew he worked in Las Vegas, so that made him a character of myth, more than a man. Her mother had told her the story hundreds of times about how he'd come to town, playing poker with the ranchers, and cleaning them all out until he had to leave town in the middle of the night, but not before becoming June's father. Barbara had told her the story countless times, each time adding more and more details as the myth grew in both their minds. Knowing he worked in Vegas she imagined he had to be dashing, and well dressed, not bent, tired, and sweaty, wearing that silly floppy hat that Ray wore every day of his life. Real Daddy was a hero. Real Daddy was a "man's man" with a Derringer hidden in his boot, and an Ace up his sleeve, and Real Daddy never called, never wrote, and never sent a check! He was too cool. She vowed that one day she would go to Vegas and find Real Daddy. He would be proud of her now that she was of the Bend. She'd made up for the mistake her mother had obviously made to loose such a man as Real Daddy!

"Well, I do love you. I love you more every minute. I'll never be apart from you." As Mike spoke, he noticed that June's thoughts seemed to be somewhere else, but no matter, her body was here, and it was beautiful! Under the multi-colored lights of the River Walk, she was positively stunning. Mike could not help but notice the admiring looks given by men as they passed the table, some even looking back for a second time! In all of his life, ever since he could remember, Buddy had bested him in every way imaginable. He could never best him here! June was something Buddy didn't have, and she was all Mike's!"

They finished their food and went walking around the river. The multi-colored lights enhanced the mood, and the moist tropical air intoxicated her as they moved along through the crowds. They moved back toward the hotel, and then went past it to the other Marriott that was situated just across Commerce Street from the one that had their room. There was a mall here and she went in, fascinated by the stores. Going into the large department store at one end of the mall, she came around a corner and confronted the escalator.

"Mike, I've never seen one of these."

Wilbur Witt and Pamela Woodward

He laughed, "You never seen an escalator? C'mon. You have seen one before."

She looked at him angrily, "How many two story buildings we got back home?"

He realized she was right. There were no two-story buildings in their town save the homes at the Bend, and *they* didn't have escalators. She gingerly stepped forward and put her tiny foot on it, but then quickly withdrew it and giggled.

"Will it grab me?"

"No, here watch." Mike stepped forward in confidence and stood on the moving stairs as they took him to the second floor of the store. "Now you."

She looked at the steps all-moving and in one brave moment, she leaped upon them, grasping the rail and began to ride, teetering, all the way to the top. She sighted the stepping off point precisely, and at the opportune moment, she sprung form the steps into the waiting arms of her husband. She laughed, and said, "Wanna do it again!" At that, she went to the down escalator and rode down and then back up. This she did about five times before she figured she'd mastered "escalator-riding," and was ready to move on to her next project.

They went from there to an ice cream shop and bought cones, even though they'd just eaten. Then they walked the short distance to the Alamo, which was situated just a little off the walk but within a city block of it. She'd only seen the Alamo in books, and a John Wayne Movie, but this building impressed her. It was closed now, but the tourists were still milling about. The old mission was lit with lights from all angles and it cast a romantic mood over the entire area.

Cigar Box

It was hard to imagine that anyone had ever actually *died* there. To June it seemed that the history of Texas had ended at the Alamo. Nothing more happened that was really worth noting since then.

She went up and put her hand on the ancient stone. "Wow. This place looks more beat up than the kitchen floor back at Fat Eddie's."

"It's older than Fat Eddie's, June."

"I know that. You think I'm ignorant. I know all about it. I know the date of the battle and everything. Ray loves this place. He told me all about it. He said they don't make men like these guys anymore. Nobody would get killed for anyone anymore. We're all too modern now. We're all too smart. Ray said it was a 'sucker' move, but that they were all heroes to do it."

Mike tried to show his sophistication, "Well, June, you gotta admit, this was one darn fool thing to do. Sit here and let five thousand Mexicans run over you?"

"She turned away from the stone, "They weren't fools, Michael. They were here because they knew they needed to be here. These guys didn't have any 'angle.' They just knew they had to hold Santa Anna off long enough to let Houston get his army together."

"Yeah, but do you really think they'd have stayed if they knew how bad it was gonna be?"

"Yeah. I think they did. Did you know that there were thirty-two men from Gonzales who got into the Alamo just before the battle just to tell them that there would be no help? They stayed because they wanted to." She looked up at the rounded top of the building, "I think Ray would have stayed."

"Even if it were a 'sucker' move?"

"Yah, even then. Ray would stay for the fight. He'd be right up on the walls."

She walked over to the sitting area in the little plaza in front of the Alamo and sat on a bench. The air was nice. She watched as the insects flew into the streetlights. To her left was the monument to the fallen of the Alamo. She just sat there and soaked it in. The building had an orange glow to it. It was surreal, almost unworldly. This building was so famous that it appeared to be a movie set. She was amazed that there hadn't been a spare stone on the ground, or a rock, or anything to take as a souvenir of the visit. She'd rubbed her hands across the face of the old mission trying to collect just one rock of any kind that she could take home and have a piece of the Alamo, but it simply wasn't to be had. Mike came over and sat beside her on the bench.

"Right over there," she pointed beyond the locked gates leading into the courtyard, "Travis drew the line. All the men but one crossed it and made the choice to stay. Ray would have crossed the line, Mike. Ray lives a long time ago. He don't play by the rules we play by. He lives back when the Alamo happened."

Mike looked in the direction she was pointing and said, "You know, recent research tells us that Travis never drew that line. That was a story that was made up by journalists to sell a story."

June smiled, "He drew the line, Mike. He drew the line in our hearts. It don't matter if he drew the line in the sand or not. Every man there knew the score, and that line was drawn when they first walked into the mission. Ray told me that every time someone does

Cigar Box

something that is good, and decent, they cross Travis's line."

"Would your Real Daddy in Vegas have stayed?"

She turned and looked sly, "Heck no! He'd have been over that wall on his way to New Orleans to deal Black Jack on some river boat!"

"Then the Alamo was the 'sucker move?"

She thought long and hard, "No, it was *their* move, Mike. They had to do it. Some seed fall here, some seed fall there. You sure are dense for a rich boy!"

Just then, an empty carriage rolled up. Mike hailed the driver and went over and gave him a twenty. June came over and Mike helped her into the carriage. "Could you take us back to the Marriott?"

The driver nodded and the couple held each other all the way back to the hotel. Once in the room Mike turned on the T. V. to HBO and began to watch. June came in wearing her panties and a "T" shirt and sat on the bed behind him. She put her foot over across the bed and began to rub his back with her big toe.

Unseen in the corner of the room Veronica and her companion watched.

"You seem happy here."

"I was happy," Veronica said as she watched June play with her husband's back.

"Did you love him now?"

"Oh yeah. Mike was wonderful in San Antone. He was like another man." She looked at the man, "His mom wasn't here."

"Ah! So there's a little problem."

"No problem, Dr. Angel. Some gotta be sheep, and some gotta be goats." She turned and walked through the wall, then in a moment she came back and grabbed him by his arm, "Hey, don't tell me you're a 'perv' Dr. Angel. C'mon, let's do the Walk!"

The spirit couple went down and began to walk leisurely about the cafes and shops of the River Walk. "How come I can't see any other ghosts here?" Veronica asked.

"Because they've all gone on. They are only on this plane for a while, and then they are processed."

"Processed?"

"Some go to a reward, some to something else."

"Hell."

"Of their own free choice, and design."

They sat on a bench and her spirit guide sat beside her. "We 'design' hell?"

"You design where ever you will go. Good or bad. Remember what Jesus said? 'Forgive, and you shall be forgiven.' The kingdom is within you, Veronica. A little piece of God, right here," he touched near her heart.

"Wonder what kind of 'kingdom' I'm working on."

"That's what we're here to find out, Veronica, but there's more at stake than just *your* kingdom. There are injustices and events that occurred long before you and I ever came along. That's part of the reason I was waiting for you at that intersection back on Sherman Road, but someone else is in the mix. You and I have to fix things a bit."

"Please excuse me for saying so, but this is all a bit deep for me."

"Not so," he smiled. "God picked you for just this particular job. He doesn't make mistakes. I have faith in you, also."

Cigar Box

"I'm a terrible sinner. You don't know the half of it."

"You are a vibrant young woman, Veronica. You don't hurt people. You just try to survive. At least you are beginning to admit you are a sinner. Look at all these people passing by. Each one creating their own 'kingdom' right now, and not caring, and when they die they go to that place they themselves have prepared all of their lives and are so surprised."

"I thought all you had to do was be saved. Doesn't Jesus count for anything in your grand plan?"

"Yes. What do you think we're doing here right now?"

Veronica rose and walked beneath an arch at such an angle that she could see the Marriott on the walk. Counting the floors with her eyes she found the floor that June and Mike were on and stood there beneath the arch staring for a long time. Her guide came up behind her and put his hand on her shoulders.

"What are you thinking?"

"Just wondering why I couldn't have just let it be. Why couldn't I just let things go as they were?"

"You were just trying to have it all."

*   *   *

Honeymoon over the couple found their way back at the Bend, and in Claudette's office the following Monday morning.

"So you want to work here," Claudette asked?

"Yeah," June replied, "I want to be a real estate person, like you.

Wilbur Witt and Pamela Woodward

The old broker looked at the sixteen year old. "You don't have high school. You are not eighteen yet, and you need to be eighteen to test for the license, and you don't know anything about our business."

"I hate school. I know how to type, and I learned to ride my first bicycle on your streets!"

"Then you aren't going back to school?"

"No. If you won't let me work here then I'll just work at Fat Eddie's and Mike and I will live in an apartment."

Claudette looked at Mike. "When are you taking your courses to test?"

"Thought you wanted me to go to college?"

"Not anymore! You got a family now! You take the real estate core and test! You need to work, not study, Socrates!"

Inwardly Claudette admired June's grit. She had more grit than Mike would ever have. She wished she could convince the girl to finish high school, but being from the old school, she knew that when June was eighteen she'd have enough "under her belt" to breeze through the courses and test for the real estate license and that would be as good as a west Texas high school diploma.

"Tell you what, you work here for a while, just to see how you do. Mike, you start the weekend classes. June, I really want you in school, but I'd rather have you here than in Fat Eddie's slinging catfish."

Mike went out to the golf course and June went right to work that very day. Her duties started simple enough. She answered the phone, kept messages, and that freed up Claudette a bit to get around town a little more than she could before. She was pleasantly

Cigar Box

surprised at June's abilities. She really could type, and fast! She quickly learned that the girl was quite a scholar at school, and hadn't quit school because she could not make passing grades, but because she was simply too bright to sit there. She loved the world of west Texas real estate more. She learned all about real estate by just being in the office. One afternoon a rancher came in and was very disturbed about his closing not happening on time. The man had wanted to sell his ranch and move out to L. A. and a discrepancy in the survey kept the closing from happening.

"What is the problem, Claudette?"

"Well, it's simple. Your original deed says the land is fourteen hundred and fifty and eighteen one-hundredths acres."

"And?"

"The new survey says it's fourteen hundred and fifty and eight one-hundredths acres. You've lost some land somewhere!"

The rancher rolled his eyes, "Well get it straight! I gotta get out to L. A.! My old lady's out there on Rodeo drive and she'll bankrupt me before I get there if you don't get this straightened out!"

He stormed out of the office and left them sitting there. Claudette told June, "Get Chip on the line for me." June called the county taxman and gave the phone to Claudette.

"Chip, I got me a problem. There is a tenth of an acre difference in a survey on a ranch I'm selling and I can't close until I find that dirt!"

"How old is the original survey?"

"Hell, I don't know," she rummaged through the closing documents, "about the time of the Alamo, how do I know? Here, about nineteen sixty-nine. How's that?"

"Ok, here's the problem. Back then; they used the old chain survey method. You remember. The boy would run along with a long chain like a football first down chain. Now, they use lasers, and satellites. Now combine that with one may be done on a wet day, and the other on a dry day."

"Ok, ok, so what. What do I do to close?"

"Put in the contract on page one under 'lot description' this; 'such and such amount of land *plus or minus,*' and that should take care of it for Marge over at the Exchange."

Claudette was correcting the contract even as the man spoke over the phone. "Never heard of that one, Chip, but I'm gonna try it. Thanks."

The next day the closing went ahead as planned with the revision on the contract. Little things like this stuck in June's mind. The dealings with land had dignity to her. The logic of it all made her feel as if everything was right in the universe. Claudette impressed her. More than anything she knew that the old broker had risen above a lot of obstacles to make her angels fly. She also was made very aware in private that the broker had a severe reading problem. Soon, June was reading all documents to her, and was actually becoming adept at understanding the subtle "in's and out's" of real estate and she hadn't darkened the doors of one class yet!

Mike had gone to the classes, however. The preliminary classes were three ten hour days of "study"

Cigar Box

in which the candidate would pass a "test" and be awarded thirty hours of credit. Actually, what it consisted of was two days of memorizing the answers to the test and the last day of testing. The questions, and answers were given in the exact order and verbiage on the test. In fact, if you could memorize numbers the math part was totally easy in that one could simply remember a few numerical answers and zip through the math part of the test. However, Mike was never very studious, even with the deck so stacked and after the first three-day class there was an explosion in the little real estate office.

"You failed?"

"Only by about five points, momma."

"You failed a fast class?"

"I'll do better next time."

"Mike, they *give* you the answers. That's all they do for two days is give you the answers and then they ask you the same blasted questions back and you fill in the blanks! People on LSD can pass these stupid classes! *I* passed those classes, and I can't READ!"

He stormed out of the office and ran out to the golf course to play a round and get his nerves under control. June was learning that Mike was not the most intellectual of the brothers in the controlling family of the Bend. Tommy was brighter, but now that she was in the family she was becoming aware that he was more than a little fond of not only smoking the smoke that June smoked with Ray, but having access to money such as he did, he also did something June had never seen; cocaine! She caught him doing a line in the rest room at the mansion one evening when he thought everyone was in bed.

"What are you doing?"

He looked up surprised, "Just a little coke, that's all. Don't tell mom."

She walked over and looked at the line on the mirror. "Never did that stuff."

Tommy saw a chance to make sure that his new sister in law kept the secret and raised the mirror to her nose. She drew back slightly, "I don't know how."

"Just sniff. It'll go in. Don't be afraid. I know you smoke grass."

"Yeah, but grass ain't this stuff." She bent down and very slightly sniffed a little bit into her nose. A small feeling of exhilaration overcame her. Composing herself, she leaned down and sniffed a bit more, and then all of it.

"Hey! Greedy ain't we," Tommy joked.

"No, you offered." She rolled her eyes. "Man! I could get used to this stuff!"

"We all do."

"Not your mom."

Tommy laughed. He watched as she let the drug take control. "How do you feel?"

"Different. Not really high. Yeah, I guess. Dunno."

Tommy became aware that he was becoming excited by the fact that June was getting high and "loosening up" before his eyes. She looked directly into his eyes and his heart leaped. He saw that she was very beautiful indeed. Perhaps it was the drug, or the moment, but he could feel her taking control of him. After a long lapse of time, he broke her stare.

"Hey, maybe you better go back to bed," he finally said.

Cigar Box

"This stay's between us, right?"

"Hey, right here in the crapper. No one will ever know."

She looked into his eyes for a full minute. Tommy was helpless; then, she pulled back and let him go. For June there were other fish to catch, and this minnow simply would not do.

She smiled and said, "Yeah," and walked back down the long hall to her bedroom.

Mike continued to struggle with the classes but lost interest rapidly. Inwardly, he was very aware that even if he didn't pass any class his mother would support him. Claudette became aware that her son would never be an agent. Each week delivered the same result, and with each week in the office June shined a bit more. The awful truth dawned and Mike finally went to work with his stepfather in construction and tried his hand at roofing. He was not a boss in any way. He wasn't much of a roofer either. He drifted through each day trying to get out of as much work as possible.

One afternoon, when June found herself alone in the office she put a CD into the computer and looked at phone listings. She clicked "state," and selected "Nevada."

Then she selected "Las Vegas." She really didn't think it would work but she put in her father's last name, and about twenty people with that last name came up. Slowly her big blue eyes drifted down the alphabetized list of first names until she saw his name, or at least someone with that same name. She looked out the glass windows in the front of the real estate office and almost trembling her forefinger clicked the mouse on "dial."

"Hello," came the man's voice on the line.

Her heart raced. She's never heard his voice before. She didn't know what to say, so she just said, "Daddy?"

"Who is this? Do I know you?"

"This is June. I live in Texas. You knew my mom," and she stopped.

There was a long silence on the phone, and then, "June? Is that you?"

"Daddy?"

"Yes, where are you?"

"I'm still in Texas. I live at the Bend now."

"The Bend. You live in the Bend?"

"Yes, I'm married."

"Girl you can't be fifteen years old."

"I'm almost seventeen. Oh daddy, it's so good to hear your voice!"

The conversation went on and on, and she didn't care who knew she'd made the call. When Mike came in from work she told him right away that she'd called her Real Daddy.

"What did he say?"

"He wants to see us. He wants us to come up and see him."

"I'll have to tell momma."

She looked disgusted, "Why do you have to tell your momma. You have to tell your momma everything. I'll bet you tell her what we do in our bedroom."

He got very angry and slapped her. Then he grabbed her by the hair and shook her head and started

Cigar Box

saying, "Don't you ever say that. Don't you *ever* say that!"

About that time, Tommy came in and ran over to grab Mike. "Hey, man, cool it. What's wrong with you?"

"She's being a bitch, that's all."

Tommy slung Mike back into the file cabinets and said," Don't hit her, ok? Don't you ever hit June!"

Mike would have swung, but Tommy had been a golden glove for two years before the cocaine took over his life. He was still a fighter, and Mike knew he was no match. He just gave that down stare he always gave at times like this. Just then, Claudette came in from the street. Studying the two boys, and knowing their ways, she asked, "What's going on?"

"Mike slapped June," Tommy said.

Claudette walked slowly over to June and looked at her face. The left side was a bit red, and the tears in the girl's eyes told the truth. She went back over to Mike, still leaning on the file cabinets. Before he could move she slapped him so hard it sounded like a rifle shot.

"Don't you ever let me catch you hitting another woman, you hear me? If you ever hit her again I'll beat you to death. You understand me?"

"Yes, momma." He rubbed his cheek and shifted his gaze to Tommy, and then back to Claudette, and then to June.

"Why'd you slap her?"

"She's been calling her Real Daddy." In his childish world, he thought that this accusation would clear him of the slapping.

Claudette turned to June, "Well, how is he?"

The girl was rubbing her face now, "Oh, he's ok. He wants me to come and see him."

"Be careful that you are not disappointed when you do. Where's he been all these years?"

"He deals blackjack in Vegas. He works all the time."

"Well, just don't bet on him, that's all. He come breezing through this town and was lucky he didn't get himself shot." She turned and pointed her finger at Mike and walked out of the room.

As Mike turned to leave, he tripped over something and fell flat on his face. June and Tommy laughed, and Mike got up off the floor, dusted himself off as best he could, and left the room.

"How'd you do that," the spirit guide asked?

"Wouldn't you like to know, Dr. Angel," Veronica answered. "I've always been pissed off that he slapped me that day. I finally got a chance to even up the score, that's all."

*   *   *

Later that evening Mike came in and went to the porch with June.

"I'm sorry about today. I never meant to hit or hurt you."

She sat in a wicker chair and stared at him. "You should be as aggressive in other areas, Mike. Beating me up won't get you through your real estate classes, or make you a better man."

Mike hung his head and looked at his feet for the longest time. "How can I make it up?"

Cigar Box

June unfolded her arms and said, "Just do what I asked. I want to meet my father. I want to at least *touch* him before he dies. Tell your mom you need us to have a week off so that we can just go and see him. C'mon Mike, he works in *Vegas* for God's sake! You'll enjoy it. God knows you have the money. We can drive out there; it's not too far from here, and we can have a great time. He'll show us the sights, and we'll have a better time than regular tourists."

Mike leaned back in his chair and actually began to take in the idea. It wasn't all that bad after all. A trip to Vegas, with a relative actually there to get you in to all the best shows, the best places was not the worse situation that could be had. His little wife may actually be onto something here.

"I'll talk to mom about it."

"No, don't *talk* to mom about it. You tell her you want to go. It'll be a week or less, and she can let you go. You *tell* her, Mike!"

The thought of *telling* Claudette anything shriveled Mike inside, but he was looking right at his new bride, and facing the challenge of the ages. He had to at least *try* to please his wife. Mike was beginning to understand that there was more to this marriage thing than just the bedroom.

"Ok, I'll tell her I want to take you out there."

Claudette sat her tea on the lawn table that evening, "I'm totally against it."

"Why," June asked?

"You'll be disappointed, that's why. You've got this scenario in your head, and I guarantee you young lady, this man will *not* be what you expect him to be!"

"He is my father!" She tried to be bold, and strong, but the old broker's glare reduced her.

"He is *not* your father, any more than that ex-husband of mine is Mike's father!"

"How can you say that?"

"Anyone can make a baby. When you are young it is incredibly easy to end up with a baby. It takes a certain type of person to be a father. Mike's 'biological' father, God, I hate that word; anyway, Mike's 'real da da' is a born-again looser! He is the biggest waste of oxygen that I know of. All these years, not one penny support, not one card, not one phone call, and now that I have a little something that fool thinks he has some kind of parental 'right' to barge into our lives and act like nothing ever happened. Well nothing ever did happen, and that 'nothing' was Mike's 'real da da!"

June drew herself up to her full height, short as she was and said, "My father is different! You'll see!"

Claudette shook her head, and smiled, "Poor little fool. I suppose you need to learn this lesson for yourself. I'm not going to stand in your way. Go! Go see your Real Daddy, and learn real lessons. I'll be waiting for you when you get back."

Claudette asked that June finish the week out at the office. Inwardly she didn't think the girl would be gone more than four days, so confident that she was that June's father would so disappoint her she would come scampering back to the Bend with her tail between her legs. Claudette could remember the man coming to the little west Texas village years ago. Barbara was happily spending her days at old Stillwell's ranch when she met the man at a dance hall

Cigar Box

one night. The affair was fast and hot, and gave lots of fuel to the gossip factories in town, but then he was gone just as quickly. Stillwell was mad, but saw Barbara again. Once a dog jumps a fence they'll jump again, and the next time she jumped she could not come back. The old rancher spent his days, and nights alone, and Barbara finally married Ray. Claudette surmised that Ray was a sight better than that worthless womanizing gambler, but she knew she could never make June understand that.

June worked through the week. Friday afternoon when the office was empty about four o'clock the little bell on the door rang and Ray came into the office. He reached up instinctively and took his old floppy cowboy hat from his balding head.

"June?"

She came from the rear of the building and said, "Ray?"

"Yeah, just coming by to wish you a good trip."

"Gee, thanks." It suddenly dawned on her that Ray was wishing her luck in the venture of going to see her real father, and she was slightly embarrassed by it. "Hey, it don't mean I don't love you Ray."

He grinned, and sat in one of the expensive leather chairs. "I know that." He looked around the office at all the furnishings. This was not a new building such as one would expect from an agency that had developed an area such as the Bend. It was expensive inside, but the outside was simply a "store front." He asked, "Hey, are we alone?"

"Yeah."

"Good. I don't want ol' Claw-dette to be hearing me talking to you." He grinned. She smiled back. He took in a deep breath. "You are the best thing that ever happened to me, June."

She stammered, "Ray, don't."

He raised his hand, "No, no, I want to say this, 'cause it needs a-sayin'. I spent some time in Huntsville, but you know that. That prison is as hard as any there is. Texas makes darn sure you don't wanna come back for a return visit. There ain't no air conditioning, no food, no nothing. When I got out I was a beat man. I wasn't tough." He looked into her sky blue eyes; "I'm a little man, June, both inside, and out. They hurt little men down there, and them boys took all the dignity I had in the world." His fingers worked the brim of his hat nervously. "Then, when I got out, I met your ma. Now your ma was pretty, just like you, June. She took me in and we started living together. You know she was pregnant with you when I met her? I saw you born. Anyway, I just want to tell you that everything they took away from me in Huntsville, you gave me back." She reached and took his hand. He went on, "You are the special part of my life. That boy over to the Bend marrying you at sixteen, well that ain't right, but that's the best you'll ever do in this little town, and I wanted it for you. I wanted you to be a fine lady, and if marrying that kid gets you there, then that's what I want."

June slid her seat over and rested her head on Ray's shoulder. "Oh, daddy. I'm not leaving you. I just gotta see my roots."

"Hell, I know that! You got spunk! Why, I wouldn't think much of you if'n you didn't go out there and at least *look* at this guy. But you know what?"

Cigar Box

"What?"

"I don't fault him for not coming around. I'm glad."

"You are?"

"Yeah! Hey, what better gift could he give me? He gave me you. A man has three relationships in his life, his mother, his wife, and his daughter. Now, his mother tells him what to do all the time, and he looks to her to take up for him. The day comes when he has to break that relationship and get a wife. Now, his wife is supposed to be equal, but believe me little girl, one or t'other in a marriage is always 'equaler,' but I suppose you're finding that out right about now, huh?" She nodded and smiled. "Then there's the daughter. A man actually leaves his wife in some ways and makes this final relationship with her. That's the best one. She *is* his equal. In her eyes he can be all things, but mostly he can just be himself, 'cause that's all she expects. That's the best one."

"Hey, I seen the Alamo."

"You did? I seen it once, too. I'll never forget it. Them guys were great. They don't make men like that anymore. People who would give their lives for a friend. That's what's wrong with this country."

"You're like them."

"Naw, princess, I ain't. I don't know if I could just sit there and let all them mad Mexicans run right over me." He laughed. She laughed.

"I think you could."

He got up and put on his hat. "Well just wanted to wish you good luck. I won't be here when you get back. I contracted a job in a place called Killeen. I'm gonna rebuild an apartment complex over there for a company out in California. I got me a crew put together now, and all the equipment I need to do it. I figure it'll take a month or six weeks, but when I get back we'll go out to catfish and talk about all the things we seen, ok?"

"Yeah, we sure will."

As he turned and walked for the door June noticed for the first time that Ray walked with a stoop. She'd never seen that before. She wondered had he always had it? Suddenly she was impelled to run to him and hug him. He was surprised, "Hey, now don't be like this! You gotta do this thing, princess!" He looked directly into her eyes and said, "It's who you *are*! You just take care of yourself and come home safe to us, ok."

"You take care of yourself, too."

He laughed, "Now what in the world can happen to an old reptile-bait like me on a rebuild job?" He kissed her on the cheek, touched the brim of his hat and turned and left.

*   *   *

Saturday morning Mike put the suitcases in the pickup and June climbed in, wearing her "501's" and her red cowboy boots. Claudette waved them goodbye and the truck disappeared around the curve and headed out for the nearby interstate that would take them to El Paso, and out of Texas. June was excited. She was just as excited about the trip itself as meeting her father. Here she'd been married only a short time and she was taking her *second* trip to a fantastic place! She eased back into the leather "captain's" chair of the

Cigar Box

truck and listened to the radio as the miles rolled off. The desert became more, and more barren, if that were possible, and soon they were through El Paso, and heading across New Mexico. After about eight hours they stopped at a motel for the night. Mike had brought some beer, and some strawberry wine coolers for June and they settled into a night of HBO.

The next day the trip continued and by that evening they were in Vegas, looking for the casino where June's father dealt Blackjack. They checked into a hotel, but found that actually going to the casino would be hard, as both of them were not twenty-one years old as yet. June found the casino, however and asked one of the people who worked there to ask her father to come and see her.

The man appeared shortly at the door. He was dressed well, as were all of the employees of the establishment. He had the same blonde hair that June had, and even had blue eyes. He was shorter than Mike, but stocky.

"You wanted to see me?"

She just stood there staring. This man *was* her father. He was her real father. She waited for some great emotion, some bolt of lighting to strike her, but none came. He was also a stranger.

"I'm your daughter. I'm June."

He stood there and stared. "And?"

"And I've come to see you."

"Hon, you'll have to excuse me. I gotta work right now. Are you staying here in Vegas?"

"Yeah, over at the Sands."

"Ok, good. I'll give you a call there." He reached in his pocket and gave her a piece of paper and a pen, "Write you room number down."

She wrote the number and returned the paper to him. "You'll get off soon?"

"About two in the morning."

"I'll be up."

He looked surprised, "Uh, yeah. I'll call."

At about two-thirty that night the phone rang. June seized on it.

"You up?"

"Yes."

"Ok, I'll be there in a few minutes, ok?"

"I'll be waiting."

About three o'clock the knock came at the door. June opened it and the man walked into the room. He had loosened his tie and appeared more relaxed than he was at his casino. "Mind if I sit?"

"No, not at all." She was still captivated by him and sat in a chair opposite the one he chose.

He looked at Mike just coming into the room. Mike shook his hand, and said, "I'm June's husband. I didn't have time to introduce myself when we first met."

"Oh, no problem. I was kinda rushed myself, working and all, you know."

"Hey, I'm gonna go down and get a sandwich, and let you two get to know each other, ok?"

"That'll be great. We'll just sit here and get to know each other."

Mike left the room and the two looked at each other. There were no words for the longest time and then June spoke, "I've thought a lot about you."

Cigar Box

"Well, I wondered about you, too. Never seen you. Didn't know you were so cute."

She blushed, "Aw, I'm cute in a Texas way. I ain't near as good looking as these ladies out here."

"These women are phony. You are not. You have a freshness to you."

"Well, what do you think? Are you glad to see me?"

"Sure, I'm glad. Just kinda stunned, that's all. How's your mom?"

"Good. She is getting on just fine."

"She still looks like you?"

June laughed, "No, she's done got fat, but don't tell her I told you that, she'll be mad at me. They tell me she used to look just like me."

He leaned back, "Yeah, she did. She was real cute, just like you. Pretty as a picture. She still living with that plumber guy?"

"Ray? Yeah, and they are married now."

"No foolin'? How long?"

"Right after I was born. Ray wanted me to have," she trailed off trying to avoid what she was just about to say.

"A last name? Hey you can say it. I kinda took off on ya, didn't I?"

"I didn't say that."

"You didn't have to. So what's your last name now, being married and all?"

"Montgomery."

"Fine name. Nice name. They built that neighborhood out there, didn't they?"

"The Bend, yeah. Big houses."

"Heard Willie Nelson played golf there."

Wilbur Witt and Pamela Woodward

"Lot's of people play golf there. They're always coming through the area."

He looked her up and down. "So, what do you want to do while you're out here?"

"Well, just found out today that I can't do much. I'm only seventeen and I can't do much of anything."

"Well, you can see Hoover dam. You can watch some of the shows. There's a few things you can do. I'll get you some tickets so you and your husband can do a little something. Can't have you coming to Vegas and going to the library."

"Why'd you leave?" She was surprised that she'd blurted it out like that. Suddenly, without warning.

He looked shocked. He'd been trying to be so cosmopolitan, and now this little girl had put the question right out there in front of him. It was a question she'd wanted to ask for a long time, and now it had to be answered.

"Can't we talk about that another time?"

"No, let's talk about it now. Why'd you leave my mom when she was pregnant?"

He leaned back, "Well, first off, I didn't know for sure if she was pregnant. Second, I wasn't real sure if it was mine."

June felt her face get hot. "What are you saying?"

"I'm saying your momma was a west Texas firecracker. You think I was her only boyfriend? She was out every Saturday night, heck, every Friday night too, for that matter. Girl, we weren't together more than two or three times."

June could feel her heart speed up. "Are you my real father?"

Cigar Box

He laughed, "Well, there's at least a chance. I mean you got blue eyes, but heck, so do half the people in town here. I *think* I'm you're father, but to be honest, I just don't know."

She started to well up to cry, and he said, "Aw now, don't cry. You just gotta grow up. You come busting out here wanting to meet me without no invite at all. Hon, I was just the most exciting person your momma ever met. She *told* you I was your father because it made her *feel* better. I was just the one who was gone, that's all. She probably didn't want to face the fact that she was pregnant by some broke-ass cowboy in west Texas. Heck, she even had an affair with that old man Stillwell about the same time. His wife had cancer and was dying and she was cleaning up his house for him. I heard she had a little fling with him. *He* might be your father for all I know!"

June reached for a tissue and wiped her eyes. "I guess I got a lot to learn. I'm sorry."

"Hey, don't be sorry. If I ever did have a little girl, I'd want her to be just like you. I wish I were your father. Now the offer of seeing the shows still holds, ok. If you and your husband want to then I'll show you around when I'm off, ok?"

She composed herself, "That's ok. We'll just look around town and go back to Texas tomorrow."

"Oh, c'mon now, don't be like that. You came out here for the truth, didn't you?"

"Just leave." She was surprised at how firm she was, and how much she sounded like Claudette now.

He sat up and looked at her, "Yeah. I guess I should."

She looked him in the eye. "I never want to hear from you again. I never want to see you again. You are nothing to me. You are a user. That's all you are, and that's all you'll ever be. My momma was beautiful! She's a sight better than whatever you got now. I'm sorry if I bothered you at work. I am June Montgomery! You are a piece of shit!"

He looked into her eyes and said, "June, everyone's got to have something to believe in. Your mother had nothing but a sandy patch of west Texas, and no future. She was messing around with old man Stillwell, and his wife was dying. She knew that the situation would end, and she'd be right back where she started. I'm not a family man. I'm not evil, hon; I'm just a man who knows I'd never be able to put up with kids, and a regular job, and all that goes with it. If your mother is happy with that plumber, and has been all these years, then she's a damn sight better off than she would have been with the likes of me."

He stood up and reached to hug her, but she drew back and said, "Don't touch me! Don't you *ever* touch me!"

Mike was coming back into the room just as the man was leaving, "Going so soon? I brought some food."

"Gotta get home. Hope you and your wife have a nice visit to Vegas, son."

He left and Mike looked at June, "What's wrong?"

"Just take me home, Mike. Let's just go home."

Cigar Box

Ray left the little west Texas town shortly after he talked to June, and drove to Killeen some four hundred miles distant arriving late that night. Killeen sits in a flat area of the state with nothing to really attract anyone there except a sprawling army base called Fort Hood. With the influx of so many soldiers the town hosts scores of apartment houses. They fell into various stages of disrepair. The usual life span for one of these buildings was about forty-two years, with them ending up gutted and vacant. This is where Ray's theory came in. He believed that if you could renovate, or even rebuild, then it was far better than new construction at new rates and prices. He had sent proposals all over the state to various rental agencies and one in Killeen had answered him. They weighed his proposal in the balance, and, like he, figured it may be better to renovate than sell and build all over again. Ray had contracted to help rebuild an apartment complex there. His crew of five followed behind him with all of the equipment that Claudette had assisted him in purchasing. The equipment would help him rebuild walls, set more concrete, just about anything just short of actually building a building from the foundation up. In time, he'd hoped to have a "dozer" and other heavy equipment required for more extensive jobs, but for now he'd get by and get his feet firmly on the ground. He'd done jobs like this before, but it was always at someone else's employ. Now he was the contractor, and he ran the show.

Ray's license was no good in Killeen, but his experience was, and he knew how to do many different things. Putting up homes in the Bend, with its west Texas flair had schooled him in many areas, and that all came in handy now. He spent the weekend sizing up the job, and Monday he commenced. This job had to be completed with all possible dispatch because the company was taking "down time" all the time the crew was doing the rebuild. Meanwhile the manager, assistant manager, and the regular maintenance men were maintained on salary, albeit the maintenance men were used with the rebuild, and they needed to get back to productive work.

All that week he progressed from apartment to apartment. The manager of the complex was amazed at Ray's expertise even to the point of offering him a job as maintenance foreman when the rebuild was through. Ray politely declined, saying that he preferred to live in west Texas and work contract labor jobs that fed him, and his family, and he was able to come and go as he pleased. Inwardly he hoped that this new venture would push on to become something larger for him, and he still hoped to rope Claudette in as a partner thereby funding his ideas of rebuilds, or even construction later down the path. Prison had left

Cigar Box

its mark on Ray, and he hated to be what he considered to be "tied down," and a regular job would do that. Add to this the fact that he made a lot more money than any "maintenance foreman" and didn't want to trade that for any false security that a "steady" job had to offer.

The week progressed and Ray began to pull ahead of his original schedule. One morning the manager greeted him as he showed up at his usual seven-thirty sharp, coffee cup in hand and tool belt slung over his shoulder.

"What are you doing for lunch today?"

"Oh, I was thinking about one of them fancy sandwiches ya'll got over on the highway."

The lady smiled and said, "Well today is boss's day, and since I'm your boss I'm taking you out to lunch. You'll eat a plate lunch today. You keep getting any thinner and you'll blow away in this wind."

Normally Ray would not go to a restaurant with any lady except his wife, but since he was far from home, and it was only lunch and not dinner he took her up on the offer. He worked the rest of the morning at his usual clip, but took off a few minutes before lunch so he could go to the restroom and clean up so he would be more presentable to the lady he would eat with. He removed his shirt and took a "spit" bath and after sniffing beneath his arms, he made his way to the car where the manager, and her assistant manager were waiting. Soon, the two ladies and Ray were on their way to a cafeteria.

They arrived about eleven forty-five and the line was not as long as they expected, but it was "boss's day" so there were more than a few finely dressed men and women eating today. Ray checked out the fare and chose a chicken fried steak, broccoli with cheese, and mashed potatoes. They went to the rear of the cafeteria and commenced to eat.

As he ate, his meat Ray noticed a pickup truck sitting in front of the building. The windows went all the way down so he could see that the man had parked but not turned off the engine by the exhaust still coming out the rear pipe. Ray was a man of instinct so he kept his eye on the man. He noticed that the man was "seething," and staring into the building. He thought the guy must be upset about something, but just kept looking up at him off and on as he ate his meal.

"How much longer do you think it will be before we'll be able to rent apartments, Ray," the manager asked?

Taking his eyes off the truck for a moment Ray replied, "No more than three more weeks. The work's going faster than I expected, and you'll be able to let some of the places within three weeks from now. Then we can work our way around to the other areas. That way the company can start to get back some of the money it's spending on the rebuild."

The lady took a bite, and continued, "Now, just what do I have to do to convince you to stay on here after the rebuild?"

Ray smiled, "Ma'am, I've been in west Texas so long I got sand in my lungs. If I didn't have them mountains, and deserts I'd get all claustrophobic. Besides that, I owe my relative a bit of money on this venture, and she'd be powerful disappointed if I was to just take a job and give up on my dream."

Cigar Box

"And what is your dream, Ray?"

He took a bite of his chicken fried steak and said, "I want to repair apartments all over the state. I think I have something to offer people, and ways to save them money on these things. I only got a crew of five now, but in a year from now I'll have a crew of ten, or even twenty, and we'll be repairing complexes as far away as Austin, or Houston."

"A man of your talents could be running maintenance for several complexes."

"A man of my talents could never punch a clock ma'am. You'd hate me. I need to work as I see fit. Also, I need that west Texas desert. I couldn't live here. It's too close! Your air is wet. Can't breathe here!"

Before he could take his next bite there was a loud crash from the front window. Ray looked up to see that the truck was now inside the establishment, resting on a table and the man was crawling out of it firing a gun at a man and screaming, "Well, was it worth it?"

Everyone in the cafeteria froze and watched the horrific scene unfold. When the first man was shot Ray thought, almost in amusement, "Well, that's one wife that guy shouldn't have messed with." In west Texas a man would shoot another man over infidelity at the drop of a hat, so the driver of the truck shooting a man at a table he'd just run over and screaming, "Was is worth it," fit right into Ray's world view.

Then the man looked around at all the people some sitting, some standing at their tables. One man rose and began to wipe his mouth with a napkin. The shooter raised the automatic weapon and fired a series of shots. The man with the handkerchief fell, and the shooter yelled yet again, "Well? Was it worth it?"

Now pandemonium reigned! People dove beneath tables, not daring to move, realizing that something was very wrong with this scene. Ray grabbed the two ladies by their arms and pulled them under the table where they sat.

"Stay down, and stay quiet." Suddenly the two ladies saw strength and authority in his eyes. He wasn't just a little man in a floppy hat any more. Ray looked for a weapon; any weapon, but he could see none. He knew that if the man would just come close enough he could break his neck. In prison he'd seen men get "Jack-Macked," where a convict would put a can of Jack Mackerel in a sock and hit another man in the head until he was dead. But he had no sock, and no can here. He had to bide his time. He watched the man progress toward a table. At the same time he looked around again for a weapon, anything he could use to take the man down. All he found was a butter knife, but that would do if the man should come close. Ray was no fool. This man had not one but two automatic pistols. Still, if he would just come near Ray knew he could push the butter knife up under his chin and into the brain case. The shooter walked over to the nearest table.

Looking at a lady and her mother at the table where he had just shot the man who had been standing wiping his mouth with the handkerchief he said, "Well? Was it," and shot the older woman in the face. She fell back and didn't move at all. He then drew a bead on the younger woman. She cried out, and put her arm in front of her face. The gun went off. The bullet struck

Cigar Box

her forearm, and as it traveled along the muscle the force slammed her arm into her face, spattering blood, and knocking her unconscious. The man bent over her and she wasn't moving, her face covered with blood. Looking around at the frightened stares the shooter yelled, "Take a look at what Bell County has done to me!" He moved to the next table.

Reaching under it he grabbed one lady by her ankle and pulled her out into the floor. As she quietly whimpered, "No, please, not me, please," he shot her once in the forehead. She stopped crying and moving. He looked at another table where a woman, her mother and child were.

He walked over to it and looked at the younger woman, holding her baby and asked, "Is this your child?"

"Yes, it is."

Motioning with the pistol he told her, "You can go."

As she ran for the door, she heard the shot that killed her mother. Ray waited for the shooter to come near him. He grieved for the people who'd already died, but he couldn't help that. This was not the first time he'd been in a tight fix and he remembered the old prison rule, "The main thing is not to panic!" He figured he could drive the butter knife up through his chin and into his brain. About that time, a Mexican man of about seventy years ran for the killer yelling, "Someone's got to do something!" The shooter casually shot him in the chest and he fell at his feet. Walking over to the table where the man had come from he noticed that the younger woman who had been there had run, and the older woman was staring at her husband.

"Is that your husband?"

The old woman nodded with tears in her eyes, not taking them off her dead husband.

"Then you need to be with him."

The man drew a bead on her head, and as she crossed herself, the shot rang out and the old woman fell over backwards. There was a crash from the rear of the restaurant and a man broke through the rear window, stopped, turned and began to pull people to safety.

Then the shooter came to Ray's table. Before Ray could move, he grabbed the assistant manager and fired a single shot. The body convulsed violently. Then he shot the manager. Ray saw the lady fall, but for some reason the bullet had not hit her in the head, but instead hit her in the upper shoulder. The shooter looked at Ray and asked, "What are you looking at?"

Ray stared at him coldly and said in a very calm west Texas drawl, "Not very fucking much!"

Looking at the assistant manager, the shooter said, "She don't look too bad, here's another one," and took aim.

Ray looked at the fallen woman. The gun was aimed squarely at her head. Time had run out for the effort to kill the shooter. His finger tensed on the trigger. Then, suddenly Ray saw another man appear. His friend Juan stepped out of thin air. "Come here," he motioned to Ray, "You can't stay here any longer my friend."

"Why?"

Cigar Box

"It's your time, old friend. I can't control this man's destiny, but I can help you. You've had a life of depravity. Save this woman on the floor. Throw yourself over her and take the bullet for her."

"Why me?"

"Because, amigo, there is no one else. You must do it. There are many things you do not understand, but you will in time."

Ray looked at the wounded lady on the floor. He looked up at the killer and then back at Juan. Then, slowly, deliberately, he lay across the lady.

"What do you know, a hero," the shooter said, and put one bullet in the back of Ray's head. Satisfied with his work at that table he moved onto the next one. Working his way around the room, killing, reloading, and killing again until the police broke into the room and began to shoot at him. He ran back to the restroom. Turning to reload again he saw the old Indian, Juan standing there staring at him."

"What are you looking at old man?"

"I am looking at a dead man." Juan extended his arm and brought his hand together as a fist and then forced it down, the killer's body crumbling to the floor in sync as he did so. Then, walking over to him he said, "Give me your gun." The man gave up the pistol like a little child. Juan took deliberate aim at the man's head and he cowered and tried to cover his head with his left hand. Juan put one bullet through his wrist and head, lay the gun beside his still twitching body and then disappeared in a puff of smoke.

*   *   *

June arrived back at the Bend less than four days after leaving for Vegas. She went to work the next day as if nothing had happened, and didn't tell Claudette a thing about her real father. She hadn't heard from Ray since he'd been in the office shortly before she'd left for Vegas, but she knew he was working the rebuild and that was what he usually would be doing. He'd get his money all saved up, and come back to west Texas, and they'd all meet at Fat Eddies for fish and talk about all that they had seen and done. She couldn't wait to see Ray because suddenly she'd realized that "Real Daddy" wore an old floppy cowboy hat and talked west Texas slang.

June began to realize a great love for this little man whom the town had pushed off to the side until they needed his talent to build their precious Bend. Claudette's husband may have been the official builder of the homes there, but Ray was certainly the knowledge behind the venture, and had it not been for him the Bend would have been a sight longer becoming a reality.

The week progressed and June was actually getting the hang of the job. It was easy to work with Claudette, for all of her reputation, and the money was very good. June was paid a good salary, and never had to really spend any money because she lived with Claudette and everything was always paid for. There was a maid, a driver if she needed one, and any little request she made was quickly catered to. Then, one afternoon Tommy burst into the real estate office with startling news.

"Some nut shot up a café in Killeen!"

Cigar Box

June was alarmed and said, "That's were Ray is." Then she thought for a moment, and asked, "Did you get the name of the place?"

"Luby's. It's a cafeteria. You know, one of them places that serve you like they did in school, but you get to eat what you want and a whole lot more of it."

June relaxed a little bit. Ray would go to a burger barn, or a greasy spoon like Fat Eddie's, but he almost never went out to a cafeteria to eat. Most likely, he was sitting in one of the apartments eating his potted meat and crackers, and drinking a beer for lunch, and was just as alarmed by the events at Luby's as she had been just now.

The rest of the day droned on and she tried to forget the event, but the news kept playing the films repeatedly. She watched as the tape of the countless white hearses carried the bodies away. She noticed the Army helicopter in the road made it ass seem like a war zone. She felt a little uneasy not hearing from her mother telling her that Ray hadn't made his usual phone call, but passed it off, and went to bed.

The next morning June got up and put on her black jeans, with a matching black shirt and her favorite baseball cap, with her long blonde ponytail running through the back of it. Then she opened the office with Claudette. The broker told her that she was going to get them breakfast over at Fat Eddie's. Claudette was fond of getting breakfast burritos with egg and sausage. June began to tidy up the rooms a bit and watched the small T. V. in the break room, which was still running film on the Luby's shooting. She heard the little bell ring in the front and went to get the sack from Claudette, but this time there was no sack.

"June, let's go back to the break room, ok?"

June retreated to her favorite "freeze" raising her chin up and saying, "Ok."

Claudette turned and locked the door in the front of the real estate office. June heard the bolt click shut. She knew that something must be up. Claudette came back to the break room behind June and sat in one of the chairs. June sat down and faced her.

"What is it?"

Claudette looked down, and then back up at June. "Just saw Deputy Dog over to Fat Eddie's. He's got reports from Killeen, June."

June started shaking and tears fell from her eyes. In a shaky voice she asked, "W...what?"

Claudette began to form tears in her eyes, too, but she composed herself and said in a slightly shaky voice, "Ray's dead. That man shot him in the back of the head, and he's dead."

June jumped up and ran to the front of the building, but couldn't remember how to open the door. She fumbled with the lock, but it wouldn't turn, and she couldn't for the life of her get the door opened. Claudette came from the break room and stood at the rear of the office away from her. June began to pound the glass, and Claudette was afraid the glass would break, but then the girl fell to the floor and began pounding the floor.

"Damn! Damn! Damn! Damn! Damn!"

She was reduced to a series of sobs and Claudette went to her and knelt, putting her arms around the broken little girl.

"Why?" June's bright blue eyes were filled with tears.

Cigar Box

"I don't know why, little sister. I don't know why. These things happen. The police killed the man. I just hope he suffered. A man like that needs to suffer. I can't tell you why hon. I just can't."

Then they both heard a tap on the glass. Looking up they saw the deputy standing there with his hat in his hands. Claudette rose and unlocked the door to let him into the room. June couldn't understand why she hadn't been able to open the door a moment before, and wondered just where she'd intended to go if it had opened. The man looked at June.

"Cat, I had to go out and tell Barbara and your grandmother first, but I was coming here next. Still, I think it's better if you heard it from Claudette, though."

"Are you sure?"

"Yeah. It was him. Ray was going to lunch with a couple of ladies. The man killed the one, and shot the other. I'll never know why, but Ray jumped on top of the lady who was wounded and took the bullet for her. Your daddy was a hero."

Upon hearing the deputy refer to Ray as her "daddy," June began to cry all over again, and the deputy knelt down beside her. "I went to high school with your dad, but you know that, don't you?"

June nodded. The deputy went on, "He wanted to be a teacher. I never will forget how he wanted to be just like Mr. Hornbuckle, our homeroom teacher. I went on to become what I am, and Ray, well he went on to be Ray."

June sobbed and raised her tear-streaked face to Deputy Dog. "You are wrong about one thing Deputy."

"What's that, hon?"

"My daddy wasn't just a hero at the end. He was a hero to me every day of his life. He raised me, and took me and my ma in. He worked hard every day, and he helped his momma cook brisket. My daddy was as big a hero as those men at the Alamo!"

"Yes, he was. I suppose he was." The deputy rose and nodded to Claudette and left.

"We need to call your momma, June." Claudette stood off from her, and let her get control of herself.

The girl was wiping her face with her hand, "Yeah, yeah, I suppose we do. I'll do it. Claudette, can we just go home for a while. Can I just go back to the house for a few minutes?"

"You can stay in your room for as long as you want, hon. This is gonna be a trying event for you. We'll get you through it, ok?"

June stood up and started to walk out of the door, but then she stopped for the longest time and stared at the very spot where Ray had last spoke to her. It was only then that she realized that the last visit was a testimonial. It was almost as if he knew. He *knew*. He would never be coming home again. He'd never spoke to her like he did on that day, and now she knew that he never would speak to her again. It was as if a large weight was setting on her right now.

They drove back to the Bend, and June didn't go to her room. Right now, she just couldn't stomach looking at Mike. Instead, she walked around the area for a while, finally ending up on the golf course, and sitting on a bench at the fourth green. She stared at the green for the longest time. The grief would come and go in waves over her. One minute she'd be racked

Cigar Box

with sobs, and the next with a numbness that would amaze her. After about an hour she walked back to the big house. Claudette was on the phone when she came in. As she hung up, she motioned June to the back porch. The maid brought some strawberry wine and poured a glass for June, but she refused.

"You drink it. You're gonna need it child," Claudette said. "Just got some stuff in. When Ray get's back here we're gonna have to make some arrangements. Your momma don't have no insurance and we are gonna have to handle the funeral."

"When's he gonna get here?"

"They gotta do the autopsy first, and then they'll send him out here."

June was incensed, "Autopsy? What the hell do they need an autopsy for? He was shot in his head! Can't they see that? I want my daddy home!"

"Now, now, they always have to do them things when a murder takes place. It's the law. I know it don't sound nice, but the state has to do it."

June looked out at the greens on the golf course, "Where was the state when Ray was taking that bullet? They were quick to judge him; send him to prison, but where were they when he was being killed?"

Claudette put her arms around June. "Deputy Dog said that he had some inside information that the police dragged that man in the restroom and killed him. He said he died begging."

June looked up, "Good. I hope it took him a long time to die!"

Four days later Ray's body arrived at the little funeral home in town. Claudette went to pick up Barbara and together they went to the home to make arrangements. The funeral director met them and led them into the office.

"Ya'll this is gonna have to be a closed casket funeral. Ya'll know that, right?"

"Is it that bad?" Claudette was hoping that they could view Ray.

"The bullet went in through the back of the skull. Blew away a part of the left side of his face. You don't wanna see nothing like that."

Barbara started to sob. Claudette had never seen the fat woman so emotional. Still she knew Barbara for what she was, and didn't believe for a moment that she was really that upset. She was just wondering where the dollars were in all of this. "Ok. Fine. You fix him up. Let her pick out a casket. Send the bill to my office and we'll write the check, ok?"

The funeral director nodded and then led Barbara into the casket room to see various boxes. Barbara looked up and down, and then picked out a simple wood casket. Claudette came in and told her, "Get what you want, Barbara. I'll take care of it."

"This is what I want. This is what Ray would want. He told me never to waste money on fancy boxes. Just put him down in whatever is needed." She looked at the funeral director, "Now don't you laugh, and don't you lie to me. I want his boots on him, ok?"

"Sure. I'll do it. I'll open the end of the casket and let you see if you want."

"No, I'll trust you. Ray wanted to be buried with his boots on. Do that for me, ok?"

"Sure."

As they went to the car Barbara asked, "Did you arrange for Ray's equipment?"

Cigar Box

Claudette looked surprised, "His equipment?"

"You know, his stuff. The things he bought before he left."

"Oh, the reconstruction equipment."

"Yeah. I want it put over at his mother's house until we figure out what to do with it."

Claudette felt her rage rise. "Well, Barbara, I have a lien on that equipment. It goes to my pen to be held in lieu of payment of the fifty thousand dollars Ray owes me."

"Ray said he could pay it as he saw fit."

"Yeah, but Ray is dead, so the equipment stays with me."

Barbara stared at her. Claudette continued, "Ok, let's get this all straight. Your little white trash con has run out. Now, you go ahead and parade yourself all over town like a bereaved widow if you like, but you are still just the trashy little bitch who shacked up with old man Stillwell when you thought you'd get the ranch, and that's all you'll ever be. Well, you didn't get the ranch and you're not getting the Bend either! That little man lying in there was far more than you ever deserved. I'll never know why he put up with you and lived in that shack. Now you know how I feel. And, oh yes, I was raised on a sand bar in the Mississippi. I know your little threat of how you'll 'jump on' anyone at the drop of the hat. Well, the hat's dropped so if you want to jump on me now you won't be getting no cherry, bitch, 'cause I been jumped on before. I don't think we have any more to say, do we Barbara?"

As if she were looking at Claudette for the first time, and taking note that she was a tall Tennessee woman, the fat woman just stood there with her bluff called.

When they left, Claudette drove to the Bend and had the maid fix Barbara a sandwich and a cup of coffee. The conversation outside the funeral home was put on the back burner as if it never happened. June came in and held her mother for the longest time. She drew a cup of coffee and sat at the table. Claudette's husband came in and got a cup.

"Well, here we all are," Barbara said.

"Yeah, here we all are," Claudette answered.

"Has anyone called Dish Bob?"

"He'll be over here in an hour or so."

Barbara said, "He came out to the house the first night and prayed with me. He said he'd be there to console me if I needed it, but that he wouldn't bother me unless I called."

"He hasn't been by to see me yet," June added.

Claudette placed her hand on June's arm, "Do you need to see him, hon?"

June shook her head and looked out through the window. "He can't bring Ray back. I just hope he don't pray for that guy that killed him."

Barbara turned to June, "Now, June, that ain't no way to be. That man was sick. He wasn't in his right mind. We need to pray for that man. He didn't know what he was doing. He didn't know your daddy. He was just in a rage. I just wish I knew what pushed him to that end."

June turned to Barbara, "I wish I'd killed him! I wish I'd pulled the trigger and seen him die! God I hate him! I hate his momma. If he has a dog, I hate his dog! How can you sit there and say we should pray

Cigar Box

for him? Pray for him to burn in hell for the rest of time, that's what I'll pray for. I wish that I could burn right beside him so I could kick his worthless ass every day for the rest of history. Don't say nothing like that to me momma. Don't you ever say that to me!"

Everyone was startled that June was so bitter. She got up and walked to the porch. Sitting on a chair, she stared at the golf course as the maid came out.

"Would you like anything, Ma'am?"

"No, no thank you. Maybe some wine. Some wine."

As she was sipping the strawberry wine Barbara came out. "I'm going to the house. If you want you can come over."

"I wanna go to Maw Maw's."

"She's all upset June."

"I know that, but I wanna see Maw, Maw."

"Ok. Ok. I'll have Claudette."

"No, I'll have the man get the car. You go on without me momma. I'll be along directly."

* * *

Dish Bob pulled up and rang the doorbell of the house. Claudette let him in and led him to her private office in the rear of the home.

"Sit. You need a drink?"

"You have some scotch?"

Claudette went to the bar in the office and opened a bottle of Chavis. "Rocks?"

"Yeah. Been a long day. You see Ray's body?"

"No. The undertaker said it was bad."

"Blowed his head off like John F. Kennedy. Terrible!"

She put a few cubes of ice into two glasses and poured them full of Chavis Regal scotch. Giving one to the preacher, she sat behind her desk in her big leather chair.

He sipped and asked, "So what do you need?"

"A bit of soul searching."

The minister rolled the whiskey around the glass and glared at her, I wasn't aware that you were in possession of a soul. What seems to be the problem?"

"Cut the humor. You are a preacher, not a comedian! I loaned Ray fifty thousand dollars."

"Hope you had collateral. He's dead!"

Claudette poured herself another scotch, "I know that. My problem is elsewhere. If I hadn't loaned him the money, he'd be alive."

Dish Bob saw the beginnings of real tears in her eyes. She was holding together well, but there was a real moment of crisis here. He set the crystal whiskey glass onto the heavy oak desk. "You didn't kill him, Claudette," he finally said.

"But if I'd not given him that money."

"He'd have been there anyway. Destiny. Remember that word. Ray was going to find his way to Killeen no matter what. Personally, I happen to know that he was working on that contract long before he came to you. He'd have been there anyway."

"Why'd he die, Bob?"

"He died because it was his time. No more, no less."

She nodded. After a moment's thought she asked, "Do you really think I don't have a soul?"

Cigar Box

The minister finished his drink, "Nah, you got one, but you keep it so darned insulated that it's hard to see it sometimes. You leave bad trouble back in Memphis, Claudette?"

She looked up alarmed. "Why do you ask?"

"Oh, no reason. Just seems that you been running from Memphis ever since you come here to these parts. Just wondering."

"I left a dead brother that died for no reason, and a white trash family. Does that answer your question?"

"Yeah. For now. Now if you'll excuse me I have a funeral to prepare." He finished the drink and stood. "The whiskey ain't working today. You notice that?" He let himself out.

About an hour later the car pulled up and June got out at Ray's mother's ranch. She walked to the house and found the old woman sitting on her sofa in the living room looking at a family album.

"Maw Maw?"

The old lady looked up, "June? Oh, child, it's so good to see you. Where's your husband, hon?"

"He's back at the house. He's taking all this pretty hard. Harder than me I guess. How are you?"

"Oh, I'll get by. Ray was my only son. He was a good boy. I knew he was a good boy even when he went to prison." She looked at June, "You know he had to jump in front of that bullet, don't you?"

"Ray always told me such a thing would be a sucker move. It was the sucker move, Maw Maw."

The old lady smiled, "No. No it weren't. It was the 'Alamo' move. Ray always believed in heroes. He'd watch that damn movie with John Wayne, and he'd cry, and try to act like he was clearing his throat, and

Wilbur Witt and Pamela Woodward

I'd laugh to myself. That was my Ray. He was the hero."

June sat beside the lady and began to look through the photo album. Ray's life unfolded before her. She noticed he had hair, and then slowly, through the years, he didn't. Even though the stay in prison wasn't noted in the book, she could tell right when he experienced it. Something was missing in the eyes. Then, almost like magic, the eyes came back a bit, and pictures of her, and her mother, and her little sister began to be sprinkled across the pages. The last picture was Ray in his suit at her wedding.

"Maw Maw, I gotta go to the barn for a few minutes, ok?"

The old woman put a hand on her arm, "Yeah, I think you should."

June walked out of the ranch house and made her way across the yard to the barn. As she approached, her pace became quicker until she was almost running by the time she got to the barn doors. She entered through the big doors at the end of the building. It seemed so strange not to see Ray here. She stared at the end of the room and squinted her eyes as if by doing so she could somehow see him still there. Then she remembered something. She ran quickly over to the side of the barn, beneath the loft where the hay was still stacked. Getting on her knees, she reached behind the hay and fumbled for a few moments until her fingers found a familiar object. Though she had never retrieved the cigar box for Ray, she knew right where it was at from all the times she saw him reach for it. She sat back on her heals and removed the big rubber band from the outside of the old box that kept it from falling

Cigar Box

to pieces. Opening it up her eyes filled with tears, and she thought she'd loose her breath. Before her was the expected bag of marijuana, but in addition to that were other things. Ray had never let her look into the box as he rolled a joint, and now, at last she could see. A lock of blonde hair was there. There was a picture of her as a newborn baby, in black and white. A picture she'd drawn in the first grade of Ray with his floppy hat. The picture was in a little girl's hand, and folded neatly. Among the items in the little cigar box was the garter from her wedding. June fell over and touched her forehead to the floor of the barn and cried.

"Oh, God! Oh God. How terrible can it be? Oh God!"

From the veil Veronica beheld the scene before her and knelt right in front of June and cried with her. The memory of this moment flooded over her and the pain returned again as if it had happened all over again. Dream Walker stood behind her and let her release it all out.

"You gonna be alright, Veronica?"

"I'll never get over him, Doctor Angel. I'll never stop missing my daddy."

The two cried together, June in one world, Veronica in the next. Though June could not see her, she cried with her blue eyes staring into the face of her own soul. It was like the two were mirror images of each other. In her grief June reached up and extended her hands to heaven. Simultaneously Veronica did the same, and for split moment the physical *did* touch eternity. A small glow formed between their hands and for the briefest of moments, June looked into Veronica's face! June did not draw back at the sight, but rather devoured it. She *saw* her! For a moment there was total understanding between the two. June and Veronica knew all history, all reason, and all expectations and results and then, as quickly as it came it went, and each were back in her own level of existence. Her companion was stunned at the power of June's soul. He almost expected them to reach out at any moment and hold each other in consolation. He imagined that it *was* at times like this that the physical touched eternity.

"She saw you," he said.

"Yeah, she saw me."

"How?"

"You're so damn smart, *you* figure it out!" Veronica rose and walked from the barn.

*   *   *

Dish Bob straightened his tie and checked his hair in the bathroom mirror of his apartment. He had to be over to the church by ten that morning and it was already past nine. As he walked out of his door he took the empty bottle of gin and put it in the dumpster. He eased into his car and started it. As the engine warmed, he opened his well-worn King James Bible and thumbed through some passages. This was to be a difficult funeral. He didn't know how many people would attend, but he'd arranged to use the First Baptist church for the event. Ray had friends, but Bob didn't know how many would show. Still, this was actually a historic event. Ray had made his mark on his way out of this world.

Cigar Box

He found his way over to the row of shacks behind Fat Eddie's, and pulled into Barbara's gravel drive. She was making coffee when he walked into the front door. He had seen her through the window and she motioned him inside, so he didn't have to disrupt the peace of the morning by knocking on the screen door. Once inside he began to look around at the innovations the little home afforded. Ray had fixed up the shack in many ways. There was bright paneling on the walls, and carpet throughout. The furniture was homemade, but very strong, and very nicely finished. Little "pretties" graced the rooms, and the ceiling was textured with the finest material.

"You like my place," Barbara said as Bob looked around?

"Why, yes sister. This is well put together."

"Every time Ray would have a little something left over from a job he'd bring it either here or his momma's place and fix up something so we'd have something nice. He made them chairs all by himself. He watched all them shows on TV about decorating and he'd try out this, or that, but he never wanted anyone to know, 'cause he didn't want anyone to know he was that sensitive."

"May I sit?"

She motioned toward one of the chairs, "You want coffee?"

"Surely. How are you feeling this morning, sister?"

Barbara stopped pouring the coffee for a minute and hung her head. She didn't cry, but it was obvious that she was struggling with it. "He'll always be with me preacher. I know he wasn't much, but he was all I had. You can't kill a man like Ray. He goes on." She turned with the coffee cup, "I really believe that, Bob."

"Paul tells us that to be absent from the body is to be with Christ. Was Ray saved?"

"I don't know. He never went to church, but in a way his church was his work."

"Our Lord Himself was a carpenter, you know."

"Then I guess that means that Ray was a little like our Lord, doesn't it?"

Bob was talking around the subject to put together the sermon for that morning. Ray had a reputation, and he didn't want to be obviously a liar when he mounted the podium. Still, Ray *had* made his mark, and a man like that needed a good send off.

"Will you be needing a ride to the church?"

"No, preacher. Ray's mother is coming over to pick me up. I'm going to ride with her."

"And June?"

"She's with that bunch over at the Bend. You know that." She laughed quietly, "Funny how we're all going to be sitting in the family section today, huh?"

"We are all in the family of God."

Barbara smiled and sipped her coffee. "He built the Bend Preacher. No matter what anyone tells you, he built it. Ol' Claudette and Bill, they took all the glory, but them houses would never have been there if Ray hadn't done it. That land shifts. We got little earthquakes out here all the time, and Ray, he knew that, so he designed the supports and foundations to roll with it. Bill didn't know shit about that, but Ray did. Every time you see one of them houses in the Bend you just better believe that it is standing 'cause

Cigar Box

Ray was there." The old preacher touched her shoulder as he left her shack.

Dish Bob left and went over to the Baptist church to begin the set up. He didn't have a regular church, but all the local preachers were partial to him because of his connection with the Bend and the proximity of the wealth that resided there. He could ask for just about any church, save the Catholic Church, and that wasn't to say that the priest wouldn't show up at the funeral, and he'd get it! Mid morning found Bob sitting alone in the First Baptist Church staring at the walls. Under his breath he prayed, "There, but by the grace of God, go I."

*   *   *

June was finishing her coffee when Mike walked into the kitchen.

"How are you feeling?"

Without looking at him she said, "How do you think I'm feeling? I'm about to put my father in the ground because some jerk couldn't get a date in Killeen, Texas!"

Mike wasn't a coffee drinker, but poured himself a glass if apple juice. "Hey, don't get mad at me. I didn't do it."

"Gonna hit me again, Mike? Seems like that's the only thing you can do right to a woman. Maybe you need to find yourself a café to shoot up."

Mike put his glass down and simply left the room. June was spoiling for a fight, and he knew she was upset. She had a right to be. He had pointed out to her the previous evening that she was in Las Vegas looking for her "Real Daddy" just a week before, and the statement had led to a big shouting match, which Claudette had to put down. The whole thing was written off as "nerves" due to the death in the family.

The casket arrived at about eleven-thirty and was wheeled into the church and set in front. It was closed, as the funeral director had requested. A few people were there, and there was some press, both local, and national, since Ray had died at such an event. The family began to arrive soon after that. June's little sister came in and put a floppy cowboy hat on the casket. It wasn't Ray's hat, that one having been lost in Killeen after his death, but it was one of his "spares" that he wore on occasion. The meaning of the hat was not lost on the people coming into the room.

As Claudette, June, and company came up in the limos the people began to all fill up the church. Angie had come down, as had Buddy. All were there in force, all arriving in limos looking like royalty. Then the common people came, and came, and came, until there was standing room only and the crowd spilled out into the street. Cars were parked all the way down to Fat Eddie's and back up again. High school girls were crying openly, and old men were wiping their eyes, too. Dish Bob looked at the crowd and was amazed. It seemed that the little carpenter had known every one in the little desert town on a first name basis. For all his crusty outward appearance, he'd loaned money to, talked to, or been a friend to just about every one in town.

The music came up a bit and began to play the standards that the funeral home played at times like this. Dish Bob sat in the area behind the casket and

Cigar Box

waited until a few minutes after ten to rise and walk to the podium.

"Let us pray." They all rose and bowed their heads. "Lord, look down upon this assembly with mercy today. We are here to commend the soul of our brother, neighbor, and friend, Raymond Clowers, to you. We pray this and all things in Jesus' name, amen."

The crowd mumbled, "Amen," and was seated.

Bob drew himself up to his full height, such that it was, and drew in a deep breath. Then his face was overcome with emotion, and in a loud voice he shouted, "How long oh Lord?" slamming his fist down hard.

The people sat up straight. Bob Continued, "How long do we put up with people such as this man who killed our brother? How long? Ray was a hard working, long suffering, humble member of our town, driven to find work in a distant city to support his family, and came to this! When I look down upon his humble casket I am overwhelmed, indeed I am not worthy to be here. I am not worthy to live, when such a man must die!

Ray walked among us for only forty-two years. Our Lord walked among us for thirty-three. Ray was a carpenter, like our Lord. He was a convicted man, like our Lord. Now I know a lot of you didn't think that I'd mention Ray's record today, but let me tell you this; the only man in the Bible that we know for sure went to heaven was a man who was being executed at the same time as Jesus! He cried, 'Remember me when you come into your kingdom,' and our Lord told him, 'Verily, I say to you that this day you will be with me in Paradise!' 'Today, you will be with me in Paradise!' Think about that my friends. And while you are thinking, think about this; Jesus told us that there is no greater love than that love that lays down life for friends! Ray didn't hesitate. Ray didn't think, rationalize, analyze, or hold back. Ray did what needed doing. He saw a woman down, and a monster about to kill her. Ray had seen many people killed that day and he cried in his soul, 'How long oh Lord? Enough!' And with that Ray saved one life." Dish Bob held up one finger. "One. How much is one life worth? One lady will have children. One lady will become a grandmother. One lady will see many more days because this man," he pointed the raised finger at the casket, "this man chose to give his life for her life. And the only thing that all of those people will ever know about Raymond Clowers is that he saved her life. Don't grieve for Ray. Grieve for yourselves. I've spoken over many a casket, and never have I been surer that a man was with our Lord as I am today. Let us pray."

As they rose and bowed heads Bob led them through the final prayer. Then the whole town began to file past the family and Ray's simple casket. When they were all finished a group of six men came up and moved the casket to the hearse outside, and the group began the three-mile drive to the cemetery. When all were there and the casket was resting on the stainless steel bars above the grave Dish Bob came over and placed his hand on the casket.

"At a time like this I'm supposed to say that Ray is not here, but that would be wrong. He *is* here. He lives in each and every one of us. He left us with so

Cigar Box

much. He doesn't need a monument, because his monument is resting in a hospital right now, with her family around her. I'm very proud to have known this man." Bob led them in one last prayer and the people began to leave, each stopping to express sorrow to the family sitting beneath the green tent. Claudette rose and walked to the limo first, without looking back. As she reached the car the funeral director came over to her and told her something. Buddy was right behind her.

"What did he want?"

Claudette was smiling and crying at the same time. "The family of the lady Ray saved called and wouldn't allow us to pick up the tab for this. They insisted on paying for it."

June was the last to get out of the chair. Mike came over to her and said, "June, let's go. We gotta get back to the Bend."

"You go Mike. I wanna stay here just a little while longer."

Looking around at the people getting into the cars, pickups and limos Mike leaned over and whispered into her ear, "C'mon baby, you don't wanna watch him go down."

She looked up at Mike, "I done seen him go down, Mike. I want to be here with him, alone, for just a little while."

"Ok. I'll leave the man with a car."

"You do that, Mike." She reached into the rear of the limo and retrieved a small object, and went back to sit beside the grave on one of the chairs as the men began to remove the lift, and shovel dirt into the hole.

All that could be heard was the west Texas wind, and the sound of the dirt as it hit the casket.

As the last car drove away, the form of June sitting beside the grave as it was covered was the last thing they saw. She was humming a tune no one could quite identify, and stroking the King Edward cigar box resting on her lap.

Somewhere In the West Texas Sand

The days turned into weeks, and the weeks turned into months after Ray was buried. The little town drifted back to normal and Ray was mentioned in passing at Fat Eddie's over coffee every now and then, but soon he faded and it was as if he had never been there. It was a little odd at first when he didn't show for catfish, or eggs in the morning, but time made the entire episode fade into history. Lives moved on, and the little grave began to grown weeds here and there. June went to the little real estate office every day, and put in her time, taking in all that she could about the operation. Mike continued to work with his stepfather, and tried again to take the real estate classes, but he was simply no good at it. He wasn't much good at other things either, and he and June began to drift farther, and farther apart. She put him in the same category as the man she'd met in Vegas, and like him, she soon lost all respect for Mike. She began to resent him more and more, and oddly enough, she began to identify with Claudette. At the funeral she'd seen a softer side of the broker, but she'd also noticed that she knew just when to stiffen her back and walk away. Also the advice she'd gotten just before the wedding had taken root and June had actually kept a wary eye on Mike at all times.

June was walking away from things now too. She really *was* seventeen now, and not just saying it. She really *was* married, and she really *did* live in the Bend. It was almost becoming her usual habit. Before, it was as if she was visiting and would shortly return to those shacks behind Fat Eddie's once again, but now she began to feel as if she belonged there. There was a spiritual attraction between her and the land of the Bend. It made her feel as if she, and it were actually one!

The day-to-day operation of the real estate market began to interest her. Real Estate was never boring to her, but alive and exciting. She was amazed by the details and little "in's and out's" of the business. Claudette told her she needed to seriously begin taking the "fast classes," and be ready to test for her real estate license when she became of age. Claudette's reading disability let June into some very private maneuvers and she learned every time she saw one of them. One such move came one afternoon when a former client called and blasted June out on the phone, admonishing her to have Claudette call him back.

"Oh, him," Claudette said, "I won't call him. He wants his 'V. A.' back on the house he sold and he can't get it."

"Why," June asked?

"Well, I put in paragraph eleven that the new buyer would apply for the loan to be transferred within a year of the closing. Well they applied."

Cigar Box

"And?"

"The mortgage company said, 'No.' they won't let the seller off the note. He's on it until it runs out."

"Isn't that dishonest. You said the people would assume the note in full within a year?"

"No, it's not dishonest. I never said they'd assume, I said they'd *apply*. They did apply. The answer was 'no.'"

"Slick."

"Slick as scum on a hot rock, child. In this business, every comma means something. Never take anyone at their word, especially a real estate agent!"

June became used to the open house duties that her job entailed. She'd fix the food, and sit in the mansions of the Bend, or a shack on the north side of the little town with equal enthusiasm! She was a local celebrity of sorts and her open houses were real events. She began to learn the history of the dream that became the Bend. Claudette showed her this history in the documents that filled the cabinets of the office. When viewed in that aspect the Bend seemed so absolutely normal, and natural, but when perceived from a realistic standpoint it was an impossible thing. June began to understand that perhaps the main reason there was only one bidder that day on the courthouse steps was that no one in the little town thought the land was worth *anything*! It certainly wasn't worth braving the cold wind on the north porch of the county court house. It was Claudette's vision that made the Bend come alive. June began to realize Claudette's genius as she studied the plot maps, and the ideas that sat silently in the office of the little west Texas real estate company now gathering dust.

June could also see how the very advent of the Bend, while bringing some construction to the area, had actually left a vacuum. There were no more homes to be built there and all the plans to expand were scrubbed. The Bend had been built and all of the construction money that could be made had been made. This very fact was what had driven Ray to Killeen. There was no work among the fat wallets of the Bend. There were very few sales, and no expansion. The Bend was settling down into exactly what Claudette had planned for it to be all along. It was a place for the privileged few to retreat when the world became too much and the west Texas deserts would keep them safe.

She could see how the wise old broker had effectively neutralized the town, and it's city officials to achieve her ends in the construction of the Bend. What June could not see was that this had led to some bitterness. When the money was new, and the excitement was still in the air, the old men who ran the town were happy, but with the winding down process they resented the lady from Memphis who had insinuated herself so dramatically in their town. The Subdivision wasn't just a mass of brick and streets, but an idea, a concept; indeed, it was Rome in its entire ancient splendor! When one turned from the interstate highway into the Bend, they turned back into time. Within its walls were the privileged few. No one dared penetrate this inner sanctum, for it in its own way was a very holy ground, sanctified by blood, and sealed for time, and eternity! It was not just a subdivision, implying that it was a part of a greater whole, but it was the whole, and it sustained itself. Its inhabitants

Cigar Box

would truly wonder why it was a "sub" division at all! It was actually larger than the little desert community it had sprang from. The Bend would recreate itself again, and again, at the will of its masters, the elite few who lived within it, and who empowered it, compelling it to greater heights.

And it would do it at the expense of anyone who dared to stand in the way! During June's tenure as secretary of Claudette's little real estate venture, she met with Juan. Juan had been around so long that no one could remember when he wasn't there. Juan was an aspiring homeowner, hoping to put a house together in the most prestigious subdivision in the state! The Bend! He submitted his plans to the "committee" which actually amounted to Claudette, and her husband, and was initially approved. He had paid for his lot in four payments. Then he gathered his clan around him to build the house a little bit at a time. He would pay in food and help to various members of his family who helped with the project. He'd skip over a lot of red tape by doing this. In skipping over the bureaucracy he attracted more than a little attention. One night a visitor came to Claudette's home.

After dinner, when the scotch was poured liberally, and the "visitor" made his pitch.

"Claudette, you know that Mexican that's putting up his place, out there on the point?"

"Why hell yes! You think I'd have a house going up out here that I didn't know about?"

The man poured a bit more whiskey and continued, "Well let me ask you this; wasn't this supposed to be an 'exclusive' area?"

The wise old broker sat her drink on the oak table, "Jim, I don't know what you're driving at, but you know as a broker with the state of Texas, I can't be a party to any such shenanigans as what I *know* you're leading up to."

"Ain't askin' you to, hon, ain't askin' you to. Just askin' you to appoint a few more 'committee' members to help you with this heavy load I know you must be carrying by now. We could hold meetings; enforce deed restrictions, and such things as that. He's out there using his family to pour concrete, frame, put in septic, hell, everything! I don't think the word 'code' is anywhere in their vocabulary."

She stared at him. "Juan's money is green. That's the only color I see. I'm from a sand bar in the middle of the Mississippi, and I don't give a damn about your codes."

About that time her husband cut her off, "Now, hon, just let Jim continue. He's not trying to hurt you. He's trying to help you."

"That's right, Claudette," Jim said, "We're just trying to help you smooth things along. I'm not interested in what that Mexican is putting up out there. All I want to do is make sure the code is adhered to, and that our property values stay right where they are. There are a lot of people with a lot of money invested here in this little neighborhood of yours, and you can't let us down, now."

"Oh, I see." Claudette saw a way out of this little trap. "Then let's go ahead and have a little vote, and form a new committee, right?"

Cigar Box

"Yeah, that's it. Now ol' Juan out there, he can even run for the committee if he wants to. We'd be proud to have him."

"Naturally. I can see how you'd be overjoyed for him to sit on the committee."

Jim smiled, "I knew you'd see it our way."

In point of fact, Claudette had written the so-called "code" with her husband, Bill, but had never actually taken it seriously. With the caliber of buyers she'd had she'd have felt like a fool trying to steer them this way or that if they decided to do something with their property, and in truth that's the very reason most of them were there in the first place is to live in peace and solitude and not be tampered with. In her mind Juan was one of the least offenders. All he wanted to really do was build a house!

Within a month Juan had more complaints against his construction than he ever imagined possible. His septic tank wasn't up to state standards, it spite of the fact that it was exactly the same as the one on the adjacent lot. (That land is *higher elevation* than Juan's land. His must be a spray type unit!) Juan's deck wasn't in conformity with the specs on the original plan. (We have the plan right here. That deck sits on ground that was hauled in and is very unsound. Why it would just slide right off into the river at the first rain!)

After such delays, and hearings, the little man was simply disgusted and left his unfinished house to be host to the tumbleweeds that blew across his property. When the fines mounted for that Juan disappeared from town, and the only reminder left was his daughter, Sabrina, still serving drinks down at the little bar that Buddy frequented. The last house to be built

Wilbur Witt and Pamela Woodward

in the Bend was at that time a foundation with gray two by fours reaching for the west Texas sky. With his friend, Ray now dead, Juan's trips to the town became fewer and fewer. Those who did know him thought they saw other worries in his eyes, but they could never quite put their fingers on it.

*   *   *

Claudette had other fish to fry. She was very aware that the Bend was tapped out. Juan's foundation was but a harbinger of the end. There was no more money to be made from the Bend. The glory days were gone as far as construction went and Claudette and her husband made their livelihoods from construction; not from what few resale homes came up in "nowhere" Texas! She had originally thought that she would have Bend II, and Bend III, but when the last home beginning she was aware that the Bend was the Bend and that was that!

Then, one day, opportunity came into the little real estate office in the form of one Mr. John Springer. Springer had made his fortune building bridges, and high-rise buildings in, and around the Austin area for years, and now in his twilight years, he was looking to retire in a secluded spot somewhere in the west Texas desert. He didn't need Claudette's building ability, only her location, but she got more than money from the old man. Since there were no new lots in the area, she convinced the older man to buy a resale and add onto it. Adding onto a home in the Bend was formidable as it was, but Mr. Springer was a formidable man. Soon the home he bought was but a

Cigar Box

core of the finished product. Still, he was aware, as was Claudette, that the Bend was history. One day he dropped into her office.

"How long have you been developing this area," he asked?

"Running up on five years or so."

"Running up and run out ain't it? I mean, lots getting a bit scarce?"

She thought a minute and nodded. Then he continued, "You need to branch out. I'm in my 'declining' years as momma here points out to me ever so often, and I'd like to take on a partner one of these days."

"What kind of partner?"

"General partner. Someone with a little investment to let come in." He pulled out some notes and ideas and put them on the desk. "I want to create a company that does the bridge thing, and the tall buildings, but also I've found that there is a pot of money to be had for contractors that can put together crews to work in the areas that the army goes to. That area around Fort Hood is involved in a lot of that stuff, and I've heard of more than one company making a pretty penny putting up permanent buildings in them war zones. Course, it takes a certain type of person; one who don't mind the 'altercations."

Claudette moved her big leather chair closer to the desk. The sound of the name "Fort Hood" rang a bell in her head. That was the place that Ray had headed for when he was killed. Even though she hadn't bought into Ray's idea, the area around the post did seem juicy. The Bend was sold out, and she needed an opportunity to expand beyond the confines of the little desert town. Otherwise she'd just end up a female version of old man Stillwell. This man just may very well give her that chance.

"What can I do for you?"

The old man smiled knowingly. He could see the hunger in her eyes. "You provide 'energy' young lady. You built this subdivision from rocks and sand, and made it one of, if not the most desirable places to live in the southwest. I need that kind of enthusiasm if I'm gonna make this project work. I built all over Texas, all over the world as a matter of fact, but I feel like this is my last round up, and I'm gonna go out good! I'm gonna go out with a bang, not a whimper!"

"I'm all for building bridges, and buildings, but I don't know about these war zones. Kinda hard to get people to go there, you know?"

"Heck, gal! This place is just chocked full of damned fools who don't mind getting their ass shot off if there's a dollar to be made! What do you say?"

Claudette leaned back in her chair. "How much for me to get in?"

"One dollar. One silver dollar."

Claudette thought the old man was crazy, but she opened her desk drawer and pulled out a Susan B. Anthony dollar from it and put it on the Pulaski desk in front of the old man. "Paid in full?"

He reached out and pulled the coin toward him. Turning it in his hand he smiled and said, "Done deal! We'll call the company the Silver Dollar Development Corporation!"

Cigar Box

Mr. Springer left the office with his silver dollar and June came into the room to talk. "That old man for real?"

Claudette leaned back in the chair, "Yeah, he's for real. That's how great things are done. A hand shake, someone's word. Texas was built on such deals. You remember how I came up with the Bend?"

"Yeah, but I know you're gonna tell it to me again anyway."

"I watched 'Dallas' on TV! I was so ignorant that I had to watch that show to see how rich folks live. I'd see a table, why I'd go out and get it. I'd see a bed, I'd get that. This neighborhood, heck child, it's just a bunch of little 'Southforks' all crammed together and built around a golf course. The fountain that sits on that first hole was something I saw on a show somewhere, and I thought that was the prettiest thing I ever did see. The way that chandelier hangs from the second story down through that hole to the first story in the country club, and them big doors, the staircase, just about everything was things that I saw other people do on TV, and I put it to use on my land. That's how I did it."

"But how did you know it would work?"

"Cause people always go for the obnoxious, kid. They never take the easy route, especially rich folks. They take the hard, silly route. Take them airplane hangers in some of the homes. Now I ask you; did you ever hear of such a silly thing in your life? Airplane hangers just so some fat cat can steer his Piper Cub down a suburban street to the runway and take off like he's got good sense."

They both laughed. "Yeah, I drew this whole place out so I could live the life style I wanted to think I could live. Does that make sense?"

June nodded her head. Claudette went on. "I looked at this land when that crazy old man forfeited it and just knew this thing would work! I just *knew* it! You know my only regret?"

"No, what?"

"I told you that. That crazy old bastard, Stillwell, went and stuck that pistol in his mouth right smack dab in the middle of my favorite picnic spot! I never forgave him for that!"

June grew dark for a moment, "Why'd he do it?"

"Do what?"

"Shoot himself like that?"

Claudette smiled and looked down at the floor, and then back up, "Only way for a rancher who gets screwed out of his land to go out. Up north, them pantywaists would have gone to court, and pissed and moaned, but Old Man Stillwell did it the way it's always done. But you know what?"

"What?"

"When he shot himself he was really shooting me!"

"Go on! How you figure?"

"Hated me that bad. He hated me so bad he blew his *own* brains out 'cause he knew it would piss me off!" She laughed, and June was ashamed of her self but she laughed right along with her. Claudette went on, "You know, your momma helped him during his days when his wife was dying?"

"I heard about that. She stay there?"

Claudette nodded, "Sure did. Night and day, day and night." The old broker let this fact soak in a bit,

Cigar Box

and continued, "Did you ever wonder about that, June?"

"No, I mean I just found out about it in Vegas. I really don't think that man I went to was my daddy."

"That's cause he wasn't! That flimsy queer come floating through here for a month or so and never really came back. No, he ain't your daddy."

June looked at her with big liquid eyes. Claudette stared back at her, "I ain't gonna say it! That's something you gonna have to go to your momma about, child!"

"She won't tell me."

"Yeah she will. It's gonna be between you and her."

"What if I am…that child?"

Claudette grinned, "Don't mean much, 'cept you are the *only* person really born in the Bend. Just think of it. Of all these hypocrites, you are the only real child of the Bend. You know, the old Stillwell house was right where my house is now. You might very well been conceived right where your bedroom is now."

June smiled. "I'm the real heir."

"No, you ain't heir to nothing! You are a relic! But you are a cute relic, and you are a damn sight better than Mike deserves. Now get back there and sort them folders and quit trying to think these high thoughts. You got a ways to go, cowgirl!"

The next few weeks were filled with Mr. Springer coming back and forth between his base of operations in Austin and the renovation of his home in the Bend. Slowly, but surely Claudette knew all the old man knew. She began her efforts with him by building a bridge for a little desert town about fifty miles to the north of her, and once her legs were steady on the deck of the new project she fanned out. Heavy construction in war zones was proving to be a lucrative business. Traveling to the Fort Hood area she found an ample supply of retirees just waiting for a chance to get back into the areas they were more familiar with than the struggle of retired life, and working at Wal Mart.

She expanded Springer's idea a bit, however, and extended it into the reconstruction business. She still had Ray's equipment, such as it was, but mostly she had Ray's *idea*! Ray died while he was rebuilding run down apartment complexes. Wouldn't it be *more* profitable to rebuild *bombed* out buildings for rich Arabs? The selling of an idea, or a project had never been a problem for Claudette, and soon she became the *one* woman the Moslems *would* talk to.

It was about this time that the Middle East exploded with the Kuwait war. Oil wells were set on fire, buildings bombed and money flowed to and from Iraq and other areas. Claudette watched the reports with a careful eye.

"I hope they don't drag this thing out too long," she told her husband one day.

"What do you mean; the war?"

"Yeah. Them buildings are looking pretty bad. I have plans for them."

He was frankly shocked at his wife's ambition. "You planning to go over there?"

She looked up from the TV, "Why hell yeah. Them rag-heads don't know what they're doing. They need direction."

Cigar Box

"They won't deal with a woman. They're all Muslim."

"I don't care. They'll deal with money. I can make them listen."

"You gonna take Mike so he can learn?"

Claudette looked up at him with mild amusement. "No, I'm going to take the man of that family with me. I'm going to take June."

"June! You're going to take that little girl with you to the Middle East?"

"Darling, just in case you haven't noticed, that *little* girl has been running that office for me down there for some time now. She's a whole lot smarter than Mike, and besides that, I can trust her. Can't trust Mike. He'd take all my money and give it to his fat 'Real Daddy' given half a chance." She paused, "Anyway, they aren't getting along so well. Maybe the separation will do them good. Make him wake up a bit."

The very next day she called Mr. Springer and proposed her idea. "It'll work, no doubt about it, but like your husband, I don't know if you should personally go there."

"Why not. It's just a big sandy, just like here. Look, you just get the men and let me worry about all the Muslims. I know where their minds are."

Springer went to make the arrangements for the crews, and Claudette told June to pack and be ready. Later that night, in bed, Mike began to question June.

"You really going over there?"

"Yeah. Your mom is going to use me to help her. Mike, don't get all messed up. It's my job."

"Yeah, but I didn't think your 'job' was going to take you that far away."

"We'll be back before you know it."

Mike reached over and began to stroke her, but she pushed his hand away. "Why?" he asked.

"Just got a lot on my mind, Mike. I can't get into it right now."

Mike rolled over and went to sleep with his face the direction of Commerce Street.

*   *   *

Claudette didn't have to wait long. The war ended and with the enemy still at the gates, she flew in construction crews and began to rebuild the city and areas needed to make the country stable again. The air was still foul from where the Iraqis had set oil wells afire during their retreat, but that didn't bother Claudette. "I grew up in Memphis," she reminded her supervisors, "and that part of Tennessee stinks! If these sand fleas want to burn up all their oil it don't matter one hill of beans so long as I get to build the country back, and they only shoot each other!"

She was a hard taskmaster. She drove the crews hard, but they loved her for it. Her west Texas flair captivated them, and made them work harder, and they couldn't help but take note of her little sidekick; a short, cute blonde she called "the Cat" who was frequently there. The "Cat" became an expert at all the broker did. She did most of her reading for her, and could actually do contracts and other legal work required by the business. In between trips to the sites in the Middle East June began to take her six "fast

Cigar Box

classes" and got ready for her state exam to become a licensed agent under Claudette's brokerage.

One night June brought Claudette's wine to her in their apartment in Kuwait.

"The Muslims would get real upset at you for sneaking this in," Claudette said.

"Not near as mad as some of the Pentecostal preachers I know." June laughed and joined in a glass of wine. "Who's that Arab who keeps coming to our site and talking to you all the time?"

"King of the sand fleas."

"A king? You mean, like a real king?"

Claudette poured another glass of wine, "Well, not like a king in England. They just shoot everybody and whoever's left, well he's the king."

The young girl sipped her wine, "Has he got a lot of wives?"

The broker looked hard at June, "You asking some questions here, girl. Why you wanna know something like that?"

"Oh, no reason. I just heard that all these Arab guys had a dozen wives."

"That excites you?" It was no secret that June and Mike did not have a good private life. The tension was in the air back in west Texas. Claudette saw how little June worked hard to keep herself very tired so she could sleep at night.

"What?"

"A man with all them girls."

June took another sip, "Just bears looking into, I guess."

"You know, June, if I ask just right I could probably get him to buy you."

"Go on! Get outta here! He can't buy me?"

"Let's think about a price. Let's see, you *are* a blonde. They like that. Course, you need the operation."

"Operation."

"Yeah. They circumcise their women."

June looked confused, "How in the world would they…OH MY GOD! NO! Do they do that?"

"Hell yes they do that. You don't think these fools are gonna let a woman enjoy herself do you. Why it would challenge their manhood! Seems that every religion over here eventually boils down to someone having to cut something off'n their private parts."

June unconsciously put her hand in her lap and gulped down her wine. Then they both started laughing, sipping more wine, and watching the moonrise over the desert. "I wish my mom was like you, Claudette."

The old broker looked at her with surprise. "Why'd you say that?"

June, now more than a little drunk said, "Oh, I don't know. I just wish it was so."

Claudette put the girl to bed and continued to watch the moon alone.

In sharp contrast was Mike, still fledging back in Texas, not passing his classes, and generally giving up on the whole thing. It was readily apparent that even if he didn't work he still lived in the Bend and would be supported. The day actually came that he didn't really care if June was in Middle East, or Austin, or New York, so long as he had his room, his golf cart and Deputy Dog's daughter on the side. June didn't care about his distance, and besides, she was so busy she didn't let it bother her. She took it as a vacation to be free of Mike's demands, and immaturity. It bothered Claudette, though.

"You messing around with the Deputy's daughter?"

"Oh, mom, don't worry about it."

She shot right back at him, "I *am* worried about it! You get caught screwing around over there and you'll blow up your marriage, my business, and this house. Maybe you need a little time in Middle East with us."

Mike looked hard at her, "I ain't going over there with all them Arabs. I'll just go spend some time back in Tennessee with my…"

"If you say 'Real Daddy' I'll shoot you where you stand! You should be past all that nonsense, and besides you are too lazy to go there and have no air conditioning."

Mike tried to act like his manly pride was hurt, but he simply stared off into space. Claudette continued, "Don't let me hear down at Fat Eddie's that you are back on Commerce Street, you got that?"

"I wasn't there."

"Don't let me hear it!"

"Ok."

Buddy came to town about this time for a visit. With the absence of affection from Mike June found it much easier to notice the older boy. She remembered his coming to the catfish house, and was very aware that he was *not* Claudette's natural son, but instead had his father's rugged good looks. Buddy couldn't take his eyes off of June. He tried not to be obvious, but the girl was on his mind the entire trip; and by the time he went to dinner with his family one night he was totally infatuated by her. The family had all gone to a restaurant in another town that was known for its history. The menu was recited and prime rib was the normal fare at the establishment. Getting ready for the evening June picked out a black dress that showed how truly lovely she really was.

"You shouldn't wear that to a dinner," Claudette warned her.

"But I like it," June said, eyeing herself in the mirror. "I want to wear it. Mike like's it."

"Just ain't proper, that's all. You should wear the one with the high collar, and accent it with that little gold cross you have."

Still looking in the mirror, June said, "Don't feel like crosses tonight. Feel like black dresses." She looked at Claudette with that sideways look she always gave when she was trying to get away with something.

"Go ahead then. I'm not gonna get in a tiff over a silly dress. Heck! Go naked if you want." And as she left she mumbled under her breath, "Mike won't notice anyway."

The family was positioned at a long table. The waitress, a lady of about fifty years came out and recited the menu. The eatery was noted for this. They all let her do her little spill and then all ordered prime rib with all the trimmings. June loved this ritual. It was one she never got to do before she became a member of the Bend, in fact she didn't even know about this place until then. Now it had become a regular part of her life. It had been a stage stop in the eighteen hundreds, and now the original hotel was the eating establishment with the stage stop itself serving as a gift shop by its side. As comfortable as she had

Cigar Box

made the Middle East it was not home, and they did not have good meat and drink. June was inwardly amazed at how spoiled she had actually become in such a short time.

As they were eating, Buddy's eyes kept following the curved of June's form, sitting opposite him. She could feel his eyes on her, and more than once returned the look when she thought no one could see. Her tan skin blended well with the black material of the dress. Her legs, perfectly formed, accented the hem, and her body filled every inch of the dress, while showing beyond a doubt that there was no fat on this body. Mike was completely oblivious to all of this, but Claudette caught them staring at each other a couple of times. She didn't say anything, partly because she was angry with her son's carrying on over on Commerce Street, and partly because she didn't want to disrupt the dinner, knowing that they were there for another reason.

Tommy rose and picked up his wine glass. "I need to let ya'll in on a little secret." He reached down and pulled his girl friend, Christina up to his side, "Me and Christine are going to be married."

Claudette used the announcement to take the edge off the "eyeballing" by Buddy and June, "Well, alert the media! Christina, you come right over here and give me a hug."

The girl of about twenty rushed around the table and began to fawn over Claudette and her husband. She had actually lived in the Bend but she wanted to marry and stay there. Tommy had been her boyfriend since grade school, and she was the only one who could really tolerate his habits.

"Now we simply must have a big wedding on the porch," Claudette said, "Your momma can afford it."

"Who's porch, dear," her husband laughingly asked. Claudette had completely forgotten protocol. She had bowled over June's parents, but this young lady's mother, a widow, was wealthy, and owned a home in the Bend."

"Oh, my gosh. I'm sorry. Christina, you will have to be married at your house I suppose."

The girl laughed and just said, "Oh, I would be so flattered to be married on *your* porch. You and momma are just gonna have to work all this out. Maybe we'll have the reception there."

Claudette rolled the idea around a bit, and, smiling replied, "Yeah, that'll work. We'll work on that."

While all of this was going on no one noticed June and Buddy staring right into each other's eyes. June began to feel her blood boil in that old familiar way, and she was walking on the edge in her mind, thinking things she should not have thought. Her heart began to race, and feelings she'd thought she'd lost came leaping back into her mind. Her husband, sitting right beside her was wading through his plate, and then turned to her without noticing her looking across the table and asked, "You gonna eat your strawberry kiss?"

She broke her gaze, "Oh, no. Go ahead Mike, enjoy."

They all drove back to the Bend when the dinner was finished and after a few drinks the various members of the family began to drift off to bed. Mike was one of the first, having consumed too much wine at dinner and topped it off with a six-pack after getting

Cigar Box

home. He practically fell over and toppled from the couch causing June to help him to bed, but shortly after that she re-emerged and went to the porch where she found Buddy having a beer all alone.

"He ok?"

"Yeah. He can't drink. Never could. But he's got that eating figured out, doesn't he?" They both laughed.

The two just sat there in silence for a little while. Buddy finally broke the quiet, "How's it going? You and Mike getting along? You happy?"

She looked at him with a suddenly mature gaze. She held his stare for a long time and then said, "No, not really."

Buddy's mouth went dry. He was on thin ice here. All the years of rivalry aside, this was his brother's wife! He noticed, quite alarmingly, that his hand was shaking. He steadied it with the other hand, hoping she hadn't noticed. June was far cooler than he. Even though her heart was pounding she didn't show a bit of it in her actions or her eyes. She *was* June the Cat! Just like a lion that knows how to kill from birth, she knew how to burn this young man down. Still, she wasn't ready to do it. She would wait just a little while longer. He'd be back. She *knew* he'd be back! He was hooked. He'd just lost his soul. She had it! She got up and began to walk toward the door. Buddy was beginning to shake so badly he couldn't hide it.

"Cold out here tonight. Maybe we'd better get inside the house, huh?"

She stopped, looked down at him and said, "Yeah, might be better if we did."

He looked up and observed her in the black dress. Her blue eyes positively glowed in the dark. As she breathed it made her body swell and strain against the fabric of the dress, and accented her form all the more. The blonde hair hung loosely down to the middle of her back, lifting here and there on the warm breeze. She held his gaze for a while, and then turned and walked inside. She could hear her heart slamming in her head, but she knew she'd save the emotion for another day. Buddy was now officially "in the bank!"

Neither one of them could see the pair standing at the end of the porch, so near, and yet a dimension apart. The man spoke first, "You were seducing him."

Veronica smiled and looked at Buddy still sitting on the porch, "Yeah, that's what you'd call it. And it was wrong, but you know what?"

"What?"

"I can feel that passion even now. I feel the need, the thrill. I know it's wrong, and I know it's something I have to live with, but I feel it, and I like it! I'm not supposed to feel that, am I Dr. Angel?"

"You don't change just because you are here. You are the same person you were back in the car. You have to want to change."

She looked at the man and smiled, "Isn't that what *you* are supposed to do? Change me?"

"No. I'm supposed to make you accept. You have to learn. You have to understand what we're up against. I'm supposed to get you to make the right choices. Juan left this town with his tail between his legs, but he wasn't beaten. That's just a real good act he has going. He is trying to trick and corner us even now. If he gets his way, you won't like it."

Cigar Box

Veronica wasn't listening. She walked over and knelt down, looking Buddy right in the face. The young man was still shaking and looking totally lost. Slowly her perfect lips formed a pout, "Oh, Buddy, been playing a game you shouldn't play?"

Her spirit guide slowly came up behind her and watched. She tilted her head this way, and that, enjoying Buddy's fear. "He knows what he wants to do, Dr. Angel; he just ain't got the guts yet."

"Maybe he has a moral."

"He doesn't have any morals. He just doesn't want his momma to catch him when he does what he really wants to do. He wants to tear that dress off of me and spend the rest of the night in my bed."

The man's eyes focused on her, "But you're *using* him!"

Veronica stood up, "And why not? All these people use *me*! They think they are in charge, but they aren't. The only one in charge is that old broker asleep in the master bedroom. The rest of these chuckleheads are just along for the ride, just like me. Remember when Claudette joked with me about selling me to the king of the sand fleas? Well these people have all been bought and paid for, by Claudette Montgomery!"

"You don't love your husband?"

"Why do you keep asking that? You want to know the truth?"

"That would be nice."

"I love position and I love money. I love whatever puts me with those two things. I hate that shack I grew up in, and I hate the way Ray worked himself to death trying to better that shack. Anyway that's what I love, and hate."

"What good is all that money doing you now?"

Her continence changed abruptly as she felt a cold shiver run down her spine, "Buddy's right. It's cold out here. Let's go!"

*   *   *

The wedding was planned about a month out. There was no long wait because Tommy and Christina had been expected to marry since the third grade. Dish Bob was called and he counseled the pair with all the seriousness he could muster. Tommy was working on jobs with his father, actually supposed to be working along side of Mike, but Mike was never there. The two siblings kept secrets, and Tommy would never "rat" Mike out during his sojourns to Commerce Street. The jobs weren't that important anyway. They were just clean up or repair. Tommy had wanted to go overseas with Claudette and June but had never had the opportunity. So, he just sat back in west Texas and watched Mike make a fool out of himself over Deputy Dog's daughter. He wondered what made the older brother want to go there with June being so beautiful. Still, he left these things alone.

Tommy had developed habits that would plague him all of his life. He had once been a boxer in the golden gloves and received two cracked ribs. The old doctor had given him painkillers at the time, and he had discovered that the drug could not only relieve him of the pain, but also put him in a state of mind he came to enjoy perhaps too much. He was a child of wealth, and privilege so while June blew a few joints with Ray out in the barn, Tommy could afford much better

Cigar Box

relaxants. He completely skipped the marijuana stage and leaped eagerly into cocaine. The lad was so bright, and so full of energy that his family never noticed. He quietly dropped his boxing, claiming that the ribs had "woke him up," and went from high school (graduating right after Mike) to work with his father on the construction sites as the Bend wound down. He was full of energy and was actually an asset to the crews, though his father wished he would be more into the *business* of building, and a little less into the labor. Though Tommy had his moments with beer, he didn't drink as much as the others, preferring to slip off for a moment, and then return.

Christina knew all about his habits, and though she didn't do the drugs, she allowed Tommy to have his way with them because she honestly loved him. To her the cocaine was just a minor flaw in an otherwise perfect man. She wasn't slow, but she let on that she was to keep people at their distance. Christina was a private girl, preferring to let only one person in her world at a time to the exclusion of all others. Tommy had the first part of her life, then her mother, and then maybe one or two others as she chose. She'd sit for long hours on her mother's porch and listen to the birds sing without saying a word, and be perfectly content with life. If Tommy wanted to sniff a little coke that was fine with Christina, so long as he was with her. She, too, was a child of privilege. Her father had been killed in a plane crash leaving a sizable amount of money, which her mother invested wisely, and the two never suffered or wanted for anything.

She was a tall girl with natural blonde hair and no shape to mention. She had a winning smile and bright eyes. When anyone talked to her she just drifted through the conversation without ever really getting involved. Claudette was intrigued with June, but Christina was just "there." Everyone knew that she would never "do" anything other than just make babies and look after Tommy, which perhaps *was* a career in itself.

Now these two drifted happily toward matrimony. Tommy actually had no more ambition in his life other than Christine, labor work, a little cocaine, and Sunday golf. He was an excellent golfer. He could have been a pro at any time, but simply never pursued it. So much talent rolled up in one person who only wanted to drift through life and be left alone.

It was decided that the wedding would be at Christina's home, with the reception *beginning* there and moving over to Claudette's home, or perhaps even the country club as things became more advanced. The details of the affair were actually much more than had been June's. June was an outsider when she married Mike, and Christina was of the Bend. Her mother was moneyed. This marriage would be more the "norm" than had June's been.

Still, June remembered the fabric that she's saved from her own wedding and gave it to Christine to help make her own gown, which was much more than June's. The invitations were sent, the gown made, and the usual commenced. Dish Bob was hired, as usual, to preside, with the usual sprinkling of lawyers, judges, and doctors, only this time no one had to put up with the people from June's side of town. It was also decided not to invite Rhonda so nobody had to go through another ordeal of her being "groped." June

Cigar Box

herself wasn't bothered by all this. She had other things on her mind, mainly in the form of Buddy, and her own crumbling marriage only so recently preformed on Claudette's porch. Mike still was slipping off to Commerce Street, much to Claudette's chagrin, and now June was beginning to catch on, though she didn't know the name, she knew there was someone else. This added the element of revenge to the feelings she was beginning to have for Buddy. She knew, had always known that the two older boys didn't get along very well, and she knew that it would be a major strike if she and Buddy were to get together. Then, suddenly she'd stop herself and wonder what in the world she was really thinking? That would destroy everything, her life, her marriage, her security, her place in the Bend, everything!

Still, Buddy brought a fire out of her that she could not ignore. She had felt no passion for Mike, as she had with the other men who had passed through her young life, but Buddy lit a certain fire that she had never felt before. She didn't really know if it was love, or just that it was so darned forbidden! Buddy was coming down for the wedding, and by the time the day arrived June had pretty much made her mind up. A little taste wouldn't hurt. They could keep the secret, and it would be just between them. Yes! That's it, a little *secret*.

The day arrived. The actual wedding was done at Christine's home. The porch was laid out very well. Christine's mother was a gentle soul who had a well kept home. Christine was her only child, and this would mean loosing her, even if it were just to Claudette's home around the corner. Angie came down from Dallas, and Buddy arrived right on time. His eyes met June's the moment he walked into the house. It was as if they already had an understanding as if he, too, had surrendered to the desire welling up within the both of them.

The reception moved to Claudette's house, and beyond to the country club as planned. Mike began the evening by eating far too much, and diving into the whiskey. At the country club, he switched to beer, but kept pouring it on as the evening progressed. Tommy was enjoying his wedding immensely. Christina had a very laid back style that everyone loved. She would agree with most anything anyone said, and would usually return any statement with the answer, "Right, right," without having really listened to what was being said at all. She was raised in the Bend. Her entire life had been wealth and privilege, and she had been conditioned for just this day, this life. She would not become a real estate *anything*. She and her Tommy would eventually buy their own home and raise heirs to the Bend fortune. June could chase off after Arabs all she wanted, Christina would stay right here in Texas and eat brisket and drink beer!

Mike fell over about eleven and Tommy broke his party for a minute to take him back to the house. After putting him to bed, and putting his boots in the closet, Tommy returned and continued to drink and make merry with his family and friends. Buddy and June actually stayed away from each other most of the evening, but as the guests began to filter home, or to guest rooms the two found time to walk out on the club's redwood deck to chat.

"Cool tonight," Buddy opened the conversation.

Cigar Box

"Yeah, not cold like the last time we talked." June returned. The light desert wind was blowing her long blonde hair gently around. It extended to her waist. She was wearing the same black gown that she'd worn the previous time Buddy had come to town. In the moonlight her hair shimmered on the black in stark contrast.

"Well ol' Tommy's married." Buddy came over and sat in one of the deck chairs.

"Think they'll work out?"

He nodded, "Yeah, they were meant for each other. Two cheeks of the same ass."

She looked out at the golf course extending away from the clubhouse, "I'm glad *someone's* gonna be happy with their marriage." It was an opening. If Buddy didn't take it she wouldn't offer it again. June didn't have time for fools, or timid men.

"You happy?"

"Told you once that I wasn't."

"How unhappy are you?"

She looked back into the country club. Claudette was gone, as were most of the people. Then, looking out over the golf course she said, "Wanna find out?"

Buddy's heart was in his throat, "Sure. Why not?"

She walked down the redwood steps to the parking lot and proceeded across it to the cart path leading out to the first green. They circled the big fountain that graced the first green, and acted as a natural barrier between them and the view from the clubhouse. She had taken this path many times since moving to the Bend. Buddy was nervously looking behind him when she laughed, and said, "They won't see you. They're all drunk." She followed the path down to the edge of

313

the course where the river met it, and formed a water hazard. Then she went down to the little extension of sand that was Claudette's picnic ground, and the last thing the rancher, Stillwell saw in this life.

"I have a dream about a night like this." June extended her arms and let her hair drift aimlessly on the cool breeze.

"You do?"

"Yeah, only it's out at Maw Maw's ranch. I'm in the shed out back; the one with the two big doors and the little side door that opens toward the house. You know the one I'm talking about?"

"Some. I never hung around Ray's much."

They both laughed and June continued, "Well it's at night, this dream. It's like it is now and everyone is like, 'over yonder,' you know. Anyway, they are too partied out to care, and me and this fella, and I can never see his face, go out back by the shed and start to kiss. Then he starts rubbing me. He kisses me some more. I pull up my dress and he turns me around. He starts making love to me in full sight of the house, but no body can see us even though they're right there. It's so strange. In the dream, even when I'm asleep I can feel it, but we never finish. I always wake up, and I never see his face. And they can't see us from there. Weird, huh?"

Buddy swallowed hard, "Yeah, Weird."

Turning, she looked up toward the country club and then back at Buddy, in his tux, still checking behind him. "Come here."

He walked over to her. They stood there for a minute, and then June took his face in her hands and kissed him. He was so stunned that at first, he didn't

Cigar Box

kiss her in return, and then he put his arms around her. They kissed for a long moment. When they pulled apart, he glanced over his shoulder. June grabbed his face in her hands and turned it toward her once again.

"Hey, I told you; they can't see us from there," she said, and they both sank into the warm west Texas sand.

It was two in the morning when they came slipping back into the house. June went straight to her bedroom and hung up her gown. Buddy loosed his tie and lay on the couch in the formal living area, fully clothed, where he fell asleep. The next day found him there still.

*　　　*　　　*

June was up bright and early making coffee. She got dressed in her "501's" and a light blouse. Mike came easing out of bed late, since it was Saturday and he would not work anyway. The smell of coffee lured him to the kitchen area. He didn't drink it, but made a cup of chocolate instead. He was into his first cup when Buddy came in, still dressed in his tux.

"Well, hey," Mike greeted him, "looks like you got in a little sand last night."

Buddy looked down at his clothes. He'd forgotten to completely brush the sand of the river off before coming home. "Yeah. Got to walking down to the river and sat down for a while. You know the place. Where momma and daddy used to eat."

June was shocked that Buddy would say that so quickly, but after thinking about it for a bit, it was logical. He could always blow off the sand as his attempt to walk off the beer he'd consumed, and after all, he *had* fallen asleep on the couch.

"Guess you're just lucky you wasn't as drunk as me. I'd probably slept down there and woke up with some dog licking me. Remember that time you passed out in the yard and the dog came over and licked you awake, and you woke up and thought the dog was in the house?"

Buddy laughed. He remembered the incident, and bringing it up meant that Mike had bought his explanation of the sand. Mike had been passed out when they returned, but still the events of the last evening were still fresh in his mind.

"Hey, I'm gonna make some eggs," June announced.

"Good idea," Mike returned. "I'll just go get my boots, and I'll be right back."

Mike left and went to his bedroom. June opened the refrigerator and began to take the eggs from a shelf. Buddy was staring at her when she turned around. Their eyes met and she said, "It was just for fun, ok? Don't ever bring it up."

Buddy actually relaxed. June was far cooler than he'd expected. He regretted what had happened now, and was happy that she was strong enough to walk away from it. "Ok," he said. "Friends?"

She smiled, "Always."

About that time Mike called from the bedroom, "Hey, where are my boots?"

While she was breaking the eggs and putting them into a big yellow bowl she'd taken down from a shelf she called back to him, "Tommy put them in the closet

Cigar Box

for you so you wouldn't loose them like you always do."

Mike walked over to the closet and opened the double doors. Sure enough, there were his boots on the floor right beneath June's gown. As he stooped to get them, he saw something on the floor that attracted his eye. Right down directly under June's gown was a small bit of sand! He checked his boots, and there was no sand on them, but he already knew that. He hadn't lost his memory from the night before, and he distinctly remembered Tommy bringing him to bed. His hand trembled as he picked some of the sand up between his thumb and forefinger and rolled it around in his hand. Then, he raised his eyes to the gown. Though June had brushed herself well she had left a bit of sand on the back of the gown. His hand slowly went to the back of the dress and pinched a small bit of the still clinging sand from the gown. He stared at it in disbelief.

June was still scrambling eggs when Mike entered the kitchen. "So, you walked down to the bend of the river, Buddy?"

Without looking up from the newspaper he was glancing over Buddy returned, "Yeah."

Mike walked around the island in the middle of the kitchen and went over near June. "Did you do some walking too, June?"

"No, I came home. I was all partied out. You know that. We woke up together this morning, or did you forget that, too?"

Reaching up, he rubbed the sand still on his fingers into her cheek, not in a rough way, but firm enough for her to feel the grit, and he asked, "Then what's this?"

She looked at him while still stirring the eggs. Buddy stopped reading and looked up at Mike. June stopped stirring the eggs and the three were there in the kitchen just staring at each other. You could almost hear the heartbeats in the kitchen. Finally Mike spoke.

"You two had a good time, huh?"

Still, there was a long silence. The look between June and Buddy told more than words could ever say. June suddenly ran from the room, dropping the bowl into the floor as she left. The two young men stood there staring at each other.

"That wasn't necessary," Mike finally spoke.

Buddy looked down at the table, "It never is, Mike. What can I say?"

Mike had never been as physical as Buddy, so all he could do was stand there and be humiliated. He finally just shook his head and walked from the kitchen, heading back to his bedroom. Claudette was coming into the kitchen, alerted by the sound of the crashing bowl.

"What's wrong," she asked, but Mike didn't turn, instead he just kept walking toward the rear of the house. She turned to Buddy, "What's going on?"

Buddy stared at his coffee. "Problem between me and June."

Claudette looked into his eyes and knew what the "problem" was. Then, she looked at the spilled eggs on the kitchen floor and *knew* what the problem was. "You had an affair with your sister in law?"

"Not really an 'affair' ma, just a 'moment."

"A 'moment," Claudette returned. "You had a 'moment' with your sister in law?"

Cigar Box

Buddy could do no more than just hang his head and sit. He was a terrible sight sitting there with his tuxedo rumpled, and still covered with the sand from the bend of the river where he'd lay down with June. Just then, they both heard a loud noise from the rear end of the house. Buddy jumped and ran from the location of the sound with Claudette right behind him, and Claudette's husband, Bill, who was just now emerging from the master suite following the both of them. When they all arrived in June's bedroom, they found her holding the side of her face and Mike looming over her.

"Well?" Mike's face was red, and he was trembling.

June looked up at him with rage, "Well what?"

"Well, why? Why'd you go down there with Buddy?" He raised his hand again, but both Buddy, and his father grabbed Mike, who offered only token resistance.

"What are you doing, Mike," Buddy shouted.

"What do you mean, 'what am I doing?' "Look what happened last night!"

"Then why don't you hit *me*?"

The answer was very plain why he didn't hit Buddy. Buddy would hit back. It was easier to hit June than to face the beating he knew Buddy would give him. He just stared at Buddy and shook. Buddy looked at June. She was sitting there on the bed with blood trickling from her nose. He noticed that there was not a tear in her eye, though. She was sitting up proud and not looking away from anyone in the room. Then Claudette spoke, "You three get outta here! Let

Wilbur Witt and Pamela Woodward

me be with her. Go out in the back yard. Ya'll can fight it out out there if you have to. Now go!"

Her husband pushed the two young men from the room and they headed for the back door of the house. Claudette went to the rest room, fetched a wet, cold cloth, and returned to the bedchamber where June was still sitting.

"Told you that black dress was gonna get you in trouble, little sister."

"Oh, mom, I been courting this trouble all my life. Men always were my downfall. Sometimes I fall a little harder than others. Maybe you should have sold me to that Arab fella."

Claudette reached and wiped the blood from her young face. June flinched a bit as it touched, and then allowed her to clean the wound.

"I'm not going to ask you why."

"You know why. Mike is not a man. He's less than a man."

"He's my son."

"So is Buddy."

"Not the same."

June looked up at her; "Buddy isn't the same to you as Mike?"

"No, no, that's not what I mean at all. What I mean is Buddy and Mike are different. You need to recognize the difference, and appreciate Mike for what he is. I get all riled up at him for being to stupid to pass the state test, but then he goes out and does up all the Christmas lights for me 'cause he loves the season, or he cooks up pork chops for everyone 'cause he likes to cook. Mike is just Mike. That's all."

Cigar Box

"Claudette, even *I* passed the state test! He's lazy, and he's stupid! But it's all over now, I guess."

The old broker took the girl's face in her hands and looked into her eyes, "No it ain't. Now you messed up, but it ain't the end of the world. We'll get past this."

June just shook her head, "I don't think so. I think I really screwed up."

Just then there was a knock at the door. Claudette reached over from the bed and opened the door. Mike was standing there, "Mom, can I speak to my wife?"

"You gonna hit her some more?"

"No, we just need to talk."

The older woman rose and walked from the room leaving the couple sitting on the bed alone. Mike reached over and slowly kicked the door closed.

"Sorry I hit you."

"I had it coming, but that's your one free one, ok. No more today, I feel bad enough. If Ray were alive you know how bad he'd beat you?"

"And I'd have it coming. I'm sorry. June, why? What did I do that was so bad?"

June looked into his eyes. "It's what you didn't' do, Mike. You treat me like I'm a piece of furniture. I just dress up your room *when* you need me here."

"But, I love you."

"I recon. I don't know Mike. Maybe we got married too soon." She looked directly into his eyes, "Mike, you never take any time with me. I'm just something you use, and then you go and get another sandwich. If you had been with me last night I wouldn't have gone to the river. You left me *alone* Mike. You left me alone!"

Inside June knew that she had planned the entire thing. She'd counted on Mike getting drunk and passing out, but she couldn't admit that out loud. She had to push it off on him. She'd been planning this for some time; only she wished she'd been smart enough to knock the sand off of the entire dress! Damn! How stupid! She remembered the sand from the SPJST hall getting her caught with her mom on that night long ago. Seemed like the west Texas sand had been drifting in and out of her life for a long time.

He reached over and put his arm around his wife, "No, we never got a chance. You were in Kuwait, or Dallas, or New York. We just need a place to call our own."

Somehow, his words struck a chord within June that resounded of truth. "You might be right. I wonder how things would work out if we were on our own."

"I think it would be much better. Maybe we need to look for another place to live. Tennessee wasn't that bad. It's a little slower than here maybe, but we could get a fresh start. We could make our own way."

As he spoke her heart began to glow. The idea or a new start rang true in her soul. "When could we go?"

"We could call dad, and he'd have us a room. We could leave tonight. It could all be over and done with, and this would be just a bad memory."

"What about my job?"

Mike laughed, "Mom just keeps you around there 'cause you're her daughter in law. You don't think you really have a job, do you?"

Cigar Box

June's pride was hurt, but she considered that a small sacrifice to get out of this mess, "No, I s'pose not. But I have my license now."

Mike just smiled and his look showed his overwhelming lack of concern for the fact that she had achieved something he never could!

"Ok, then. Now, don't tell mom, OK? I'll go over to a pay phone and call dad in Tennessee and let him know we're driving up." Then, reflecting on what he'd said and knowing that leaving without telling Claudette anything would not work he continued, "You tell mom that we're going away for a day or so, and when we get there we'll get clothes and all."

June nodded her head, and Mike left the room. She sat there for a moment and looked through her bedroom window at the Bend. Standing, she pulled the lace curtains back and peered out through the window. Her face was still smarting from the slap. She was pathetic. Standing there in her 501's looking at all she'd ever wanted in life. The Bend! Her dream! Gone! Why had she done such a thing? She knew why she'd done it. She'd done it for the passion, for the moment. If only she'd gotten all the sand off her gown. If only she hadn't lied! She could have told Mike that she went and found Buddy sleeping on the sand and helped him to the house, but she didn't do that. She lied, and there in that lie was her undoing. Just then, she noticed someone coming into the room. It was Angie. The older girl sat on the bed. June turned from the window and looked into her eyes, and for the first time began to cry, but not for the adultery she'd been caught in, but the fact that for the first time she realized that she'd lost the Bend because of it.

"Feeling alright?"

"Yeah. I'll be ok."

"You need to learn to cover your tracks little sister."

The words surprised June. Angie wasn't condemning her, or fussing, just telling her to learn to hide it all better.

"That's odd, coming from you. You're Miss Perfect."

The words weren't meant to sting, but they came out that way. June was sorry immediately, "I'm sorry, Angie. I didn't mean it to come across like that."

"Oh, no problem. The key word there is 'Miss.' Did you ever wonder why I stay in Dallas. There's a need here in the Bend for my specialty. What with all these fat cats with bad backs down here, I'd clean up, but then, I couldn't live the life I choose to live."

June shook her head, and the doctor knew that what she was driving at was far beyond the young lady's understanding, so she continued, "Did you ever notice that I never come down here with a boyfriend?"

Slowly the realization came to June, and her eyes widened. She didn't draw back from Angie, for she'd known her all of her life, but she froze a bit.

"You are a lesbian?"

"Yes, I am. A little gift from loosing my dad at a young age for a Christmas present, and watching my mother die of cancer. I am gay. And my denial took my childhood, my pride, my very soul, until I went to Dallas to attend Medical School, and it was there I realized just who, and what I truly was. I come home now, enjoy my family, and go back to Dallas and help my patients and live the life that I choose to live. June,

Cigar Box

you made a mistake, but I'm the first to tell you, you are a woman of passion and my brother-cousin, Mike, well, hon, he ain't got it! Never will have it. You just need to learn to dust off a little better, that's all."

She leaned over and kissed June gently on the cheek, "Now that's a 'sister' kiss, you understand? Buddy's made enough problems 'round here without us having another scandal."

She winked and June smiled.

No one noticed when Buddy silently slipped away early that evening to try and find peace in the arms of Sabrina. He wondered why he hadn't spent last night in her place. It certainly would have not had the repercussions that the liaison with June had caused. Still, there was a captivating factor about her. His emotions tumbled violently between shame, and a strange attraction.

Sabrina exploded, "You screwed June?"

Buddy could do no more than hang his head. "I wish you wouldn't be so blunt."

The girl put her hands on her hips and shook her head, "What would you call it then. Please don't use the word, 'love' for what you did. Do you know how bad that is. You're Catholic. I'm Catholic. You come over here and sleep with me, and then you do something like that?"

Buddy reached for her hand, but she snatched it from him. Then, after several moments she sat on the sofa near him and slowly put her arms around him. "The Catter has always been a man trap. You knew that. Why did you fall for her?"

Buddy looked into Sabrina's eyes and knew he'd found his life partner.

In San Antonio Tommy and Christina were blissfully ignorant of all of this. True to tradition they had slipped away just after the reception, and after Tommy had bedded Mike down and put his boots in the closet, and drove to San Antonio. Claudette had not called them and disturbed their honeymoon. They would find out soon enough when they returned.

At twilight Claudette and her husband were taking some wine on the porch, the very porch where June and Mike had been married.

"Hon, I'm sorry this had to happen," her husband said as he poured the wine into her glass.

"Trash."

"Pardon?"

"Trash. Just like Memphis. That's why I left and came here. My people were all trash. Just doing anything that came into mind. Sleep with a cousin; kill a brother, just anything that come into their pointed little heads. I thought I'd put enough desert between me and that kind of behavior so that I never had to look at it again."

Bill knew that he had to take the blame for Buddy's behavior. Buddy was *her* son when he achieved, and he was *his* son when he made mistakes. Though Buddy was not her natural child she had raised him, taken him to all his band practices, wiped his nose when he had a cold, and now she was shamed with him.

"I'm sorry."

"Ain't no sorry." She fought for a moment to control herself, and then, choking slightly, she said, "That little girl was a bright light for me. I had hopes for her. I *really* thought she'd be just like me. Lord, I

Cigar Box

could see it in her eyes." Claudette looked away briefly and wiped her eyes. "She'd work her pretty little butt off in that office, and now…this!"

They looked out over the greens bordering their property, and Claudette whispered quietly, "Whore!"

*   *   *

Later that evening Mike and June silently got into the new truck while the family was sleeping. They forgot to mention to Claudette that they were leaving, in spite of Mike's intended dodge. June made sure that her "501's" were in the truck, and she was wearing her new red boots. As they drove through town, she noticed Buddy's truck parked behind Sabrina's trailer. The lights were off and she knew they two were together. She felt unexplained jealousy, but quickly swallowed it. She was in enough trouble already. Mike went through the town's single red light and drove toward the interstate. June watched as the blinking red light receded in the rear view mirror. All of her dreams were receding with it. All of her hopes, her ambitions, and yes, a bit of love. A torn understanding of love she'd found somewhere beyond the second hole last night; a tangle of emotions that rose within her upon seeing Buddy's truck at Sabrina's home. Before her lay Memphis, and uncertainty. They passed the cemetery and she strained to see Ray's grave, but could not. Behind her lay disgrace, and the only real home she'd ever known. She looked at Mike, driving through the night. She almost wanted to open the door and leap out and go running back to Claudette's house, begging for mercy. He could never support her in the style of the Bend. She didn't know what to expect when he got to "Real Daddy's" house. She'd never met "Real Daddy." She'd met hers, and was not impressed. "Why do men have to be such children," she asked herself as the pickup truck turned onto the interstate, and headed east.

Memphis

"Real Daddy" was sitting up waiting when the pair arrived in the wee hours of the morning. June was looking very rough from the trip to Tennessee. The major part was the trip through Texas. They lived in west Texas, which was as far away as east is from west. The trip through Arkansas didn't really take all that long once Texas was out of the way. The entire trip June could feel imaginary bonds pulling her back to the Bend, yet she knew that the very reason she was living in the Bend at all was driving the truck that she was riding in!

Mike was silent most of the trip. As the events of the last few days soaked into his mind he drifted from rage to hurt, and back to rage again. He, too, was leaving the security of a home he'd grown up in to go to his biological father's home. He wasn't a high school boy anymore. He was facing real issues here, and Claudette wasn't there to pull him out of it. He imagined her rage when she found what he'd done. June would just stare through the window at the countryside, and he'd drive, faster than the speed limit, and stare at the road. The landscape had turned from the deserts of west Texas to the prairies of central Texas, to the Pine trees of east Texas. Texas is like five states rolled into one. June got to roll across all five in a four-wheel drive pick up truck!

"Ya'll can sleep in that room," Real Daddy said, as they walked into his shack. "So this is the little lady?" he said, eyeing her up and down. June felt dirty as the fat man looked at her.

June thought that the home she'd had with Ray and her mother was bad, but this was *bad*! The wood frame shack hadn't been painted for at least ten years. The roof was history. As you walked across the porch, it creaked; a far cry from the exquisite porch that had entertained guests the night of her wedding. The floors were equally bad, and it was dirty! Every single piece of chicken Real Daddy had ever eaten was somewhere on the floor, and the stench rose into the air from it!

"I deserve this," June thought. "This is my reward for what I've done. I'll get by. I'll make do."

They slept for a long time, getting over the rigors of the trip. Mike's father went to work, and came back, and they were still sleeping. Then, the following day they woke and went to talk with the older man.

Mike's father was very critical of June and made his feeling known very soon.

"So you like to fool around, huh?"

She flashed her eyes in disgust at him and said, "Hey, I made a mistake. Like you never made one, huh?"

Addressing Mike as if she wasn't in the room at all he replied, "Smart mouth on her ain't it?"

Cigar Box

Mike took the cue from him and said, "Yeah, and it gets smarter all the time."

"Well, you just keep that little mouth shut around here little lady. There ain't a place' round here for you to slip off to and mess around." Everything he said was designed to be a humiliation for her. Ed didn't like women. He hadn't liked women since his divorce from Claudette and he used that event to explain every failure in his life. He sat around and put on more weight and told everyone that it was all Claudette's fault.

Claudette's reputation in Memphis was not the image of the highly motivated and successful real estate entrepreneur that she enjoyed in Texas but of the skinny girl who left home and divorced her husband (a scandal in itself) and went "out west" to "whore" around with "some builder." June was her running buddy and so therefore she, too, must be just as bad, if not worse than this evil woman who had "ruined" poor Ed! June was now officially paying not only for her sins, but any real or imagined sins that Claudette may or may not have committed too!

"My smart mouth will talk anytime it wants," June said, trying to gain some small bit of her respect back.

Suddenly, Mike lunged across the table and let go of all the fury he had built up on the trip from Texas to Tennessee. The slap sent June reeling backwards onto the wooden floor. Mike was upon her in an instant, "How's your mouth now, bitch? How's that mouth now?"

She looked at him with absolute hate, "Ray would kill you."

Grabbing her by her long blonde hair, he pulled her up. "Yeah he would, but you know what? That dope-smoking looser is just a little bit dead, now ain't he?"

Ed was leaning forward laughing with fiendish glee. He was actually drooling while Mike slapped June. She looked at the man and loathed every cell in his body. Still, she "deserved" this. At least it couldn't get any worse. At least this was the immediate reaction and she reasoned that it had to let up after a little time. She couldn't have been more wrong.

Thus began June's long journey into purgatory. Each day was a new ordeal, a new challenge. Ed made her life a hell when Mike wasn't there and when Mike *was* there then they both made her miserable.

She wasn't actually "in" Memphis, but a little outside of town on the northern edge. There wasn't much to the area, just a convenience store with gas pumps and a clerk that thought he was Don Juan, and a little white Pentecostal church. She went to the church the following Sunday after her arrival. Mike wouldn't go, and Ed hadn't been to church in years. She sat in the back, but soon the preacher's sermon warmed her heart and she began to actually relax. After services she stayed a bit and chatted with the people, who were genuinely friendly, wanting to know where she was from, and why she had come to their area. She began to feel as if she were being accepted, perhaps even getting past the events in the Bend, perhaps even the Bend itself. Ironically, the readings that Sunday were centered on the rich man and the needle's eye. June began to wonder if perhaps the Bend itself had put her in the position she had found herself in. It seemed to

Cigar Box

her as if for all the money and comfort there was something inherently evil about the Bend. It was as if there were some long-standing inequities that rested there and must be answered for.

Arriving back at Ed's shack she genuinely had a glow about her and came into the house very happy. Mike and Ed were just beginning to stir and both were roaming around without shirts.

"Where'd you go?" Mike asked.

"That little church down the way. I saw it the other day and I thought I'd go there."

Ed moved about the shack throwing papers, and candy wrappers around as he found his old recliner chair and TV remote. Turning the TV on and beginning to flick through the channels he acted as if June were not even there. She cleared a spot and sat on the sofa, if it could be called that, and started to watch the flickering screen with him. She could feel the tension rise for a few moments. Then, almost without looking at her, Ed asked, "Did you tell them you were a whore?"

June could feel the absolute evil coming off the man. She could honestly feel that what she had done was far less than this man's attitude. She had *committed* a sin; he *was* a sin. He was something foul living in a rotting body that used good air other people could put to better use.

"Why no," she replied. "I usually take Sunday off."

Ed sat there in his dim-witted way and let the statement soak in. Then he said, "Mike took care of that little smart mouth last night, didn't he?"

"Yeah. I'll bet you took care of Claudette's smart mouth too, didn't you? That's why she lives at the Bend and you live here."

"That's 'nough," Mike interceded. "You show respect for my pa."

June looked at Mike, "Oh God! Respect? For that? She pointed at Ed. "And since when did you use words like 'pa' Mike? You started talking like that when we got here. Well it's not cool Mike! It's stupid!"

She jumped up and ran from the room to one of the two bedrooms only to find it full of candy wrappers and old food. She looked through the smoky glass to the high grass outside and began to cry. This was too much. Even a shack behind Fat Eddie's was better than this. She slowly began to actually hate Mike and Ed. She now understood why she'd cheated. Perhaps she'd seen this side of Mike all along. All the time in the world at the Bend would not take the trash out of Mike. She felt like this was God's reward to her for her adultery. In eternity Veronica, and her ever-present companion discussed this.

"I deserved it."

"God doesn't deal like that. He didn't punish you for what you did, you punished yourself."

"How can you say that? Look at this filth! Look at this shack! I was in the Bend, and God put me here because of what I did with Buddy."

The man looked at her and smiled, "You would never have thought it so bad before you had lived in the Bend, but now it's terrible. Why didn't you just clean it up?"

Cigar Box

"Because I'm not their slave! They are pigs. Both of them. I know now why I did what I did. Look at them, sitting there in their Lazy Boys stuffing themselves with 'fat boy' food! Disgusting!" She puzzled for a moment, "Aren't their hearts supposed to blow up after a while?"

"But you deserve it?"

"Yes, I did. I wouldn't have been here if I hadn't led Buddy off that night."

"Key phrase there, June. *You* led him off. You don't think this was a fifty-fifty arrangement?"

She smiled and looked at him. Then she replied, "Buddy didn't control anything. I did! He'd never have had the guts to come on to me if I hadn't led him far enough away from the others. I did that. Did you see him run right back to that Mexican? He'd have never messed with me if I hadn't led him in."

"Why did you 'lead him in?"

"'Cause I wanted to, that's why. I wanted to be away form Mike for a while, with his endless food-fest, and I wanted to feather my nest a bit. Mike wasn't going to make anything of himself, and Buddy always had that drive. He kept hanging around that bar keeper and never seemed to want to settle down."

"What did you think was going to come of this? Surely you must have known Claudette would never condone it. And you don't need to think too lowly of that *barkeep.*"

Veronica smiled, "Dr. Angel, I ain't upset over what I did, I'm upset over getting caught! If I hadn't had one too many glasses of wine that night I'd have checked that stupid gown better and that sand would not have been on that floor."

"Didn't you think of spiritual repercussions?"

She sat down on the steps of the shack and looked at Dr. Angel. "Dr. Angel, are you religious?"

He laughed, "Now that's a bit of a question isn't it? I mean, look where we are!"

"I know where we are. That don't mean nothing. That just means that we're still alive. We're still conscious. That don't prove the Bible, or nothing like that."

"How can you accept what is happening to you right now, and not believe?"

"Because I'm in control of me, that's why. You look at things and think that God makes it happen, but I see things and think that's just the way it is."

"Veronica, there is an order to the universe. For every plus there is a minus, and for every evil there is a good. There is a great check out counter in the sky. We all go there."

"Don't wanna talk about it!"

"You have to. That is what we're here for."

"Don't want to. You worry about it."

"You have to worry about it, June. There are other things involved here besides just you."

"Are you talking about my son?"

The man nodded. She continued, "He is innocent. He's no part of this."

"He is a big part of this. In fact, he is the core of this. He is the main reason for all of this. Everything goes back to him."

"Even he can't be free."

"Perhaps. It all depends on you."

"Explain."

Cigar Box

"I waited over twenty years at the intersection for that car to come along. I had to make payment for my errors, but the man who sealed me was more at fault than I. He put me there to hide his own guilt. Then he kept me there to make sure that your son died in that wreck. He transcends time and space, and he keeps going back there to 'tweak' the results a bit more. The only thing that's screwed up his plan is the fact that we left the scene and with all the layers of reality he can't tell who the real Veronica is. That's why he killed Ray."

Veronica froze, "He killed Ray?"

"Yes. He thought it would bring you back to that level and he'd be able to identify you and place you back at the intersection. You still don't understand, do you?"

"No. Why is it so important that I be with you, seeing all this."

"Because the person I met back in Memphis was a self centered little wench. She'd save herself no matter what. I'm trying to make you understand why you can't save yourself. You must save little Mike. This man; this shaman will stop at nothing to keep his power. He's been double crossing his own people for over one hundred years!"

"What do you mean?"

"Watch."

In a moment of time Veronica found herself back at the bend of the river, only the time was different. There was no subdivision; in fact, there was no ranch. The grass was wild, and very tall. In the little clearing where Claudette had eaten her tuna sandwich with her husband, and where the rancher, Stillwell would spend

Wilbur Witt and Pamela Woodward

lazy afternoons with June's mother, and where June would commit the act that drove her from her beloved Bend was a camp filled with Indians.

"Who are they?" Veronica asked.

"They are Comanche. They come here in the spring migrating to the milder climate of the Davis Mountains. This bend of the river is very sacred to them. Look! See the children playing."

She walked over to the children. They were so happy; so relaxed that she wanted to be with them. There was a young girl playing among the stones, by the bend of the river. The maid looked alarmingly like Sabrina. Features of timeless beauty etched into her face as she ran her hands through the clear water of the bend of the river. Her hair was long and black. She was very healthy, and very happy. Veronica watched for the longest time and then turned to the man and said, "It's really their land isn't it?"

"Yes, it is. People like your father, Mr. Stillwell, took it from them illegally. But he didn't do it all by himself. He was helped by someone these people trusted."

She watched the girl a bit more. "We have no right to it."

"And if you have no right to it, how could you have 'lost' it?"

She pondered for a moment, "Can't loose what was never really yours, huh?"

"No, you can't."

"How does this all relate to my son?"

"All wrongs become right in time. It depends on who writes the history. In his generation, it *will* be his

Cigar Box

land. He will be the rightful owner because of his sister."

"Who?"

He pointed to the girl playing with the water, "Her great, great, great grand daughter."

"Sabrina?"

"Sabrina's daughter. You know that your child is not Mike's son, don't you?"

Veronica stared coldly at him, "Yes, I guess I've always known."

"That makes the girl the descendant of the Comanche. Your son is her half brother, *and* he is the descendant of the Stillwells. You see? Little Mike is the true blend of both cultures and will be the rightful master of the Bend because Buddy's daughter by Sabrina is half sister to your son. If Little Mike lives then he will grow to be the master of all that Claudette has assembled. Yet, within his heart will beat the love for his sister. In time the land will return to the Comanche. But someone is there who does not want him to have that power. There is someone who stands to loose a lot if little Mike grows up."

"But the land has been sold. Dr. Angel, even *you* can't understand how locked up ol' Claw-dette has that land!"

"Sold but will return. All that you know of as the Bend will be brought to nothing in the end. All the homes will one day be gone, and all the people will move away."

"How can that be?"

The man smiled, and said, "You ask too many questions. Just know that for now, you must make the right choice. If you make the right choice the person who wishes to harm little Mike will not succeed."

"Yes," she pointed to the little girl still playing in the rocks. Slowly a smile spread across her face and she whispered, "Little Mike's sister."

"Yes, his sister. She is the reason little Mike is the shaman. He is her brother. This is the mistake the shaman made. He did not know the affair between you and Buddy, which put Mike in this position."

She nodded and knelt to watch the little girl play among the rocks. Veronica reached down and played with the sand between her fingers. Just then another man came walking across the sand toward the little girl and stooped to pick her up. His back was to Veronica, so she couldn't see him until he turned. It was Juan!

"It's Juan," Veronica said.

"Yes, it is. He was the shaman, or witch doctor if you will. He would make the deal with the whites that drove the Indians off their land, and he'd even desecrate their graves so as to seal their souls here for eternity, and none of them could progress. And as long as no male heir comes along, he lives. But, like I told you, because of the complicated series of events that led to the birth of your son, and Sabrina's daughter, little Mike is actually the shaman now, and the old man simply missed the point because he had blonde hair and blue eyes. Now he is feverishly prowling time and space to make sure that little boy does not survive Christmas morning in Memphis, because if he does the shaman dies!"

*   *   *

Cigar Box

The phone rang back at the real estate office in west Texas. Claudette picked it up, thinking it was Mike, but instead heard the warped voice of Dish Bob on the other end.

"Claudette?"

"Bob?"

"Claudette, come get me."

"What's going on Bob? Where you at?"

"I don't know. Claudette, I don't know where I'm at. Come get me."

"How can I come and get you if I don't know where you are?"

The phone went silent for a few minutes and then another voice came on the line, "Is anyone there?"

"Yes. This is Claudette Montgomery. Who is this?"

"Deacon White. The Reverend seems to have had too much to drink. Can you come over here and get him."

Claudette was at the same time appalled and amused that someone of her wealth would be called to pick up a drunken preacher, but it did take her mind off of Mike for just a while so she said, "Sure. Where are you?"

The man gave the address of an apartment in a nearby town and Claudette drove there to get the preacher. Upon arriving, she found that Bob was asleep on the couch.

"Can't he just sleep it off here?" she asked.

"Oh, no! He can't stay here. He's in sin. He's drunk."

Wilbur Witt and Pamela Woodward

Disgusted, she helped Bob to his feet and led him to the car. He began to come around. "Got too much again."

"You get too much a lot, Dish Bob!"

"Ghosts."

She looked at him puzzled, "Ghosts?"

"Yeah. They come back, Claudette. They have been chasing me for years. Chased me all the way from Anthony, New Mexico. All the preaching in the world don't get rid of them."

"Whose ghosts?"

"Someone dear to me. People can haunt you even while they're still alive, in fact, sometimes that's worse. I can generally drink the dead ones away." Then he paused, and continued, "And I saw June tonight."

"She's gone, Bob. She's not here. How'd you see her?"

"Before I came here I was down by the bend of the river. I saw her standing there with a man. Before I could call out to her she disappeared like a puff of smoke. Claudette, that scared me. Got to drinking right after that. I can't tell these people that story they'll think I'm crazy."

She looked firmly at the fat preacher, "Bob I don't buy a single word of that shit. You are what you are. You got a booze problem. That's all there is to it."

Dish Bob didn't take offence, but continued to stare out through the window at the passing desert. "Claudette, you are going to discover one day that the all mighty dollar is not alive. Remember the man who built the extra barn in the Bible? One night the Lord came and told him his soul was required of him. All your money won't save you on that last day."

"If you really believe that you need to quit passing the plate."

"When was the last time *you* tithed, Claudette?"

She stared out at the headlights processing the road at eighty miles an hour, "When I gave Ray that fifty thousand!"

"And no ghosts chase you?"

"No, I don't have time for that shit!"

"Claudette, there are things going on in this old world you can't put your finger or your checkbook on. I didn't start out to get drunk tonight. I tried to go back to my place and was going to call it a night when suddenly I saw ol' Juan step out of the wall."

She looked at him, "You mean you don't *remember* drinking. If you saw Juan step out of a wall you'd been drinking bubba, no two ways about it. That poor Mexican's been gone since the committee shut him down."

Dish Bob did not back up, "No, I wasn't. It was like he was looking for someone. I don't think he knew I could see him."

"And that's the ghost you saw tonight?"

"Yeah. That's them. I dove off in a bottle and woke up with a phone in my hand calling you. I didn't really know where I was at, but I knew I wasn't going back to that place again."

There was no more conversation between the two all the way back to the Bend. She let Dish Bob sleep it off in her guest room that night. The next day they had breakfast together with her husband, Bill. Claudette brought up the previous night.

"Tell me again what you saw, Bob."

Dish Bob concentrated on his coffee for a minute. "Claudette, I know I drink a bit, but I never drank so much that I seen things, and I wasn't drinking until *after* I saw what I saw yesterday. I saw Juan! He come through the wall, looked this way and that, and then just stepped back through it. Damndest thing I ever did see! I seen it, Claudette, I *seen* it!"

Claudette sipped her coffee, "I saw something like that years ago."

"You did?"

"Yeah, right after my brother died. I was pretty irritated at Ed, but even though I'd said I was going to leave I didn't have the nerve or the money. Then one night I was sleeping and woke up, or rather, something woke me up, and I sat up in bed. Now mind you, I'd never seen old Juan before this, but the man that I would come to know as Juan was standing at the end of my bed. He told me to take Ed's paycheck and my boys and go to the Pecos Valley in Texas. God! I didn't even know where the Pecos Valley was, but the next day I woke up and Ed stupidly left his money in his other pants. I took all of it and just got on a bus."

"That the bus you got off of here?" Bill asked.

"Yeah. Craziest thing I ever done. Just getting on a bus like that.

"How'd you know what town to come to?" Bill asked.

"I didn't. I just rode 'till I run out of money. This little town was it for me."

"And you saw Juan?"

"Yeah. I saw him."

Cigar Box

Bill sipped his coffee, "I've heard stories about him. You know, no one knows how old he is. He was old as hell when he had that little girl Sabrina. Now I guess he's older than hell. He's some kind of spiritual leader of those Mexicans that run with him. Never hurt anybody I guess, but it gives me a chill. You now all this land used to be the Comanche land?"

"Yeah," Claudette said, "but it's *our* land now. Those Indians just need to get it through their head that all that crap's over and done with. You think ol' Juan is pissed off about all that?"

"Lot's of people are. Still all pissed off about loosing the land. Still, *this* land is special to them. It's holy in some way to them."

"Well, I'll tell him just like I told old man Stillwell. Get a mortgage!"

Dish Bob and Bill laughed as they drank their coffee.

*   *   *

Life drifted on in the Bend. The weather turned cooler, but in west Texas there is no change of seasons, only summer and "not summer." Still the cooler winds from the panhandle seemed to bring blessed relief from the desert heat. Every year the newer inhabitants of the Bend swore that the weather was getting hotter each summer and that it was some kind of "global warming" coming about to end the world, but it wasn't. It was just plain old west Texas summer! The social life there abated some and the deer munched the greens unmolested. Those events seemed a lifetime away to those still left in the area. Where a generation ago Barbara's affair with old man Stillwell was the talk of the town now the scandal of the "Catter" was the topic of choice. She'd done it at the Bend, in fact at the very bend of the river where they'd found Mr. Stillwell's body way back when. Like all royalty, the inhabitants of the Bend were watched closely for any flaws or imperfections that may arise. June had provided much entertainment, not just because she was in the Bend but also because she was *from* the other side of town. While outwardly folks talked about the issue with strict Baptist distain, inwardly they were proud that little June had given the rich upstarts of the Bend a run for their money.

There was talk that Claudette had spirited them away in the middle of the night and supported the pair until the scandal died down. The other camp of Bend-watchers said that the old broker had banished June from the Montgomery family and that Mike, in his lusting stupidity, had chased after her, abandoning all his inheritance and lifestyle. Then, too, there was a contingent of young cowboys in town who could privately testify that a liaison with June was not all that hard to arrange and that they had frankly been surprised that she'd "jumped the fence" and gotten into the Bend in the first place!

Dish Bob sobered up as he did periodically, and he made it a point to go out and see after Ray's grave. He felt a strange kinship to the dead plumber. He, too, had known all the stories about June and had wondered how many Ray had heard, and how many he believed. It amazed the fat preacher that such a hard man could be so soft when it came to his little girl, even an adopted little girl. Ray was the one person in the

Cigar Box

world who believed that June was as pure as the driven snow and while he lived no man in the little town had the guts to tell him otherwise. June had kept her private life well concealed from her stepfather and her many boyfriends were glad!

One night, in the cool of autumn, the phone rang in Sabrina's mobile home and she picked it up knowing it would be Buddy on the other end.

"Hello," the expected voice came.

"Hi."

"Been thinking things over a bit. I think more and more I miss the Bend."

"You stirred things up a bit, Buddy. I just imagine your momma is still pissed off at you for what you did to June. You know she's having to live with Mike's slop daddy up in Memphis?"

She could hear Buddy breathing on the other end. "Sabrina, what has happened has happened. I wish I could go back and change it, but I can't. I knew I wanted to be with June at least once when she wore that blasted black dress the first time."

"Buddy, that's not it. You hate Mike. You wanted to hurt Mike! You took the only thing he felt like he had in his life. You profaned their lives, Buddy. I don't know what to think of you. Used to, when we were in school, I thought you were the best looking, smarted guy in town, but now; Buddy, Tommy has more class than that!"

"Don't say that. Please, Sabrina, don't say that. I'll admit this rivalry thing has gone a bit too far, but that's all it is, a rivalry. It ends now! I've realized something."

"What?"

"I love you."

Now there was a long silence on *her* end of the line. "Will you still love me when the Catter wears another black dress?"

"Sabrina, I think there have been enough black dresses in my life. I want to just come home. I want to work with mom and do the best I can for you."

Sabrina felt the goal of a lifetime within her reach. Not the Bend, but Buddy. Her love for him was unrelenting, but she couldn't let him know that. Not just yet. She had to teach him a lesson or she'd never feel comfortable when June was in town.

"I have to think it over, Buddy."

"Sabrina, I'll be here when you think it over. I'll do anything you ask. I'll move back, or if you want, you can move here. You call the shots."

"Buddy, why don't *we* call the shots, ok? I think that will be much better." She softened, "We'll get beyond this. I promise. We'll make it."

Buddy felt as if a huge press had been lifted from his heart. The chains that June had placed there had been severed and finally he could really come home.

"What do you want me to do, Sabrina?"

"I don't know just yet. Maybe you need to talk to Claudette."

Buddy felt his heart go like wax, but he knew this was the only way. Claudette did call all the shots. He didn't want to end up like Mike, exiled from home. Even though Mike had done it to himself, Buddy wanted the Bend, the golf course and Sabrina.

"I'll get with her. I love you."

After a long silence Sabrina answered, "And I've always loved you, Buddy."

Cigar Box

Tommy and Christina marked all their days as a new experience. The "scandal" didn't affect them one way or another. Tommy was struggling with his coke habit and Christina was struggling with Tommy. She was finding that knowing him as a boy from the neighborhood was far different from being married to him and seeing him in all of his various moods. While he wasn't abusive in the way that Mike was, he was concerned more with his drugs than with Christina and therein laid the major problem. All of this, of course, had to be kept from Claudette who would loose the rest of her mind that she had left from the June/Buddy incident if she ever found out that her "baby" was on drugs. Claudette didn't believe in any "rehab" she believed to throwing people to the wolves for as long as it took to bring them to their senses. Tommy and Christina did *not* want this! They had a good life in the Bend and they wanted to keep it that way.

They'd made contact with June in Memphis, but Ed kept this to a minimum. June's heart leapt when the first call from the Bend came, but soon it became apparent that this was a solo effort on Tommy's part and had no official "sanction" from Claudette. June began to really understand the gravity of what she'd done. Repeatedly she chastised herself. If only she'd gotten *all* the sand off that silly black dress! If only she'd not worn that silly black dress. If only she'd not lain with Buddy. Ultimately she was realizing if only she'd *not* married Mike! She would sit for long hours and watch the moon, remembering the moon in Kuwait. Inside she'd laugh about the "operation" and then she'd plunge into deep depression as she realized that those days were gone forever. She felt like a sailor who realized he'd never go to sea again.

Claudette found herself missing the spunky little blonde, but she was deeply disturbed in what had happened to her family. She'd sit in her office for long hours staring at contracts she could not read and remember how easy, and unashamed it had been when June was around. Like June, she stared through the window of her bedroom and saw all her dreams vanish. She had the idea that all the boys would follow in her footsteps. She envisioned a great family corporation spanning worldwide based right here in the Bend. The only thing that was spanning worldwide was her family being more and more broken up. Slowly, but surely Claudette was discovering something in her heart that she'd never known, forgiveness. Not all at once, but ever so slowly she realized that if Buddy, June and Mike would just come home that perhaps they would all be able to make it just work out!

Bill handled his grief alone. He never let on how her really felt. He, too, had had a soft spot for June, but he knew that her name "Catter" was a well-earned one. He'd heard the stories around Fat Eddie's and he knew that most of them were true. The same blood that flowed thorough Barbara's veins flowed through June's, only more concentrated, and more deadly! Barbara had lost the Bend before it *was* the Bend, but June had been there, lost it, and Bill knew that she wasn't just sitting up at Ed's in Memphis eating pork skins and forgetting. The way he saw it June was a deliberate manipulator. Her manipulation had failed, but if he knew June, he knew she had more tricks in her bag, and he also knew that she was more than a

Cigar Box

match for the hillbillies she now found herself in the midst of.

He watched his wife brood over the situation and he knew that this thing must be resolved. Claudette didn't know it, but her "edge" was going away. She wasn't landing the deals like she'd been doing. Her aggressiveness was waning and it wasn't because she was getting old. If was because her mind was now preoccupied with family instead of business. Bill wondered if it was possible for a shark to starve, or grieve itself to death, and all the while, he watched Claudette doing just that! She needed some big project, some *cause* to spur her into action again.

The family would wander down to Fat Eddies to eat fish on Fridays, but it was empty. Ray was gone. Mike was gone. June was gone. Buddy and Angie were *always* gone but now it seemed as if they were a little more gone than usual. They sat there and ate the fish as if they were condemned, and this was their last meal. Each one feeling as if the eyes of the town were on them, which indeed they were! Not far from Fat Eddie's Sabrina poured beer and waited for Buddy to spring the question on Claudette about his return. For the first time her entire world, her very life depended upon Claudette's mood, and suddenly the old broker didn't look that stable to her. Sabrina had dropped by the little real estate office and been surprised by all the clutter, and dust that had accumulated. If Claudette or Bill were not in the office simply was not open. There were even rumors that they were planning to close it down. Claudette no longer solicited listings, not even from ranchers whom originally had been her stock and trade. Everyone imagined that her investments were doing well, but like Bill, the town knew that Claudette was in a period of mourning and all were waiting to see just how she'd come out on the other side.

How she would come out of this slump truly rested in Memphis. Though she hadn't confided in Dish Bob, Claudette did have ghosts. Now June had taken off and gone right back where Claudette's ghosts were. June was with the one person in the world that Claudette loathed! She knew Ed was pounding away at June, not that she didn't deserve it, but she still didn't want anyone to put up with him. As Mike had grown older, he began to put on weight like Ed and Claudette had fought tooth and nail to keep it off him. She didn't want a "little Ed" around her. She could just imagine how he must be blowing up now up there in Memphis all pissed off at Buddy and Ed throwing every slur and fried pie he could find at him! She wondered inwardly if Mike was like Ed in his private life too. If this were the case, she really couldn't blame June for looking around. Then, she'd hate herself for thinking such a thing. Still, as a woman, she realized that Buddy had Bill's rugged looks, and perhaps more. Maybe June had been attracted to Buddy just as she had been attracted to Bill. Why hadn't she married Buddy then? He was never around. Buddy took off to Houston looking for fame and fortune. She found herself wishing he'd call and want to come home. She knew that Mike's internal jealousy would make him return if he knew Buddy was back sopping up all the gravy. Claudette was beginning to worry that perhaps she was thinking a little too much about all this and it was costing her business.

Cigar Box

Springer had been "on" her about moving forward, and she couldn't confide in him as to what the real problem was. He perceived her as strong and able and she didn't want him to see her at a weak moment, but just as she thought she had a grip, the whole thing would come crashing in again and put her down. It would take her a long while to get back up. There had been offers for her to buy out some smaller west Texas builders but she had sat by and let the deals lapse. This had alarmed Springer, but he'd trusted her judgment.

So, in her own way, June had brought the pomp and ceremony of the Bend to its knees. What had spawned in the sand of the bend of the river now spread like a cancer threatening to paralyze and destroy everything that Claudette had built, and she didn't even seem to care. Somehow, someway, this had to be resolved. What good were a big house and a fortune with no one there to enjoy it? Claudette found that she was haunted by the specter of the rancher Stillwell staring at her from beyond the bend of the river with the top of his head blown off and the slow realization that perhaps one day she, too, would understand what drove him to put that gun in his mouth. She began to think that perhaps, as some had said, the Bend *was* cursed. It was as if there was a debt to be paid, and that all that lived there paid it in installments, just like a mortgage; a mortgage to the Devil to be paid in souls. As she stared through her bedroom window to the bend of the river beyond the second green, the broker was determined to *refinance* that note!

Contrition

While the controversy swirled around her back at the Bend, June marched through her hiatus of penance in Memphis. She figured that she deserved whatever Mike dished out, and so she bent down low to the ground and began to endure. Truly in her heart she thought that if she just bore with all the challenges that everything would eventually work out, and one day Mike would just figure that her sin had been covered by her acceptance, and suffering. Two things weren't in June's mind, however; things that she could not possibly know, such as Mike's mental condition, which at best was angry, and at worse were cruel and sadistic. He wanted to pay her in full for her mistake, and never mind that he had had his fling over on Commerce Street, June must pay! Deep inside he harbored deep resentments against his brothers, mother, and stepfather, just about everyone except "Real Daddy," whom he identified more and more with every day. The second thing she didn't count on was a queer sickness that began to overtake her each morning, and as soon as the sickness became apparent,

Cigar Box

the horror of the ramifications became clear, not only for June, but also for the internal politics of the Bend itself, for June was with child!

Whose child? Mike's, or Buddy's? Mike's liaisons with her were few, and far between, and never properly consummated, while Buddy had been with her but once, but it was an exquisite once. A once that rang in her heart still. A once that she felt within her soul, even as they rose from the sand of the bend of the river and tried to sneak, and lie, but no use. Her head was filled with wine that night, but also with a consuming fire that took her common sense, and caused the sand to fall accusingly to the closet floor. She still recalled the jealousy she had felt upon seeing Buddy's truck parked behind Sabrina's trailer. As the weeks progressed, June knew that she simply *must* make Mike think that he, and only he were responsible for the condition she now found herself involved in. She began to be nicer to him, and began to make him feel more in control of his, and her life.

This was in spite of Mike's "Real Da Da" who challenged her at every point. He hated June, and made no secret of it, all the while trying to slip a peek at her in the shower, or coming from her ramshackle bedroom that he provided grudgingly in his shack. He would listen as Mike made love to her, and leer at her in the early morning hours, but June would never say anything about it because she thought it to be her "penance" for her "sin" and therefore it was allowed. She felt violated! Whenever "Real Daddy" was in the room she could feel him undressing her with his eyes. She hated to bathe in his shack, but she did so if for no other reason than to wash off his eyes. Oh, but if she could pluck them from his fat head!

And he was fat! God was he fat! He was a literal pig. Why did God let such a pig live? June could readily see just why Claudette had divorced him. He was five foot nothing, and weighed in excess of three hundred pounds. He kept a beard because he thought it made him look "cool," and he smelled like vinegar. No, vinegar was a polite way of putting it. He smelled like piss! One big fat pool of walking piss. His house, if you could call it that, was really a tarpaper shack in the outskirts of Memphis. He prided himself in saying things that he thought was "country" like, "Git in there and cook up some of dem good grits." He pronounced grits, "greeits," so as to drag out the word and make it even more obnoxious. She hated that, and she hated him, but then, again, he hated her.

Each day Mike would go to work, in construction, and "Real Da Da," and June would sit in the little shack on the outskirts of Memphis and hate each other. And what made it worse was as each day passed Mike became more like "Real Da Da." He had always been abusive, but now he had a cheering section. He would routinely slap June, and "Real Da Da" would just laugh and cheer him on! He was so uncouth that once when June asked him if he ever had a girl friend, he replied that he went to a local gambling hall on occasion and "got some of that stinky stuff on him." June was appalled! For real! She had never met whiter trash than "Real Da Da!"

Finally, about a month into her pregnancy she told Mike about it.

"Are you sure?"

Cigar Box

"Sure, I'm sure. You think I'd be wrong about something like that?"

"Well, I don't know. It's the first time, you know."

"I know, Mike! I'm pregnant, ok?"

Mike began to take care with her as far as slapping her around, and called Claudette to let her know that she was about to be a grandmother. Claudette was thrilled. Actually, she thought that this would bind the couple together. She had taken a bit of a "hit" when they left in the middle of the night to flee to Memphis, but she'd forgiven that, viewing the facts of the events preceding the leaving. She didn't see how Mike could really stay in the Bend at the time, with the affair out in the open such as it was. He didn't have the courage to confront Buddy, so to run away was just about all the choice that he had in the matter.

June began to show her condition, and Mike began to find interests elsewhere. The nightlife in Memphis was appealing to a man who perceived himself as wronged, and one night he listened to a blues singer put out some lyrics that touched his soul, albeit in the wrong way.

>Lord, she's had the nightlife
>Long 'fore she had you
>And you might think she loves you
>But I got you some news.

>That woman been in the fast lane
>Since she was seventeen
>And you might thing she'll settle down
>But the years done made her mean

Wilbur Witt and Pamela Woodward

She's a cheatin' woman
And cheatin' woman ain't gonna change
No matter what you call it
It gonna petrify your brain

You go running to your family
Say this gal gives you the blues
And they say, "Get away, boy
We done told you what to do!"

Then you turn to drugs and whiskey
To neutralize the pain
And every time she plays
You'll shoot that poison to your brain

Cheatin' woman
Cheatin' woman ain't gonna loose
No matter what you call it
It gonna boil down to the blues.

When she finally up and leaves you
Well it's gonna be too late.
Cause then you'll hear the devil
Just a laughin' in your face

Better hear the words I'm singing
Cause I won't sing you wrong
You won't find no better words
Than what you're hearin' in this song

Cheatin' woman
Cheatin' woman ain't gonna change
You can try to cope
But it gonna run you plumb insane!

Cigar Box

And it did run Mike insane! In time, he found diversion in Memphis in the form of a Creole girl that promised him the earth, moon, and stars, and he brought all his fears, and hate home to June. He was careful not to hit her in the stomach, and careful not to leave any marks on her. "Real Da Da" watched with glee and the young couple fought night after night over the same thing. He had a natural hate for Buddy because that was not his natural son, and he had an axe to grind from way back when Claudette had left him standing stupidly at the Memphis bus station and headed out to an unknown future in west Texas. In time "Real Da Da's" attitude drove June to a confrontation with Mike.

"We need to have our own place."

"Why?"

"We are living with your father."

"We lived with my mother, and that didn't seem to bother you at all."

"That was the Bend. Your so called 'father' is white trash."

"He is a good man. He works hard, and he tries."

"He is a pig! You know he's a pig, and if you don't know that, then you are a pig, too!"

Mike moved to hit her, but June didn't back down. "Mike, get me my own place or I swear, I'll find some way to get it for myself. You are a sex maniac! You can't do without me, and you know it. Just get me my own place!"

Mike finally capitulated and let her rent an apartment, though not far from "Real, Da Da." It was down the opposite end of the highway leading out of

Memphis, near Sherman road. Sherman Road was a red dirt road that really went nowhere. Near the apartment was a four-lane highway that fed Memphis. June never really took any real notice since she didn't drive.

It wasn't much of an apartment. It had a combination living and dining area with a kitchen that had a bar, if you could call it one, but it served for a table because the kitchen had virtually no room for one. It had one bathroom, a far cry from the luxury June had known at the Bend. She had adapted so quickly that she'd forgotten the little shack behind Fat Eddie's. The bathroom became more, and more important as her pregnancy progressed.

Mike's attitude was better when they moved into the apartment, in spite of it's size, but in a short while "Real Daddy" began to come over to "visit," and his mental state went sour again. "Real Daddy" would go straight to the kitchen and pick up anything that was out in the open, cookies, candy, or whatever, and proceed straight to the couch in the living area and commence to eat and leave droppings all over the floor, and in the couch. June was always in a state of agitation over this. Then Mike would come home from work (which was often because he didn't like to do the labor) and the two, father and son, would take off to Memphis where "Real Daddy" would fill Mike's head with more of his own failures, convincing the boy that he, too, was destined to the same fate.

In "Real Daddy's" mind, June wasn't just a cheat, she was the worse example of womanhood that could ever be. But then, "Real Daddy" thought all women were in that area just in different ranks of depravity.

Cigar Box

He liked to look at women, whom he did often, but he used only the physical sight of them for satisfaction. He considered them only for "use" and didn't ascribe any humanity to them. June noticed his lecherous ways right away, and used it to torture him. He was spineless and would never approach her, but he'd leer at her. She knew that if Ray were alive he would have already been to Memphis to whip "Real Daddy" with his big leather rodeo belt.

She found herself remembering more, and more about Ray as her pregnancy progressed. She'd go into the tiny bedroom and open the old cigar box and look at its contents. It somehow brought her closer to Ray. He had kept it so secret from her during his life, and now, after his death, it brought him nearer, and nearer to her in spirit. It was the soft part of Ray. In life, he had been the brutal ex-convict that everyone in town was afraid of, and in death, the cigar box had revealed him a gentle man who simply loved his little girl.

There was also the town she was living in now that bothered her, too. The Bend was situated in the west Texas desert. The air was cool in the winter and hot in the summer, but it was "light." There was no humidity there. Here it was humid, and hot in the summer, and the winters were downright *cold* in this place. She could readily see how so many blues artists came out of this area because it was so depressing to her. San Antonio had been full of life, but this place was full of stagnant air. She could easily understand why Claudette had left here!

She tried to ease the boredom, and loneliness by taking walks around the town, but it did was no use. To her it was all "closed in," and going out just made it all the worse. So, she sat in the tiny apartment just off Sherman Road, and watched the TV, and became more, and more depressed. Each week, as her body grew larger she looked at herself in the mirror with disgust. She would emerge from the shower, which she never took when "Real Daddy" was over, and stand there nude, rubbing her hands over her belly, but instead of joy, she felt sadness. She was sad because she wasn't quite sure just *who* the baby's father was. She hated herself secretly for this because she actually hoped that the father was Buddy. Her disgust for Mike was growing at such a rate that any form of revenge would do at this point. She couldn't know that her emotions were playing on her because of the hormonal ups and downs she was experiencing at this particular time in her life, but if she'd know it wouldn't matter. She genuinely *hated* "Real Daddy," and Mike was running a close second.

One day Mike came in late, claiming to having had to work late, which she knew was impossible; one, because in his construction job there were *no* late hours, and two, Mike was too lazy to work late even if there *was* overtime to be had! He proceeded to the kitchen and opened the refrigerator.

"Got anything to eat?"

June got up and waddled into the kitchen, "I'll fix some of that beef stew we got."

"I'm tired of you just opening a can. Can't you *cook* anything?"

June just proceeded past him to get the can opener. As she passed him, he reached out and grabbed a hand full of her long blonde hair the hair that had so

Cigar Box

attracted him before, and pulled her back, hurting her neck.

"I said, can't you COOK something?"

She pulled free and stood there in the middle of the kitchen looking at him. "You hit me, Mike, and I swear I'll put your ass in the county jail! I'm not going to put up with it anymore. I don't care *what* that worthless daddy of yours says."

Mike reached up and took her by the chin, placing his thumb, and forefinger on each side of her jaw, squeezing it until her lips formed a sort of "kiss."

"You call the police and I'll kill you. You got killing coming, whore."

She jerked back and ran to the living room with Mike in hot pursuit. When they got there, he shoved her down on the couch where "Real Daddy" liked to sit and eat up all the cookies in the apartment. Grabbing her wrists, he pushed her arms up above her head and lay on top of her. She struggled and fought, but Mike was too heavy for her.

"What's the matter? I ain't Buddy? Come on *wife*, be nice to me. You had such a good time with Buddy you didn't even have sense enough to wipe the sand out of your dress when it was over."

"Let me go, Mike. Just let me up. I can't *stand* being held like this. Please let me up."

He then held both of her wrists in one hand while he reached down and fondled her body. June was repulsed! She began to cry and turn her head away from him when he tried to kiss her. Finally, he gave up and got off her. She sat up and brushed her long hair out of her face.

"Why did you do that, Mike?"

"Because we're married, June! I have a *right* to do whatever I want to you."

She shook her head in disbelief. "Mike, I'm not your property! You have only those rights I give you. You'd get more out of me if you'd just be nice to me. There was a time when I loved you, Mike."

He looked angry. "What? You don't love me now?"

"How can I? You just held me down and ran your hands all over my body against my will. Is that why Claudette left your daddy?"

"What does my daddy got to do with this?"

"You're becoming just like him, Mike. You're even getting fat just like him. You aren't the guy I met years ago."

"We were kids years ago."

"It didn't seem to bother you that I was a child at City Park!"

"You were different then."

"I'm the same girl now that I was then, Mike. You changed. When you came back from Memphis after that first trip you were turning just like your daddy. You weren't the same anymore. I don't know if you can ever be that Mike for me again."

"Why did you sleep with Buddy?"

She threw up her hands, "Oh! God! Mike, I made a mistake, ok? I did something after a few glasses of wine that I shouldn't have done, and I'm paying for it now. I think this is God's punishment for me, and I'm enduring it, but just don't throw it up to me, ok? If you were so mad about it why didn't you go to Buddy?"

"I didn't want a big family incident."

Cigar Box

"We didn't have a big enough incident as it was? You were just scared of Buddy, that's all. 'Cause he used to kick your ass all the time when you were kids."

Mike jumped up, but June stepped back, "Don't hit!"

He raised his fist, but put it back down in helpless rage. He contorted his face and put it right in front of hers, "Whore," he hissed.

"Yeah, I'm a whore."

"Bitch."

"I'm a bitch, too."

"I hate you so bad."

She gave him her "blank" stare and said, "Then you need to quit throwing me down on the couch and feeling me up then, don't you?"

Mike turned and went out the front door of the apartment.

*   *   *

Claudette held a letter in her hand, while sitting at her desk in the little real estate office. With up most difficulty she deciphered the words "pregnant," and "due" telling her that there was about to be a blessed event in the family. She remembered how easy it had been when June worked with her and read everything for her. But, surprisingly there was no joy in this, because of the scandal that had spread itself though the little town. Buddy had called and spoke with her, and Claudette was finding herself fighting on not one, but two fronts. Just yesterday Sabrina, the waitress from the pub had come to the office. She, too, had news of a "blessed event." The political punch that her event carried could not be measured. Her father, Juan, had virtually been swindled out of his measly lot at the Bend, indeed his partially finished house stood among the others at the far western end of the subdivision. Now here was Juan's daughter pregnant by Claudette's stepson. "Step!" She'd never referred to Buddy as that, but right now, she was angry. To be perfectly honest, her anger would subside, and she'd cool down. She *was* Buddy's mother. She had raised him. What to do? There must be a solution. First she had to let Buddy know in Houston that she knew Sabrina's condition. Once that was taken care of, she'd handle the other problems.

Other problems! This unborn child put Sabrina in striking distance of the entire fortune that Claudette had amassed. It put that child on an equal status with the yet to be born child in Memphis. Claudette was amazed. It was almost Biblical! Just then, the phone rang.

"Mom," Buddy's voice came over the phone.

"Yeah, what's up?"

"Well, I know Sabrina has been there by now. You know what's up."

"What do you want to do?"

After a long silence Buddy spoke. "Well, mom, I've been around Sabrina all my life. We went to school together. I guess I got to just admit that she's the one for me. Now, I don't want no big wedding, but I do want to relocate and try to work in the company with you and dad."

About half of her upset evaporated at those words. The fact that he wanted to 'do the right thing' touched

Cigar Box

her as a woman, and the fact that he wanted to come into the family business touched her as a proud mother.

"Ok, ok, drive out here. I'm going to go over and talk to Sabrina tonight. We'll do something quick, and I have a plan that may smooth a lot of other things over. It's gonna be ok, Buddy."

The sound of his mother saying, "It's gonna be ok," calmed Buddy down. Claudette was in control. Everything was going to be alright."

That evening, after the pub closed Claudette found her way into Sabrina's trailer park. The girl lived in a small blue trailer on a muddy street. As Claudette approached, she could hear the music from the radio playing inside. She knocked on the metal door.

Sabrina appeared in a moment, trustingly opening the door even before checking through a window to see who was there.

"Miss Claudette?"

"Yeah, hey got a minute for a visitor?"

"Sure, yeah, come on in." She stepped back to let Claudette enter.

The mobile home was well kept. The young lady had even placed potpourri around the home, which gave it a most unexpected fragrance. There were pictures of family all over the walls, including a picture of Sabrina's father, Juan. Claudette noted that no matter how old the pictures were, Juan still looked the same. From yellowed black and white photos to recent color snap shots, the man seemed to never change. "Like a Mexican Dick Clark," she mused to herself. Claudette motioned to a chair in the living room and Sabrina bade her to sit.

"Nice place," Claudette said looking about the room. "How's your father?"

"Oh, working. He's always working. Following the crops from the valley to Kansas and back again."

Juan's business had been harvesting. He owned several machines, and his family, and employees began the season in the Rio Grande river valley and followed the maturing crops all the way through the Panhandle plains of Texas into the wheat fields of Kansas, and then back again to begin all over again. Sabrina had stayed in the little town because she liked the lighter work of the pub as opposed to the rigorous life of a farm laborer.

"He is getting on, ok?"

"Yeah." The girl's eyes betrayed her feelings. It had been a bitter pill to swallow when the "committee" had forced Juan to cease construction on his home in the Bend. They had filed the appropriate lien on the property to stop the construction, and even though Juan was not in debt for his home, he was effectively "dead in the water," at this point.

"Listen," Claudette continued, "what would your father say if I could help that home be finished?"

Not in a sarcastic way Sabrina asked, "Why didn't you do that before?"

"Because you weren't carrying my grandchild before."

The young girl sat back. She hadn't expected Claudette to be so forceful. She now understood how this woman had become just who she was.

"My child makes the difference?"

"Has Buddy talked to you about marriage?"

Cigar Box

"Yes. We want to be married, but not at one of those 'Bend' things. I just want to be married and get on with my life."

"We can arrange that, but I don't want to act as if I'm just sweeping you under a rug."

"I know better. Hey, if it means anything I know that you weren't directly responsible for what happened to my father's house."

"Your father is a good man, an honest man. I admire him. There were just too many people in the way."

"Aren't they still in the way?"

"Where my family is involved I will move them *out* of the way."

"Ok, how will you fix it?"

"Ask your father to call me, and I'll tell him."

Sabrina agreed, and they talked for a couple more hours, mainly about "baby" things. As the conversation progressed, Claudette began to like Sabrina. The girl was down to earth, and hard working. She had made her own way, and Claudette *had* to admit that when Sabrina became pregnant it was at her own house that she paid for with her own labor.

The next day the phone rang again in the little real estate office.

"Miss Claudette?" Juan's voice said.

"Yes, Juan?"

"Yes. Sabrina said you needed to speak to me."

"Yes, Juan, I have some things to tell you. Did you know your daughter is expecting a baby?"

"Yes, my Sabrina told me. She told me it was Buddy's baby."

"What does that mean to you?"

"What do you mean? It means that I will have a grand child. It is a blessed event. Sabrina told me that she, and Buddy are to be married."

"Yes, this is true. Juan, you are about to be a member of the family."

After a long silence Juan spoke, "What do you want, Miss Claudette?"

"Juan, I want to give my son, Buddy a wedding gift. That gift would also be for Sabrina."

"Such as?"

"The house you are constructing at the Bend."

"But my house will never be finished."

"Yes it will, and there will be a guest house on the grounds for you when you visit your son in law."

"How will you make the committee agree to that?"

"Trust me, I will. How much do you think is a fair price for the land, and the home?"

"Oh, Miss Claudette, I don't know. That is your business. My land is paid for, and there are no contractor bills against it. Only the committee's liens. I do not understand these things. I wasn't hurting anyone. My building is sound. I was using my family to finish it."

"I'll do a market analysis for you, Juan, and we'll come to a fair price."

"Miss Claudette, do you think you can really finish this home?"

"Yes, Juan, I can."

"Then I give it to my daughter as a wedding gift. To her, and her new husband. I give it if you can finish it."

Claudette was aghast! So many had coveted land in the Bend, and now this simple little brown man just

Cigar Box

gave it away in one simple act of love. It was something so removed from her mindset that it took a few minutes for her to realize that such an act could really be done. Then she spoke again.

"Juan, I will have to approach the committee before you can give it to them. We must get those liens off the title. Your title has a cloud on it, and it must be removed."

"I can't even *give* it away to my little girl?"

"Yes, but let me work on it. I'll get back with you. The main thing is, do we have a deal?"

"If Buddy marries Sabrina that land and the house will be their wedding gift from me."

"And your wife, and family do not mind?"

"My family will do what I ask of them."

"Thank you, Juan. You'll be hearing from me."

"Thank you Miss Claudette."

He hung up the phone and walked out from his motor home to look at the desert. More things were on Juan's mind than the home he had began in the Bend. True, he'd wanted to finish it, but he, and only he know that returning to the Bend had a double meaning for him. Long ago, as long as long, he'd conspired with the whites and that conspiracy had cost him his land. It had cost his people the land, too. And something more. He had been shaman! Helping the whites cheat his people out of the burial ground that was on the land put a curse on Juan. He could not die until a new shaman came along. At first it was of no matter, for he thought he'd live a normal life. Then, he began to know that he did not want to die. One by one all the witnesses to "Quanah" died and the old Comanche shaman became Juan the Mexican. His powers increased with his incredible age and as his people died they were buried in the city cemetery, their souls forever locked at the bend of the Pecos, never to ascend, or descend, until the new shaman could be found. And none was found, for Juan's family seemed to have a curse of the birth of man-children. They all died at birth or very young. Only sons-in-law lived in the family. As each generation came and went it became harder and harder to keep the new shaman from being born. Of late, Juan began to feel in his heart that another was to be born, and he supposed it to be from his daughter Sabrina. If it were born, then it too would follow all the others, and takes its place at the bend of the river.

Unaware of all of this, Claudette immediately went to arranging a meeting with the six members of the "committee." They put it off a bit, but eventually they met at the country club to talk with her. The scotch was brought in, and they all sat around the big oak table and talked."

"Gentlemen," she began, "I am purchasing Juan Sanchez's home for my son Buddy."

This parcel was an extreme sore spot with this committee so the first statement was, "Now, Claudette, you know the problems with that place. Why do you want to even get involved with that thing?"

"Because my son needs a house, and it's a eyesore such as it is."

"Well, what about the deed restrictions; the violations. What are you going to do about them?"

She took a sip of her scotch. "Gentlemen, I want a list from this committee of all the violations. I will correct them. I don't care if it is some violation that

Cigar Box

you all discovered after the construction ended, and you filed all the other liens, just list 'em out for me, and I'll get it done. If you want me to pull up the septic system and sling it out in the middle of the Interstate then I'll have my crews go in there and do it, but after I conform I want a letter from this committee that I can take to the courthouse and lift those liens so my son's house can transfer deed! I expect no other obstacles to my project. I will use regular contractors to do the work and I assure you that I will do it right."

The committee chairman smiled his best 'west Texas' smile, and asked, "Now Claudette, that's a pretty tall order, a-fixin' up that house like that."

"Don't you talk down to me, Jim! I built the Bend. I made it what it is, when you, and others like you were telling me the lots wouldn't even sell. Now we both know what the bottom line is here. You didn't want Juan Sanchez in the Bend, and I think that's despicable! But, you win. You kept Juan out, but you better NOT try and keep my own son out. Do you understand me, Jim?"

"Hey, hey, climb down Claudette. We want you to have the house. We'll draw up a list, and meet you here next week, during the regular session, ok?"

"Fair enough!" She slugged down the scotch, turned her glass over on the table, and walked from the room.

When the next Thursday came, they all convened once again, only formally this time. The chairman spoke to Claudette through the authority given him by the committee of the Bend.

"Claudette, we have a letter here for you to give to Chip down at the county tax office so he can remove them two liens from that house you're buying from Juan. Now we assume this house is to be in Buddy's name, correct?"

"Yes. His name, and anyone he may marry."

"And when will this closing be done?"

"Within forty five days from today. I have the paperwork in my office. Are there any other problems with the house, other than those two items?"

"None. In fact, upon inspection of the property we discovered that the septic, and the foundation now conform. I guess Mr. Sanchez corrected those items before he stopped the project, wouldn't you say, gentlemen?"

All members of the committee concurred with the chairman's appraisal of the situation. Claudette knew the story, though. The first thing they asked was that they wanted to be sure that Juan would *not* be taking residency in the Bend. The next statement proved that in actual point of fact there never *had* been any problems with Juan's home, save he was a Mexican. This was one more good reason to keep Buddy's impending wedding a secret until the transfer of deed. Still she had one more order of business.

"Mr. Chairman, I would like to submit a change on the original blue print," she turned to the owner of the local survey company who had accompanied her to the meeting and retrieved a set of blue prints used for home construction. She then reached across the table and handed the prints to Jim, the chairman and said, "I would like to include a guest house on the land so Buddy might entertain. This house will be smaller than the deed restrictions require, but I ask that it be exempt because it *is* simply an out building, and

Cigar Box

actually increases the value, and size of the property by giving more living space."

The chairman unrolled the blue prints and looked at them, "Rather large, though, wouldn't you say, Claudette?"

"Oh, no more that eighteen hundred square feet. Buddy has many friends in the Houston area, and he will frequently have visitors. Also, I myself may put guests there on occasion when we have a 'do' over at my house."

The chairman nodded, and one by one, the six committee members signed the blue prints thereby accepting the little house into the Bend.

*   *   *

Meanwhile, back in Memphis June was growing more and more impatient with Mike. His late night sojourns were becoming regular, and she knew what they were. He wasn't working, she was sure of that. There had to be a girl out there somewhere. She was now too large to go out and look, and she didn't have a car anyway. She was closing in on nineteen years old and still didn't have a driver's license. She thought it a paradox not having a driver's license, and at the same time being a licensed real estate agent in Texas! Mike totally controlled everywhere she went, everything she ate, and every visitor she had. Lately she'd been reduced to eating Vienna sausages in her bedroom, while watching soaps on the little portable TV set she had on a stand at the end of the bed.

Mike had long stopped trying to make any kind of love to her, even the two minute "special" he would

Wilbur Witt and Pamela Woodward

perform during a commercial. She figured her size, and his constant anger kept this from happening. He continued to be upset, seemingly more, and more each week over the baby, which *should* have been a source of joy for the both of them. Weren't babies supposed to bring people together? Inwardly she suspected that he knew the child was Buddy's, and this brought on the resentment that he was experiencing now.

Then, in the very pit of misery, June had guests that brightened things up a bit. Tommy and Christine came up to see her. She felt the surge of joy within her soul such as she'd never known before. Christine had news, too.

"It's gonna be a race between us."

"Race?"

"Yeah." The slim blonde pulled her blouse back from her swelling belly. "What 'cha think about that?"

June stared in amazement, "You're pregnant!"

"Well, yeah! You didn't think little Tommy was gonna let his brothers have the only babies, did you?"

June cocked her head and asked, "Brothers?"

"Oh, you ain't in the family secret are ya? Been up here in this mosquito breeding ground too long! Buddy's done knocked up Sabrina down at the pub. They're sneaking off to the J. P. to get married soon. Ol' Claudette's buying the 'Juan' house for them, only they ain't letting on that it's Sabrina that's moving in there. What cha think about that?"

"Super cool," June laughed. She was working in Claudette's office when Juan lost his battle to the committee."

"Wanna know the funny part?"

"Yeah, let me in."

"Claudette's building a 'guest house' on the land, too, only it's gonna be over eighteen hundred square feet, and ol' Juan's gonna just *live* there in the off season."

"How the hell did she get that past the committee?"

"She didn't tell them about Sabrina. She led them to believe that ol' Buddy is just a comin' home like a good boy to work with his momma, all 'cause he's so put out over what happened between you and him." She looked over her shoulder to make sure Mike didn't hear that last statement. "Claudette told me that she thought they just was in a hurry to get at the scotch and passed it right on thorough. They signed the blueprints *right there* at the meeting with out even thinking about it. Ol' fat ass Jim was the first one to sign!"

The two girls giggled uncontrollably. In the kitchen, Mike and Tommy discussed things also.

"Hey, man, you need to just come home. Buddy's coming back, and you up here with that fat assed daddy of yours is a bit much."

"This is my family."

"He ain't your family. He ain't nothing."

"I can't forget what happened."

"Well get over it, man. June's about to have a baby, and you're kinda 'locked in' if you get my drift."

Mike looked at June sitting with Christine in the living room, "I ain't locked into nothing. I'm seriously thinking about divorcing her."

Tommy shook his head, "Now you know you can't be divorcing June the Cat. Mom'll just move her back to the Bend *with* that grandbaby and support her, and you'll just be up here swatting mosquitoes with fat boy."

The idea of June being back in the Bend, and him being in Memphis was a startling thought for Mike, yet he knew it was true. He knew his mother's attitude, and he knew that she would forgive any sin to see, and hold grand babies. Working every day, even the little bit he did, and having to pay rent was beginning to tell on his nerves a bit.

"Yeah, you might be right. Still, that's a lot to forget."

"Hey, she's June the Cat, man. Did you think you married a virgin?"

"Yeah, I know, but I thought she'd settle down after we got married."

Looking around to make sure the girls were still in the living area, and out of earshot, Tommy said, "Maybe *you* should have settled down a bit, too. Them trips over on Commerce Street weren't cool, man."

"Wasn't as bad as what she did."

"Hey, dude, bad, is bad. Women, well they're the 'whores,' but we men can be sluts. You is a slut, bro!"

"Well, maybe it'll work out, but it'll take time."

"Well get your 'Real Daddy' out of it. If you want my advice you need to clear him out of your life. Dude, he owes you *money*!"

The day passed easily enough, with Mike taking them out to a local steak house. They all feasted just like the old days, and June missed the Bend even more. She couldn't get a glass of wine here, and really knew she shouldn't be drinking because of her advanced pregnancy, but still, such problems never arose in the Bend. For a few hours the problems that had plagued the couple seem to go away, and Mike even laughed, but then, when Tommy, and Christine drove away to

Cigar Box

visit Nashville the same old darkness came back. It was as if Mike was putting on a show just for Tommy and his wife, and the old anger was still there, just hiding for one night.

June entered her last trimester, and began to get ready for the advent of the baby. No matter who the father was, she inwardly laughed thinking that someday Buddy may be "Real Daddy," she was about to give birth, and her instincts kicked in. She bought a crib at Wal-Mart, and she and Michael assembled it. He treated the occasion as a necessity rather than an expected joy, but no matter. June made the most of it. She put up little things in the second bedroom of their tiny apartment, but lamented that had she been in the Bend, Claudette would have allowed her to paint clouds on the walls, and do other things that here she could not do because she would loose her "deposit" of two hundred and fifty dollars. Even that was a laugh. Two hundred and fifty lousy dollars. They'd spent that on *drinks* in one night back in Texas.

Most of all, at this time, she missed Ray. Even though this would not have been a blood grand child to him, he would have been "Grand paw!" Ray would have made a great grand paw, too, she thought. If the baby was a boy he'd teach him to shoot and hunt, and nail sheet rock, and if it were a girl, well, there'd just be another cigar box, now wouldn't there? She could close her eyes even now and still see him telling her good bye that day in the little real estate office when he went off to Killeen. Why did he have to go? She wondered why Ray hadn't killed that man, but she began to realize that by his actions, Ray proved that it wasn't in him to take a life, but to save one. She wondered what the woman that Ray saved that day was doing now. She hoped that the lady was making the most of the gift her stepfather had given her.

Her once clear complexion was going bad on her these days, and her face was fat, too. She was so busy calling "Real Daddy" fat that she'd failed to notice her own shape. Not just her stomach, but her legs, face, arms, everything! She resolved to get her shape back after the baby was born.

Mike drifted farther, and farther away, and she decided more, and more to be done with him once the baby was born. She would get a job. She had looked at Wal-Mart, and thought that the jobs there may be easy to get, even if she didn't have a high school diploma.

About 10 days from her due date, June began to have pain. Not knowing labor pains she roused Mike, who grumbling, took her to the hospital. After many hours, it was announced to be a "false labor," but the doctor warned that June was most certainly going to deliver within the next five days. This prompted Mike to call his mother who flew immediately to Memphis to be with June during this time.

"Real Daddy" came around about twice, But Claudette put him in his place to badly that he opted to stay out in his shack and ride this one out. June was very grateful for this, for with all of this discomfort, and out right pain, she didn't think she could take much more of "Real Daddy."

In the following days Claudette got a chance to talk to June in detail about her life in the Memphis area.

"You like it up here?"

"Heck no! I'd rather be back behind Fat Eddie's."

Cigar Box

"Then why do you stay?"

"I thought it would help things between me and Mike."

Claudette drew a long breath. "Nothing can help that but time, and I'm afraid that Mike is becoming more, and more like his father. You can't be held responsible for that."

"You're not going to go on, and on, about 'why' I did it?"

Claudette laughed, "I *know* why you did it. You got hot pants after a few glasses of wine. Get over it!"

"I did, but Mike didn't."

"Well, he'll have to." Then she thought a moment, "No he won't. His dad never did."

"You fooled around?"

"No, but I left him. Same thing to these hillbillies up here. They think they own their women." She walked over and peered through the window, "My brother was killed not far from here. There's an intersection off Sherman. Got killed Christmas morning. He was Angie's dad, you know?"

June nodded, and Claudette continued, "Then her momma died, and she came up to live with me. She didn't like the real estate though, didn't take to it at all like you did. You gonna keep your license, June?"

"What good is it gonna do me up here?"

Closing the blinds the old broker said, "Who says you're gonna stay up here. Aren't you tired of this yet?"

"Damn tired Miss Claudette. I get a little more wrung out every day."

"Well, you remember my fireplace?"

"Teach the angels to fly?"

"Yeah, and the first place I flew was straight outta here!"

June's face showed a little pain, and Claudette asked her if she felt badly. The girl said she didn't, but in about five minutes the look came again, only stronger. Claudette was amazed at how strong June was, because at this point the older woman knew that this was the real thing. June the Cat was about to have a kitten! Mike was nowhere to be found, as usual, so Claudette loaded June into her rented car and sped off to the hospital she knew so well from her two trips there. June's water broke just after arrival at the hospital, and the next two hours were painful, but well done for the girl. Soon there was a little boy crying in the nursery named Michael, and already nicknamed, "Little Mike."

"Real Daddy" came rushing down *after* the baby was already born and made a big deal over his first grand child. He scrubbed up real good and went in to feel the baby's head to confirm the presence of bumps to confirm its "DNA" was definitely in *his* bloodline. Then he disappeared to an "all you can eat" food bar and began to eat himself into a stupor.

Claudette made all of the phone calls needed, and then went alone to the nursery to see the baby. She didn't check the little guy for anything, but was genuinely amazed at him. He was a first grand child, and the first grand child of the family that formed the Bend. *That* made him special. *That* filled his lungs with the winds of destiny. He would never be a part of this trash in Memphis! He would be *home*! If Claudette had her way, this baby would never know

Cigar Box

what "Real Daddy" even looked like. He would know only freedom, and wealth.

June was alone in her room that night when the nurse brought the baby to her. She took Little Mike in her arms and held him close.

"Hey, hey, little man. You gonna be momma's little man?"

He looked up at her with unfocused eyes.

"Well, let me let you in on a little secret, ok? When momma gets her wind back, it's gonna be out with the old, and in with the new. You and momma gonna make it! You gonna be my little buddy!" She was surprised that she'd said the word "buddy," but no matter. This baby was a "buddy" in many ways.

The baby smiled, but June knew it had to just be gas.

Breaking Away

Buddy relocated to his mother's home in the Bend about a month after the meeting with the committee. He took up residence in the bedroom vacated by June, and Mike. Immediately he had to begin real estate classes in order to achieve his license, and to Claudette's glee, he excelled in the courses, and passed the state test with embarrassing ease. She admitted to herself that Buddy and June did have that trait in common. They could test on anything, and always come out on top. She admired them for that, and felt more secure now with not one but two of her family sporting a license. True, June was in Memphis, for *now*. On the other side of the coin, however, this only made her angrier with Mike who could not even pass the first course.

Sabrina was kept in the darkest halls of the family secrets. It wasn't that Claudette was ashamed of her, but instead that she wanted no glitches when it came time to transfer the deed to Juan's home. The official "cover" for Buddy was to let the now well-known scandal about Buddy and June explain why Mike had

Cigar Box

to leave, and now Buddy returned to get into the family business. Claudette's dyslexia was well known, and it was understood that she needed a family member to work with her to help with paperwork, and the intricacies of the real estate market. June had actually come up a notch or two with her brief, but well preformed duties in the real estate office, and her abilities to turn out documents, and research were commended by the west Texas real estate community.

Sabrina kept her job at the pub, and her condition a secret in complete concert with the family's wishes. She was a practical girl who didn't mind keeping her head low if it meant that she would have the ultimate gain in the end. She even imagined that she would miss her job at the pub where she got along well with everyone, and she was more or less happy with the work. Still, she knew what had happened to her father, and this wedding would ultimately right that wrong.

Buddy, being Claudette's stepson was a Catholic, as was Sabrina. They both decided that the "J. P." wedding would do for now, but that as soon as it was practical they would go to the parish priest and take the necessary steps to solemnize their vows. They felt as if this move would go a long way with Juan and his family who would bear the civil ceremony only so long as they knew that the Catholic rite was defiantly in the future.

There was absolutely no preparation for the wedding. The preparation, instead, was for the transfer of deed from Juan to Buddy. Behind the scenes, naturally, there was an understanding between Claudette, and Juan that upon the marriage Sabrina's name would be added to the deed. There was also a small adjustment in the blue print change that Claudette had slipped past the committee. They insisted that she make a covered walkway between the main house, and the guesthouse, thereby bringing all the living space beneath one roof. This she gladly did chuckling to herself that it would make it that much easier for Juan to have morning coffee with his daughter on rainy days.

Juan's house was not bricked, and the sheet rock walls had not been "taped and floated." Claudette moved gingerly on this getting all of the paper work in order before actually committing any real money to the project, not that she could not afford it but knowing that it put up a good pretense to the committee. The only problem remaining was the actual "sale" of the house and land. As agreed Juan was going to donate it to his daughter's dowry, but such a move involved no money, and would expose the plan to the closing company, where "big mouthed" Shirley would alert the committee to the move. Claudette covered this very simply. She would actually buy the property for an agreed amount, and after the closing, Juan would endorse the check back to her. She made him understand that he was in no way bound to give the check back, but that if he did, then it would truly be a wedding gift to his daughter, and that Claudette would see to it that the bride's name appeared on the deed when all was said, and done.

The day of the closing came. Claudette met with Juan and his daughter at the house itself and did a "walk through" although none was actually needed. Juan explained many things he liked about his home,

Cigar Box

and some things he would have done differently, had he had the experience, and money that Claudette had.

"You are much more experienced in these things, Miss Claudette. It is truly God's will that you, and your family finish this house."

"I don't know about that, Juan. I just know that we *will* finish it, and that you *will* have a place in the Bend."

The man looked across the desert to the river bend. "This land is sacred to my people. Did you know that, Miss Claudette?"

"The Mexican people?"

He smiled, "No, I'm only part Mexican. My roots are Comanche. For as long as there has been water in the river my people have come here to camp, bury their dead, and prepare for journeys in search of food."

Claudette was amazed. "You are Indian?"

"Mostly. Not all, but I am descended from Quanah Parker. Same tribe. I have some white in me too, if you count Quanah's mother, Cynthia Ann." Juan skirted his true roots.

"You said, 'bury their dead.' Is there an Indian burial ground around here someplace?"

He nodded.

"Where?"

"You'd be surprised." His smile told her it was nearer than she cared to think about. She didn't know the exact ramifications of the advent of the Bend sitting smack dab on top of a bunch of dead Indians, but she's save that debate until *after* the wedding. The idea of bull dozing the entire Bend down and making it a state park horrified Claudette, but then, again, it would serve the committee right. But, like Scarlet

O'Hara, she wasn't going to think about *that* today, she'd think about it tomorrow!

Changing the subject she said, "I'm going to connect the guesthouse with the main house by means of a covered walkway."

"How long will it take you to build the small house?"

"Ninety days. We'll hurry it up."

"When will my daughter and Buddy actually be married?"

"It will take me no more than thirty days to finish the tape and float, trim and brick up this house. Then we'll run to El Paso and get them married."

"And they will present themselves as man and wife?"

Claudette smiled, "Well, we won't have a 'coming out' at the country club, but they will commence to live in the house, while construction goes on at the hacienda, and they will be out front about it."

"You will loose a lot of friends, Miss Claudette."

"Juan, these people are my friends because I'm the biggest frog in their little dried up pond. I tolerated that silly committee; Silly men, in their silly hats. They would never have even *known* about such a place as the Bend if I hadn't rubbed their greedy little noses in it. They'll buck and roll, sure, but in the end they'll swallow it because they really *have* to! I'm building too many bridges, and buildings around the world with Silver Dollar for them to talk too loud! Piss me off too bad, and I'll take it all to El Paso. Juan, the Bend is *me*!"

The little brown man appreciated her strength, and was glad his daughter was going to be under the watchful eye of such a lady. He already knew this strength, but didn't let her know why. He hadn't found Veronica and her spirit fiend yet, and he knew that time was running out. He had to play along with this game and portray the offended, caring father. If things didn't go well back at that intersection Juan wouldn't have to worry about this house much longer. He'd be a dried up relic!

"Do you feel a kinship to this land, Miss Claudette?"

"Juan, I don't know what I feel. Forces I still don't understand brought me here. I had a vision of someone, who looked a lot like you, who led me here."

"Me?"

"Yes, and he told me how to get the money to come here."

"There is much injustice on the land of the bend of the river. For years, centuries, my people came there to pray, bury their dead, and prepare for the journey to find food. When the whites came this was all gone in less than a generation, and all that we were was no more."

"You can't live in the past, Juan. Your daughter will make a good way for herself."

"I know she will, but you can see how they system works. We are all hiding here from men who would not even let me build a house."

"Just silly men in their silly hats, Juan, just silly men in their silly hats."

*   *   *

If June had any spirits they weren't helping her right now. She was back in the tiny apartment, and now tied to a baby all night, and all day! Mike was making his rounds about the Memphis area, and June was powerless to stop him in any way. At least before she was simply bored, now she was bored with a baby to boot! It was not that she didn't love the child, she did, but she was only nineteen, and this was a big responsibility for the little "catfish girl."

Mike had a new love interest in the city, and he spent long hour's away "working." June was in the tail end of the "suffering" stage of her relationship with Mike, and was just about to turn around on him, but he couldn't see it. For all these months as her figure slipped away, and the mosquitoes ate her flesh, June had figured she had "this one coming" because of her transgression with Buddy, but now the baby was born, and she thought that the pain of birth had more than paid for whatever mistake she'd made on that riverbank so very long ago. She was locked down right now, but that Super Wal-Mart down on the highway was beckoning her, and sooner or later, she was going to heed that call!

To add to this Mike's income wasn't what it should be. Where June had been used to the Bend, and all the privilege of being there now there were "bills" and there was no check down at the real estate office to handle it. Lights went off, and lights went on. You'd use the rest room, and the toilette would not fill up. The TV developed a "blue screen" from the overdue cable bill more often than she cared to remember, and she was hungry! It was hard to believe that there was a time in her life that she went into the kitchen at the big

Cigar Box

house in the Bend and opened a beer and made a bratwurst sandwich just because she *wanted* to! Even in the shacks behind Fat Eddie's place she could always get a meal. To be hungry! What a come down. And the apartment got dirty. How in the world did such a hovel get so dirty? In a word, (or two words) "Real Daddy!" The cookie crumbled the same. He came over everyday, and sat and ate, and ate, and ate. Where was the maid now?

She wondered how people lived very long in such a state. Never mind the fact that in Ray's shack it was more cramped, and dirtier, but that was Texas! This was humid, filthy Memphis! One day, about two months after the baby was born she put him in the stroller and started for the Wal-Mart. It was about two miles from her apartment, but the walk felt good to the girl who'd run wild on the west Texas desert. She was amazed at how good it made her feel, just *going* somewhere, and trying to *do* something. She followed Sherman Road to the highway, and then walked along the edge, facing the traffic until she got to the Supercenter. A Wal Mart is a very big deal for folks in the south, almost a holy thing. It is a cultural center, a gathering place, a place to blow off steam, hob-nob, or do whatever one desired, and it was *air-conditioned*! Gloriously so! She felt it was worth the long walk just to be able to stroll around in the cool air.

This particular Wal-Mart was taking applications, something she hadn't even checked when she started her walk that morning, and she filled out the paperwork. About the only thing she was qualified for was "night stocker," where she would be on the "ten till six" shift replacing stock purchased the previous day by patrons. Everyone who was anyone came there to shop. In fact, there was a real estate agent who made his entire living right there. "Big Fat Buddy," did nothing but shop at Wal-Mart, and when people saw him they knew who he was and would approach him for various real estate needs. He didn't even use the local MLS, or multiple listing service because everyone just *knew* that you just didn't buy nothing 'less you bought it from "Big Fat Buddy!" June even considered approaching "Big Fat Buddy," but was informed that he only employed his children, and grand children, and she was *already* a member of *one* dynasty. She didn't need to slide over to another just yet!

After leaving her application, June gleefully ran back to the prison she lived in. When Mike wandered home that night, she told him her achievement.

"I applied for a job today."

"What? Where?"

"Wally-World!"

"What the hell are you gonna do down there?"

"I'm working nights as a stocker."

"Who's gonna watch the baby?"

She looked in total amazement, "Why *you* are, Michael!"

He looked gut shot, "Me?"

"Yeah. I don't go to work until ten, and by then your little construction job should be over for the day, right?"

He was caught but came back, "But you need to be here for the baby."

"You can be here for the baby until I get home at six, Mi-chael!"

Cigar Box

He had no response for her. He hated having to be home by ten, and it definitely cut into his night life, but how could he object when she was working and helping to pay the bills, and combined with that she was so excited about the job he couldn't stop her momentum. He could not see that the momentum was pushing him right out of the door of the little apartment on Sherman Road.

Within another month, June had her first check. It wasn't much by Bend standards, but it beat Mike's check, and it was *steady*. Mike's was construction, and came in when he worked, and if he worked. Now, if you combined that with his liaisons in Memphis, you got very little steady income. First, June caught all the bills up in the little apartment. Then one day she made a momentous decision. Mike was out late, as usual, and she called the locksmith. Within an hour both the front, and back door of the apartment had shiny new locks, and Mike's possessions were literally on the curb. Slowly, meticulously, June poured gasoline over the pile, and waited for "lover-boy" to wander in. When he finally pulled into the drive he stormed over to the pile, reeking of gasoline."

"What the hell is this?"

Smiling, June flicked a match onto the pile, which exploded and said, "A fire!"

As he tried to save his meager possessions in vain, June retreated toward the apartment, locking her brand new locks behind her. When Mike had totally lost the battle of the flame, and his temper, he ran to the apartment, only to be enraged even more by the locked door that *his* key no longer fit. He banged, and banged, and was still banging when the local volunteer fire department showed up and put out his duds. He was yelling and cussing, and the alcohol on his breath led him to a night in jail when the police arrived, and June didn't have to do any more than watch her television that no longer had the blue screen.

As the fire department cleared the ashes, June rocked her "Little Mike" and said, "Out with the old, and in with the new, little man."

*   *   *

In El Paso Claudette was putting together a fast wedding at a large hotel. She may have had to hide Buddy's wedding from the Bend, but they didn't know about El Paso, and she could certainly "walk the dog" here. She arranged for a ballroom to provide the setting, complete with a wedding cake at one end, and a "D-J" to provide music for the few guests that were involved. Her old friend the talk show host came, as did Mr. Springer, but other than that few members of the actual Bend community were involved.

On the other hand, Sabrina's family turned out in force! Claudette quickly learned that these people were not by any means "poor relations." They all booked the best rooms, and had the best of food and drink delivered both to their suites, and to the wedding reception itself. Their gaiety gave the marriage a definite air of a Mexican fiesta. Buddy found himself quickly trading shots of Tequila with his new brothers family, and just as quickly learned that they had had much more practice at this than he had. Tequila has a way of "sneaking in the back door" of your mind and making you crazy. Bud's craziness was confined to

Cigar Box

repeating to his new in-laws about how wonderful the Mexican people are.

Sabrina was beautiful! She was as lovely as she had ever been. Her dark skin contrasted perfectly with the white gown that her parents had provided her. Beneath the veil her dark hair could be seen. Her eyes eagerly darting from person to person in the ballroom, it seemed as if she knew each and every one on both sides of the family. The ones she wasn't directly related to she'd served beer to in the pub, and knew practically every thing about them. Being an only child she considered her cousins her closest relations, almost like brothers and sisters. Two of her brothers had been still born.

One other person was slipped into El Paso that day. His lips were sealed, and he would never betray the family that called upon him whenever he was needed. "Dish Bob" performed the ceremony with the same gravity that he would have had he been back at the Bend. After all the words were said, he took a bottle of the Tequila and retired to his private suite. Claudette could not help but notice the little man seemed to be more reclusive than usual, but no matter. The reception was still going on. She'd worry about that later.

The reception carried on until one in the morning, and then adjourned to the various suites the party had booked. Surprisingly there were no loud conversations, no harsh words, and no fights. Juan had full control of all areas of his family, and they showed him the most respect. It astounded Claudette that he could be so well thought of in this circle, and so beat down by the so-called "committee" at the Bend.

"My father is a Holy Man," Sabrina told her near the cake.

"I believe that," Claudette said.

"No, I mean he is our 'Holy Man.' He is a healer, mystic, all the things that you whites would consider special. It is a gift, brought down to him by our ancestors. Our family will bring their sick to him, and he heals them. If you need a spirit guide, he will call them for you. He can read the future."

"You think a lot of your father, don't you Sabrina?"

"My father is the most special of all men. If only those men on the committee knew how special they would have paid for his house themselves just to have him there with them."

Just then Tommy came up behind them, "Hey, Sabrina, if your dad's a Holy Man, can he get me some of that stuff they smoke in them pipes?"

She turned, and with mock seriousness she replied, "You laugh, Tommy Montgomery, but you'll see the day when you call my dad."

Claudette excused herself and went up to her suite. On the way, she passed Dish Bob's room and tapped lightly on the door. In a few moments, the little round man appeared and invited her inside.

"Party over?" he asked.

"No, you know me. I'm no late nighter."

He led her to the balcony where the now half empty bottle of Tequila was sitting between two chairs. "Want a touch?" He asked.

She nodded and he fetched another shot glass. As he poured the shots Claudette licked the space between

Cigar Box

her left thumb and forefinger and sprinkled salt on it. Then she picked up the drink, licked the salt, downed the shot, and quickly bit into a slice of lemon resting on a saucer.

"Hooooooweee!" she exclaimed. "This stuff'll make you see visions!"

"Always works for me," the little minister said.

Claudette sucked on the lemon for a bit and then asked, "What's on your mind tonight, Bob?"

"Just looking over to those mountains a bit. See that road running up there?"

She looked out toward the rust colored mountains and saw a winding highway in the distance. "Yes."

"That's Trans Mountain freeway, and beyond that is Anthony, New Mexico. I used to live there."

"Why don't you live there now?"

"Well, me and my wife, we were both ministers of the faith, you understand? But my Charlotte was born under a wandering star. She heard another voice, not my own."

"Cheated on you?"

"Worse cheat there ever was. Spiritual cheat! She heard a voice in Waco, and went there to follow it. She's there still, and there's nothing I can do about it."

"You need help with that? Maybe a lawyer?"

"Claudette, there are some things in this life you simply cannot buy. I can't buy her out of there, or talk her out of there. The cult has a hold that I cannot break. I don't normally let it bother me, but now and then, like now, I see those mountains, and I know I used to be over there, and things were so much different. I was a minister."

"You still are."

"Yeah, but not like then. Even my name, 'Dish-Bob,' is a joke."

Claudette sat her shot glass down, "Bob, you are *not* a joke to me. That's why I come to get you when you get drunk. I do it 'cause I'm your friend. I'm sorry if you ever thought that. You are right! You and I both have ghosts in our past. It doesn't make us any less of a human being. You carry your load well. I wish I carried mine as well."

She rose and excused herself from the suite.

Juan went from room to room drinking toasts to his daughter, and his new son in law. The drink did not seem to have any effect on him, and many went to bed before he did that night. But, by three in the morning, Juan decided to retire and went to his more modest room to lie down. The TV was on when he came in, his wife having left it on as she fell to sleep. Gently he reached over her and took the remote control and turned it off. Then he went to the rest room to clean up before retiring.

The restroom was nice, and large. It had a tub, and a shower, with all the little soaps, and shampoos that a large and luxurious hotel provides. Juan washed his face and hands to break the drink's hold on him and very quickly regained his sobriety, which he, if no one else knew he'd lost that night. Still, it was a special night. His Sabrina was married, and married well! No father could be more proud. This was going along with his plan. He wanted Sabrina to be a Montgomery. It was important for her to be one. The child within her would be a Montgomery and then all the wrong would be right! Sabrina had no brothers so no one could take Juan's place as the spiritual leader of his

Cigar Box

clan. He prayed that the child she carried would not be a male. If so, the curse would continue, and it would be still born, for Juan would see to it that it was. He looked into the mirror at his eyes. So much going on behind those eyes. Each time he smoked the sacred smoke, and ventured into the spirit world the duo eluded him. The plan had been a simple one. The car would go through the intersection. The boy would die, and his link to Juan would be broken. Claudette would die in a crash in Texas at the same time, and her power would be broken, and he, Juan Sanchez, Quanah, would be living in the Bend, back on the sacred soil, and then perhaps the curse would be lifted! It was all so simple! How had that Dreamwalker just messed everything up? He shook his head, and dried his face.

Then, as he dried his face he saw another reflection in the mirror. There were two forms standing behind him. Quickly he turned and in a low, but firm voice he said, "I see you, Dreamwalker! I can see where you stand! I have searched for you after you left the place where I sealed you. And you have the whore with you!"

Veronica's spirit guide stiffened, and she stared at the old Indian with disbelief. "He can see us?"

"Yes," Dreamwalker said. "He has that ability. This is the man who left me at the intersection of Sherman Road. This is the man who brought Claudette to the Pecos Valley, killed your stepfather, and this is the man who wants your son dead!"

Juan continued, "What have you to do with me? Why are you here, Dreamwalker? Why did you not stay where I put you?"

"I'm not here for you, I'm here for the child who was just born!"

"The child that will be born is more important."

"They are sister, and brother."

"The souls of my ancestors are forced down by the foundations of the Bend! They cannot be brother and sister. He is the son of Mike and June Montgomery!"

Veronica asked, "How does he know Sabrina's child will be a girl?"

"He really doesn't," Dreamwalker said, "but he is prepared for every eventuality. If it is a male he will kill it just as he has all the others for one hundred and fifty years, and if it is a girl he has hedged his bets by killing your son."

"You missed something old man," Dreamwalker said, "June Montgomery has added something into the plan you never counted on!"

"Nothing has been added! Nothing has changed! He is the descendent of the man who took our land! His grandfather is Rancher Stillwell, and his father is Mike Montgomery!"

"He is the half brother of your grand daughter to be born. You know what that means."

The old Indian rubbed his chin. He had not thought that Dreamwalker had figured this all out.

"My son is not related to this mess," Veronica said.

Dr. Angel turned to her. "Yes, I'm afraid he is. In your heart, you know that Little Mike is not Mike's son. He cannot be. Mike can have no children. Little Mike is the product of your liaison with Buddy at the bend of the river that night. Within her womb, Sabrina carries a child, who is also Buddy's child, and that makes Little Mike its half brother. If that child is a girl

Cigar Box

that makes him the next *male* descendant of Juan here. Not only that, but he completes the circle by making the family of John Stillwell and the Comanche nation his people robbed one and the same tribe. So by his birth and the girl's birth the Comanche have returned to the land. The land that Juan helped rob them of!" Then, looking at Juan he continued, "You thought that I didn't know that, didn't you? Juan here is the very man who gave the bend of the river to the Stillwells. If another shaman is born, no matter who it is, it rights the wrong, and returns the land, only Juan knows that the whites did not do the wrong; he did! He robbed and then murdered his own people, and now he keeps their souls in a sandy purgatory down on the Pecos. Sabrina has had tests, and those tests have said she's going to have a girl, but girl or boy is doesn't matter to Juan, because for all his posturing and groveling before the whites he will kill both of the children before he will allow another shaman to be born. Isn't that right, Juan?"

"Then my son will get the Bend?" Veronica butted in.

"No."

"But you just said he is the heir."

Dr. Angel glanced at Juan, "He will take Juan's place. As he grows and realizes who, and what he is, he will be instrumental in returning the Bend to the rightful owners, the Comanche, and the homes will be razed to the ground, and the souls of the dead will finally rest. All but Juan's soul, which will go where it really deserves to be. Little Mike will seal *him* there, just as he seal so many others down through time!"

"He will NOT!" Juan raised his voice for the first time.

"He will! You know he will." He turned back to Veronica, "Juan here manipulated his original plan. Remember how I told you? Now, during this conversation he is finding out who your son really is, and he will go back and change the circumstance of the accident so as to remove your son, only he didn't count on you. When he caused my wreck his entire plan was to cause my sister, Claudette to come to west Texas, solely to buy the Stillwell Ranch. He didn't know the accident of little Mike's birth that puts him as shaman at that time. He knows now, but though he can manipulate some things he can't change you. He can't touch you or little Mike. You have a special place in all of this and he can't touch you or little Mike. He can only set up the reason for little Mike's death, but he can't kill him out right, because if he does he, too dies at the same time. Little Mike will replace him."

"He is *not* our tribe."

"Yes, he is. Buddy has made it so. When you sealed me all those years ago, old man you made one error. You knew that a female could never be shaman, and you would remain. It has to be a male child. No female can take your place if there is any male to take the mantle, and June's child is that male child. You thought you would regain the land by building your house near the river, right on the sacred site, but it will not be so."

Veronica Spoke, "But what if there is no shaman. What if Juan dies?"

"That's the rub. You don't know how old he is. He is the shaman until the next shaman comes along.

Cigar Box

Juan here is the very shaman that lost the bend of the river to the Stillwells."

"Silence," Juan shouted.

"I will not be quiet! He traded the land, legally, to the first Stillwell for money, whiskey and gold. He lied to his people and they were forced off their land. Now he comes here pretending to be outraged at the loss of the land, when in point of fact he is the very one who lost it!"

"Don't they know?" she asked. "Can't they see?"

"They know. Remember the little Indian girl and her people at the bend of the river? Do you think they were history? They were the souls of the dead he has imprisoned much as he did me on the opposite side of the river. He holds their souls there. If he looses his battle here those souls are free, as will be mine, and they he will go where he knows he really needs to be."

Juan pointed to Veronica, who was still surprised that he could see her and charged, "She cannot give life to a shaman! She is marked with the 'dirty nose' sign!"

"Her nose will look a lot cleaner when her son takes your stick away from you, old man. And when he does you have to release me. You swore! And since you swore you will either release me, or take my place back at that intersection. You know the deal. If you break your word you must take the very curse you passed onto me. You *used* me, Juan, to grieve my sister and then you lured her to the Pecos Valley. All along you have lied, and manipulated. But you have manipulated yourself into a corner now old man. Soon you will be all in, and Michael Montgomery will be shaman!"

"You are not strong enough to fight me, Dreamwalker."

"Then why am I here at all, and not back in Memphis?"

Juan stared right into Dreamwalker's eyes, "The bastard will die!"

"I know that one must die, but it will not be the one you wanted."

Veronica stepped forward, "Why do you want to kill my son?"

Juan would not speak, but she pressed and then he spoke, "I do not hate your son but you need to understand that your houses sit on our sacred ground. I will have that ground back."

"And for that, you kill my son?"

"I will do what I need to do."

Veronica put on her best "freeze" and looked at the old man and said, "Then, old man, *I* will do what *I* need to do. You will not get my son!"

Juan tried to stare her down, but suddenly his blood ran cold and he saw Veronica's soul as it truly was. He fell back against the wall. He got up and looked at Veronica. Reaching out his hand he tried to touch her face but the blue flash drove him back, once more, into the wall.

"You have power!" He stared at her in amazement.

"I don't know what the hell you're talking about."

"Dreamwalker, you will loose." Suddenly Juan disappeard in a puff of smoke.

"He's going back to the crash site," Dreamwalker said. "He's going to try to make it happen without me or you there."

Cigar Box

"Can he?"

"No. You are here, and you've taken your soul with you. He is powerless against that. He has thought he could put me back there, and you, but he now knows that you have power over him. He'll just get the same blue flash he got here. Come, we need to get away from here. I don't want to be here when he comes back."

Dreamwalker and Veronica turned and walked through the wall.

*   *   *

June was working her job at Wal-Mart each night bringing home her wage. The wage wasn't the carte blanche check she'd had at the Bend, but she wasn't broke!

Working had never bothered her. Being a catfish girl at Fat Eddie's was hard work. Carrying all the fish on the trays, and standing on her feet in a tuxedo for four to six hours on a Friday night was very tiring, but she'd done it, and she'd made good tips at the job. This new job was eight hours a night, but it was well regulated. She had breaks, (something Fat Eddie never heard of) and she could work at her own pace. She had a natural energy that put her leaps and bounds beyond her co-workers. She found that she actually had to slow down to keep in step with the people around her.

She made friends readily, also especially one girl, Crystal, who had a winning smile, and began to show her what little "night life" there was in the suburb where they lived. While Mike got into Memphis quite often with "Real Daddy," June had been a prisoner in the apartment. Still, when she began to spread her wings to fly she found that she didn't want to fly very far. In reality, her experience was the SPJST hall, and the country club at the Bend. June quickly discovered that she really *was* a little pampered princess of the Bend.

And then there was the "Doc." He wasn't a real doctor, just a med student at college, but he was the shift leader, and had that air about him that attracted June. He couldn't help but notice the little blonde who was on his crew right away, and began to let her know just who he was and where his roots were, trying to impress her. His parents lived in Little Rock, and he was in his first year of med school, which meant absolutely nothing to June, whose experience at higher education was the real estate school back in west Texas. To her he either *was* a doctor, or he *wasn't*. He was in something called "med" school; therefore, he *must* be a doctor. That, and all the other members of the crew called him "Doc," so there you have it. He must be a doctor!

The "Doc" was very taken by June. She was far prettier than the usual for this shift. He made sure that he paid special attention to her, giving her easier work, and took every opportunity to help her along. June found herself becoming very attracted to him, and eventually he became her regular ride home in the morning when the shift ended. She didn't actually *need* a ride, Crystal would have taken her, but since he offered and she was a bit tired, she accepted.

Crystal's little sister watched Little Mike, but June never picked him up at the end of the shift, waiting until about noon, or one in the afternoon to walk the three blocks to Crystal's house and get him. Crystal's parents didn't mind helping the girl at all, and the tiny bit of money June gave the girl, just out of high school and not working, helped the family with small necessities.

For three weeks June never invited the Doc into her apartment. She always thanked him and got out of the car and went into her home, waving good-bye, and he waving dutifully back. Then one night at work something happened.

"Oh!" June reached and grabbed the small of her back. She had just lifted a box to place it on a shelf and felt a "pull" in her back.

The Doc came running over, genuinely concerned, "You ok?"

"Don't know. Felt something hurt."

He pressed his fingers gently on her back, "Here?"

She winced, "Yeah."

"You've pulled a muscle, that's all, but don't do any more lifting. Go to the back and sort for the rest of the night. Sit down. That way, you'll get the time in, but won't aggravate the condition anymore, ok?"

She nodded her head, and went to the area in the rear of the store that was used to receive goods and prepare them for display in the main store. She spent the next three hours doing that. When the shift was over the Doc took her home.

"Are you going to be all right?" He looked concerned.

"Yeah, I think. It still feels tight." As she opened the door, she winced again.

"Let me help you in, ok?"

Wilbur Witt and Pamela Woodward

She nodded her head. He came around to her side of the car and opened it. Reaching inside he took her by the shoulders and helped her out. By now she *was* limping a bit, and he let her lean on him while they went to the apartment. When they reached the door she retrieved her keys, but he took them and opened it for her. Instead of turning to say good-bye she allowed him to help her inside.

Inside the apartment was clean, and smelled very good. June was fond of her candles and had burned them at key areas of the little apartment giving it a mystic odor throughout. The furniture wasn't expensive, but it was adequate. He helped her to the couch and eased her down.

"How do you feel?"

"Hurts. Kinda tight, you know."

"Do you have any lotion here?"

"Um hm," she pointed, "In the bathroom. On the counter."

He went to the bath and found the body lotion there. Coming back into the living room he told her, "Turn over on your stomach."

She started to, but he stopped her and said, "Here, let me help." He took off her red jacket and began to unbutton her blouse but she raised her hand. "Hey, I'm a doctor, right?" June studied his face for a moment and concluded that he must be right, and she *was* in pain so she moved her hand and allowed him to unbutton the blouse. Then he gently flipped her over onto her belly and reached up to unsnap the bra. As he did so her arms moved ever so slightly to stop him but with a slight effort he placed her wrists above her head and continued. Then he urged her gently to raise her

Cigar Box

body up so he could remove the bra, and opened the bottle of lotion.

"Now, exactly where does it hurt?"

She reached behind her and pointed to an area at the bottom of her back and slightly to the right. He reached under her and unsnapped her pants and eased them down to expose a bit of her butt. This time she offered no resistance. Then putting a bit of the lotion in the palm of his hand, he let it warm.

"Just relax, June. I'm just going to lightly message your back. I want the muscles to relax. You haven't torn anything just strained it, and if we can get the muscle to relax you'll be better in a couple of days."

The advice was true, but the young man's heart was beating very hard as he gazed down upon the most beautiful woman he'd ever laid eyes on. It was hard to keep his hands from trembling as he began to rub the lotion into her skin. He kneaded the muscle gently between his fingers and she began to relax. He rubbed the lotion into the rest of her back, and the upper part of her butt and she closed her eyes and practically fell asleep. When he was finished, he went to the bathroom and washed his hands. Coming back, he found her lying comfortably on the couch.

"Now, I want you to stay right here all night, ok?"
"Ok."
"Don't move until you get up in the morning. Then, take a warm bath and call me at my apartment. I want to check this muscle before you come to work tomorrow night. If you're still sore, we'll figure something. I don't want this condition to get any worse."

She looked up and smiled, "Thanks." He reached down and gently patted her head. Then, he let himself out, the perfect gentleman.

*   *   *

Buddy, and Sabrina arrived back at the Bend about three days after their wedding. They flew in on a private plane, having spent the usual time on the River Walk in San Antonio where they flew by jet right after the wedding. The house was not quite complete so they spent a little time with Claudette and her husband in their house. Sabrina became very useful to Claudette in a short time. She was quick, far quicker than the broker had thought she'd be, and she showed an interest in the family business. Unlike June, she refused to take any pay insisting on a sandwich here and there instead of money, feeling privileged to be at the Bend at all.

Her absence at the pub soon let out word of just what had transpired and the expected phone call came about a week after the couple's arrival back in town.

"Hello."

"Claudette?" It was the chairman of the committee.

"Yes?"

"We need to have a little meeting with you whenever you have time, if you don't mind."

"Oh, no problem. What does it concern?"

"Well, we have a few questions concerning the house you just purchased for your son, Bud, and we want to clear these matters up."

"Matters?"

Cigar Box

"We'll touch base with you then. When can you make it?"

"I'm free tonight, if you all can get together."

"That's a bit soon, but I think we can swing it. About seven?"

"Sure. At the club?"

"Yeah, that'll do fine. See you then."

As she hung up the phone she realized what it was that was on the committee's mind, but she honestly didn't see how they would do anything about it. No one could be that crass! Still, in the back of her mind she was acutely aware that these men were all her customers, and she had sold them a bill of goods, and that they could be right and expected a certain delivery of those goods. Still, they were wrong trying to exclude someone from a neighborhood based on their ethnic background. This was indeed a very touchy situation. Once she had capitulated and looked the other way while the committee ground Juan's construction to a halt, but this time she couldn't do that. In addition to that, there was a bit of ego here. She *was* Claudette! The Bend *was* her "baby." Who were these men to try and tell her *anything*? She bristled when she actually thought about it. Where were they when this area was filled with prickly-pear cactus, and rattlesnakes? These were some of the same idiots who gave her the third degree at the very *idea* of the Bend. She began to brace herself for the meeting.

Claudette arrived at seven o'clock sharp. The members were already there, seated around the big oak "closing" table, with their glasses filled. They had chosen the main dining room in the country club, with the lit fountains still flowing where they could see them through the large windows situated at one end of the room. She came into the room and closed the door behind her. She then sat at the table in the center, and directly across form the six men. She looked up at the chandelier hanging from the second story with all the plants around it as it penetrated the first floor. They began to fidget, and look about. Claudette smiled and said, "Boys, what's wrong? Ya'll look as nervous as a pack of whores in church!"

The chairman spoke first. "Well, Claudette, we understand that Buddy went and got himself married."

"Yes he did. I believe you know the bride. That little girl that pulls beer down at the pub."

They nervously looked at one another. "Yeah. We suppose that they'll be moving into the home soon?"

"Uh, yes they will. Any problem with that?"

It was a direct challenge, not just at the committee, but also at the chairman himself. Claudette was effectively putting him on the spot. He had to respond directly now.

"Now, now, Claudette, that ain't the problem, and you know it."

(That *was* the problem and she *did* know it!)

"Then what *is* the problem? What are we all doing sitting here on a Tuesday night?"

"Well, we just want to make sure that the project is proceeding along the way the blueprints say it's supposed to. You know there were numerous violations concerning that property before?"

She leaned forward and looked him dead in the face, ignoring the other members of the committee whom she considered sidemen anyway, "Then why didn't you bring those facts up at the last meeting? In

Cigar Box

fact, you didn't have any problems at all when my son purchased the home from Juan Sanchez."

"Well, other things have come to light since then."

"Such as?"

"Well, that deck for one thing."

"What about it?"

"We didn't notice that on the blue prints."

"It's there."

"Well, we just need to see it."

"Where is your copy?"

"We don't have it at the present time. Seems to have been misplaced.

"No problem, I have my *signed* copy in my office. I'll bring it to the next regular meeting of the committee."

"Then there's the core sample of the foundation." The core sample was the sample of the cement used to put in the foundation, which was put aside for an engineer to verify the quality of the cement. A smashing process to determine just how much stress the cement could stand before giving did this.

"What about it?"

"We don't have a record of it."

"Let me check on that. Is there anything else?"

The embarrassed men looked at one another, looking quite like the Inquisition itself and then the chairman said, "No, nothing else, I guess. Is the construction proceeding on schedule for you?"

"Yes, it will be finished within the week. We're laying the carpet on Thursday. My son and my daughter in law will be taking occupancy Monday."

"And the little guest house, how is that doing?"

"It'll be a bit longer, but they don't need it to move into the main house."

"That's nice. Will Juan and his family be visiting from time to time?"

"From time to time, yes." Then she lost her temper a bit, "Oh damn it! What's the problem between you and Juan, Jim? Are you gonna sit there and tell me the man can't visit his daughter when he's in town? You know how he works. If he wants to stop by for a few days to see Sabrina what's it to you?"

"Now, settle down, Claudette. We didn't say anything like that. Just making sure that the guest house is not used for a permanent residence, that's all."

"And where the hell does it say *that* in the deed restrictions?"

"Well we did let the house into the Bend in spite of its undersize status."

"It is *not* undersized, it is connected to the main house and thereby contributed to the overall square footage of the property."

"I don't understand. It's a house. It's a totally different house! How can it be part of the main house?"

"You need to learn to read blue prints, Jim. If it's under one roof then it's just one big house! I thought I was the only dyslexic here."

"Ok, ok, no problem. We'll just get those two issues resolved and there'll be no problems. Just making sure, that's all."

Claudette rose, "So if there's no more 'making sure' I'll be needing to get to my house, ok?"

"Sure. You ain't gonna have a drink?"

Cigar Box

"No," she patted her stomach, "trying to get back my school girl figure." She turned her dry glass over on the oak table.

They all laughed, trying to lighten the atmosphere. Claudette did not go home, however. She went straight to her office in town and pulled out the blue prints of Juan's house. Sure enough, the deck had been added on the spur of a moment. It wasn't on the print at all. It wasn't that big of a deal, and had this not been such a supercharged issue she could have skated the whole thing by, but this was not the case. She picked up the phone and called the local architect.

"Mitch, I need you to come to my office."

"Right now," the voice on the phone asked?

"Yes. I have a minor matter that I need you to handle with the up most candor."

"Sounds serious."

"It is if you consider my pride is on the line."

"Is serious. You got some beer?"

"Got a fridge full right here."

"I'll be there in ten minutes."

True to his word in ten minutes, the man was tapping on the glass of the little real estate office. Claudette let him in and got him a beer from the fridge. She unrolled the prints before him.

"Mitch, I want you to put me a deck on these prints."

"On the completed prints? Why?"

"Because that dumb-ass committee is looking for a flaw in my project."

"Why don't you just let me draw up plans for a deck and present them to the committee and get formal approval?"

"Because the deck already exists."

He sipped the beer and leaned back, "Oh, I see. Didn't we have to redraw the plans for the guest house?"

"Yes, as a matter of fact, we did."

"Let me check in my office. You know, it very well could be an oversight on my part that the deck didn't get put on those plans. If that's the case I'll be happy to explain to the committee that it was my oversight, and you, through no fault of your own proceeded in good faith."

Claudette smiled. "Yes. I like that. Then you just submit a set of plans with the deck on them, right?"

"Sure, no problem. We'll tell them that with all the work we did on the guesthouse it was just a mistake not putting the deck onto the plan. They'll probably buy off on it. I mean, what are they going to do? Make you pull the deck down. Piss you off over a few sticks of wood?"

"Well, they're after the foundation, too."

"What the hell's wrong with the foundation?"

"They say they can't find evidence of a core sample."

The architect smiled. "Old Juan probably had some of his cousins pour that thing, and there probably *isn't* an inspection."

Claudette slapped her forehead, "What was in his mind? I'm beginning to understand why the committee didn't want him in the area. Why didn't he get the core sample?"

"Never intended to sell the house. Probably gonna move in there and live there until he died, and then the kids, and grandkids would be there, also."

Cigar Box

"I wonder how many other corners he cut."

"Don't know, but you need to find out. You know the deal. You make that house pass VA standards, and that way no one can ever mess with it. It'll be at the highest standard in the country."

"I'll have to call that engineering firm and have them drill a core."

"Four cores."

She nodded. It would cost her. It would be a pain to do it, but she could conform. "I'll call them first thing in the morning."

"Oh, don't sweat it Claudette. Those people most likely did a good job. The samples will pass. You know what Davy Crockett told Jim Bowie at the Alamo, don't you?

"No, what?"

"When he saw all them Mexicans running up on them he said, 'Gee, I didn't know we were pouring concrete today, did you?"

Claudette shook her head and grinned, "I can't say something like that. I'd just have to put my license on the table."

"Hey, I'm not saying anything bad about the Mexican people. What I'm trying to tell you is that they do know that work. Them cores will be perfect. You ever hear about when they brought the Pieta to the U.S?"

"What the hell is the Pieta?"

"It's that statue that Michelangelo did of Mary holding Jesus."

"Oh, yeah. What about it?"

"Well, they x-rayed it to see if it had any flaws. Now ol' Michelangelo said it was a perfect block, but they x-rayed it anyway. You know what they found?"

"No, what?"

"It *was* perfect. You know how he knew?"

"I know you're gonna tell me."

"He hit it with a hammer and listened to it. He could tell that there were no flaws in the basic stone. Them guys that poured that concrete are the same. The experts can check them cores 'till Jesus comes back, but I'll bet you a case of beer that that foundation is perfect!"

"I hope you're right!"

"I am. That concrete is harder than the heads of that damn committee, I'll guarantee you that1"

Claudette laughed, and shook her head. They finished their beer in quiet.

Wednesday morning came and she made the call to the engineering firm. Arrangements were made to have the firm take the necessary samples to test the strength of the concrete. They had to do it over a period of time so she couldn't have that information for the committee at the meeting the next day, which was Thursday. In addition to that, the plans weren't ready so Claudette went empty handed to the men that Thursday night.

Swallowing her ego she began, "Gentlemen, you were correct in assessing that there had been no core samples taken. I have taken the appropriate measures to rectify this situation, and these samples will be taken and tested by your next regular meeting."

Cigar Box

The committee appeared pleased that she was being to cooperative, and the chairman asked, "And the deck?"

"I've met with Mitch, and he said that when he drew the revised prints to include the guesthouse that he obviously overlooked the deck, which was the other improvement I included. He is bringing those plans to your next session also."

"Thank you."

"In addition to that, I will personally see to it that the home is inspected and passed to VA standards."

"But there will be no loan," Jim said.

"I don't care," she replied, "I will have a VA inspector check it and I will get the paper. It will pass those standards. Is there anything else you need, Jim?"

Jim was caught. Claudette had out flanked him. True, because of the deck he could have demanded that she pull it down, but he just didn't feel like taking her on head to head over a silly redwood deck!

The meeting ended agreeably, and Claudette went home. As she walked in her husband was just making a bologna sandwich.

"You want one?"

"No thank you. I just had me a big plate of crow."

"That bad, huh?"

"I practically had to back up on every single thing."

"Did you really think that you'd control the Bend for the rest of your life?"

Claudette sat on a stool and motioned her husband to give her a wine cooler from the fridge. "No, but I didn't expect a simple house construction to humiliate me like this one did."

The man came around and sat beside her and began to eat his sandwich. "Aw, hon, don't let it worry you none. When they see all them peppers growing in the back yard you'll get your revenge."

Claudette sipped her cooler, "I hope they all get hemorrhoids!"

When The Grass Isn't Green, and The Water Don't Flow

In Memphis, for June the weeks turned into months, and the months turned into the better part of a year. The Doc began to come over a lot, but she didn't date him, partly because she was just disgusted with the whole situation, and partly because there was a little part of her that secretly longed for reconciliation with Michael. He, for the most part, was living over at his "Real Daddy's" house, and gave her few calls. He had gotten into the nightlife in Memphis now, and June knew that he still had a pipeline to Claudette, and money no matter what he said.

She had cut her hair to shoulder length. It had been beautiful when she was sixteen, but now it was just a bother, and the shorter style would be easier to keep up. The weight she'd picked up during her pregnancy was now all gone, and left her a striking, full-figured woman, where a girl had once been. Her eyes were still the eyes they'd always been, but she was beginning to notice age creeping in, even at eighteen, going on nineteen, she was old for her years. Inside she knew that she'd left all innocence in the sand by the bend of the river the night of Tommy's wedding, and whenever she'd try to get over that night she'd just pick up Little Mike, and look him in the face, and with an intuition that only a mother could know, she'd realize the awful truth. Then she'd think about it, and wonder was it really innocence she left, or just the deception? June realized that she'd played the same games all of her life, and this one just blew up in her face, that's all.

Claudette hadn't punished her for her action, though. In fact, she had frequent contact with her, and even talked of business, and Texas. Time was healing the wound, but there was still a scar. Mike was still over at his father's shack, and she was still alone. Sometimes, at night, she'd peer from her window, and squinting her eyes, she could almost see the mansions of the Bend rising in the distance. She could almost taste the wine, and smell the meat being roasted. The pain inside was real for her. Opening her eyes a little more, she'd see reality come crashing down upon her, and realize all too soon, that she was not in the Bend, but in this cesspool of a town.

While Claudette did stay in touch, her mother, Barbara never called, or wrote. It was like June's usefulness was over for Barbara and she had moved on. June wondered; was that it, or was it just Ray's death, weighing so heavily upon her that she had withdrawn from life. Barbara seemed to fade in memory and Ray became more and more clear to her, even in death. It seemed to June as if Ray had actually been her father, and her mother was more of a stepmother. Ray took all the sense of family she had

Cigar Box

to the grave. She never even saw her little sister, who now had gained a lot of weight, just like her mother, and people in the little west Texas town had a hard time believing the two were in any way related. Once in a very blue moon the phone would ring, and her sister would be there, but the connection was fading fast.

A decision was coming up on her these days. Divorce. She knew that she had to bring closure to her marriage with Michael if she was ever to move on to any type of life, but she just couldn't bear to let go of the last shred of the Bend. Deep in her core the desert sand still stirred her soul, and she still considered herself a member of that family that formed and made the Bend what it was. Yet, the Doc was knocking at her door both literally and figuratively. She had studied the Doc, and now she wasn't very impressed. True, he was in medical school, but it was only his first year, and he could turn out to be anything, even a dogcatcher. There was no guarantee of anything with him. Oh, to hear him talk about it he was going to be another Salk, but she didn't care about that. He had told her his family had money in Little Rock, but she was concerned about how much, and she couldn't imagine anyone in Arkansas having anything but bug bites. She knew what Claudette had because she'd seen it! She'd *been* to Kuwait, and seen the Arabs fall over hell and back to gain the attention of the builder from west Texas. All she'd seen the Doc do was talk!

Still, each night when he brought her home, she was nearer to a decision concerning him. One night when he walked her to the door, as he turned to leave she gently took his hand.

"Don't go. Not tonight."

He turned and looked into her sky blue eyes. "You want me to come in?"

"Yeah. Why don't you come in for a bite of supper? I got some ravioli in the box."

"Ok."

She toyed with his emotions for a moment. *He's so easy* she thought. She leaned closer to him and let him put his arms around her. Looking up at him, she said, "And why don't you stay for breakfast?"

It wasn't very long before she made the choice to move into the Doc's apartment because it was bigger than hers, and they could share expenses. He had an apartment not very far from her place just off Sherman Road. He never mentioned any more permanent arrangement than just that, and even had her sell her furniture and put the money on the utility bills, and use it to buy some food the first month. She was disappointed at how little her furnishings brought. Then she started saving for the lawyer and the divorce. Even though the Doc never mentioned marriage she figured she might as well be ready should the idea ever cross his mind.

Not that living with him was very bad, because it wasn't. Unlike Michael, he did come home at night, mostly because they worked the same shift. She was frankly amazed at how he maintained his college hours, and his workload, and began to admire the man who was only in his first year of medical school. He never hit her, but he had a way of demeaning her at every possible turn. He made a lot out of her lack of formal education, and was not impressed by her real estate license that she still held in the state of Texas.

Cigar Box

In fact, she'd wondered about her renewal, and that led her to call Claudette one afternoon while the Doc was away in school.

"Hello."

"Hey, Claudette, it's me, June."

"How are you? Doing ok?"

"Um, yeah. Getting by."

"You still like it up there?"

"Hey, what's there to like? I exist."

"Mike said you moved in with some guy."

"Yeah. He's a doctor. Well, he's gonna be a doctor. He's in school right now."

"Well, you done real good for yourself. How's my little grandson?"

"Growing like a weed. Over a year old now, you know."

"Well, what can I do to help you, June?"

"I was wondering if I could renew my real estate license. I want to keep it going, you know. I don't want to loose it."

"Well, you can't do it up there. You must come down here and take a fast class, or maybe two. You know you been gone a long time. We talked about this when you were pregnant, remember?"

"Isn't there any way I could just take it here and send down the paper?"

"No. You must take a course in the state of Texas. You got any problems with that?"

"Well, I just gotta get the time off, that's all."

"It's a bitch working for a living, huh?"

"Yeah. Maybe I could get a weekend off soon. Sometime before Christmas. That would be nice. It would be nice to see home around that time."

Claudette saw her dream of reconciliation within reach for a very small price. She asked, "You need some help getting here, hon."

June was overwhelmed with emotion. Claudette had let down all the guard and let her know that she was in fact still a member of the Bend, and she could come home, but then just as quickly June put her guard up.

"I can get there. The Doc can bring me."

"June, there is a room in my house for you, and for my grandson, but not for your boyfriend, ok?"

"Ok."

"Now, do you really want to renew your license?"

"Yes."

"Ok, I'll get in touch with the real estate commission in Austin, and find out what it is that you need to renew. Then I'll make the flight arrangements from Memphis to El Paso, and we'll pick you up in a private plane. You can stay here that weekend, and then you can go back. Is that ok with you?"

"Yeah, that'll do. I can do that."

"Anything else on your mind?"

She wanted to discuss her divorce plans, but she shelved that idea for later. Claudette was in a giving mood, and she didn't want to ruffle her feathers too much. She had been down right civil about this whole matter, and June knew that she needed not to burn that bridge just yet.

"No, I'll be fine. Just check on that. I'll give you my number and you can call me when you know, ok?"

"Ok."

"See you then."

"Ok, bye."

Cigar Box

As she heard the click June could feel the longing in her heart for the west Texas sun, and the bend of the river. She even longed for Fat Eddie's catfish, which she hated, but she'd eat it now, just to see everyone back home. Then a feeling if extreme sadness came over her when she suddenly realized that o*ne* person wouldn't be there; Ray. The fact settled over her that she'd never see him sit there and eat the catfish again. She'd never be his little catfish girl, and give him extra ever again. Tears rolled down her cheeks as she felt the utter finality of it all. Suddenly the gunshots seemed very near again, and she again knew who her "Real Daddy" was. If only Michael could feel what she felt now! In bitter tears, she wondered why Ray had to die, and a fat slop like Mike's father still walked the earth and used up good air!

She didn't let it possess her, though. She wiped the tears away and forced the images from her mind. Going to the kitchen she began to make a tuna sandwich. She had made the tuna salad earlier so that the Doc would have something to eat when he came in from school. As she ate, she watched little Mike crawl across the floor, and begin to make real efforts to rise and take a step or two. She was amazed at how much he *did* look like Buddy.

*   *   *

By this time Buddy was watching his own baby, a girl, wiggle in her bed. Sabrina had given birth three months before. The mystery over its sex was now over. Buddy was working with his father and Claudette with the real estate and construction, and was turning out to be a real asset. The guesthouse was finished. Juan had been in town for the birth of his granddaughter, and stayed in the house during that time. He seemed genuinely happy that he had a granddaughter, and grandson. There had been no rumble from anyone, and Claudette hoped that whole issue would just fade away. Her grip on the politics of the Bend was loosening with every day. She began to get reflective at this time in her life. She even found herself taking walks down by the bend of the river, and remembering the picnics she'd had with her husband. She stared at the houses of the Bend across the river. This was the last thing Stillwell ever saw. She'd felt badly about the old man, but she'd never told anyone.

He was part of the reason for her loyalty on the phone to June, and not Michael. Claudette had a sense of history, and she knew that June was indeed the only person who was really *from* the Bend. There was so much of June in this land, and so much of the land in her! It literally projected her persona onto anyone who'd known her. The little catfish girl had indeed made her mark. Claudette felt sorry for her. She felt sorrier every time she sent a check to Mike to pay for his hot checks, or feed him, and inside knowing that she was feeding "Real Daddy," too! How could she fault June for what she'd done? True, it had been wrong, but it was just a reaction of a young girl to a bad situation, and too much red wine. So much history was rolled into that bend on the Pecos. Stillwell died there, she'd romanced there, and June had fallen from privilege there. Claudette could not see the souls of the dead staring at her from beyond the veil, and if she could it would have made her no matter for she was a realist. For her there was nothing beyond that veil buy oblivion. The darkness of death. Let fools like Dish Bob, and Juan Sanchez puzzle over the after life, she would make money, and enjoy this life until it was taken from her.

Only one spiritual thing drove her. At this time in her life, Claudette wanted all of her children home. Tommy was here it was true. He, too had a little girl, but Mike and June were not here, and Claudette didn't see how they ever could be. She couldn't turn against Buddy. He was working hard, and Mike was just on the dole now. Buddy had gotten his real estate license, and Mike had not. Buddy had married his first love, and Mike had lost his. As she looked at the sand near the river she could not but help to think what would have been had June the common sense to make sure all the sand was wiped from her gown that night.

Angela wasn't here either, but it wasn't the same. She's always been a bit different, and her life in Dallas seemed to suit her. When she *did* come to the Bend it was always a festive occasion, and everyone enjoyed her visit. That was good. There were never any problems, never any prying, never anything said or done to spoil the occasion. Then, she just went back to Dallas and the world that she told no one about.

Claudette looked out over the river. This bend possessed her! It had drawn her here. It owned her; she'd never owned it. Still, she could not help but feel that she was just a cog in some kind of cosmic wheel that ground on and on, and never let up. It had killed Stillwell, and how many others. How many of those ghosts she and Dish Bob had talked about stood on the other side of the river, and waited in eternity for her to cross over? But, to quote he own words, she didn't have any time for that "shit!"

Two stood there for sure. Veronica and her guide looked at her that very day as she pondered her existence.

"What do you suppose she's thinking," he asked?

"Power, money, things like that."

"You don't suppose she's thinking about her life? Maybe God?"

Veronica looked at him and shook her head, "Get a life, Dr. Angel. Oh, I'm sorry; bad choice of words."

"No problem. That's what we're here for, Veronica. So you and I can have life."

She stared at him, "You get weirder the more we go along."

"No, you are coming to understandings. Do you know what this is all coming to? Do you know why we're here?"

"Something to do with that patch of ground over there, Doc. Something I gotta give back to that land. That sound odd?"

He shook his head, "No, Veronica, not at all. Not at all. The Comanche thought that this land would be theirs so long as there was green grass, and the water flowed in the river."

Veronica knelt and picked up a bit of sand in her hand, "Well, Doc, I've seen this desert turn as brown as old Juan's ass, and I've walked across that river on dry land in August. Them Indians needed to understand that sometimes the grass ain't green and the river don't flow!"

"Maybe they understood it better than you know, Veronica. Why did you go to Tennessee?"

Cigar Box

"It was the right thing to do. I had to stand by my husband."

"Yet, in the final analysis you didn't."

She looked at him, "No, I suppose I didn't, did I?"

"You were living by a code that was imposed on you."

"What do you mean?"

"You don't really love Mike."

"I suppose not."

"Yet you went to Memphis with him because it was the 'decent' thing to do."

"Yes."

"Wouldn't it have been more decent to just end it and be with Buddy?"

She looked at Claudette sitting on the sand across the river. "Dr. Angel, I suppose she and I are trapped into the same game. She plays it her way, and I play it mine. I feel that we are being pushed into that chute, like a bull, and soon the gate will open, they'll stick a cattle prod up our asses, and we'll run out. Just like ol' Claudette said."

"Then you are not in control?"

"No, not really. I'm probably acting just like my grandmother, or her mother. There is nothing new, Dr. Angel. We just change clothes, that's all."

"What will you do when we go back to Memphis?"

"That's where this is all heading, huh? I gotta go back and get back in that car."

"You've known that all along. What will you do now?"

"I don't know."

"You don't?"

Wilbur Witt and Pamela Woodward

"Of course not! You're talking about death, Doctor Angel."

"Well, I'm dead. What do you think of that?"

She looked at him, gave a little chuckle and said, "And it didn't make you a damn bit smarter, now did it?" She rose and walked off.

*   *   *

In the physical realm, June was sitting in her apartment in Tennessee thinking seriously about a divorce. It would sever ties with Claudette for sure, and that was definitely a deciding factor. She wasn't ready to make the jump to dump Michael for good. Still, there was little Mike. No matter who his "Real Daddy" was, he was still related to *someone* who owned *something* at the Bend. Then it hit her. She was becoming just like her mother. Her mother had manipulated to get her married to Michael, and now she was actually formulating plans to move her own son back into that same arena! She was suddenly disgusted with herself. Then, that very thought made the divorce decision for her. She firmly made up her mind to see a lawyer.

On the Monday following the conversation with Claudette she went into Memphis and spoke with a lawyer. The man put all the options before her and then told her the problems.

"From what you've told me your in-laws are going to fight this. Young lady, they will put everything they have toward securing this child of yours for themselves."

Cigar Box

"But Mike and I don't love each other. How can they just run my life?"

"Because they are rich, my dear. Rich people don't like to be pushed around. Your mother in law is a power broker. Do you know what that is? Have you been so close to the flame that you can't see the light anymore? You are about to tell Claudette Montgomery to suck a lemon! That little boy sitting there is part of their family, and you cannot ever dissolve those bonds."

"What do you suggest then?"

The attorney stroked his chin, "Well, I suggest that you take that free trip to Texas your mother in law offered. You use this trip to mend some fences so that if you do embark on this course of action she will not just drop a ton of money on some attorney in this town that can put me in the dirt. We try to tie this all up nice and neat and there will be no surprises when you walk into family court."

"I kiss Claudette's ass?"

"Well, in a word, yes. You placate the old girl. You let her enjoy her grandson. June, you are lucky. From what you've told me here, today you're at least guilty of adultery, and a DNA test can prove it. In spite of this, your mother in law still cares for the child. And you want to know something else that I think?"

"What?"

"I think she still cares for you. She wouldn't have fooled around with you talking on the phone, much less offered you a free trip home if she wasn't willing to work things out with you."

"I'm going to have to talk to my boyfriend about that."

"Keep him low key, honey. Back in Texas, you may be able to hoot and holler and run around with boyfriends, but here in Tennessee there are laws against that behavior. Your mother in law is from Memphis, and you can bet your bottom dollar that she knows all about Tennessee law. She's showing restraint here, if you want my opinion."

"Isn't this divorce between Michael and me?"

"Money is power! You are divorcing the Montgomery family. Pull back gently from them, June. These people play for keeps. You think just because you know them they are like everyone else, but they are not! These are the kind of people who can ruin you, everyone, and me. You take my advice, June. Play it cool.

June went back to her apartment stung. Her pride was hurt. Claudette had actually reached all the way up to Memphis and touched her life, using her own son to do it! It was hard for the young girl to reconcile the woman she'd eaten breakfast burritos with in the little real estate office with the "power broker" that the lawyer was describing. What infuriated her was the fact that she knew that Claudette was holding Michael up during all of this. On his own he'd fizzle out and go away, but his mother was strong enough to keep him standing long after he should have been on the canvas.

"I've got to go to Texas for a week," she told the Doc that night.

"Why?"

Cigar Box

"Claudette wants to see her grandson, and I want to see my momma."

"Well, I gotta get us both time off from work and."

"Just me."

He looked stunned. June was resolute. Her face was expressionless. He had never seen this side of her, and he didn't like it. "Why just you?"

"Look, Doc, I don't need any problems with Claudette, ok. I have to talk with her, and smooth things over if I'm ever going to be free to live my own life. Mike's still over there living with his dad, and it's going on a year since we were separated. My son is a year and a half old, almost, and I need to make some moves."

His ego kicked in, "Why do you have to 'smooth' things over down there. My family..."

"Your family can't hold a candle to what Claudette can do!" She was amazed she'd blurted that out. She'd never challenged his family like that. In its own way, it showed her pride in still being a Montgomery.

The "Doc" bristled, "You don't know my family!"

"I know, but I know Claudette, and I know your family can't fight her in court! Look, Doc, she flew me from Bosnia to Paris for lunch. Does your family do that kind of stuff?"

"You don't know what they do."

"Well, I know they don't do that! Now, deal with it. I have to go. I have to see her. What are you so worried about? My husband is *here*!"

"He's not going to go to Texas to see his mother on Christmas?"

"No, he's going to stay here and visit his father's parents. He goads Claudette like that, and she gives him more money trying to buy him back down there."

"I don't want to find out that you two are meeting there, ok?"

"Don't worry about it."

She was amazed at his total calm. He left the room, not saying a word more on the subject. In a few days, the expected call from Claudette came with the information she needed to reinstate her real estate license. She would have to take one "fast class," and that, with forty-five dollars would renew her license.

Claudette made the flight arrangements for both little Mike, and June. She flew out of Memphis on December 12th to give herself enough time to arrive and get settled before going through the three day class required. The classes consisted of a Friday, Saturday, and Sunday, with a test being given on Sunday to get results to be sent into Austin to renew the license. Claudette would use the three days to be acquainted with the baby.

When the plane landed at El Paso June took a "hop" to the airstrip at the Bend, where she found Claudette, and much to her surprise, Michael also waiting to pick her up.

"What are you doing here? June asked as she came out of the private plane.

"Don't I have a right to visit my mom on Christmas?"

"I suppose you do, but don't think we're sharing a room."

Mike got a sour look on his face, "Are you going to stay for Christmas?"

Cigar Box

"No, I'm going back on Christmas Eve. I want to be home for that."

Claudette ignored the obvious jab that Texas was not June's home in her mind. Mike reached over and picked up the small suitcase she'd brought, and took it to the car. It was but a short trip around the end of the runway into the estates of the Bend. Soon the big garage door was opening and June was once again inside the home she had missed so much. Nothing had changed. The inscription was still on the mantle. She wasn't teaching many angels to fly these days. It seemed a lifetime since Claudette had first shown her the brass plate.

She went to the bedroom that was waiting, and hung her clothes in the closet. Sitting on the bed, she wondered why she'd ever agreed to leave at all. She actually left the clean, clear air of the Bend for the mosquito-infested life in Memphis! The maturity she's gained was obvious as she sat there. Suddenly, she didn't feel any animosity toward her husband, only a fatigue that would not go away with just one night's sleep. She realized she was beyond the lust that drove her to the bend of the river that night, and beyond all the petty arguments that pervaded the family now. She now knew that she, and Claudette were closer than she had previously thought. She imagined that somewhere in Claudette's past was a Buddy, only she had kept hers buried beneath the sand. Just then she noticed that one of the mini-blinds was still bent where she'd bent it taking her last look at the Bend before leaving with Mike that night for Memphis. No one had ever fixed it. It was like a little memento of her life there, a monument to her having been in that room.

She emerged from the bedroom to find her husband and mother in law in the kitchen. Claudette was doing one of her rare moments at cooking, and Mike was sitting on a stool at the island in the kitchen. Little Mike was clinging to Claudette, excited about the contents of the skillet, which was a blend of Mexican, and American flavors. June walked out to the porch and sat in one of the lawn chairs. It seemed like an eternity since her wedding had been here. Could one mistake put so much time between people? She heard the French doors open and the maid appeared with a bottle of strawberry wine. She was overwhelmed. It was like she never left. It was like Memphis never happened at all. The woman placed the wine, and her glass on the table as if she'd always been there. She poured a glass, and sipped the red liquid. As the wine relaxed her, Mike came out and sat beside her.

"Penny for your thoughts."

She sipped a little more of the wine, "I'm sorry, Mike."

Michael reached over and took her hand and looked into her eyes. "That's ok, June. Don't let it bother you."

"But it does bother me. I shouldn't have done it."

She squeezed his hand and said, "Mike. I should have shown a little more restraint. A little more understanding."

He reached for a glass and poured a glass of her strawberry wine. "Maybe I'm the one who needed to show some restraint. I cheated first, June."

"I know."

He looked surprised, "You know?"

Cigar Box

"Yeah, Commerce Street, Deputy's daughter; yeah, I know."

"Why didn't you say something?"

She smiled, and sipped her wine, "Hell, Mike. A man will be a man. I didn't fault you for her as much as I faulted you for ignoring me. You should have loved on me more, hon."

He was amazed at how old she looked right now. So "Texas!" She seemed to have come a thousand miles in his mind to this point, and she was his little "Catfish girl," once again.

"Man, I thought that was a real secret."

"No more than when we went to City Park. Whole town knew it." She smiled at him.

"I'm sorry."

"Don't be. Ain't your fault, Mike."

They looked out over the golf course. June poured another glass of wine. "Mike, let's just come home." Little tears brimmed in her eyes as she said these words. It was all that she could do to just say them before she choked on them.

"What?"

"Let's just come home, Mike. Let's pick up where we left off, and raise our boy. Let's just come home."

He fumbled with his glass, and looked down. His mouth reached for the words, and then with the greatest effort he said, "I…can't." He hung his head and looked at his feet, holding the wine glass very tightly as he did so.

She looked at him, puzzled, "What do you mean, you can't? Do you like working odd jobs up there? Do you like Fat Daddy telling you how to do everything? Hell, Mike, your mom supports you now anyway. What's the difference?" Then realizing what she'd just said, she said, "I'm sorry, Mike. That was cruel."

The young man was visibly shaking. He raised his head and stared at the greens and said, "All my life, June, Buddy bested me. In school, on the golf course, in everything I ever did. When I saw him looking at you at dinner, I knew I'd bested him. I had something he couldn't have, and now, he's had it. I just can't do it, June. It's not that I don't love you, 'cause I do, but Buddy has beaten me. I can't come back and let the whole town laugh at me."

"Ray would have got over this."

"Cause he would have shot Buddy!"

Smiling, she sipped her wine, "This is true."

They sipped the wine and sat in silence for a few moments. June finally asked, "What are we going to do?"

"Well, I'm going back to Memphis. Maybe one day I'll come back, but it'll be a while."

"I'm coming home, Mike."

"That's your choice."

"I'll be waiting for you."

"Maybe some day."

"I'm sorry. I never meant to hurt you."

"Hey, that's ok. I just gotta deal with it."

June finished her wine and went to her bedroom. Within a few minutes, Mike came to her. That one night, the couple was as perfect as any couple could be. Mike had his little catfish girl back, and June was truly in love if only for one night.

* * *

Cigar Box

The next morning Claudette was again in the kitchen making breakfast when June walked in. "Mind if we have a talk?"

"You got the floor," the broker said, without turning away from the stove.

"I want to come home."

Claudette knew she'd won. Her face did not betray her victory. Instead, she just turned and looked at her. "Think you can?"

"Oh, yeah. I can do it. Been through worse than this."

"Where you gonna work?"

"Kinda thought I'd work for you."

Claudette let the silence soak in for a while, and then said, "You gotta stay away from Buddy." Then she looked back and smiled. June smiled back.

"I don't think that'll be a problem, mom."

"Damn straight it won't be. Sabrina'll cut you!"

Mike came into the kitchen right about then. "What ya'll talking about?"

"June's moving back to Texas," Claudette said, not looking up from the eggs.

Mike sat down at the island and said, "What you gonna do for a living?"

June replied, "Well, I kinda thought I'd pick up real estate."

"Mom, you gonna go for this?"

"Yeah."

Mike got up and went straight back to his room. June just sat there and drank her coffee. Claudette stirred eggs, and the world turned. Finally June spoke, "Maybe I'd better just stay in Memphis."

"You'll do no such a thing! You'll get your things and come home. Mike will be where ever you are. You renew your license, and just come home! You move in here. To hell with him! He'll come to his milk." She put the eggs on a plate, "We need you June! You are a part of us."

Breakfast was silent. After it was over June walked down to the bend of the river. The same place she'd lain with Buddy and where the rancher Stillwell had ended his life. The spot where the little Indian girl had played with rocks on a lazy summer day. She reached down and picked up a bit of sand. This sand decided so much. Her entire life was this sand! She walked over to the water and reached into it, so clear, and cool. Drawing up a bit, she sprinkled her face with it. After all these years she was still amazed that this water had no taste. It was so pure. She knelt, and rested on her knees, looking at the Bend. All she could do was miss Ray.

That Friday she went to the fast class. It was incredibly boring. Basically what it boiled down to was two days of memorizing the test, and one half day of taking the test. She was amazed at the hypocrisy of it all. How could the state of Texas fall for this? Yet, inwardly, she was glad that it did. It enabled her to come back and pick up her life. On Sunday she took the test, and passed it to no surprise. Claudette mailed in her certificate, with her payment. She discussed her plans with her after that.

"I'm going to break off with Doc. I need to come home. Do you have a place I can live?"

"You'll live here."

"Here?"

Cigar Box

"Yeah."

"What about Mike?"

"When those mosquitoes eat his ass enough, he'll come home." She smiled at June, "I'll just cut him off and let him depend on his Real Daddy for a little bit. He'll come home." She winked.

"Guess I should hang my things in the closet, huh?"

"Guess so."

"I'm leaving before Christmas, ok?"

"Just wind it up, say goodbye to your friends, and come here. Mike will be right behind you. He's staying 'till New Year's anyway. Hey, hon, he'll probably never go back."

Before she left, June found her way out to her mother's house. She was appalled by how she had fallen back. The house was a mess. Dishes were in the sink, and the house was very dirty. Her mother was fatter, and unkempt. She visited for a few minutes, not even an hour.

"You get out to Ray's grave much?" she asked.

"No. Not anymore. It makes me sad. I don't there now."

"You need to keep up his flowers."

"You keep them up. I don't have the time."

June realized that the woman she'd known as her mother was not as much of a mother as Claudette, and that she'd never loved Ray; or else she'd have gone out to fix the flowers on his grave. Late in the day, on the day before she flew back to Memphis, June went to the little graveyard at the edge of town. Ray's modest little stone sat in the corner of the lot. He was a *hero*! She couldn't believe his life was reduced to this. She knelt, cried, and then picked up a rock. Slowly, deeply, she scratched the words on his stone, "Real Daddy."

*   *   *

Twenty-four hours later, she landed at the Memphis airport. No one was there to meet her. It was in stark contrast to her landing in El Paso not long before. She got a cab to take her to the Doc's apartment. She expected him to be gone to Little Rock for the holidays but to her surprise, he was there when she put her key in the door.

"So, you got home," he greeted her.

"Hey, don't go there, ok. I need some sleep."

He went to the bedroom and retrieved a blanket. Returning to the living room, he threw it, and a pillow onto the couch and said, "There! You and your bastard can sleep there. I'm not going to throw you out tonight, but tomorrow, you need to find someplace else to live."

"Tomorrow's Christmas."

"Then, merry Christmas, bitch! I took your things over to your father in law's house. He told me that Mike was in Texas. You two have a big reunion?" He turned and went to his bedroom and slammed the door.

June looked around the apartment. Everything that was "her" was gone. She picked up the phone and called Crystal.

"Hey, I'm back."

"You at Doc's?"

"Yeah."

Cigar Box

"Hey, he took your things over to Mike's dad's and dumped them on the porch"

"I know. He just told me."

"Yeah."

"Hey, could you go over there and get my things? And, pick me up in the morning?"

"We'll be there. You don't worry; ok?"

"Ok."

"June lay on the couch, but she didn't sleep that night.

* * *

A few hours later Veronica and her spirit guide found themselves once more at the Bend standing at the off ramp of the freeway. She could see the car with Claudette and her family approaching in the distance. Also, she could see another car exiting the freeway down the ramp, and coming onto the access road. It was apparent that the two cars were on a collision course, but the traffic light was there to stop either one or the other. It was only then that she noticed that the light was signaling green on all sides; a serious malfunction.

Claudette's car whizzed under the freeway and through the light just as the other car came from the ramp onto the city street. The collision was inevitable, but just as in her case the cars froze in time. Veronica walked over to the colliding cars. Claudette was driving and seriously had not seen the approaching automobile from the freeway. Mike did see the car, and his mouth was flying open to say something. Sabrina likewise, was staring through her window at the racing car. Buddy sat beside her, and their daughter was in the rear seat also. Veronica studied each face for a long time. She was amazed at how she could now take this as so normal, yet she did! They were in the exact same position that the car in Tennessee found itself in, only worse. She figured the speed of the approaching car must be even greater than the one in Tennessee because of its exit from the freeway. The impact would be much worse, and she knew that all occupants within Claudette's car would be likely killed.

She peered through the window at Sabrina's daughter, supposedly safe within the confines of the child seat that was firmly attached to its seat belt. She was the image of her mother. Just like Little Mike, she was playing, and completely unaware of the impending crash. Then she looked at Claudette, who appeared to be concerned with something else other than the car. Probably some deal going through her head, or some idea. Was she thinking about June's impending return to the Bend? Was she putting together another "big deal" in Bosnia, or New York? No matter, because in the next instant she would be in eternity and for all of her conniving, and maneuvering she would simply have to answer for her sins just like everyone else! What was it the preacher had said? She remembered the scripture, which surprised her; "Thou fool! Tonight thy soul is required of thee!"

She looked at "Dr. Angel," and said, "Gonna be two big car wrecks on Christmas, huh?"

"Possible. It's up to you, Veronica."

"And now I have to make some choices."

Cigar Box

"It's actually very simple. Actions, both God's and men control the universe. Man has choices that he makes based upon the situation God has created. How many times have you read in your Bible where God repented of some course of action He had previously planned to take because of the action of someone?"

"So my action will dictate what happens here?"

"Yes. A selfless action goes a long way with God."

"Selfless action? A perfect act of contrition."

"You must give something up. Veronica, in your entire life, you have never done anything that you didn't benefit from directly. That's what the journey was all about. Look at the selfless actions you have seen. Look at Ray. Veronica, you must make the free choice to die for all these people."

The gravity began to sink into her conscious. "If I die, then they all live?"

He nodded his head. She turned and walked back to Claudette's car. "And my son?"

"That will actually be the deciding factor. He is the principle reason for all of this. Juan knows where we are now. He knows we must come back to that intersection. I've shown you all I can show you. It's all up to you now. But come, let's go back to Tennessee."

Veronica then found herself sitting back in the car in Tennessee. Suddenly she was aware that she was no longer "Veronica" but "June" again. Everything was just as it was before Dreamwalker had taken her out. He was sitting there beside her, just the other side of Little Mike. She looked at the Bronco still frozen in time, touching the door of the car. Then she looked at her friend Crystal. She could still see the reflection in the girl's eyes, as she accepted her death. She looked out of the window at the driver of the Bronco. His eyes were intense, concentrating. He was doing all he could to avoid the crash, but there was no use. His wife's mouth was frozen in a shouted warning, "Car!"

June turned to the man. "Now What?"

"Now you make the choice, June. You make the choice based on what you have learned."

"To die?"

"Remember the car in Texas? Remember how it, too, is about to have a crash? You looked into their faces, also. A crash is going to happen. It is a moment in time. Only you, depending on the choice you make now, that crash will or will not happen. You must make a perfect act of contrition. That act of contrition will cover not only your sins, but also the sins of your ancestors, and a great wrong will be made right. Your death will cover a multitude of sins. Juan knows that, and that's why he wants you to live and the child to die. The wrong that sealed us both to this intersection for time and eternity will simply cease to exist. At that moment *you* will be the one changing history. At this moment, you hold that key in your hands. If you choose to live then your son will die. Juan will win. His father will die also, and Claudette, and Buddy. Sabrina and her child will die. That makes you at least an heir to their fortune but not of the land. That is a done deal. Before long a case will be made and the land will go back to being sacred anyway. Juan will win. What we're deciding at this intersection is which shaman will make the choice of what to do with the Bend, little Mike or Juan. I called you Veronica

Cigar Box

because that's the name of Sabrina's child. She is your spirit child. If you choose to give your life now your soul will rest with her and she will live your life for you. You have the ultimate choice before you now. Juan needs you to save yourself, and thereby kill all these people, leaving him as the shaman of his clan. He's betting on it, June. Don't let him win."

"Then why can't Juan just let us all live and put his case in court?"

"It is not as simple as that. With little Mike being who he is he takes the *spiritual* control of the land, which is just as important at the *physical* control of it. If there were no little Mike then yes this would be so, but remember, all history is a series of various time lines and Juan is manipulating them masterfully. But he can't manipulate you. He has to let you make the choice. That's the stickler in his hide. He can't force you."

"Why me? What did I ever do to deserve to make this choice? Why did you wait all these years for me?"

The man looked slowly to Little Mike and then back to June's tear filled blue eyes, "I had to wait for you, June. Juan saw to that. But while I waited I took in everything and ran it through my mind. Juan sealed me from heaven, but not from earth. When I saw you I froze the scene, took you out of the car, changed your name to Veronica and led you through your life to make you understand. He was looking for 'June' and not 'Veronica.' I hid you from him until you began to see what you needed to do. If I'd given you this choice at first you would have just taken the easy way out, but now you have grown spiritually and the choice is more profound. You now understand that you son is the powerful link in this entire matter. Your actions concerning him will be the deciding factor. That's the choice. If he lives then he will decide the fate of the Bend. He will replace Juan. He will be the spiritual leader of the tribe, and the court case and all concerning it will have to go through him. He is the shaman. Juan also knows this, and he knows if little Mike is the leader the Bend will survive and he will loose."

"My son?"

"The *true* heir. The shaman! What happened to me the night that I died; the accident that killed me, drove my little sister, Claudette to the desert, and eventually to the Bend, where you met Buddy, and Buddy met Sabrina, was orchestrated by Juan. That's how he works. The injustice committed so many years ago was to be made right. But the injustice was initiated by Juan and covered all these years by lies! Now we have perfect justice. Juan locked my soul here; at this place for the time it took to wait for the arrival of the child who would return to the Bend. He just never thought that I would grow spiritually after he left me here. Then, when he came here the morning of your accident and found me gone he realized he'd underestimated me. Remember how I told you that he could go back and change things even after they were done? When he found out for sure whom little Mike was at the Hilton in El Paso that night he went back and decided to kill little Mike, only he didn't count on one thing. He never counted on you making the unselfish choice and giving your life for that of your child. There are many possibilities, many time lines, but Juan knew the child must die. He knew if Mike lived he would be shaman, and that he, Juan would finally die and all the souls would be released."

"Pivotal?"

"He is Buddy's son. You know that. His half sister from Buddy's marriage to Sabrina is the descendant of the Comanche nation that used the bend of the river centuries before the white man came along. He is also in direct line with John Stillwell, whose family purchased the bend of the river from Juan. This makes the child the only true, and moral heir to the sacred ground of the bend. You must make the free choice for him to live and complete the circle. You must undo Juan's treachery."

"But the Bend is *sold*. There are so many owners now. Dr. Angel, you just don't understand real estate."

"I understand the law concerning Native American burial grounds."

"All the homes will be gone?"

"Remember when I told you that the day would come when the homes would be gone?"

"Yes."

"And the sole, surviving custodian sits right here." His hand brushed the child's blonde hair. Juan carries a stick given him by his father, and given his father by his father. Little Mike will take that stick. After this, Juan will loose his life force and he will die, and little Mike will be shaman. And, being that he will control the land that is the Bend. In effect it will still be Montgomery land, but in the blink of an eye it could all revert. Sabrina is Comanche, but she knows her daughter cannot be shaman, only the male can, and she cannot dispute that. Little Mike will take the stick."

In a very small voice she said, "And I must die?"

"One unselfish act, for many lives, both now, and in the past. All those people that really mean something to you are in that car, and he represents all the people of the past and future who will have their lives entwined with the Bend. At this moment in time all those lives are on the line. Depending on your choice, they will live...or die. Depending on you we will all ascend or be locked forever in Juan's grasp. All these years he has been keeping a grip on his tribe. Any time a man-child was born that stood a chance to be the shaman he would destroy him, and lock his soul on the nether side of the Pecos. You don't understand just how he was fooled this time, so let me tell you. You had an affair with Buddy. That affair produced little Mike. Then, Buddy married Sabrina, and that union produced the girl, Veronica. Now, Veronica cannot be shaman, so Juan didn't worry about her, but in all his schemes, in all his wisdom he did not know about you and Buddy, and Mike is Veronica's half brother and that gives him the right to be shaman. Juan transcended time and space, and that's important for you to know, *time* and space. When he realized that the shaman had been born he went back in time and sealed *me* to the intersection. My job was to make *sure* that little Mike did *not* survive the crash, because if he *did* he would be shaman, and Juan would die. His evil hold on the Comanche would end, and me and all the souls on the other side of the Pecos would ascend, just as he would descend."

"But why must someone die," she asked. "Why can't we live?"

"As I told you, God created many timelines, but there are rules. There is no time line that allows both

Cigar Box

you, and your son to live. One of you must perish. Juan's spell is strong enough to assure that. The whole reason for me showing you your life, and asking you all these questions is that you must make the free choice to give up your life for that of your child. It *must* be an unselfish act. Otherwise it will not work, and that very unselfish act will undo what Juan has done, but that act will cost you your life."

"What if I choose to live?"

"Your choice. You will live. You will haggle with Claudette's husband, but you will win eventually, maybe even become another Claudette." His hand reached down and stroked Little Mike's blonde hair, "He will join me, and all the others and we will be here at this intersection, and all the wonderful things he would have done will never be done. Juan will win. He will have locked the soul of the true shaman here for eternity and Juan will live another hundred years. He's very old, you know. The car will crash into the car in Texas and they will all die in the engulfing fire that follows. But you will live."

"My friends?"

"No. It is their time. Their lives been demanded on that part, and they will go to their judgment. This does not involve them. It involves you, and your choice. June, saints are chosen from before the beginning of the world. God so loved you that he left this free choice to you, and He will honor that choice. You are a very evolved soul. You gave birth to the shaman and the soul of the shaman is a very powerful one. It doesn't just come from linage but from God. Sabrina's daughter is not that. Mike is. This is what is wrong. Juan is trying to force God. He can't do that, but still the entire thing rests in your hands now. The soul of the shaman is what Juan saw at the Hilton. When he tried to touch you he touched the skin of the mother of the shaman and at that moment he knew for sure! That's what caused him to fall into the wall that night. He knows that."

"She will save herself!" They both looked up at Juan standing near the car. "She will take the path she always takes. You, Dreamwalker are about to learn the weakness of the whore. She will let the boy die and she will run like a gazelle to the next boyfriend, just like she's always done!"

June looked over at Juan, "I think you have misjudged me Juan. You don't know me. You never did. Nobody did. My mother made me what I was. But I also sang in the church choir. I also went to Christmas parties. I have friends who love me. Men have used me, but I have used them. I've don't a lot of things, but I would never let my son die just so some old fool could have some field of bones back."

Dreamwalker said, "He leaves his body to do this. This is only his soul. His body is back in Texas. If you make the right choice you will blind his soul and it will not find its way back and they will find him dead."

He looked into June's eyes. The man realized that he was looking at a soul in torment. She was struggling against her base nature. But he saw strength also. Spiritually there was a bit of Claudette within her. Also, there was the spirit of the true shaman within her, and likewise within her son, still frozen in the Mazda. Seeing all of this, suddenly Dreamwalker was calm. He realized that God in all His wisdom *had* chosen the right soul. She had been the lion, but now

Cigar Box

the lion lay down with the lamb. And all depended on her now. He could say no more. He knew that she had the strength to rise above what Juan Sanchez thought of her. He felt like a lawyer who had given concluding arguments to the jury of eternity, he rested his case.

"Contrition," June repeated back to him. "How come I know just what that means?"

Her right hand reached and stroked Little Mike's hair. She reached around him and picked him up. He "came alive" in her arms, wiggling and saying, "Momma," as she brushed his blonde hair away from his face."

"Hey. Hey, little man. You gonna remember me? You gonna remember what I look like?"

The little fingers reached for her nose, and he said slowly, "Nooooose…"

She fought back the tears. "Yeah…nooooose. And cheek…And eye…and." she lost her control for a moment and cried, holding him to her. She looked at Juan. Then she wiped her eyes and sat him in her lap. "Hey, little man, listen, ok. Momma's gotta go away for a while, but she's gonna be watching you, ok? I want you to know that. You love Momma?"

The child repeated, "Noooooose."

"Do you love Momma?" June's voice was wavering badly with emotion.

He smiled and rubbed her face. She leaned very close to his ear and whispered, "Hey, I'm gonna go and teach the angels how to fly. Can you say that?"

He didn't know what she wanted him to do, so she repeated, "Teach the angels how to fly."

"Anels to fly…"

"Teach the angels how to fly."

"Anels...fly."

She sat up straight, put on her best freeze and said, "Yeah." She kissed him and held him for the longest time to her breast. She saw the man's eyes looking at her, and she said, "Hey, if I got an eternity ahead you can give me a second to kiss him good bye, ok?" Then taking a deep breath, she turned and with one deliberate motion, she handed the baby to the Dreamwalker, who took him to his breast and stepped out of the car. There were no blue sparks this time. He closed the door and looked at June sitting on the passenger's side of the rear seat. With a quick nod he walked across the road to the cyclone fence that surrounded an equipment rental business, closed today for Christmas. He took the boy and threw him forcefully against the fence across the road, causing him to bounce back to the pavement, breaking a leg. The baby "froze" in time again. The man turned, took one last look at the car where June sat.

She reached down to the floorboard and picked up the cigar box. Opening it, she reached and took the ring from the ring finger on her left hand and placed it inside the box. Looking at the contents one last time she looked at her "Dr. Angel."

"I can do it," she mouthed.

"I know you can," he mouthed back.

She then looked at Juan and said, "You *loose* old man. I just killed you!"

Juan screamed, "No!" and then disappeared in a puff of smoke.

A cluster of rainbow lights formed around "Dr. Angel," and he faded from sight. June watched as the

Cigar Box

lights rose to the heavens, and slowly, one, by one, disappeared from view.

In Texas, the car with her mother in law approached the overpass that held the off ramp to the freeway. As she moved through the green light Michael saw the car bearing down on them.

"Go! Go! Go! Go! Go!"

She pushed the accelerator and the Buick skirted effortlessly to safety.

"What in the world do you think was on his mind," Mike yelled.

Buddy looked back at the intersection and said, "Hey, all the lights are green! Somebody needs to call the city and let them know that they need to get a crew out here!"

Sabrina felt a sudden coldness within her, and instinctively turned and put her arms around her baby. "Something terrible has just happened," she said, and the tears began to flow.

Back in Tennessee, June was still staring at the sky where "Dr. Angel" had gone. She saw that Juan, too was gone, but she didn't think he went to the same place that the Dreamwalker had gone to. She looked across the road to where her own baby lay. She knew that Little Mike had to have some injury. She saw him lying there on the asphalt. Then, turning, she looked once again at the Bronco as it bore down upon her, suspended in time. Then, in a flash she was again rolling down the road leading to the four-lane highway. Lois pressed the gas pedal and moved the speed up to about forty-five miles an hour. June watched the trees begin to rush by. She reached up and poked Lois with her finger, "Hey, run by Mike's, ok? I wanna see if his dad is still there. I'll get my clothes."

Crystal looked straight ahead and said, "I don't think that's what we need to be doing right now, June. Maybe you need to talk to Mike about this. I think there are some unresolved issues here. He was holding on to a little bit of you when he kept the boots and jeans. He was really using the clothes just to get you to come back over."

"Then why didn't he say that in Texas? I'm not going to meet him in that shack.

Lois half turned, and continued to drive down the road, but she noticed that something was wrong in the back seat now. The baby was not fastened into his seatbelt anymore and June was just looking at her with a slight smile on her face. There was a crazy look on her face, too. As if she were contemplating something that no one else in the car could know.

"Where's the baby?" Lois asked, taking her attention away from the road. From her vantage point as driver, she could tell that the child was nowhere in the back seat, or even in the floorboard. "Where's the baby, June?" she raised her voice a bit more.

The Bronco came suddenly into Lois's field of vision on her right. Instinctively her foot hit the brake and the little car skidded to a stop in front of the oncoming vehicle. June looked right at it and saw the vehicle bear down on her. Drawing a breath, and steeling herself for the impact, she closed her eyes and whispered, "We're gonna teach the angels how to fly"

She never heard the crash.

Epilog

June's body arrived on the day after New Year's. It was cold in west Texas and a dry wind was blowing from the northwest across the dismal prairies and deserts she had once called home. The hearse brought the body to the funeral home, the same one that had received her stepfather, and the mortician began preparing her. Not long after her arrival, Claudette showed up in the parlor of the funeral home. The mortician, David, an old friend and resident of the Bend, met her.

"How are you feeling today, Claudette?"

The strain showed in her face but she pulled herself together and answered, "Well, about as good as can be expected I guess. You got her ready yet?"

The man's face showed concern, "Claudette, I don't think this will be an open casket affair. The impact messed her up pretty bad."

The news hit the old broker like a freight train. The very idea that one so beautiful could be mangled beyond recognition tore at her heart. Slightly choking she asked, "You can do nothing, David? Isn't there some kind of makeup, some kind of plastic you can use?"

He motioned for her to sit, "She was crushed Claudette. Her body was torn from one end to the other in that back seat, heck, I'm not sure if we got everything in there. There's no way. What we need here is a nice portrait of her to rest on top of the casket so that people can remember her as she was. You don't want to see her as she is now."

Claudette nodded, and nodded again, and then just sat still. A slight sob escaped and she pulled it back, looking up at the undertaker with red eyes. Knowing his old friend as he did, David the undertaker went quietly into his office and retrieved a bottle of scotch with two glasses. He handed her one of the glasses and she took it with a trembling hand. As she sipped the liquor she said, "Don't tell anyone I was this upset, ok?"

He smiled and nodded, "Ol' 'Claw-det' has a heart after all, huh?"

She finished the drink and poured one more, "Yeah." She swallowed hard. "David, this is just as upsetting as when my brother died years ago. It's as if the two events are linked together, at least in my mind."

She finished the drink and then asked. "Have you got her in a box right now?"

"Oh, yes. Why?"

"I'd like to spend a moment with her before the circus begins."

He nodded, "Just give me a minute."

He went into the back of the building and returned, motioned her into a viewing room and left her alone.

Cigar Box

Claudette walked over to the simple wooden casket and gently rested her hands on its lid. Ever so slowly, her head nodded. "Well, little sister, I guess I got fetch my own drinks now, huh? June bug, I never ask why, I just endure, but I'm here to tell you, this is hard to take. You done went and got yourself in a mess I can't get you out of. David tells me that you are pretty messed up so we gotta keep you in this box, but you and I know you aren't here. You're out there with your daddy, Mr. Stillwell at the bend of the river." Her hands began to shake a bit and she sobbed for a moment. David came back and eased behind her. "I'm ready to go, David." He was amazed at how old his friend looked now.

Mike and Buddy sat on the porch looking out at the greens. "If I hadn't sent her back," Mike started.

"Don't say that, "Buddy said. "It was just a bad accident. Wasn't your fault, Mike. You two were getting back together, but things like this take time."

Mike put his head in his hands. "I gotta get over to the hospital. Little Mike is getting better. They say his leg is gonna mend perfect. I just don't understand how he was thrown free like that, but I thank God for it."

"Miracle, Mike. Some things just can't be explained."

Buddy noticed a cigar box on the table. "What's that?"

"What?" Mike asked.

"That cigar box."

"Oh, it came from the wreck. Dad, I mean Ed sent it down to me. It was in the floorboard of the Mazda June was killed in."

Buddy went over and opened the lid. "There's nothing in it."

"I know. I don't know was in it, but the impact threw everything out. I just know it was hers because I saw it out at Ray's mom's ranch."

"What was in it then?"

Mike smiled, "Grass."

Buddy smiled and shook his head, "Ray! That old bastard."

The two young men sat and looked at each other for the longest time. Then Mike spoke, "Why did you do it?"

Buddy drew a long and ragged breath. He stared at the floor of the porch and then slowly, ever so slowly, he lifted his eyes to Mike's and said, "I fell in love with her."

Buddy's answer was so honest, so pure Mike was taken completely off guard. Then, so slowly Mike's eyes began to tear up and he said, "Don't you think that I loved her too?"

Buddy shook his head, "I know you did. Mike, I know you did. I just want you to know that if I could go back and undo anything in my life that I've ever done it would be that night out at the bend of the river. She was the sweetest gal, Mike. Man, she was really one of us, you know?"

Mike smiled through his tears, "Yeah, you remember the spider bite." It was an old story about when June got a spider bite on her behind and ran out into the lunchroom at school pulling up her dress and screaming about it.

"Mr. Sims put some Skoal on it," Buddy began to laugh.

Cigar Box

"Hey, the old bastard didn't have to rub it in, did he?" Mike added. About that time, the door to the main house opened and Tommy and Christina stepped onto the porch.

"What are you two idiots laughing about?" Tommy asked.

"Oh we were just remembering June's spider bite."

Tommy smiled and said, "Buddy, you weren't even there! You'd done graduated.

"That spider bite was legendary little brother!" the older boy added.

Then Mike began to really laugh, "I can still see her ignorant ass going up and down the escalator in San Antonio. Up and down. She damn near wore me out."

Tommy laughed, "On the escalator or at the Marriott?"

"You men are awful," Christina said.

"Come on, Chrissie," Tommy nudged her, "you got a story. Whup it out!"

The tall lanky blonde thought for a minute and then said, "I remember the time she told me she used to think panty shields were like a chastity belt."

"Oh, God!" Another voice came through the door. They all looked around to see Sabrina coming out with them. "Are you assholes sharing stories about June?"

"Why hell yes. You got one?"

"I am a lady. I did not *run* with the Cat!" Their faces all fell, and then she added, "Except this once."

"C'mon, c'mon, give it to us," Buddy urged.

Sabrina grinned sheepishly, "Well, it was about the time she went to that Christmas party, the one out in the boonies. Well, ya'll remember Janey Miller, don't you?"

Buddy asked, "That chubby red head that turned Mormon?"

"Yeah, that's the one. Well, this was in her 'virgin' period where she didn't do no drugs or anything. Anyway, she gets about three quarters lit on some beer, which she *swore* she didn't drink and went to sleep on the couch. Now all the parents are out getting stoned, right?"

"Christina added her usual, 'Right, right."

Sabrina went on, "And so the Catter, she sneaks up quiet as a mouse and she's got this big damn 'fattie," she held her fingers apart demonstrating the size of the joint she was referring to, "and she's got this piece of clear plastic hose with her. She slips this hose up *under* the pillow where Janey is sleeping and begins to huff smoke through the hose so that Janey is breathing the smoke in her sleep."

The little crowd began to laugh and wipe their eyes. Sabrina went on, "And by and by Janey stirs. The Cat runs to the kitchen. Now I didn't know it, but she's stole the ceramic Jesus from the nativity scene in the yard, you see, and she's got it in a Dutch oven."

They all began to laugh louder. "And," Sabrina continues, "Janey gets up, *messed* up," the crowd is virtually howling now, "and stumbles to the kitchen and here's the Catter, just shoving the baby Jesus into the oven, looking over her shoulder, asking Janey, 'Hey, could you get that bar b que sauce on the top shelf, please?"

Cigar Box

Tommy began to laugh so hard he slip down the wall he was leaning on. Christina just held her head and chuckled, "Oh, my God! Oh, my God!"

Sabrina began to wipe tears out of her eyes and finished, "Janey ran out the back door, into the desert. It took us *hours* to catch that silly bitch, and when we did all she would say was, 'We gotta file a police report!"

The young people spent the rest of the morning telling stories and remembering June. A gentle calm settled over them and for a while it was as if June had never left them, but was, and would always be, right there.

Slowly the others did drift back into the house leaving Mike and Buddy alone once again. Mike had something he wanted to ask Buddy, but he wanted to be alone.

"Buddy, I want to have her cremated."

"Why?"

"I got a plan. I'll explain it to ya'll, but you gotta stand with me on this one against momma, ok?"

"Sure, but it ain't nothing weird is it. I mean you don't want us all to roll her up and smoke her or nothing like that?"

"No. I got something better in mind, and if June were right here I'd think she'd go along with it."

Claudette objected a bit, but not near as much as they expected. She conceded that it was Mike's area to decide to do so as he wished. They communicated their wishes to the funeral director who made the arrangements, which would be completed after the memorial service.

Wilbur Witt and Pamela Woodward

The day of the funeral came. It was cold, so very cold. June was big news in town and everyone showed up. Dish Bob mounted the podium and began to speak, his voice wavering from time to time, but all in all, he put on a good show. When the service was over Mike rose and went to the microphone.

"I know all of you expected that we'd all go to the cemetery now, but we aren't. For those of you who wish to be with us in the final part of June's funeral please meet us at the bend of the river at noon on June 21st. We will finish then. Thank all of you for coming, and we'll be at the house should anyone wish to come by."

They all retired to the big house in the Bend. No one had seen Juan since the news about June had arrived. This didn't alarm anyone because he frequently took trips to Mexico and would be gone for days or even weeks. Even though he hadn't been there for the funeral it was no matter because he hadn't been seen since *before* June's death. The last person to see him was one family member the night before her death, and it was assumed he had left that evening. The afternoon passed and the conversation finally tapered and everyone went home. When Buddy and Sabrina got home the phone was already ringing. Sabrina answered it and then dropped the phone. Buddy rushed over to her.

"What is it?"

She looked at him with a tear-streaked face and said, "They just found dad dead. He's been in his house all along. Mom had gone to see her sister and when she returned he was just sitting there in his chair dead. They think is was a heart attack."

Cigar Box

They buried Juan. Spring came and began to warm. The cactus flowers bloomed, the storms came and went and the hot weather set in. On June 21^{st,} a good-sized crowd met on the sandy shore of the bend of the river. It was the same place where Stillwell had died; the place where June had been with Buddy; and the place where Claudette had picnicked with Bill and the little Indian girl had played among the rocks in the river.

Dish Bob spoke: "We commit June Montgomery's ashes to the bend that spawned her, and her memory to our hearts; Ashes to ashes, dust to dust. We pray that she don't go far. Save us some strawberry wine. We're all right behind her."

Mike came forward with the old tattered cigar box with a rubber band around it. Buddy stood beside him at the edge of the river as he removed the rubber band and opened the lid. Then, slowly the two brothers turned the box over and let the fine, gray ash fall into the gurgling waters of the river. Christina and Sabrina stepped forward and took some rose pedals out from a bag and sprinkled them into the water with the ashes. Then, they all watched as the pedals floated down the river into the distance. Angie picked up her Spanish guitar. Gently stroking the strings she sang:

When I die
I may not go to heaven
'Cause I don't know if they'd let cowboys in.
But if they don't
Just let me go to Texas, Lord
'Cause Texas is as close as I've been.

She choked slightly, and before she could continue a young cowboy picked up the chorus and began to sing, as did another, and another, until they were all singing, watching the rose pedals drift down the river, while behind them, as they sang, little Mike, and his half sister played in the west Texas sand.

The End

About the Author

Pamela Woodward and Wilbur Witt have written three novels. Cigar Box is the latest of these. They "Team up" on their writing efforts, telling the story to each other until it "cooks" they reside in North Austin. They blend their varied experiences into the stories they weave.

Printed in the United States
1436500001B/7